DOLL'S EYE

The Doll's Eye plant, also known as the
White Baneberry.

The highly poisonous white berries resembling
eyeballs, dangle from bloody stems as if they
were a serial killer's trophy.

This is a DARK romance. It contains dark content and sensitive situations that may be triggering to some readers. Only for those 18 years and older.

This book is dedicated to every crazy bitch out there. Sometimes, it's okay to embrace it.

They think it's still a man's world.
To them, we're pawns.
Used for our lineage and reproductive systems.
We're expected to stay silent.
But it's us women who birth heirs and raise kings.
We give life.
And we most certainly can take it.
They tried to dictate my life as if it weren't my own.
But I carve my own path.
Leaving a crimson trail behind me.
Everyone knows that a woman who knows their worth is a dangerous woman.
I don't need a title or throne to know that my blood is imperial.
Add in scorned fragments and shards of betrayal.
They didn't break me.
They made me into a pretty little poison.
I will always be seen as harmless.
But even the devil has a pretty face.

Ciao—Hi
Vaffanculo—Fuck off/you
Stronzos—assholes
Babbo—dad/father
Piccolina—little one
Bambina—baby
Merda—shit
Ti amo, mia piccola guerriera—I love you my little warrior
É abbastanza!—That's enough!
Mia famiglia—My family
Sta' zitto!—Be quiet!
La mia sorella preferita—My favorite sister
sorellina—sister
Amatissimo—beloved
Signoa—Madam
Grazie—thank you
Buonasera—Good evening
Buona notte!—Good night!
Bella—beautiful
Regina—queen
Cara mia—my darling
Cazzo—fuck
Come sta?—How are you?
Sto bene, grazie. E lei?—I'm well, thank you. And you?
Entra!—Enter!
Bordello—whorehouse/brothel
Cara—dear
Gattina—little kitten
Fica—cunt
Dolcezza—sweetness
Baciami—kiss me
Ti voglio—I want you
Perfezione—Perfection
Seducente—seductive/sexy
Mi ecciti—You're turning me on.
Che cosa?—What?
Calmati, amore mio.—Calm down, my love.
Amore—love
Bene—good
Salve!—Hello!
Nonno—Grandfather
Nonna—Grandmother

Cazzata!—Bullshit!
Sti cazza—Fuck that
Porca troia—Fucking hell
Mi sei mancato molto, amore mio—I miss you so much my love.
Sposami—Marry me
Ti amo—I love you
Ti amo tanto—I love you too
Mi amata—my love
Potrei guardarti tutto il giorno—I could look at you all day.
Zhopu porvu margala vikoliu, suka—I'll rip your ass and poke your eyes out, bitch. (Russian)
Porcas—Pigs
Zaychik—bunny (Russian)
Mio Dio—My God
Cogliones--Balls
Mia cigna—my swan
Mio re—My king
Cuore mio—My heart
Che cazzo!—What the fuck!
Pompinara—Cock sucker
Mangia merde e morte—Eat shit and die
Siamo fatti l'uno all'altra, amore mio—We're made for each other, my love.
Cornuto—Cuckhold
Bastardo—Bastard
Ti ammazo—I'll kill you
Caro—dear
Madonna—Madonna/Oh, God!
Santo cazzo Madre di Cristo!—Holy fucking Mother of Christ!
Prizak—Ghost (Russian)
Da—Yes (Russian)
Fratello—Brother
Siamo fatti l'uno all'altra—We were made for each other.
Chooch—Jackass

Alessia

It's almost wrong we're even here.

Organized crime families all rallied at a gala that is raising money for the new hospital being built as if we're trying to save lives. Between all the families collectively, we place at least one body in the hospital on the daily. I guess that's why a new hospital is necessary.

But we'll all write a big check, shake some hands, and the city will deem us as gods rather than the demons we truly are.

I've never been one for fancy dresses, but in the ballgown I'm wearing tonight, I feel like a real princess. A powerful and beguiling one. On the outside, I look like just another pretty woman. Soft and simple. But what no one knows about is the gun and throwing knives I have concealed under my dress. They checked every single man for weapons upon arrival, but I walked right through without any suspicion.

Foolish men. They'll always underestimate the absolute power and threat of a woman.

"Alessia Bonetti," a deep voice causes me to spin around, coming face to face with the eldest son of Angelo De Luca, Massimo De Luca. A sadist to some and the devil himself to the rest. The stoic look on his face doesn't change when his cold gaze makes an obvious trail up and down the length of my body.

"*Ciao*, Massimo." *Hi*. I close the gap to kiss each cheek. He smells like whiskey, mint, and something I can't put my finger on. Not at all like the fire and brimstone I imagined he'd smell of.

"You have certainly grown up," he murmurs flatly as if it were something I was unaware of.

"I have." I glance around the room, finding it challenging to keep the polite smile on my face when looking him in the eye.

"Afraid to speak with me alone?" There's the slightest jest under the smooth baritone.

I find the courage to meet his gaze and exude confidence in my stature. Especially now that his proximity had gone unnoticed. He's over a foot taller than me and twice as wide as my petite frame, and he thinks his size will intimidate me.

"Of course not," I say firmly without blinking.

He seems to find humor in my bravado as one side of his mouth tightens, and I try to ignore the fact that I find him handsome. Massimo is not someone you find attractive. You find him chilling.

His dark gaze journeys down my body again, and I feel my skin pebbling. Not quite sure if it's from fear. "You should wear dresses more often." His eyes lock on mine. "It's deceptive."

"Deceptive, how?"

"To everyone, you're just another beautiful and *fragile* woman."

I fight the urge to cross my arms for comfort. Why does it feel like he's inside my head? "And you? What do you see?"

He takes a long pause before answering as if trying to see me crack. "I see a lethal woman that looks sinful in a dress." He raises his glass in salute as my heart races, and my breathing stops. "It was nice seeing you, Alessia." His eyes brighten for a moment before he turns and walks away.

"Who was that?" My sister Gemma comes up out of nowhere.

I shake myself from my stupor and suck in a breath of air. "That was Massimo De Luca." I snatch the champagne glass out of her hand and down it.

"*That* was Massimo De Luca?"

I nod my head.

"Oh, *wow*. Are you okay? What did he say to you?"

I clear my throat, not looking at her. "That he liked my dress."

I can't deny Massimo's domineering presence had shaken me. However, that fear he evoked unlocked a dormant part of me, igniting a surge of empowerment and ambition.

CHAPTER ONE

Alessia

"Will the gentleman be leaving with you?" my driver asks as I climb into the back of the car.

Sighing, I slouch down in the seat. "No, he won't."

"Home then?"

"Yup."

We're pulling away from the club when two of my father's men exit it scouring the street. I'm tempted to roll down the window to flip them off, but they're just doing their job. And it isn't them who I'm upset with. It's me.

No matter how hard I try, I can't suppress the *mafiosa* in me. It's who I am, but if I want a relationship with a man at all, then I need to rein in my Italian gangster some. I'm not even looking for a serious relationship because, as the daughter of Marino Bonetti, it is my obligation to marry a man of my father's choosing.

So, for now, I'd like someone to pass the time with and experience some normalcy until then.

I thought Maverick could be that someone, but I should've known. I mean, his name was *Maverick*, and he wore polo shirts. I don't know what I was thinking. Well, he was really hot, that's what I was thinking. We started dating a couple of months ago, and everything went fine. He was pleasant, fun, and pretty good in bed. He wasn't the best, but he left me satisfied almost every time.

My phone starts ringing with a call from my brother. *"Ciao."*

"I heard another one bites the dust," he muses.

"Vaffanculo." Fuck off.

He chuckles over the phone, and I crack a smile with him. "So, what happened this time?"

I let out a dramatic sigh. "Oh, you know. The usual," I murmur and inspect my nails.

This time he more than chuckles. He actually laughs. It's a rare sound to hear from him these days.

It wasn't always so hard to make Tullio smile or laugh. He used to be jovial and easygoing, even though he was the oldest of our siblings, born and bred to be the head of the family someday. One of the biggest crime families on the east coast. But then he met a girl, fell in love, got her pregnant, and they were engaged to be married. He was mad about Agnella. It caused quite a stir in the outfit since Tullio was already betrothed to another, but nothing could stop love.

Not even death.

Agnella was in a fatal accident and died only days before their wedding. My brother hasn't been the same since. His refusal to ever marry left our father disgruntled, but at the end of the day, our father would never force us into anything irrevocable.

"Stop laughing at me, Tullio!"

"Well, stop going out with *stronzos!" Assholes.*

"Who the hell am I supposed to go out with? I'm not going to sit around like a nun and wait for my *betrothed.*"

"I do not need to know that," he mutters.

"I didn't mean save myself. That ship has long sailed. This isn't—"

"Okay, okay," he rushes out, making me giggle. "Pain in my—so, are you on your way home?"

"Yes, I am." Unfortunately. I was hoping I would be heading home with Maverick right about now to have some mediocre sex.

"Good. *Babbo* wants you here. We're entertaining the De Luca's tonight."

I sit up straight. There are only a few reasons why we would be having the De Luca's over and why I would need to attend. "Should I bring a bottle of champagne?" I ask dryly, hiding the hurt in my chest.

The warning in his grunt tells me just to shut my mouth and get my ass home.

"See you soon," I mutter before hanging up.

On the ride home, I conjure up several theories. One thing is for sure: The De Lucas are there to discuss solidifying both families once and for all with a marriage, making us both a stronger, unconquerable force.

There are six of us Bonetti heirs, and only Armando has married so far. That leaves Tullio, Santino, Gemma, Paolo, and me. My father would never ask Gemma, my twin sister, to even consider an arranged marriage, so she's out of the equation as well.

Tullio was set to marry Sarita De Luca before he met Agnella. When he broke off the engagement, breaking his word, shit went down between our families. It drudged up old matters that should have been buried along with the past, and it was bad for a while.

Things finally settled down once we handed some of our territory over to the De Lucas to pacify Angelo and make amends for what was broken.

Now, here we are, once again, making an attempt to cement the bond between the two families through another marriage proposal. It could be Tullio and Sarita again, but I doubt Tullio would sound so chipper on the phone if that were the case. Which still leaves quite a few more options.

Based on age and availability, we have me marrying Ezzo, the younger of the two De Luca brothers. Or it could be either Paolo or Santino paired with Sarita or the youngest of their clan, Vita. But my guess is Ezzo and me. Why else would they be calling me in?

No matter how hard I try to prove myself, I'm still only seen as a female. Change has been impossible to make in terms of tradition and status in the life of the mafia. The world around us continues to evolve, yet we're still trying to come out of the Golden Age. Women are most important for their bloodline and dowry. Not to mention a fruitful uterus.

But I was born to prove them all wrong. Once I secure my place next to a man in power, they will see exactly what I, as a female, am capable of.

Thoughts of Ezzo being the one chosen for me stampede through my head as I pull up to the estate. I can actually consider myself lucky if that's my fate. It could certainly be worse. He's a good-looking Italian known for being charismatic and a lady's-man. Too many women in my position are arranged from the moment of birth and bound to a much, much older man who is not only ugly with a gut but cruel too.

He's seven years older than me, from what I recall, though that's still a boy to me. Men don't even begin to grow up until their thirties. I'll definitely have my work cut out for me, but I'll make a man out of him in no time.

I'm greeted by a couple of our men, who open my door and escort me inside the large estate where I reside. Only Armando moved out when he got married, and the rest of us most likely won't leave until we get married ourselves. Except for Tullio, since he will eventually take over as head of the family. Some of us have a small condo in the city to escape to sometimes, but this is home for all of us.

The estate was built by my great-grandfather and handed down to my grandfather and then my father. We're the first generation to reside solely in the States. We have property and family in Italy, which we visit quite often, but this is where we were born and raised.

"Mmm." I inhale deeply as I smell some of Mamma's home cooking. I didn't have much of a dinner before heading to the club, and her food was calling my name. I know that when I enter one of the rooms where Father tends to entertain, there will be some hors d'oeuvres made by Mamma for me to devour.

When I turn the corner, I take a deep breath and run my hands down my dress. My palms are already clammy, and my heart is racing with nerves. I've been prepared for chosen marriage for years, but it's hard to believe the moment might already be here at twenty-one.

The double doors to the room are wide open as both of our families mingle. Every head in the room turns when I enter, and it's all the confirmation I need. They were waiting on the bride-to-be.

Thankfully, I'm wearing something somewhat tasteful. My dress, adorned with rose gold pearls and jewels, is short with a small slit on one thigh, but I don't have any cleavage showing, and the cream-colored, slouchy cardigan covers me up. Add in the rose gold luxury brand emblem buckle on my white belt, and you have a sexy yet classy ensemble. It's something acceptable by mafia royalty standards.

However, Angelo De Luca and his oldest son, Massimo, don't seem to approve. Angelo looks at me with disdain, and Massimo looks at me with indifference. *Aw, well, I can't win them all.*

Ezzo seems to like what he sees, and I guess that's all that really matters. His eyes practically absorb every inch of my body, a little heat behind his gaze. It doesn't do much for me, but still feels good to be admired.

As I traipse around the room to kiss ass and make nice with our guests, I feel a heavy presence weighing on my backside. Feigning oblivion, I continue to move about, but the curiosity chips away at my fortitude. Especially when I finally meet the invader head-on and learn that Ezzo's gaze isn't penetrating right through me.

Massimo De Luca blatantly stares at me and does not flinch when I catch him. His eyes remain impassive, and his face remains stony. He's again trying to intimidate me, like he did years ago at the gala.

He rattled me then, and he rattles me now. But I was always taught to face my demons and never run from them.

With my shoulders back, I go to him, never letting my eyes waver from his. "Massimo." I give him a kiss on his cheeks. Each move with confidence. "Nice to see you again. It's been years, hasn't it?"

His hazel eyes are much lighter than I remember. He's also much taller. Even with my four-inch heels, he towers over me, which isn't hard to do since I'm barely over five feet tall. But he is massive in height and fills his suit with solid muscle. The strength of this man...

"It's been quite a few, Alessia. They've been good to you." My skin lights up with goosebumps from the same baritone in his voice I can still remember so clearly. One corner of his mouth ticks as if he notices.

"*Piccolina.*" *Little one.* My father approaches me and places a kiss on my cheek and a hand on my lower back. "We'd like to have a private discussion with you." Angelo comes to join our small group sipping on a glass of dark liquid and still looking at me with disapproval. Tullio isn't far behind him, looking grave. *Oh, shit.* I glance around and quickly discover that Ezzo is not joining us, which means...I turn my gaze back to Massimo, and he's still watching me with an empty stare.

"Right." I gulp. "Lead the way, *Babbo.*" Tullio replaces my father at my side as we head out of the room and down to my father's office. I can tell he wants to wrap an arm around me for comfort but knows I will give him shit for it later. I don't need these pompous pricks thinking I'm at all diffident.

I know I can opt out of this arrangement or choose not to agree to it, but I promised my father that I would do whatever is necessary for the good of the family and the empire the several generations before us built.

If that is marrying Massimo De Luca, then that is my sealed fate.

CHAPTER TWO

Alessia

We all file into father's office, the doors closing as we take our seats.

Tullio stands at my father's side as he takes his rightful place behind his desk, and Massimo stands stoically at his father's side as he takes the seat next to me. The room grows eerily quiet, and the tension thickens as we all mentally prepare ourselves for the forthcoming business transaction.

I haven't felt so uncomfortable in my father's office since I was caught smoking weed when I was thirteen. Other than that, I've always loved being in here. Visiting my father while he worked tirelessly day in and day out to continue our family's legacy. I'd bring him lunch from Mamma and come pull him out to join us for dinner each evening. Sometimes, I sit on the worn loveseat with a book just to listen to his voice as he conducts business. It's always been hard for him to find a lot of spare time for us, so I'd make time for him.

Many conversations surface my mind as I drift off momentarily.

My persistent pleas for more involvement. This is where he broke the news to me about allowing Gemma to go to college and that I was to stay here.

It never bothered me that Gemma was taller than me and smarter and more popular. But it hurt knowing that she has always been favored.

Whatever the reasoning behind that decision to keep me home, it was the right one. I'd get nothing out of college for what I want with me life.

"Over much discussion, and after the failed attempt to unify the families with Tullio and Sarita." He throws Tullio a stern look, but Tullio stands there unmoving. "We came up with another suitable partnership. You and Massimo."

I swallow down the lump in my throat and keep my focus forward. "And has everyone agreed to this?" *Meaning has Massimo?*

"Yes, everyone is in agreement," my father confirms.

"And you, *piccolina*?" Angelo chimes in with a condescending tone.

I turn to meet his eye boldly. I refuse to show any weakness to *anyone*, let alone Angelo De Luca and his unwarranted rancor towards me. "Yes. For the sake of our family and the city, I accept this decision." He holds my gaze like I will succumb and be the first to break. I don't. He may be the alpha in his family, but he is not someone I will ever submit to. I submit to no one but my father. And even then, I'm not so easy to bend.

His face twitches as if he finds me amusing, and he turns his beady eyes back over to my father. My eyes leave him to meet hazel ones. I don't know why I remembered Massimo's eyes being much darker. Maybe it was his soul I was thinking about. But there are many colors that make up his irises.

This time, I am the one to break first. His intense stare is too much for me, and that's unsettling. I wish it were Ezzo they wanted to pair me with. It wouldn't be difficult to earn the upper hand with him, but Massimo, one look from him, has me mentally furling in on myself.

I look at my father again and realize he and Angelo have been talking, and now I'm lost in the conversation. I ask to be a part of the business, yet here I am, sitting in on an important meeting with the De Lucas, and I can't concentrate on the discussion. All I can think about is my husband-to-be, and his potent stare is jarring.

Massimo De Luca has an ever-growing nightmarish reputation. Not much scares me since I learned how to shoot my Glock 43 and carried it with me before I was old enough to wear lipstick or drive a car. I'm also a master at knife throwing and have done tons of fight training. Even a man of Massimo's size and stature doesn't really intimidate me, but he does. He's so handsome it's frightening, and his voice alone is spine-chilling. He has this intensity and regal air about him that irradiates, sending me tingles and raising all the little hairs on my body. As if he were a powerful king in another life with actual powers and there're still pieces of him inside.

The graphic rumors about the deranged De Luca could be only rumors. But rumors stem from somewhere, right? Supposedly, his bedroom preferences are something to gossip about, as well as his mercenary skills.

Tying women up and demeaning them. I even heard he likes to put collars on them like dogs. Good luck putting a fucking collar on me. I'm a bitch that *does* bite, and I'll fucking bite his fingers off if he ever came at me with one. Fuck. That. I will be a good wife, and I understand he will one day be the boss, but I am not, nor will I ever be, a submissive.

Then, they are not so much rumors as they are tales about him and how very dirty he gets his hands. His very large and calloused hands. They could easily choke the life out of you and snap your neck. They say he's totally sinister. Not batting an eye as he clips fingers off one by one or when he literally peels the skin off whatever unfortunate soul got tangled in his web. Or how he will crush bones with his bare hands or gouge eyes out with his thumbs. It's...*sick*. You have to be some psychopath to stomach the things he's accused of doing.

But every time I overheard the hushed whispers, my curiosity was manic. The idea of seeing him in action to discover for myself how accurate those rumors were filled my cheeks with scorching heat, and the pit of my stomach tingled.

But all fear him, and in our world, to be feared is to be respected. Fear gives you protection.

We wrap up the meeting, and without much of a goodbye, Angelo and Massimo are led out of the office by Tullio, leaving me alone with my father. He lets his mask fall a little, softening his features for me. Switching his don hat out for his father hat.

"It's okay, *Babbo*. It's not the worst match, really. But I'm curious. How the hell did this happen?"

He sighs and stands up. "It came as just as much a surprise to me too. *Piccolina*, come sit with me." I go over and join him on the nostalgic loveseat. "You know you do not have to do this. I would never force you. You remember that?"

"I know, *Babbo*, but I did just agree. Tullio already broke his word, and there would be no way to salvage anything between our families if I also broke mine. I know Tullio had his reasons, but I would never break my word. Not after I gave you mine, and now them in agreement to the marriage. It's set in stone as far as I'm concerned."

He gets this blissful smile in his eyes as he strokes my cheek tenderly. "I am so very proud of you, *bambina*. I could not ask for a better daughter."

"That's because you already have one," I mutter. "Literally a better version of me."

The lines between his thick brows deepen as they come together, making him look so much older. "You don't really think that do you, Alessia?"

I shake my head and look down at my hands resting in my lap. "Gemma has always been your favorite, and it's okay. I know you still love me."

"Alessia. Look at me." I know better than to disobey him as I meet his gaze. "Do you really think that?"

"It's not something I think. It's something that everyone knows. Why you've always been more gentle with her, let her go to college, why you give her more affection."

"*Merda.*" *Shit*. "Alessia. You remember what your name means?"

I nod my head. "Yes. Defender. And Gemma's means precious stone." Mamma waited a day or so to choose our names based on their meaning. She wanted to learn our personalities first and give us a fitting name.

"Did Mamma ever tell you that I named you?"

I frown at him.

"I was the one who decided to call you Alessia. The defender. Do you want to know why?"

"Yes." I am so enthralled by this piece of history that I want to sit here and make him speak for hours. Give me every single detail of those first few days I was alive.

"Since the day you were born, you would find a way to comfort your sister when she'd cry."

"Mamma said I hardly ever cried." I smile a little.

"That's because your sister would, and it seemed like you were always trying to be strong for the both of you. Be her defender. I saw your strength from those first moments, my *piccolina*. I am gentler with Gemma because she needs it. I could have sent you away to college, but I know where you would always want to be, where your heart will always be. Your mother and I have always wanted to shelter our girls from this life, but I don't think that is possible with you. And as for affection." He scoots in closer and wraps an arm tightly around my shoulders, squeezing me, making me grin like the little girl he somehow always makes me feel like. "You should know why I do not shower you with affection like I do her."

"The same reason you don't with the boys?"

"To make sure you are prepared for this life, I mustn't be soft with you all. It does kill me to withhold my love from my children, you must know that. To refrain from hugging you when I feel the urge. To restrain myself from comforting you when you need it. But it has to be one way or the other. I cannot give you both, and if I was wrong to think this is what you have always wanted, then I am terribly sorry for that."

I'm the one who has had it wrong for all these years. So very wrong. My father was trying to find that balance between being a father and being a boss with me. It's easier to do so with my brothers since he was raised in the same fashion, but women don't typically want to be included like I do.

"You weren't at all wrong, *Babbo*. My life is being a Bonetti, and a part of its legacy."

He gets this beamish smile on his face and kisses my cheek. "That's my girl. *Ti amo, mia piccola guerriera*." *I love you, my little warrior*. "Massimo will be good to you. He gives me his word. But if he isn't, you do not hesitate to tell me."

"I can take care of myself."

"That I know you can, but I will always be your father. I would never forgive myself if I married you to a monster. So, you must promise me if he tries to hurt you."

"I will tell you if there is something I cannot handle, *Babbo*. I promise."

CHAPTER THREE

Alessia

Once I told Gemma the news, she insisted on flying home the very next morning.

She's appalled at the prospect of me marrying Massimo De Luca and thinks of me as some victim being forced into this no matter what I tell her, and when Gemma gets like this, it's hard to get through to her. So, I called in our cousin Fia, who is our best friend, for reinforcement.

As soon as my sister walked into the door this morning, there was yelling and screaming in rapid Italian between all of us. Tullio is the only one out of my siblings who isn't upset with the arrangement because he knows damn well I would speak up if I were not on board. I've never been one to keep my thoughts and opinions to myself, especially if I am unhappy about something.

The rest of my brothers are riotous over Massimo's being much older than me. He isn't wrinkling, and yes, he's technically old enough to be my father, but he can't be more than thirty-nine years old. The men are to marry by forty, and my brothers seem to miss the fact that I am a woman. One beyond my chronological years.

Mamma was just as upset as Gemma and tried to talk me out of it until late in the night last night, but she, too, knows me well. She knows that I cannot and will not be forced into something I did not want to do or forced out of it. And if I have my mind set on something, then that's it. It's done, and no one can stop me or change my mind. I'm always more willing to learn the hard way if necessary.

Looking around at my family arguing about me and my future, I've had just about enough of it.

Heading over to a chair, I stand up on it and open my lungs. "*É abbastanza!*" *That's enough!* The whole room falls silent and turns to me. "*Mia famiglia.*" *My family.* "I was a part of this decision, and I agreed to it knowing exactly what I was agreeing to." Armando and Paolo open their mouths to protest. "*Sta'zitto!*" *Be quiet!* "I am not a child. I'm a woman, and I will do what is expected of me just as is expected of each and every one of you. When you are called to step up, do you not? Now, it's my turn. I will marry Massimo De Luca, strengthening us as a whole." Paolo and Gemma now look sheepish, but Santino and Armando still look upset.

Tullio remains reticent, most likely blaming himself for this. If he went through with the original arrangement, I would not be asked to do this. But I am not upset about this, nor am I with him. I'm elated to finally be able to step up and show my importance. To not only marry into another eminent family, but to someone who will become a capo.

Gemma and I finally head up to my room to be alone as Fia follows us. "Well, that was entertaining," Fia muses as she plops down on my bed.

My sister remains meek as we both climb up to join her. "Gemma, I promise it's okay."

"How? How can you be okay with this? You're being forced to marry Massimo De Luca. He's...he's..."

"Scary as fuck?" Fia fills in for her.

"Yes! Scary as fuck!" My eyes widen in faint shock at the profanity she never uses. "You've heard what they say about him! *I* even hear what they say, and you know I stay out of that business. But people still talk. He like...ties up women and beats them!"

Fia giggles as I roll my eyes at her dramatics. "He doesn't beat them, Gem. It's called BDSM."

She jerks her head back. "What the hell is that?"

Fia laughs, and I shake my head at her innocence. She's in college, for goodness sake. How is she still so sheltered? "It's like bondage, dominance, submission, and masochism?" I think out loud.

"I think there's also discipline and sadomasochism in there somewhere as well," Fia adds, and I raise a questioning eyebrow at her. She shrugs her shoulders with a guilty smirk.

"Wait, what the hell are you guys talking about?" Fia and I both laugh at her. "It's not funny!"

Doing my best to sober up, I look at her. "It's a kink, Gemma. Yes, he might tie up women and like to use toys and such in the bedroom, but he doesn't *beat* them." I purposely leave out the part of him putting collars on them because she would actually die. And this is all hearsay. It could all be total bullshit for all we know. None of us have slept with the man. *Oh, God. I'm going to have to sleep with him.*

"Okay, so maybe he doesn't *abuse* women, but what about all the other things? He's killed so many people!"

"I've killed too," I state flatly.

Her whole demeanor softens as she remembers my brush with death a couple of years ago. "Yeah, but you were defending yourself, Less. That's different. He does it for a living and with his bare hands. And he likes it!"

"He might like to be more *hands-on*, but it's what *Babbo* has enforcers for. He might not be doing the actual killing themselves like Massimo, but he might as well. So, if Massimo is a bad man, so are *Babbo* and our brothers." Her body deflates as she heavily sighs, and I know I need to be patient with her. "Gemma. I know this is hard for you to understand, but I need you to trust me. Trust that I know what I'm doing and that I'm perfectly happy with my choices. Just be thankful this will never be asked of you." I take her hands in mine. "You get to meet someone normal and fall in love like a normal girl, and that makes me so happy for you."

"*Babbo* would let you do that too if you told him it's what you wanted."

"It isn't, though. I promise I am not being forced into this nor do I feel obligated to do so."

She shakes her head. "I just can't let you—"

"You have to, Gemma. This is my decision, and that's final. I will not be talked out of it," I say firmly, and she studies me for a long moment.

"Seriously?" I nod my head without blinking. "Ugh!" she groans. "You are crazy, you know that?"

"I do," I state arrogantly.

Fia snorts. "And so does half the east coast."

Anyone relevant that didn't know me by name sure as hell learned it two years ago. A man who worked for the Gallos made the grave mistake of trying to take me in an empty banquet room at an event, not knowing exactly who I was. Not only did I kill the bastard, but I made sure to send a message.

After getting the upper hand in the struggle, I cut his limp dick off with one of my pocket knives and stuffed them in his mouth to choke on. Then, using the same knife, I carved my initials into his chest, legible enough to read.

The dude was low on the totem pole, and I'm like royalty, so the Gallo's did not seek revenge. If he were higher up in the chain of command, they might have taken out one of our own in retaliation, but they knew better. The bastard got exactly what he deserved, and everyone learned I am no rose.

That was the first and only life I have taken, but I know it will not be the last. Leaving my family's estate to marry a De Luca, I will no longer have full protection from my brothers.

"And you're wrong." Gemma gives me a sad smile. "No matter how normal I try to be and how far I go, I will always be mobbed up. Nothing can change that."

It's true. She'll always be connected to the mob. And if any guy were ever to hurt her, they're dead for sure. I can't even keep track of the number of guys who have been given a good beatdown if they in any way mistreated me. Meaning, unlike a princess. And anyone who has stuck around long enough was given a mock execution as a test. No one has made it past either of those. They all ran for the hills. It never bothered me, though. I don't want a pansy. If they can't handle my brothers, they can't handle me.

"You'll find someone good enough and brave enough to stick around one day knowing who you really are."

"Maybe date someone else who is mobbed up," Fia suggests.

"No way! I don't want to date a gangster! I want away from the mob, remember?"

"It doesn't have to be a made guy. It can be a soldier." She shrugs.

"So, I'd always be worried if they were coming home alive or in a body bag? No, thank you." She scowls.

"It doesn't have to be a soldier necessarily. Just someone who would understand this life. Someone who wouldn't judge you for who your family is. Someone connected but not entirely involved," I say.

"Yeah, someone who isn't directly connected but in the know," Fia adds.

Gemma waves her hand around. "I'm not even looking for someone right now. I'm still in college, and I'm enjoying it. That's enough for me for the time being." She sighs. "So, a wedding."

My head starts whipping side to side. "I'm not there yet. Massimo and I have yet to meet one-on-one, so I'm not even considering the wedding."

"Do you at least know when you're supposed to be married?" Fia asks.

"Within a year." Upon agreement.

"Wow. In one year, you will be Massimo De Luca's wife," Gemma says dreadfully, adding a shiver at the end.

"He isn't that bad!" I chuckle.

"He certainly isn't bad-looking," Fia mutters, and I bite back a smirk.

"What! You two are insane! How can you see anything about him that doesn't shake you to the core?" Gemma exclaims.

Fia and I exchange a look, then break out into laughter as Gemma officially thinks we have lost it. "Oh, I think he makes my core quiver alright," Fia jokes, making me laugh harder and giving her a playful swat.

"Hey, that's my fiancé you're talking about there." We keep laughing.

"What is wrong with you two?" Gemma stares at us with great consternation.

"Oh, I'll explain it to you when you get older," I tease.

She growls and climbs off the bed. "I need some alcohol if I'm going to hang out with you two all day."

CHAPTER FOUR

Alessia

I'm headed into the kitchen when I stumble upon Armando and his lovely Italian-tempered wife, Lesina, arguing as usual.

It's gotten to the point where we're all so used to it that they don't even bother to stop when someone enters the room, and we don't turn right around to avoid it. It's almost like background noise at this point.

The woman is hardly Italian but has totally embraced the whole Italian mob wife persona. Using this fake-ass accent and always throwing a fit over nothing. Gets her hair and nails done weekly and uses my brother as her personal ATM. She wasn't so bad in the beginning, and they seemed like they were really in love. Then, after a year of marriage and one baby later, all they do is fight, and all she does is spend his money.

But who am I to say? Maybe they are still in love, and this is just their relationship. They might both get off on all the fighting. It's not like you can really judge a couple when you have no idea what goes on behind closed doors.

I overhear Lesina telling him to 'ask your sister', and I know what's coming next as I grab a drink from the fridge. Lesina is standing there with her hip popped and her arms crossed over her recently enhanced chest.

"Alessia, my beautiful and wonderful sister," Armando lays it on thick as I give him an unamused look. "Can you do us a solid and watch Alba for a couple of hours? I have to be in *Babbo's* office, and Lesina here made plans tonight."

"*Important* plans," she adds, and I give her a tight smile.

One of the unspoken rules within the family, no matter how much we despise someone's significant other, we are to be civil with them. Especially after they've gotten married. They're officially a part of the family, and we stick together.

"Yes, I can watch Alba." I concede because, one, I fucking love my niece to pieces, and two, why would I let her go off with her mother, who'll try to pawn her off to someone else?

"Thank you, *la mia sorella preferita*." *My favorite sister.* He smooshes my face in his hands and plants a wet kiss on either cheek before I shove him away and wipe it off.

Lesina smiles in victory. "She's in the other room, still asleep in her car seat, and the diaper bag is next to her. Thank you, *piccolina*. You're a doll." She gives me two air kisses and plants a big kiss on Armando's lips while he relishes it. They both murmur gross words to each other, and then she sashays out of the kitchen gleefully as if the heated argument never happened.

Armando watches her the entire way, then looks at me with this goofy look on his face, which quickly drops when he sees mine. "What?"

I put both hands up. "Nothing. I didn't say anything."

"You sure you don't mind?"

"I'm sure. Go do what you need to do."

"Thanks, *sorellina*." He gives me another sloppy kiss, which earns him a punch in his arm, making him jump away and hiss as he holds the area with a pinched look on his face. "How do I always forget how hard you can hit?" He backs away.

"Maybe now you won't forget," I warn playfully, and he finally leaves.

It doesn't take long for little Alba to wake up, and I go get her. Hugging her close to me and consoling her. She knows who I am by now since I have her at least a couple of days a week, and she's now almost eight months old. Cutest age ever. Well, I've said that every week since she was born. Every age being my new favorite.

"*Amatissimo*," I murmur and kiss her soft curls, inhaling her sweet baby scent. "I missed you, baby."

After putting a dry diaper on her, I have her settled into the highchair, and I'm feeding her some snacks when I feel a heavy presence nearby. The hairs on the back of my neck stand, and I'm on high alert. Even though it feels like danger, I know it can't be. I'm safer here than anywhere. The estate is heavily guarded, and we have state-of-the-art surveillance around every corner. You would need an army to infiltrate our barriers. Or a rat inside.

Turning my head slowly, I find Massimo standing at the kitchen's threshold watching me. In his bespoke suit, he perfectly fills out his light but intense gaze, his brown hair perfectly styled, and his neatly trimmed facial hair about two shades lighter than the hair on top of his head. He is definitely a great-looking man, but who knows if the beauty has any depth.

"Massimo," I say casually, then turn back to Alba. I should get up to properly greet him, but I don't trust my knees not to wobble at the moment. "Oh, my goodness. You're almost out of blueberries, aren't you, my precious *bambina*," I say in a gentle tone with a genuine smile.

"Aren't you joining us?"

"Joining you? Where?" My mouth pops open in surprise when Alba gobbles up more berries. "You little piggy."

"Finalizing some of the terms as a result of our marriage."

I don't turn to let him see the crestfallen look on my face. I'm the one making the sacrifice here, and I'm not invited to learn of the outcome. My father acts like he understands my commitment, yet I'm left in the dark even when it directly involves me.

"I have to watch my niece." He isn't allowed to see my vulnerability or my cards played.

No matter how much dedication I show, my place will always be with the children or in the kitchen. In this case, both.

"Massimo. How are you?" I hear my mother politely say from the same direction.

Saved by the bell.

"*Signora*. I'm well, *grazie*." *Ma'am. I'm well, thank you.*

My mother enters my periphery as she glances back at the man who will soon be her son-in-law. She has an amicable look on her face, but I can sense the uneasiness underneath. Then she focuses her attention on Alba.

"Alessia." His voice sends that tingle down my spine. I face him with poise, as always. "I think you should join us. This is about our families and what we will both benefit from our union." His hands are now stuffed inside the pockets of his dress slacks. Standing there looking like the model on the cover of a mafia magazine. If there were such a thing.

"I think if *Babbo* wanted me there, he would have asked me himself." I turn back and avoid looking at my mother's face.

"*I'm* asking you, Alessia. If you would please join me at this meeting. As my fiancée, I would like you there." My gaze jumps up to my mother as my heart does this weird little flapping inside my chest. She only stares back at me as I silently plead with her. Finally, after moments of disquiet, she throws her head to the side as if telling me to go.

Taking an inconspicuous deep breath, I stand to my feet and wipe my sweaty palms down my tight-jeaned thighs. I hardly wear jeans, but I wasn't planning on seeing anyone other than family tonight. "Thank you, Mamma." I give her a kiss on her cheek and then one to Alba before joining Massimo at his side.

I hope he doesn't think I'm going to hold his hand or anything.

He glances back at Mamma. "*Signora.*" Then he places his hand on the small of my back, and I flinch a little from the tension I'm instantly fraught with. I have to force my legs to move on autopilot, heading out of the kitchen and through the house. Neither of us says a word the entire way, but his hand remains touching me. I've never been so aware of another person's simple touch before.

Just before we head into the room, I stop to face him. I have to crane my neck back to look him in the eye. The very handsome face looks down at me with relaxed features, but he's not at all placid. He displays no emotion as usual, but the more I inspect him up this close, the less threatening he seems.

Moments tick by as we stand there staring at one another. Studying, deciphering, contemplating. There are quite a few things I would like to ask him, but I let the first thing that comes to mind tumble out of my mouth without much thought. "Why?" *Why what, though?* I know this wasn't his decision. It was up to our fathers. So, what am I asking?

"Because you are like no other woman, Alessia. You're not content to be a manipulated pawn in the game. You're a strategic player controlling the board."

The lump in my throat doubles in size. I'm unsure what question he answered, but I'll take it either way.

Through our short encounter at the gala, he made me feel more seen with only a handful of words than I have ever felt. Could I possibly be more to him than just a last name or leverage?

Shaking myself from my thoughts, I lick my suddenly dry lips. "I appreciate you seeing me, Massimo."

There's a slight tilt to his lips and a flash of warmth in his eyes, but it disappears as quickly as it appears. But it was there. "I'd like to take you to dinner tomorrow night. Discuss terms of our engagement, just you and I."

"Okay." I glance at the open door, but we're angled, so no one has noticed us yet. "You sure about this?"

"It's because of your future with me that we are meeting. And you are a Bonetti, no?"

Tilting my face back up towards him, I actually crack a smile. "I am."

CHAPTER FIVE

Massimo

I was a bit vexed when I learned that Alessia would not be present at last night's discussion.

I'm not sure what her family's intentions were for leaving her out, but to me, it made her seem more like a transaction than an equal part of the arrangement. By the time I succeed the De Luca empire, she will know she is a queen. Not a mafia princess nor a mobster's wife.

When the discussion over the sex trade had begun, I stole a glance over at her. And when I did, she was unruffled. Looking just as regal as she had when she entered the room, and it deadened.

It has always been in our best interest to solidify her family with mine since our territories are so close, and we're two of the original families, even before the notorious original five. Not to mention our influence in Italy.

Tullio and Sarita would have been a conciliatory match, but they would only empower us by name. Although I lost much respect for Tullio, I was content with the marriage not going through.

There were plenty of suitable options for me out there. Ones that made more sense; age-wise, money-wise, and connection-wise. But I was thinking more strategically. I wanted someone who could make us a power couple and best suit my ambition.

My father was against my decision from the start and still is. He has some nonsensical vendetta towards the Bonettis that started way before the first failed arrangement. Eventually, I was able to convince him that this would be most beneficial.

I last spoke to Alessia three years ago, but that was not the last time I saw her. She unknowingly demanded my attention and became a permanent fixture inside my head.

But my decision became absolute when she so gruesomely killed one of Gallo's men. The other families labeled her as unstable and untamable, but all I saw was her tyrannous potential.

Alessia is perfect, and it was her I wanted.

Us two together, we will build an untouchable empire.

Since then, I've stood back, giving her as much time as I could spare. But it's time to execute my plan and secure this alliance.

And as soon as I can get this wedding planned, the better.

Pulling up to the Bonetti estate for the third day in a row, I head inside to pick Alessia up for our dinner date. I'm keen on getting her alone and to be able to give all of my focus to her.

After being checked at the door for weapons, I'm led in through the house and towards the voices. Over the years, I've noticed how different our two families are. They're close to one another and still live here at the estate. I care for my siblings, and some could say we are close, but we don't spend much time together, and I am the only one who lives full-time at the estate, considering it will be mine someday.

When I enter the kitchen, my eyes land on Alessia right away. Her toned legs are on display, and a red velvet dress hugs every curve of her petite body. Her ass plump, and the curve of her back accentuated. Her long, dark hair is worn down in big soft curls down her back. And with the heels she's wearing, her calf muscles are more defined. All I can think about is how delicious it would be to bite into them and how many times I can wrap her hair around my fist.

They urgently take notice of my presence, and the atmosphere becomes restless. Everyone except for Marino, Tullio, and Gemma seems to be here. All together as a family, not at all looking like the mobsters they are known for. If you weren't aware of the concealed weapons they wear as an essential, you wouldn't take any of them as a threat.

"*Buonasera*." *Good evening*. I dip my chin and place my hands casually in my pockets. They all say hello to me and begin talking amongst themselves again.

Alessia heads my way with a pretty smile. "Hello, Massimo." I lean down for us to greet. She rests both hands on my shoulders and mine automatically go to her hips, causing her to tense under my touch. Soon my touch will make her quiver. It will take some time to ease her into me. A woman any less than her I would have to break and reconstruct into a woman fitting for a life at my side. Not Alessia. She may need some softening, but she's ready.

I'm reluctant to let her go, but I manage to. "Are you ready?"

"I am." She turns to shout, "*Buona notte*!" *Good night*! They respond with their goodbyes, and all eyes remain on us as we turn to leave the room. I'm sure her brothers abhor the thought of their sister being alone with me.

"Was there a special occasion tonight?" I ask as we head for the door.

"No." She shakes her head, and then she smiles up at me. "Just a typical night at the Bonetti's. You come from an Italian family, Massimo. Don't you all spend too much time together?"

"I can't say that we do. Not like that, at least." I hold the car door open for her, let her slip inside first, and then join her in the backseat.

"Do you have family dinners?"

"No."

"Hm." She glances out the window. "I guess that's good for me then."

"Why is that?"

She turns her smile over to me again. Even in the dark, you can see the golden slivers in her eyes. "Because I won't have to split them between our families once married. It'll be hard not living there anymore." She sighs. "I couldn't imagine not going to family dinners often."

The car is hushed as I try to think of the last time we all sat down as a family to eat. I can't even remember our last Christmas when everyone was there. My father has always been nothing but a boss to us growing up, and our mother hasn't been herself for years. They had an arranged marriage, and my father used her for power, money, and heirs. After he got those from her, he completely neglected her. Multiple affairs and verbal abuse when she sought any attention from him. So, she resorted to anti-depressants she now depends on. Numbing herself into a docile and meek woman.

Any time Marino Bonetti is seen out of the estate for any reason involving an audience, he usually has his wife on his arm, and she seems earnestly content. It could be for show. Whether it's authentic or a ruse, I respect Marino for it. Whether Alessia and I learn to love each other or not, I will do my best to appease her, and I hope she will give me respect in return.

I bring her to one of our family restaurants in the city for our first date. It's fine dining and the best Italian food the city has to offer. She might beg to differ since her family owns one in the city as well, but I personally put a lot of passion into this place as a tribute to my late grandmother.

We indeed turn heads walking in. I'm bringing a Bonetti onto De Luca territory, and not just any Bonetti. The beautiful and fierce Alessia Bonetti. Her hips swaying, chin up, back straight. Brimming with confidence and wearing an invisible crown showing off the royalty she naturally projects.

Word of our appearance and engagement will spread quickly. No one would be foolish enough to voice their objections, and everyone would know that she is under my protection now.

Pulling out her chair for her, I take my own on the other side so I can see every muscle twitching on her beautiful face, which glows underneath the warm lighting. I study her while she settles in and takes a look around. Her full lips are a rich natural color, her nose is small and straight, and those bold copper eyes complement her olive skin and dark hair.

I tear my eyes away from her when a bottle of our finest wine is brought to us, and two glasses are poured.

Once we're alone, she turns her attention to me. "So, now that we have the business side of things squared away, shall we discuss the terms of our marriage? What do you expect out of me as a wife, and what do I expect out of you as a husband?"

One corner of my mouth hitches up, and I use a sip of wine to cover it. I do admire her brazenness. "Ladies first." I recline back in my chair casually.

She smirks. "How about I tell you what I want, then you tell me what you want, then we can negotiate?" I nod once. "Leading up to the wedding you may have your freedom to do as you please, with whomever you please, as long as you are discreet. Preferably outside of the city. And I will make sure to be discreet as well." *Not happening.* "After we are married, I expect you to be faithful to me, and I promise to be faithful to you. I will fulfill my wifely duties to you, of course, starting the night of our wedding." She pauses. "Oh, and I require us to have separate bedrooms. No need to encroach on each other's space."

"Wifely duties..." I muse.

"Yes, as in sex. And I require the same. A woman has needs as well. I refuse to have a sexless marriage. It's a must."

No problem there, bella. Beautiful. "Anything else?"

"Yes." She sits up straighter. "I am not some debutant where I'm there just to smile and look pretty with my head in the sand. I refuse to be oblivious, and I want responsibilities. I'm not talking about how to perfect some family recipe. I'm valuable. Not only am I a great shot, I'm also great with numbers and very—"

"Yes." I stop her.

"Yes, what?"

"I think you've made your point, and it's now my turn." She narrows her eyes at me but doesn't argue. *Smart woman.* "I require fidelity from this moment forward. I won't expect you in my bed until the night of our wedding, but I will certainly welcome you if your womanly needs are too hard to ignore." I let myself smirk a little as she mirrors one back. "We most definitely will not have a sexless marriage and I do know how valuable you are, Alessia. It may have been your womanly physique and angelic face that made me look, but your intellect and ferocity have kept me captivated." Her face softens. "For years, I have waited to find someone who could be my queen, and that's you, Alessia. You will be my *regina.*" I sip my wine as I watch her gape at me, speechless. "Oh, and yes to the separate bedrooms, but only until we are married. Once we're married, I will not have a separate bedroom from my wife." I want her within arms reach.

She blinks several times trying to process everything, then she mentally shakes herself. "Wait...Until we're married? I'm not living with you until we are."

"That will be a problem for me, *cara mia.*" *My darling.* "I'd like you close by so we can get to know each other before the wedding arrives."

"I'm sorry, Massimo. That is not going to happen," she says firmly. "I will stay at my family's estate until we are married, and that's final."

"I will give you one more month at home."

"Is that when we will be married? One month?" she challenges with one eyebrow raised.

"That depends. Could you throw together a royal wedding that quickly?"

"Doubtful. It'll take months to plan."

"Shame." We're quiet for a long moment, neither willing to back down. "How about this? One month, you move into my estate, in your own bedroom, but you may see your family as much as you'd like."

She leans back with both eyebrows arched. "As much as I'd like? Oh, how generous of you, Massimo. Why don't you tell me what other kinds of privileges you will bless me with?" she sasses. "Will I be allowed free-range of the estate or permitted to certain parts? Will I be allowed to come and go as I please, or will I need to ask for permission first before stepping foot out the door?"

"Now, you're just being childish." She scowls, and I find even that attractive on her. "Of course, you can come and go as you please, and as far as the estate goes, I have my separate wing. Private from my mother and father, so it would be best if you stick to our side." She doesn't say anything as she's clearly unsatisfied. "I know it will be difficult to leave your home and your family, but you will eventually have to. If you want to try to make this work and have an amicable marriage, I would like it if you and I spent time together leading up to our nuptials, preferably in the evening. If you prefer to have dinner with your family, then so be it, but I would like you to come home afterward. I work long hours, so that's all I could spare for you unless it's a special occasion." I take a breath. "And you said you would like responsibilities, no? How am I supposed to start giving them to you if you are not there?"

That obviously piques her interest. "You'd start giving me responsibilities before we're married?"

"I could. Not much until we're official, but I would love to see what you're capable of. I could also teach you some things if you would like to learn." She nods her head. "Then one month, Alessia."

Her chest rises and falls as she takes a deep breath in and then out. "And you won't try and control me, Massimo?" Her voice is abnormally raw.

"I will never try to control you, Alessia. I enjoy your ferocity and will not try and tame you. If anything, I'd like to give you wings, not clip them."

Her nostrils flare as she stares at me. My eyes meander around her face and down the slender column of her neck, anxious to sink my teeth into it. "Okay."

"Then we agree to everything we've discussed?"

"Fidelity from this moment on, frequent sex starting the night of the wedding—"

"Or whenever you want."

Her copper eyes dance in delight as she shakes her head with a smirk. "I move into a separate room at the estate in one month, and we will share a bedroom once we are officially married. Did I cover everything?"

"I would also like you to always have one of my men with you whenever you leave the estate. Starting now, that is. If you are not inside your estate or mine, I want you protected." She opens that sassy mouth of hers, and I hold a hand up to stop her. "I know very well how capable you are in protecting yourself, but I would like you as safe as possible, Alessia. Being a Bonetti already gives you enemies, when everyone discovers we are to be married, they will double in numbers."

With a heavy sigh, she holds her gaze with mine. Thinking, plotting, deciding, analyzing. "Seems like I'm not getting anything I want."

"Aren't you? I see that your father knows you aren't some *debutant*, only good for marrying off for his benefit, but he's still stuck in his ways and very old school. You're still a woman and will never get the respect you deserve." Her face hardens, but she must understand that I'm only giving it to her straight since she doesn't comment. "I promise to make you feel useful and use you to your utmost potential. Isn't that something you want?"

"It is."

"And sex, of course. You require sex, and I am willing to uphold that end of the deal." My antics to lighten the mood seem to work as her face softens again, and she cracks a smile.

"Starting the night of the wedding."

"I'll leave that entirely up to you, *cara mia*." She tries to hide her smile with her drink. "Are we in complete agreement now?"

"I'd say so."

"Then, in that case." I reach into my pocket and pull out the jewelry box. Her eyes bore into it as if it were a snake ready to bite, cautious but unafraid. Splitting the box open, I present her with an engagement ring. Those brown eyes of hers widen as she gawks at the large diamond ring. It wasn't easy to find a ring fit for my queen.

"*Cazzo.*" *Fuck*, she says on an exhale, and her eyes dart up to mine.

"May I?" She clears her throat, and it looks like she's wiping her hands in her lap before giving me her left one. I cradle it as gently as it is delicate and slip the ring into place. It fits her perfectly in size and character. She certainly wears the ring well, as diamonds do not get much more regal than this.

"It's beautiful," she says, looking down at it. "Thank you, Massimo."

"You're welcome, Alessia."

CHAPTER SIX

Alessia

"**W**ow. Holy mother Mary." Fia beams down at my ring as she obsesses over it. "I mean...*wow*. I just..."

I giggle as she tries to find words for it, and I don't blame her. I was speechless as well when he gave it to me. It's at least a seven-carrot pear-shaped diamond on a rose gold band. The large diamond against my small hand makes it look even more massive. It'll easily split through meaty flesh if I were to punch someone in the face with it. And I love it.

"Yeah, it's pretty amazing, isn't it?" I pry my hand from hers, and she pouts. Sighing, I walk over to the lounger and lie down.

"So, tell me everything. Did you guys kiss goodnight or anything?" She plops down in the lounger with me, making me scoot to share.

"No, we didn't kiss goodnight. It was more of a business dinner than a date."

"Whatever. Spill."

"We kind of went back and forth discussing our union."

"And...?"

The scent of the chemicals from the indoor pool fills my senses as I reflect on my time spent with Massimo last night. When I got home, I went straight up to my room to take time to myself. He muddled my brain and made me feel things I was not expecting to feel. Not for Massimo De Luca. He's supposed to be cold and calloused, yet he made me feel warm and tingly.

Knowing my exuberantly persistent cousin won't let it go until I give her what she wants, I give her some minor details about last night. Enough to keep her satisfied.

"Oh, shit. You're supposed to move in there in a month? When's the wedding?" She turns on her side.

"Still haven't even started planning that, but you know how extravagant those things must be." Not nearly enough time to prepare myself for Massimo mentally.

"And why does he want you to move in so soon?"

"To get to know each other better," I say, using air quotes.

Her eyes are wide as she becomes stock-still. Most likely in shock. "Wow, okay. I don't even know where to start. So, it seems like you agreed to all of *his* terms."

This is why I didn't want to give her the *full* details. The gist alone makes me seem as if I were manipulated. "They weren't so bad. He's promising to let me be a part of his family's business and teach me things. He's actually looking at me more than just part of a transaction, Fia. He's going to treat me like a real partner." I get really serious about this next part. "He said he wants to make me his queen."

Not a chess piece, but a player.

"And you believe him?"

"Why would he lie? I agreed to marry him before he said any of those things."

Massimo may be menacing and capable of deceit, but I also see honor in him. Sure, he'll manipulate when it suits him, but if he knows anything about me, he would know I won't be taken with wool over my eyes.

"Then this may be better than you ever thought, right?"

"I really hope so," I say quietly.

"What are you worried about then? Besides the obvious."

I'm quiet as I contemplate, my eyes cast downwards. What am I so afraid of? I've been preparing for this for years, and I've never really been afraid of anything. I've been trained for the worst, and I'll always have my family to fall back on and protect me.

"Wait. Alessia." I look up at her. "Are you afraid of falling for him?"

Damn. How does she know me better than I know myself? I wasn't even aware that I could actually fall for Massimo. He's never really frightened me, so I was able to look past his savageness and see the sexual appeal he has to offer. But after last night's one-on-one, it uncovered more layers to him, and that honestly worries me.

"What if I do fall for him, Fia?"

"God forbid you fall for your husband." She rolls her eyes. "Why the hell would that be a bad thing?"

"You know there is no way out of this marriage other than death. What if I fall for him hard, and he never returns my feelings? I will spend the rest of my life in love with someone who isn't in love with me."

"I see what you're saying." She screws her lips to the side. "But hey. If that's the case, at least he agreed to stay faithful to you, right? So, you wouldn't have to worry about him fucking around on you."

Only if he really is a man of his word. Tullio is one of the best men I know, and even he is capable of breaking his word. Massimo, I'm just getting to know, and although my instincts tell me I can trust him, with his word, it's not for certain.

"I sure hope so." I sigh. "There's no point in worrying about the inevitable, though. Like I said, I'm stuck with whoever Massimo turns out to be."

"Have I ever told you how thankful I am not to be important enough ever to be married off?" she teases, making me smile.

"Shut up," I mutter and stare at the glass panels above us. "Oh, and we're having an engagement party soon. We need to go dress shopping."

"You know I'm always down."

"Yeah, you are, you little slut."

"Fuck off." She punches me in the tit, making me grunt and laugh. "I'm not that slutty!"

I laugh even harder. "Sure you're not!"

She joins me in laughter, knowing how damn promiscuous she is. But she's my best fucking friend.

CHAPTER SEVEN

Alessia

Massimo insisted on having the engagement party at his estate, which was shocking. You only know who your enemies are once they make it abundantly clear.

My father and I had planned on doubling security between our men and theirs, but Massimo was quite incisive with his tactics. Quality over quantity. He wanted only those of our most trusted men as security for the party. There are extensive background checks on every person hired to work for or under us, and there are eyes everywhere, but having so many employed, sometimes one rat slips through undetected.

I've seen Massimo twice since our date a couple of weeks ago and received the official tour of their estate. The entire place was dead quiet, which is never the case in my home. I had to block out the maudlin feelings I felt crippled with. To no longer come home to comforting chaos. Instead, I'll be met with chilling silence.

So far, we've remained professional. It might sound crazy to a stranger that I'm terrified of falling in love with my fiancé, but so would an arranged marriage. My life is certainly in a world separate from reality. Not only am I very privileged, but I'm exempt from the law. Hell, I got away with murder. I wasn't even the slightest bit worried about getting arrested.

"You are definitely the prettier twin," Gemma says after I slip into my evening gown in front of the floor-length mirror.

I give her a dry look in the mirror. "You're kidding me, right?"

Her eyes widen in offense. "*You're* kidding *me*, right?"

"You girls are equally the most beautiful women in the world," Mamma says as she looks at us both in the mirror with a warm smile.

"You have to say that because you're our mother," I retort lightly.

"And because it's true," Fia chimes in. "You're twins," she teases. "Duh."

"Yes, my brother is certainly a fortunate man," Sarita says from where she's sitting.

I came over to the estate early to check on things and help make sure it all goes smoothly, so Massimo gave me a room to get ready in. Mamma, Gemma, and Fia came with me. We had some people come in to do our hair and makeup, and I invited the De Luca women to join us. Sarita politely accepted the invitation, and Vita not so politely declined.

I glance at her through the mirror and again take in her appearance. She's hard not to gawk at. Sarita is absolutely stunning. Tall, leggy, dirty blonde hair that falls into silky waves to the middle of her back, big, bold blue eyes, full pouty lips, perfect set of teeth, and dimples when she smiles. She's a knock-out.

My brother was an idiot to fuck things up with her. I get that he fell in love, and supposedly, it's something you can't help but *come on*. How could he have even looked at another woman when *that* was supposed to be his future wife? Hell, if I were told to marry her, I wouldn't hesitate to accept.

"Thank you, Sarita. Will your mother be joining us?"

Her perfect smile and posture never falter. "I can't be sure. She knows where we are, so I'm sure she'll come to us at some point before the party starts."

Nodding my head with a smile, I reach for my glass of champagne. "Don't drink too much before the party, *piccolina*. You don't want to greet your guests drunk," my mother chastises.

"Oh, Mamma." I roll my eyes.

"Massimo is going to drool over you in that dress, like for real," Fia says, and I feel my cheeks heat at the thought of him finding me attractive on any given day.

I give a nervous chuckle. "I don't think Massimo is the kind of man to drool."

The women all chuckle, and I glance over at Gemma. She still finds every opportunity when we're alone to ask me if I'm still sure about this. I feel like she's under the impression that I might be brainwashed or something. We may be twins, but we're polar opposites regarding what we expect out of life.

Walking to her, I take her hand in mine, reassuringly squeezing it. "I'm okay, Gemma. I swear. Please stop worrying about me," I murmur to her.

"Just please promise me, Alessia. If you have any doubts at all, don't go through with it. You have time. And if you do go through with it, please *please please* tell *Babbo* if he mistreats you. Don't let your pride get in the way."

"I promise I won't let myself become a weak and pathetic woman," I muse, and it seems to work as she smiles. "I can take care of myself, you know that. Plus, we have four older brothers who taught us not to take any shit."

"Just don't think you can handle everything on your own."

"Okay, I promise."

We're all sitting around sipping on champagne and chit-chatting when I decide it's time to get down there. My perfectionist needs me to check to ensure everything is under control.

When I hit the top of the steps, I stop in my tracks, and so does Massimo, who is ascending them. His hazel eyes grow darker as he takes me in. My dress is a black silk floor-length gown. It's strapless with a deep neck plunge and form-fitting down to my upper thighs, where it then falls loosely. There's a slit on one side that goes up to my mid-thigh to show off one leg and my black strappy heel. I had felt beautiful in this dress, even though it's simple with no frills, but with the way Massimo looks at me...to have a man like him slip down his mask without thought or control...it's empowering and somewhat intoxicating.

As he checks me out, I do the same to him. He's wearing a classy black suit with silk lapels and a silk bowtie. He fills everything out to perfection. His broad shoulders are the sexiest thing ever. So strong looking and masculine. The muscles in his arms and chest are hard to hide, and I cannot wait to see what he looks like unobscured.

His feet begin moving, the space between us dwindling. He stops on the step right below me. So close. Closer than we've ever been before. I can smell the fresh, manly scent coming off him and the hint of mint from his breath. Even with him a step lower and the heels I have on, he's still taller than me and twice the width. I wonder what it'll feel like to have his massive body over mine. Lips parted, hair askew, heavily breathing. *Okay, need to get my lady parts in check.*

"You look devastating, Alessia." The depth in his voice has my stomach doing flips.

Keeping my features cool, I reply, "Thank you, Massimo. You look very handsome." *Agonizingly* handsome.

His lips twitch as he tries to bite back his smile but gives me a handsome smirk. He turns and offers me his elbow, and I loop my hand around the crook of it. Pretending not to take notice of his massive bicep, I hold onto the railing with my other hand, and we descend the stairs together.

"Were there any problems today with setting up?"

"None at all. It came together nicely."

"And what about security?"

"I have Monte and another one of my guys who will be on you all evening. Do not leave the room without them," he says sternly.

I understand the severity of having a detail on me tonight, so I ignore the instant agitation of feeling scolded like a child. "Got it."

"The Gallos are coming," he says when we reach the ground floor.

I come to a halt and look up at him. "The Gallos? Why—"

"I'm sorry if that makes you uncomfortable, but they would be insulted if not invited." I glance away and swallow hard. "Hey." His voice is abnormally soft. When I look up at him, I find his head bent down some, and the look in his eyes is almost warm. "You have nothing to worry about, Alessia."

My sudden apprehension abashes me. It's unlike me to let anything other than valor and gut show, but the thought of facing the Gallos has somehow caused an unwelcome trepidation. Perhaps it's the reminder of taking a life, and how much I enjoyed it...

I paste on a confident smile and chuckle. "I appreciate your reassurance, Massimo, but I'm not worried about facing them." I propel us forward, and he continues with me, but I can feel him stealing glances at my profile.

He was lucky to die at my hands. The barbaric things my brothers would have done to him if he succeeded at violating me, he would be begging for hell to come and take him. I was merciful.

But I know the Gallos still hold a grudge against me. It all circles back to me being the wrong gender. If it were a man to commit the crime, all would be forgotten and forgiven. But since I have a vagina, I'm not supposed to protect myself or spill any blood.

But I am unlike anything women are portrayed to be.

I *can* protect myself, and I *will* spill blood.

CHAPTER EIGHT

Alessia

Since I took Massimo's elbow, he has not let me go the entire evening. Always a hand on me in some way as we mix and mingle with our invited guests. A hand at the small of my back, a hand on the back of my arm or elbow, a hand on my hip.

Then, he did the most bizarre thing when he excused himself to use the restroom. He softly kissed my cheek just before brushing the shell of my ear with his lips to whisper to me. Every cell in my body went haywire, and he walked away as I was stunned into a statue momentarily. Afraid to move in case I might crumble.

I somehow managed to avoid touching my cheek where he pressed his lips, leaving it blistering from the heat. Quickly, I had to remind myself that people were watching, and I needed to harness some aloofness. I can't let anyone see the way he already affects me.

But when I jumped back into the conversation, my voice was slightly shaky.

From one single kiss.

When he finally returns to my side, he carries a lot of tension with him. I'm not sure if he looks upset or possibly even a little flustered. I don't know him well enough to tell the difference yet, and that bothers me.

As soon as I find the opportunity, I pull him away for a bit of privacy. "Is everything okay?" I search his face for any signs that could tell me when something catches my eye. I swallow hard as my nostrils flare, and my hands are already shaking from restraint.

"Everything is fine," he mutters, not looking at me and screaming guilt.

"You might want to go change your shirt. There's lipstick on the collar." Lipstick that does not at all match the color I am currently wearing. My words are tight, and so are every muscle in my body. "And I'd appreciate it if you did it before anyone sees it."

His eyes remain reserved when they snap down to mine, and I want to fucking kill him. "Alessia—"

"Don't. Not now. We can talk about this later. We have people watching. Excuse yourself and go change your shirt." Turning with a forced smile, I walk away and do my best not to walk right out of the door and scream. My temper can be a ruinous flaw. Sometimes, it is impossible to rein in when it burns like molten lava inside of me.

It's not just humility and anger I'm feeling; it's jealousy, too.

What a fucking *stronzo*! We had an agreement, and he already broke it. An agreement *he* insisted on. I gave him the opportunity to fuck around before we got married, and he opted out of it.

Trust has to be earned as it is, so to break that already before it's even built is setting us up for a strenuous road ahead.

And to dare try and make a fool out of me at our fucking engagement party. I already want to shank his ass right here in front of everyone. Luckily, I didn't catch him in the act, or I would not have been able to restrain myself.

If he thinks he can do whatever the hell he wants and I have to follow the rules, he has another thing coming. I will not stand by and behave like a good, obedient girl while he's out there making a mockery of me. Fuck. That. And fuck. Him.

Plucking a new glass of champagne off a tray, I glance around the room to find who the whore might be. Obviously, a woman wearing red lipstick and someone with a death sentence.

I continue scouring the room, smiling politely at anyone I come in eye contact with when my gazing gets put on pause. Arianna De Niro. Rumors about her and Massimo being an item a few years ago sizzle as her red-painted lips are curled up into a dazzling smile directed at me. My vision is polluted with murderous rage as I use deep breaths to calm myself. I'm a Bonetti, and I will not lose it on some hussy that messed around with my fiancé at my own engagement party. She knows better than to disrespect a woman in my position since she, too, is the daughter of a capo. Not a well-respected one, but one no less.

It seems my reputation has not made an impression on her as it should, and she needs a little demonstration.

Downing my champagne, I begin to make my way over to her. Our eyes locked, and a smirk now mocking me on her face. She will not get away with this— "Alessia." A strong hand wraps around my upper arm, and a deep voice in my ear stops me. "I can explain. It's not at all—"

My glower snaps up to his. "Oh, I think I'll have Arianna explain it to me," I coo and try to pull away from him, but he doesn't let me go.

"It's not what you think. I said I would not touch any other woman, and I meant it," he practically spits at me as if I should be the one on trial here.

To everyone else, it looks like I am leaning into my handsome fiancé getting a little cozy, and when I open my mouth, my words are passionate, but not in a loving way. "Your word doesn't mean shit. How the *fuck* did red lipstick get on your collar? Someone would have to be awfully close to you for that to happen. You think I'm stupid? I know you and her used to be a thing, and she happens to be wearing that exact color on her whorish lips. Not to mention the fact that when you came back, you were slightly flustered and wouldn't even look at me. Those are not hard puzzle pieces to fit together. They fell into place all on their own. Now, if you'll excuse me, I must remind someone what happens when I feel disrespected." I place my hands on his chest and smile up at him coyly. "Care to join me?"

"My place is at your side, *cara mia*," he says evenly as if no longer perturbed. Taking one of my hands from his chest, he laces his fingers with mine a little too tightly as a warning. I squeeze his hand right back, and we journey the short distance to the lovely Arianna.

"Arianna, how are you?" I walk right up to her and kiss each cheek. "Thank you so much for coming."

"I wouldn't have missed it for the world," she purrs, then turns her attention to Massimo. I watch them out of the corner of my eye as I greet the others around. "Massimo." She smirks at him over her glass of champagne and sips from it.

"Arianna. Good to see you again," he responds dryly, his voice as level as usual.

"Your dress is lovely, Arianna. It's very...pageant-like. Something only you could pull off." A few people chuckle around us as I smile at her. Hers fades a little, and she stands straighter in her red sparkly gown. She looks like that big-boobed cartoon chick in that one movie married to a rabbit. "I do love a good red dress. Easier to conceal blood splatter." I bat my lashes as everyone chuckles.

"So, are you as savage as they say?" she responds as if it would offend me.

"I'm only savage when I feel disrespected," my words come out smoother than honey.

"I know I certainly would not want to be on the receiving end of your wrath, Miss Bonetti," a man of little importance says from somewhere around the small group gathered.

"You definitely wouldn't," I agree loudly, my eyes still locked with Arianna's. The little bravado she had left disappears quickly, and she looks like she might tuck her tail and run. And I do love a good chase. "Well, we do have other guests to get around to." I tear my gaze away to address the others. "But thank you all for being here. Come, my love." I tug at Massimo's hand that I'm still adhered to, and we walk away without direction.

I pry my shaking hand away from him, and he puts his at the small of my back. "I need a private moment with you," he rumbles in my ear, and I try to calm the rage his voice is amplifying. I have never practiced such great self-control before. I should be picking her teeth out of my knuckles, but here I am, acting like a dignified lady.

Why am I not angrier with *Massimo*? He's the one that broke my trust.

"I don't want to be alone with you right now," I say defiantly with my eyes averted.

"I will drag you out of this room if I have to, Alessia," he threatens.

"And make a scene?" I taunt. "That wouldn't be very kingly."

He sighs heavily, then gives my upper arm a firm grip. "Last chance to come with me willingly," he growls, and I heed his warning. The last thing we need is my brothers coming to the rescue and an all-out brawl to begin.

"Fine," I say through gritted teeth. "Lead the way, *sweetheart*."

His grip on my arm doesn't let up in the slightest as he steers us out of the room, and he tells the guys to hang back as we disappear into a darkened hallway. There, he pins me against the wall and hovers over me as I glower up at him. His arms caging me in and trying to use his massive size to make me yield. I could knee him in the balls or head butt him, but something makes me want to stay.

"I gave you my word on something, and I need you to understand that when I give it to you, it's as good as me signing a contract in blood."

"Then why the fuck was there lipstick on your collar? Please explain that to me," I sneer. I am dying to know what kind of bullshit he'll try to feed me.

"I do not need to explain anything. If I tell you that nothing happened, then nothing happened," he snarls in my face, his patience waning.

"You didn't say that nothing happened."

"Fine. Nothing happened. Happy?"

"Oh, I am over the moon," I say acerbically. He stays right there in my personal space, and I find myself studying his lips. Remembering what they felt like on my cheek and wondering if he had to scrub red lipstick off them before rejoining me, causing the anger to revive. "Are we done here?" My voice isn't as strong as I intended it to be, and I catch him glancing down at my mouth. "We should get back, Massimo," I rasp.

His nostrils twitch. "We can go back whenever we damn well please. It is our party. They'll just think I had to steal a moment with my fiancée because I can't keep my hands off her." My breath hitches, and I find myself breathing harder. My body is craving something indescribable and something almost too overwhelming to handle. "Have I told you how stunning you are, Alessia?" His warm breath fans out over my face, and when he gently uses one rough finger to make a path down my jawline, I completely melt against the wall, now holding me up. "The most stunning thing in the room. I really can't keep my hands off you, and you're getting harder and harder to resist." A lump forms in my suddenly tight throat, making it impossible to say a word. How did this conversation abruptly make a complete one-eighty? How did he just win the upper hand? "Knowing that you are now mine, no other woman can steal my attention from you for even a moment. Even when we are not in the same room. You may be inclined to wait until our wedding night, but know I want you and only you. The wait will be more than worth it, so I can wait, Alessia. I can and I will. Do not question my faithfulness again, or I'll have to put you over my knee and remind you of your place."

The rage is back with a vengeance, coiling tight and ready to snap. "My place?" I blurt in a shrill voice.

"Your place is with me, and as your man, I need you to trust me and my word, or I'll have to mark your pretty little ass with the hands that belong to you."

What the... My man? The hands that belong to me? Can you actually own any part of Massimo? Wait...over his knee?!

I should be appalled, but I'm so fucking turned on and dumbfounded.

"Do not question me again, Alessia," he reprimands.

"Do not threaten me," I hiss, and he has the audacity to find it humorous.

"It's not a threat, *cara mia*. You will soon learn that I make no threats." He leans back some but still has me trapped. "Now, do you think you can rein in your temper some and let this thing go? Or do you need to get the rest of your tantrum out of the way? I could help you with that, you know." His lips are still slightly curled up at the corners, and his eyes have a playful gleam.

"I think I can handle myself, thank you."

"Shame," he muses and stands up straight, dropping his hands from the wall, and I take a deep breath. "Shall we?" He holds a hand out, and I ignore it as I walk past him. Just as one of my feet steps over the threshold, my hand is gripped tightly in his as he leans into my ear. "You're trying my patience, *piccolina*. Do you actually want that spanking, or are you truly incapable of controlling that beautiful temper of yours?" My skin bristles with goosebumps.

"You have no idea what my temper actually looks like, Massimo. If you did, you would see that I am most definitely in control of myself right now. That out there was tame compared to my tantrums," I say lowly.

When he lets out a chuckle, he tries to hide it behind a fist, disguising it with a cough. My head whips around to get a look, and wouldn't you know? The madman is capable of smiling. His white teeth are perfectly straight, and there are crinkles around his eyes. He's absolutely magnetizing.

"You'll definitely keep me entertained, won't you, Alessia?" He glances down at me with a slight smile.

I can't help myself as I try to fight back my own smile and totally fail. Putting a damper on my inner turmoil. "Seems like you will keep me entertained as well, Massimo." And certainly a challenge.

The fact that he was able to use my hormones against me to prevaricate the situation and turn me on instead, he already has some hold on me that I need to take back. I will not be his submissive in any way.

I will be his equal, or I will be his worst nightmare.

CHAPTER NINE

Alessia

"Calm yourself, *piccolina*. You go relax until your fiancé gets here," my mom says, still trying to shoo me out of the kitchen.

Massimo is coming over for dinner tonight, and I don't understand why I am so nervous. This is *my* territory.

The party was four nights ago, and I haven't seen him since we said goodbye at night's end. But his presence isn't needed to continue to mess with my head and, most certainly, my body.

Every time he placed a kiss on my cheek or brushed his lips against the shell of my ear to whisper something, I wanted to turn my head and catch it on my lips—to feel it burn my lips the way it burned my cheek. And as the night went on, the more I found myself leaning into his every touch—enjoying it, anticipating it. Fia even said he and I looked like a real couple, which I refused to comment on.

Then I keep thinking about Arianna's lipstick stain on Massimo's collar. I don't think he plans to explain himself to me, and I do not plan on letting it go. He thinks he's entitled to my trust. You cannot force someone to trust you just like you cannot demand someone to love you.

"I don't want to relax, Mamma. I can't. I need something to do," I whine, and she clucks her tongue in disapproval.

"Go. I mean it."

Sighing, I turn and leave the kitchen to head into the other room. I grab a seat next to Salvatore, Tullio's six-year-old son, and my nephew. "Hey, Sal." I ruffle his hair, and he ducks out of the way. I chuckle and wrap an arm around him to give him a squeeze.

Glancing over at Tullio, I find him watching me. His guilt is palpable, but I hold no grudge against him. Yes, if he married Sarita, I wouldn't be marrying Massimo, but it would be someone else from another family.

I give him a sanguine smile and engage in conversation like normal. As usual, Alba ends up on my lap and becomes my responsibility, especially since Gemma isn't here to share the duties. My brothers love giving the little princess love and attention, but she's mine once everyone has had their fill. I don't mind, though. She's my girl, and I honestly cannot wait to have kids of my own. There's no hurry, though, since I am only twenty-one.

Which reminds me, Massimo and I haven't talked about kids yet, and we probably should discuss it. He'll most definitely want an heir or two, but how soon? And how many?

My father finally graces us with his presence and says Massimo is now pulling up to the estate. He looks at me, but I remain blithe as I talk to Alba and smile at her.

I keep my focus on her as a distraction when Massimo enters the room, and I hear everyone greeting him. The mood changes, my brothers slipping somewhat into mobster mode now that there is a De Luca on our turf. He may be family soon, but until then, we all must remain wary.

There's a mixture of English and Italian going around, and I overhear him saying he brought over two bottles of his family's wine. I must admit, it's the best wine I have ever tasted. And the food at his family restaurant is neck and neck with my mother's cooking. However, I would never dare ever to say that out loud.

Standing up with Alba in my arms, I smile up at Massimo as he approaches and allow him to brush his lips across each cheek, titillating my skin. "Massimo."

"Alessia." He looks down at Alba and gives her a tiny but warm smile.

"I guess you haven't officially met Alba yet. The newest Bonetti princess."

"She's beautiful," he says, still looking at her.

My mother comes whirling into the room. A paragon of an Italian mother and hostess. "Massimo, *come sta?*" *How are you?*

"*Sto bene, grazie, e Lei?*" *I'm well, thank you, and you?*

"I'm wonderful. Dinner should be ready soon. I hope you're hungry. Lesina, honey. Come give me a hand." I open my mouth to offer my help, but my mother gives me a look that stops me.

Lesina silently begs me for backup with her eyes, but she's on her own. I'm occupied with taking care of *her* baby at the moment, so she can pretend to be an actual part of the family for once. When she realizes I won't be bailing her out, she cements on a fake smile and follows my mother out.

"Come, let me get you a drink, Massimo," my father says, leading him to the bar.

Santino comes over to sit next to me. "You okay?" he murmurs, throwing an arm along the back of the couch.

I nod my head, smiling. "I'm fine."

Santino is the taciturn one, but that in no way means he's soft or easy. He's quiet because he's busy observing and absorbing. Making him the most perspicacious, able to see and hear what others won't. It's why our father relies on him most for his useful information. Armando would be considered our best soldier physically, but Santino is downright scary. Yet, ironically, he's the most sensitive of all my brothers.

"I still don't like this," he grumbles and eyes up Massimo from across the room.

"I know, Santino, but you'll have to get over it."

"It isn't final until you're married. You have plenty of time to change your mind."

Why must I continue to repeat myself?

"That's not happening. It's hard enough to be respected as a woman in this world. If my word doesn't mean shit, then neither will I."

He sighs and rubs his jawline. "Is that why you're really doing this? To earn more respect?" I don't answer him. "I'm just saying that no one would judge you for changing your mind. Arranged marriage is so old school, and things are slowly changing."

Too slowly...

"I appreciate your support, Saint, but I'm doing this. Accept it." I glance over at Massimo and catch him staring. "It could be a lot worse than Massimo De Luca."

"You better tell me if he wrongs you in any way."

I don't bother telling him how I can take care of myself. I know they only love me, but I'm beginning to feel like a broken record. "I promise I will."

Family dinner is just as you would expect in a big Italian family. It's chaotic. Everyone talks too loudly and over each other, insults are thrown, serving dishes of Mamma's cooking are passed around the crowded table.

Our aunts, uncles, and cousins come over for dinner at least twice a week, and it only gets crazier. And when our grandparents come from Italy to visit, it is insane. My grandma, aunts, and mother start preparing for dinner shortly after breakfast, making enough food to feed an army.

Massimo sits beside me, and I feel how tightly spun he is. To him, this may be quite a shock. I mean, we're gangsters who thrive on crime, yet we sit down as a family to eat. We even bow our heads as Mamma says a quick grace.

I can't help the giggle that bubbles up when Mamma scolds Massimo for taking a polite serving. Only she could get away with treating Massimo like a child, and he cracked a smile rather than a skull.

"If it weren't for the intensive training I do daily, I'd be fat as hell," I murmur over to him.

His smile widens some as his eyes make a leisurely trail down the length of my body. "Intensive training, huh?" he asks, and I nod my head.

"She's also lethal with a knife of any kind," Armando interjects, obviously eavesdropping in on our conversation. "So, keep her away from pointy objects if you're in some kind of a tiff."

"Scary as shit, more like it," Paolo mutters, and Tullio smacks him on the back of the head at the same time Mamma chastises him for cursing at the table. "I'm sorry for cursing, Mamma, but it's true!"

"You're just jealous because you have terrible aim," I tease him, then look over at Massimo, grinning. "He couldn't hit the target with a knife if it were six feet away."

"And you?" His eyes are full of intrigue.

"I could hit it with my eyes closed," I reply smugly.

"I'd certainly like to see that." We lock gazes for a moment until Armando speaks again.

"It's how she got the name 'little psycho.'" A bunch of them start snickering as I glare at my annoying brother.

"Hey, I told you not to call her that!" Mamma reprimands. "You know I hate that. Now apologize to your sister."

I raise both eyebrows at him with a smirk. "I'm sorry for calling you psycho," he says half-heartedly.

I think it bothers Mamma so much when they call me that because she's concerned there might be some truth to it. She's from an affluent family, but she'd rather have her head in the sand than know what really goes on around her.

After we're all overly stuffed and all the wine is consumed, the boys clear the table while the rest sit around and chat. My father and Massimo are the only two still withdrawn, remaining in boss form. Neither of them willing to show their hand.

Yet, I sense that Massimo will learn to breach my carefully constructed walls.

CHAPTER TEN

Massimo

I placed Alessia's room across the hall from mine. Close to me, but not close enough.

I'm not accustomed to having to harness any of myself. If I didn't believe in the words I fed her about having a somewhat happy relationship myself, then I would have her tied to my bed already. Claiming precisely what is mine.

The night of our engagement party, she had me so close to unraveling. I do not lose control, and I do not let myself become emotional. But her accusation of me touching any other woman beside her infuriated me. She has no idea how hard up she has me and how badly I wanted to fuck Arianna just to release some of the fucking tension Alessia's presence alone has festered in my fucking balls. One good release, but when Arianna threw herself at me, I turned her down even though it was painful.

I sent over some of my men on move-in day, which was three days ago, but when they arrived, her brothers had already handled it and sent them away. I appreciate the protection her brothers provide her with, but she's now my full responsibility. She's *mine* to take care of.

I did give her my word that she would be able to have dinner with her family as much as she'd like, but I also told her that I'd like to spend time with her, preferably in the evenings. Yet, she has been gone every night so far, not returning until late.

My cousin Monte is on Alessia duty for the majority of the time, so before heading over to my father's side of the estate for a quick meeting, I ask him where I might find Alessia.

Just before entering the room, I hear laughter coming from it. Alessia's laughter, and it puts a smile on my face to hear it. It's a girlish sound, exposing her more gentle and feminine side. The regal air around her subsiding briefly when she lights up like that.

It's inherent for us to keep our emotions far from the surface, and I know that since Alessia is a female trying to be seen for more than just her body as a vessel, she feels as if she has to try even harder. She's risen to prominence through her own efforts, but her irascible temper is a strong emotion she must learn to conquer.

Making my presence known, I walk into the room, and Alessia and Monte stop mid-conversation. "Massimo. I was beginning to think we would never cross paths here." She comes to me and kisses me softly on either of my cheeks, her ambrosial scent surrounding me.

"I know I haven't been able to see you settled in, but I'm hoping you could spare one evening to have dinner with me." There's a slight bite to my tone. Almost feeling jealous of her family for getting all her time.

"I suppose I could spare one night," she says cheekily and goes to sit back down on the loveseat she was occupying. "Since I haven't been given anything to do, I get a little stir-crazy. It can get quite lonely in a big place like this with no one to talk to. Other than my trusty guard dog," she muses, looking at Monte, and he chuckles. The playfulness they seem to already have with one another slightly irks me.

"I thought you'd like time to settle in first."

"I'm settled."

"Good, then we can discuss more over dinner tonight."

"Very well then."

My feet are rooted to the floor as she stares back at me. Waiting for me to say something else. Daring me to. Now that I'm here with her, I don't want to leave yet. This is my first conversation with her in days, and I'm at a loss for words.

"I have to go meet with my father, and then I have to run out for a while."

"Sure." She opens her book and looks down at it. As if dismissing me, and I, for some reason, want her attention back.

"Would you like to go with me?" Her head snaps up, and I elaborate. "Out, that is." I won't force Alessia to deal with my father's company if she doesn't have to. She deserves respect, and my father refuses to acknowledge that.

Her eyes dance with curiosity. "And where will we be going?"

"Out," I state vaguely.

"And what kind of attire would this outing require?"

"Nothing you wouldn't want to get ruined," I muse, though she'll only be there as a spectator.

Her eyes squint in devious appeasement. "Hmm. Okay then. I'll go change and be waiting for you."

"I'll come find you when it's time to leave."

"Sounds good."

Heading to my father's office, I think about Alessia. The way she always presents herself and the confidence she emanates. Dignity and esteem glowing from the inside out making her come off solipsistic, but so secure in it that it makes everyone else a believer.

My father and I don't work side by side like we used to. We haven't worked in the same room in probably a decade or so. He leaves specific duties and responsibilities to me, which I execute independently. We meet a few times a week, but typically, we work separately. I even have my own businesses that he is not a part of.

Even though it had hardly been ten minutes spent with him, I still feel a pounding in my head, which I always get whenever he's around. If it weren't for the customary succession we all abide by, I would have ventured out on my own years ago. Breaking from my father completely.

"*Entra!*" *Enter!* Alessia calls out when I knock on her bedroom door.

I walk in to find her perched on the edge of her bed, pulling on a pair of boots that come up to her knees. She switched her pretty dress out for another pretty one, yet less vibrant. "Should I be packing?" she asks with one eyebrow hitched.

"If it makes you feel better but isn't necessary." I'm unsure if it was a test, but she stares at me for a long moment, then shrugs her shoulders and goes over to her dresser to pick up her Glock. She checks the chamber and then the safety before tucking it into her thigh holster. I drink in the olive skin there that looks smooth to the touch, anxious to mark it up.

Dropping her dress down, she grabs a light jacket and comes to stand in front of me. "Alright, I'm ready." Her ethereal smile is indeed deceptive.

"What about you?" she asks, looking at my suit as we head downstairs.

"I don't have any attachments to this suit." My suit evokes a sense of functional uniformity.

We slide into the backseat, and it feels natural to be with her as if we've been doing this for so long. Whenever we speak, it isn't to fill the silence. And when we're silent, it's comfortable.

"So, since my trainer isn't able to come here to train me, I need a new one," she says as we pull away from the estate.

"You can use ours. I'll have that set up for you. Give me a time and when you'd like to start."

"Awesome. Thank you."

"You're welcome."

"So, who are we torturing today?"

I surprise everyone in the vehicle when I throw my head back and laugh out loud. "What makes you think that's where we're headed?" She gives me a dry look, and I shake my head in amusement. "Fair enough. There's someone with some loose lips." I don't give her anything more, and she doesn't ask. Only nods and looks out the window as if we're driving to the park.

"So, the warehouse in the city?" I see her smile in the reflection of the tinted window.

I fix my eyes forward while giving a disapproving grunt. The warehouse is a fairly new location of ours located boldly in the city with an underground level. Not something that that was broadcasted. What else does the little vixen know that she shouldn't? It should be unsettling, but I find myself impressed.

I keep a protective hand on the curve of her back as we enter the building, flanked by a few men. She's still her chipper self as we head for the stairs going down. Her bravado never faltering.

The *stronzo* on trial thought it was a free-for-all for him and his buddies at one of our *bordellos*. Our *bordello* isn't what you would describe as a whore house. Yes, it's for the sex trade, but it's where the women are prepared and trained to be auctioned off to our high clientele. Only those at the very top of the totem pole may send out invitations.

His buddies were already taken care of, but he is detained until I have personally confirmed there is more loose ends to tie up. Peeling my jacket off and rolling up my sleeves, I stand in front of the bloodied and soiled man hanging limply. His arms stretched above, tethered in chains, and his head slumped forward.

I give his cheek a few taps, which he only flinches and groans in response. "Wake him up for me, will ya?" I tell one of my men and step back. Spotting Alessia, I almost smile when I see her standing there with a lead pipe in her hand, itching to use it. I arch an eyebrow at her, and she arches hers right back with a little gleam in her eyes. "Would you like to take a crack at it, *cara*?"

She slaps the lead pipe into one of her palms a few times, and my cock grows stiff in my pants. She's fascinatingly deviant. "May I?" she asks sweetly.

I move aside and tell my guy to as well. He looks from me to Alessia, and when I release a growl from the back of my throat in warning, and he instantly moves. I'm enthralled as Alessia stalks forward with the pipe still slapping her palm. Her heels clicking on the floor, and her pretty dress swaying with her hips. She had tied her dark hair back into a sophisticated bun at the nape of her neck, her elegant features unveiled.

Without any hesitation, she speeds up her steps, cranks the pipe back, and swings forward with all her might like a baseball bat, hitting her target and kneecapping him. All you hear is the sound of bone crunching, and it works like a charm as the guy's head snaps back, and he begins howling at the top of his lungs. Now, wide awake and alert.

The guys in the room all hiss and grimace, knowing how fucking painful kneecapping is. Alessia has this gleeful smile on her face like she's a kid who just ate some cotton candy or some shit as she walks away from the man, and I swear she looks absolutely illusory. As if walking out of my darkest and dirtiest dream.

"You're welcome," she chirps, and I rub a hand over my jaw to try and hide my grin.

"You've done this before," I murmur as she walks past me.

"Nope. But I have always wanted to." She smiles at me over her shoulder, and I can't hide the grin from my face this time.

"Little psycho," I mutter under my breath and turn back to the still-howling man.

"I heard that!" she sing-songs from behind me, making me swallow a chuckle.

One of my guys stuffs some fabric into his mouth when he doesn't stop squealing like a pig. "Jeremy, is it?" The guy is panting around the gag, and his eyes look wildly around the room. When they land on me, they grow twice the size. "That was a subtle wake-up call from my beautiful fiancée." I gesture to Alessia, and his eyes bounce from her to me. "Yes, she is the one who took a pipe to your knee, which you will never get back, unfortunately. That was just her warm-up, I'm afraid." His eyes continue to frantically look between me and my stunning queen somewhere behind me. "It's also nothing compared to what I will do to you."

Having Alessia there worked out better than I predicted. It's one thing to hear the rumors about me wielding my power around in the form of torture and dismemberment; it's another to actually witness it. I'm not the kind of boss to sit behind my desk barking orders and sending my goons out in representation of me. I'm a boss who is not reluctant of the dirty work.

Alessia was even more zealous when I let her take the pipe to his second knee. He had already begun singing like a canary once I was done with him, but I couldn't deny her such a simple pleasure.

After I gave the orders to take care of him and his brother, Alessia and I walked right out of there, slipping into the backseat of the car like we were on a date. It's dead silent for a few moments and I'm almost hesitant to look at her. As soon as the adrenaline wears off, she might panic.

"So, what's for dinner tonight? I am *starving*."

For the second time tonight, and the second time in God knows how long, I bark out laughter that ricochets off the windows and closed doors of the vehicle.

This woman could be the best thing that has ever happened to me, or she could be the worst.

My uprising or my downfall.

But her danger is too intoxicating to ignore.

CHAPTER ELEVEN

Alessia

I'm bored. Like really fucking bored.

Massimo hasn't given me much to do yet, but I get it. Until we're married, I'm still a Bonetti, a once rivaled family. But it doesn't change the fact that *I am bored*.

The De Luca estate is like a freaking tomb. None of his other siblings live here, and his mother might as well not. She hides in her room every day, and I've only seen her once since the party. The two short encounters were depressing. Her mind is no longer lucid, and she's like an empty shell of a once beautiful woman.

Thankfully I've had no run-ins with Angelo. I'm not afraid of the man, but I'd rather keep my distance and not have to see him if it's not necessary. I have no idea what the hell I've done to earn such animosity from him. If he hated me so much, then why the arranged marriage?

I also find it peculiar that he and his father don't work closely together like my father and Tullio. From my understanding, that's what you do. You work under your father until it's time for you to take over. It's as if two separate De Luca empires are being run.

Armando is the only one to reside off our estate, but he's over the house every freaking day. There's always someone around and stuff going on. Never a dull moment at the Bonetti's. Maybe Massimo will let me get a dog or something to keep me company and give me something to do.

Monte is decent company and helps with the loneliness, but it's also his job to hang around me. Poor guy got put on babysitting duty. At least he isn't terrible to look at. Nice brown hair with style, handsome face, nice smile, easy on the eyes, tall, and I'm sure very fit underneath. He's also amusing and makes me laugh a lot.

We're going to my family's for dinner tonight, and I can't wait. It's been four days since I've seen them, and it feels like weeks. Massimo and I have had dinner together every night and then enjoyed a nice little nightcap afterward, but that's all it's been. *Nice*.

I had more fun with my first kneecapping and watching Massimo play operation on a live human being than any dinner I've had with him. At least then, he laughed. *Twice*. So I know he's capable of smiling and laughing.

When our eyes meet, I feel something vital pulling me towards him, but he manages to quickly disconnect it as if something is holding him back. I thought he was thawing out for me, but he seems to be freezing me out now.

The wedding planning started a couple of weeks ago, and surprisingly, Massimo is giving me the green light to do whatever the fuck I want. I was almost positive I had him pegged for being administrative like me. I guess he probably doesn't care much because I wasn't his first choice as a wife, and this is a marriage of convenience and not love.

Walking into my family's home, I bask in the scent of Mamma's cooking and the clangor of my family being their obnoxious selves. We're bombarded with greetings and love when we enter the room, and I'm pleasantly surprised to see Fia and her family here.

Dinner goes by in the same fashion. Loud banter while Massimo watches us like we're creatures from another planet. I understand his restlessness now more than ever. Our upbringing couldn't be more opposing even though we really are from the same world.

Before we arrived tonight, I asked Massimo if it was alright that I stuck around for a while after dinner. I offered to let him leave and got a ride back later. His agreement to stay with me was unprecedented.

I could be hallucinating, but I swear Massimo is enjoying tonight. We're all congregated in the sitting room off the kitchen, and Salvatore chose the seat next to him. Sal looks like a grown man talking to him right now. His chest puffed out, and one ankle crossed over his knee, mirroring Massimo. I can only imagine what their conversation is like. Salvatore is so mature for his age, and well, Massimo is Massimo. Even Tullio has difficulty being warm towards his son, and he isn't as stern as Massimo.

Massimo looks so relaxed at this very moment. His tense and massive shoulders aren't as stiff, and the lines between his brows are faint creases, not crevices. This proves that he is, in fact, capable of being human.

I sit and observe as Alba makes her way around the room by holding herself up on things. She has grown so much over the past month, and it only makes me realize how much she'll keep growing and how much I'll be missing. She's so close to walking, and I hate that I won't be around for her first real steps.

She's inching closer and closer to Massimo, and I'm eager for his reaction. When her hands make it to his knees, I stifle a giggle as I watch the two of them stare at each other. Both trying to figure the other one out. Friend or foe.

After moments of staring him down, she starts babbling away at him, and he cracks a rare smile. Not a smirk or a vicious grin. Gleaming white teeth and crinkles around his eyes kind of smile. His large hand tentatively reaches out to stroke her soft brown curls on top of her head like petting a kitten, and the look in his eyes when he does it makes my heart do that weird flapping thing in my chest again.

We still have yet to talk about children. I'm too chicken-shit to start that conversation. Children come from sex, and no matter how sexy or handsome I find him and how much I want to climb him like a tree, I'm terrified of it. I've always been the controlling one sexually, but I've never been with a true alpha before, and Massimo is definitely a true alpha. Am I ready to give up that control? Will *I* be able to handle *him*? The shiver down my spine only frightens me more.

It's getting late when we finally say our goodbyes and return to his estate. I guess I should start calling it home now.

"Massimo." I look at him, and he gives me his undivided attention. "We haven't discussed our terms of reproduction, and I think we should." My voice is steady when I'm shaking inside.

His lips twitch. "I agree." He pauses. "Ladies first."

"Obviously, we should have children. You need an heir, and I would like to be a mother someday. But I'm still young and would like to wait a few years."

"How many years are we talking?"

"Well, I'm just going on twenty-two, so I do have a lot of years left on my maternal clock. There'd be no reason to rush things."

"How many years are we talking?" he repeats.

I guess I am beating around the bush here. "Six." That'll make me about twenty-eight. It's a good age to start having children, I think.

"Three."

My eyes widen. "Five."

"Four."

I cross my arms over my chest. "Four from now or from the wedding?"

He tries fighting the humor he finds in this. "From the wedding."

Damnit. His negotiating skills are annoying as fuck. "Fine. Four years from the wedding, we'll start trying for a baby."

"We'll have a baby. Four years from the wedding, I want a baby."

Hearing Massimo say, 'I want a baby,' makes my uterus quiver. "Let's compromise."

"We already have."

"No, we negotiated. Now, we compromise." He dips his chin, telling me to go on, and I hate how endearing I find his smirk. "Four years from *now*, we start *trying* for a baby."

Chuckling, he rubs a palm along his perfectly groomed facial hair. "Alright, *cara*. Four years from *now*, we will *try* for a baby."

"Agreed." I grin in victory. "You know, I kind of like negotiating with you." It's refreshing. Usually, it's way too easy in getting my own way.

"You're the only one who would ever say that."

"You're not as scary as everyone thinks you are, too."

"You found me scary?"

"No, but I was unsure how much of the rumors could be true. It's only been a couple of months getting to know you, but something tells me you are above abusing women."

"You thought that I abuse women?" His head cocks to one side.

I shrug. "Rumors say you're a little rough with them." I don't elaborate.

"I don't harm women," he says gravely, and I believe him.

I believed him before he even spoke the words.

CHAPTER TWELVE

Alessia

Massimo left town and was very evasive about his agenda.

Not only was I slightly offended when he didn't invite me to join him, but when he wouldn't give me any straight answers, it immediately had paranoia peaking.

"Business," he said. And when I asked, "Where?" he said, "Out of the country." After, he looked at me like I was this pestering child he couldn't be bothered with. He has yet to discover how pertinacious I can genuinely be. Once we're married, I will demand to know *everything*.

Not at all able to sit around the vapid and dull estate, I go to my family's to have lunch with Mamma and Monte in tow.

Thankfully, he gives us privacy as we sit in the tearoom over-looking the grounds at the back of the property. "There aren't any gardens at Massimo's," I say, staring outside. It's warming up, and I'm looking forward to the summer. I absolutely love the warm weather and basking in the hot sun.

"You could ask him if you can get some plants put in," Mamma suggests.

Sighing, I sip my tea as I obsessively ruminate about where Massimo is. He's been gone over a day and has yet to call or text. I keep reminding myself that this isn't a normal relationship where we can't stand to be away from each other.

"What's wrong, *piccolina*? You seem a bit forlorn. Talk to me."

Mamma always knows when something is plaguing us. I hope to be a wonderful mother like her someday. "I'm afraid, Mamma." She is the one and only person in the world I would splay my heart for. To admit my doubts and fears so openly. Let her see my vulnerability and see me at my weakest and lowest.

"Of your feelings for Massimo?" I nod my head. "Why, *bambina*?"

"I feel like I'm already falling for him and barely know him. I know our relationship is based on an arrangement, but I don't know. I wish it felt like a little more than that. I can't expect him to somehow fall in love with me someday, but I hope he'll at least learn to care for me and love me as family."

"What makes you think he isn't falling for you too?"

"He's not." I shake my head.

"How do you know?"

"I just do, Mamma. The little time we spend together, he's...cold. I mean, not cruel or anything like that, and there's been a few rare moments where he warmed up to me. I just wish I knew how to make him do it more often. Let his guard down some when it's only the two of us."

"Maybe he's afraid of the same things as you."

"Massimo isn't afraid of anything," I state matter-of-factly.

"Okay, so maybe afraid is not the right word to use. Maybe apprehensive." We're quiet for a moment. "Would falling in love with your husband be so bad?"

"Could you imagine *Babbo* never loving you back? Marrying him, falling in love with him, and spending the rest of your life with unrequited love?"

"It wouldn't be ideal, but if he at least let me love him, it's something I could live with, especially if I had no other choice. It'd be better than to be at war with myself, trying to fight a losing battle."

Mamma and I are different people, though. She's soft, kind, and much more accepting of things than I am. To imagine a life of being in love with someone who did not return those same feelings sounds like a despondent one.

No, I need to get a better hold of my feelings, which are rapidly growing for him. If I can put a leash on my temper, I can certainly put a leash on my emotions all around.

During the four days that Massimo is gone, I spend most of my time with my family. Hanging out in my father's office just to be with him, spending time with my brothers and Fia, cooking with Mamma, watching my niece, and even having a few nightcaps with Monte when I wasn't quite ready to call it a night.

It's evening when Massimo finally comes home. I'm on the outdoor patio enjoying some wine when he walks out. Monte jumps to his feet as Massimo looks between the two of us as if he caught us doing something wrong. Only the guilty would so quickly jump to conclusions like that.

"Hey, Massimo. How was your trip?" Monte asks, and Massimo goes from disgruntled to surly in a matter of seconds. "I'll, uh, give you guys some privacy." Monte turns and leaves when Massimo refuses to acknowledge him.

Massimo watches his retreat, then turns to me as I sit and wait for him to make the first move. He eventually does, kissing me on either cheek. I open my mouth to ask him about his trip when he beats me to it.

"Monte isn't for your entertainment," he all but growls.

"No? Pray tell, who is, Massimo? I wake up, train, then wait around the rest of the day until you have a couple of hours to spare me," I say evenly, holding onto my cool. Using that leash I gave myself a pep-talk on.

"You have the freedom to leave and do whatever it is that you want."

"Whatever I want, huh? Is that what you were doing these past few days?"

He frowns down at me. "What are you trying to say, Alessia?" Right away, he's getting defensive.

"Where were you really, Massimo? If you remember correctly, I did permit you to be with other women until we were married, and it was *you* who wanted to be monogamous without delay. What I am not okay with is sneaking around behind my back." I'm quickly spiraling, and I can't stop. That leash is now pulled exorbitantly taut. "At least be man enough to tell me the truth to my face."

"Are you accusing me once again of infidelity?" he raises his voice slightly.

"Yes." I spring up from my chair and jut out my chin. "I'm not an idiot, Massimo. So, do not treat me like one. If you want to be with other women before we are married, then just admit it and stop being a pussy about it." Spinning on my heels, I storm up the steps and into the house before I can lash out anymore.

"Alessia, we are not done talking," he bellows out after me, and I ignore him. "Alessia, if you know what's good for you, you will stop and face me."

What's good for me? *Oh, hell no. Have fun watching my backside, Massimo, because that's all you'll be seeing before I slam the door in your face.* I can feel his presence still somewhere behind me as I ascend the stairs and stomp to my room. I don't run, but I do keep a swift pace.

I'm about to slam my door shut when he charges me—spinning me around and using my body to forcefully close it. He looks deranged and out of his mind, his gaze darkened, and a lock of hair out of place. A shiver billows through me from the sex appeal he's currently projecting.

"Twice now, you have accused me of being a man I am not. If I tell you I am not to touch another woman ever again, then I mean it. I let the first one go since we were still very new, and the situation did not look good for me, but I will not let this one go."

"What the fuck is that supposed to mean?" I hiss.

"It means you need some correction."

"Excuse me?!" I practically shriek.

"Did I not tell you how I will put you over my knee if you question my word again?"

"You wouldn't fucking dare."

His glower turns into a sinister glee, and I swallow hard as my mouth dries up. He wouldn't really put me over his knee to spank me, right?

"Come take your punishment like a good girl, Alessia." He harshly grips my hand in his and pries open the door. I try to yank my hand back, but he's too strong. I dig my heels in and squat low to the ground making it more difficult for him but not impossible as I'm pulled into the hallway. "Alessia. I am warning you right now. Your pretty ass will be upright for me over my knee one way or another."

"I will not let you spank me like a child!" I keep struggling against his grasp.

"If you would stop acting so childish, I wouldn't have to." He keeps pulling me by my hand, and if I don't want to be dragged on my face, then I have to move my feet because he isn't delaying.

"No, Massimo. Do not spank me!" Where the hell did all my training go? There are so many ways I could get out of this, but I'm in too much of a panic to think straight. "Get the fuck off me!" I scream as we get closer to his room.

We reach the threshold, and my training suddenly kicks in. But in the blink of an eye, I'm yanked against his body, my arms pinned down at my sides, his arms like a steel cage around me so that I'm entirely immobile.

I begin thrashing and struggling with all my might, and he chuckles. "My feral *gattina*," he muses, and I pause to growl at him. "Are you done yet?"

How the fuck did he catch me so damn quickly? I hardly had time to strike, as if he anticipated my exact moves. "Not even."

"The harder you fight me, the harsher your punishment will be."

"You will not *punish* me, Massimo. I did nothing wrong. You are the one sneaking around behind my back and lying to my face!"

"You are the one accusing me of being disloyal. I will tie you up if I have to."

That gets my attention as I freeze up inside his arms. "I'll fucking kill you."

"Oh, my wild *gattina*." He's able to remove one arm to stroke my hair while still keeping me in his confines. And if I weren't so incredibly enraged at the moment, I'd be impressed. "I'll reward you afterward if you're a good girl."

"Massimo. I am warning you right now. I will blow your fucking brains out if you even try—"

My feet leave the ground as he carries me trapped against his body. I hear the door slam shut, and the panic *really* begins to set in. I've heard about the shit he's into, and I will not be one of those submissive bitches that gets on my hands and knees crawling towards him wearing a fucking collar! *I'm not a fucking animal. I am goddamn royalty!*

"Massimo! Put me down!" I thrash more when he heads towards the bed at full speed. "No! Okay, no! I'll let you spank me! I'll let you! Just put me down, okay?! Do not tie me up!" The thought of being so helpless really begins to send me into a tailspin. "Please, Massimo. I'll let you do it. I will." I'll kill him for making me sound so feeble.

He stops and looks down at me, frowning. "Calm down, *cara mia*. It's not as bad as you think."

"Tying me up and spanking me? It's demeaning!" My voice is so high-pitched it almost squeaks.

His eyes somehow grow even darker. "You need to start trusting me, *cara*. I will make you if I have to."

What? Make me trust him?

"Now, only this one time will I give you a choice. But it will never happen again. You either be a good girl and take your spanking over my knee, or I can restrain you."

My nostrils flare as I take a deep breath in and out through my teeth. "I'll go willingly," I snarl. He will pay for this...

"Pity." His arms loosen around me when he decides that I will no longer fight him or try to run. I refuse to be restrained, so I'll go along with it. But I *will* find a way to pay him back. Drug him and tie him up to give him a good spanking. Maybe stuff an apple in his mouth and hogtie him.

"What are you smiling at, *gattina*?"

I wipe the smile off my face. "Nothing."

Not taking his eyes off me, he sits at the edge of his bed. It's my first time in his bedroom, and I glance behind him at the bed we'll soon share. When I look back at him, there's a slight smirk teasing his lips. "You sure you don't want to be restrained?" he taunts.

"I'm sure."

I exhale loudly before going to his side. The glower on my face causes my jaw to ache from how hard I am clenching my teeth. Already feeling mortified and indignant, I lay across his lap.

He is so going to pay for this.

He doesn't waste any time. I feel the fabric of my dress lazily slide up my legs, exposing more of my skin. The cool air hits the backs of my thighs, and when my dress is around my waist, I squeeze my eyes shut as the cool air hits my panties, realizing they're wet. It's no secret I have a few screws loose, so of course I am so turned on.

My eyes pop back open when I feel him blow air at my crotch, taunting me and amplifying my humiliation further. He murmurs something I can't decipher and starts to pull my panties down slowly. "Hey!" I start struggling against him, and he binds my wrists together with one hand behind my back. "What are you doing?!"

"You think I'm going to spank you with anything in the way?"

"You think I'm going to let you touch me without my permission?!"

"If you think I'm a man who needs to take anything that isn't given to me, you have so much to learn, *piccolina*."

"Do not call me *piccolina* when you are about to spank me," I growl. It's bad enough he's about to spank me like a child, but to call me the name my family calls me? That's just disturbing.

"Very well, *gattina*."

I huff out a breath. "Fine. You can pull my panties down, but can you please stop restraining me?"

"I think you've run out of chances, baby." His voice takes on this gravelly tone that makes my eyes flutter shut once again. Thankfully, he can't see my face to catch it. He already knows I'm wet; there's no need to spur him on further.

His free hand yanks down my panties, and they dangle around my ankles. The cool air hits the wetness pooling between the apex of my thighs. *Please don't comment on it. Please don't—*

I hear him take a deep breath through his nose. "You smell delicious, *gattina*. You can try to deny you want this all you want, but your *fica* says otherwise." *Cunt.*

Oh, fucking kill me now.

He palms one of my ass cheeks, and I find myself relaxing in his lap. His hand abandons it for only a second before it connects with it again, hard and fast. The slap of skin to skin bounces off the walls making it echo. I bite down on my bottom lip to silence myself. He can punish me, but I will not let him get a peep out of me while he does it. But *fuck*, that stings.

After he slaps me, he rubs the area, diminishing some of the sting, and it isn't so bad now. Maybe I should pretend it is so that he doesn't increase the tensity of it. No, fuck that. Nothing will infuriate someone more than not giving a reaction when they're looking for one.

He slaps me again in the same area, and I don't know if it's because it already hurts there or if he hit me harder, but it definitely stung more. He kneads the area and then slaps me again and again. All in the same spot.

"My handprint looks beautiful on you, *gattina*." He roughly kneads the area, basically groping my ass. I can feel the heat growing unbearably hot between my legs and wish I could somehow get some friction going there without him knowing. "Tell me, is this so bad? And don't lie to me, Alessia. I will know."

"It's not so bad," I mutter grumpily.

"Do you like it?"

"No."

He chuckles. "Liar. I'll let you get away with just that one because I'm sure you're a little confused right now." He starts palming the other cheek.

"What's so confusing about you being a sadist?"

"Sadist, hmm?" He brings his hand down on that unmarred cheek and then palms it. "What is your impression of a sadist?"

"One who gets off by hurting and humiliating someone."

"What is so humiliating about this?"

"Seriously? I'm being spanked like a child. It's undignified."

"You don't really think of it like that, do you?" I don't answer, and he furthers his point by blowing air between my thighs again, making me suck in a breath. "You're telling yourself that," he murmurs lowly. "Tell me to touch you, *gattina*," he rasps in a slightly pained voice, and my eyes flutter behind my closed lids to the sound. His massive erection has been digging into my belly since I laid over his lap, so maybe he is in slight pain.

"You already are." My voice trembles, and I lick my lips.

"You know what I mean." *Whack!* I flinch a little at that one because he caught me completely off guard. When he palms my cheek, the tip of his thumb comes awfully close to where I'm desperate for his touch. He must have still managed to gather some of my wetness as his thumb leaves a wet trail on my cheek. He spanks me three more times, and by the time he stops, I'm panting, and the fire between my legs is searing. More so than the reddened skin on my ass.

"I can see how frustrated you are, Alessia. I can help you with that. It won't take long," the smug bastard says as he plays with my sore cheeks.

"I can take care of that myself, thank you very much."

He grows ultimately still under me; his hand stops groping. "What's stopping you then? By all means, take care of that."

The thought of touching myself in front of him is tempting. It would be a much better orgasm than if I were to run into my room right now and rub one out alone. But he's already caused enough damage to my pride and dignity for a lifetime. I will not allow him anymore.

"I've taken my punishment like a *good girl*. Now, let me go." The breathiness is gone from my voice as I growl.

He sighs and shifts a little to reach for my panties and slides them back into place. "Well, if you change your mind..." He pulls my dress down and stands me up. "You'll know where to find me."

I have the compelling urge to tell him to go fuck himself, but I'm sure that would earn me another spanking, and I would not be able to resist him a second time. So, with my tail tucked between my legs, I run out of his room without a glance back and lock myself into mine.

Going straight for my bed, I don't even pull my panties down as I shove my hand down the front of them and get myself off to thoughts of Massimo spanking me and touching me.

CHAPTER THIRTEEN

Massimo

M y wild kitten has been avoiding me now for days after I turned her perky ass red.

I can still see her glistening pussy and smell her pungent scent. I knew she would enjoy her spanking. The mixture of struggle and rage turned her on.

It won't be long until I can adequately claim Alessia. And I don't mean by our espousal. I mean showing her how her body is owned by me. The only man capable of understanding and managing a woman of her nature, and vice versa. A wild being like her needs to relinquish control every once in a while. To feel overpowered.

I did enjoy the submissive women I've had in the past, but to finally have a woman worthy of a challenge will more than keep me satisfied for the rest of my days. So far, this union with Alessia Bonetti has not been disappointing at all.

Leaning back in my chair, I sigh and run my hands through my hair frustratingly. It's been so long since I've had sex, and although the wait for Alessia will be over soon, it's not soon enough. Rolling my head around on my shoulders, I decide to see where my *gattina* is right now.

I've had enough of her silent treatment. I'm the one who should still be furious with her for accusing me once again of being a perfidious man. I warned her once, and she defied me. Questioned me. Doubted me. Mistrusted me.

Pulling up surveillance, I look at her bedroom first. When I do, I'm on my feet, instantly wrathful. She and Monte are in her room...

With. The. Door. *Shut.*

How dare either of them slight me in my own home? What the fuck would people think if they saw them go into her bedroom and shut the door behind them? My men would lose respect for me; my staff would start whispering, and rumors would spread. People would think that my fiancée is fucking my cousin. Another man. *A fucking foot soldier!* That will *not* be tolerated. Monte should know better, but he's about to be taught a hard fucking lesson.

Storming into her room without knocking, they stop laughing from where they're sitting. Monte's eyes widen when he sees that it's he who is targeted. "Massimo?" I hardly even register Alessia's voice. Monte has just gotten to his feet when I grab him by the collar and use my fist to make quick contact with his face, not at all holding back. I'm seeing red as I imagine him and Alessia fucking behind my back and under my own roof.

"Oh, my God! Massimo! What the fuck!" Alessia shrieks behind me as I literally toss Monte as far as I can and go for him again. His face is already bleeding, and he begins sputtering as he tries to scramble back and get his feet underneath him.

"You dare disrespect me in my own fucking house!" I roar. "With my fucking woman!" His head starts shaking, and I snatch him up by the shirt. This time, my fist plunging through his skull with seemingly absent resistance, splattering blood chaotically. "You think just because we are family, you can get away with it?" I feel bone crunch under my fist when I drive my fist into his face again and again in a fit of rage.

The thought of anyone getting near my woman is unfathomable. It drives me into such a rage I cannot see straight. I lose all control. I can barely even breathe. My actions and emotions are out of my hands and driven solely by fury. I'm unbalanced and crazed, out for blood.

My fist keeps pounding until my air supply gets cut off by something tightly wrapped around my throat, choking me. My instincts have me grabbing at it with my hands, but it's so tight around my neck I can't get a grip on it, and it must have been strangling me for a while because my head is already getting light and spots are dancing in front of my eyes. The adrenaline from the rage is wearing off as I'm vastly weakening, and I get yanked back. Then it's released, and I'm choking and gasping for air. Disoriented and confused as to what the hell just happened.

"Are you done now?" Alessia snaps, and I see her feet on the floor right in front of me, but all I'm able to do is cough and choke. Her feet leave my sight, and I can faintly hear her muttering something behind me and then calling for my men to come to help her.

Turning over to sit on my ass to try and catch my breath, I see two of my men rushing in with their guns drawn, seeking out the danger. It takes them a moment to assess the situation as they first look at me, then they see Monte, a bloody mess on the floor, and rush to him.

"Yeah, he's still got a pulse," I hear Alessia say, shaking me out of it some.

I'm still trying to squeeze air through my now sore throat when she looks over her shoulder at me. And when her eyes meet mine, she gives me a look I have never seen from her before. There's fear in her gaze. From what, though? Me? No, she can't be afraid of me for that. She knows what I am capable of, and I've watched her kneecap a man with a lead pipe and enjoy it. But defending my honor and hers, that scares her?

The guys lift Monte's limp body, and I watch Alessia follow them out. I don't try to stop her mainly because my vocal cords aren't fully functioning yet, so I sit here and sulk instead. It's then that I notice the scarf sitting on my lap. It must've been what was around my neck, and I chuckle now, realizing what the hell happened. She knew she couldn't possibly fight me off him, so she strangled me with a scarf to subdue me.

Crafty woman.

Dusting myself off, I get to my feet and head back to my office to occupy myself with work. Not carrying even an ounce of compunction with me either.

CHAPTER FOURTEEN

Alessia

T hank God Monte will live. With some reconstructive surgery, he'll be good as new in a few months. And I'll ensure it comes out of Massimo's pocket to cover the hospital bills.

What the fuck made Massimo go all Hulk on his cousin? I thought he was actually going to kill him. He almost did!

So, okay. I did know that closing my bedroom door with another man inside wasn't entirely appropriate, and I don't know why I even did it. Was I so starved for Massimo's attention that I used my only friend and ally here to provoke him?

Instead of heading to the stairs for my room to hide, I change directions and head for Massimo's office. We need to clear the air, or at this rate, one of us will end up killing the other. Or another unfortunate soul will get caught in our crossfires.

I give a firm knock on his door, and I am too irate to wait for permission to enter. As soon as I do, I look around the room to be sure we're alone before slipping inside and closing myself in. He only gives me a short glance from his desk, and I take notice of the red and purple rings around his neck. I almost laugh, but I don't because I don't *actually* want to die today. I was choking the fuck out of him for a while before he even noticed.

"Monte will be okay, by the way. In case you care at all." *Damn, girl. Provoking him even further? You do want to die today, don't you?* He doesn't bite as he ignores me, and for some reason, that stings. Can't he just smarten up and see I only want a little of his attention? I take in the dried blood on his knuckles and shirt that he didn't even bother to clean. "So, is this how it's really going to be?"

He slams down his pen and leans back in his chair to finally give me his full attention. "If you think I owe either of you an apology, you are a stupid woman."

My chin hits the floor as I am flabbergasted with his impertinence. "You almost killed your cousin with your bare hands for a closed bedroom door!" I exclaim, and his eyes narrow on me.

"So, you *did* know what you were doing." *Shit.* "You purposely provoke me, and you think I am the bad guy here? Yes, I almost killed my cousin, but that is on *you*." He points a scolding finger at me. "You knew damn well what you were trying to do, and that is not the way to get my attention, *gattina*."

"Can you blame me!? You insist that I move in here so we could get to know each other, but I still barely know you because of the little time you give me. You remain all business! Is that really going to be our marriage? Strictly business? Or do you think you could ever give me more?"

"I told you that you are welcome in my bed anytime."

"I don't mean—" I clench my fists and growl. "I mean, can't we be friends too? Talk about things that don't involve money or violence. Go out sometimes? Like a real couple? Massimo, I know this isn't an optimal situation, but you're stuck with me. Don't you want to enjoy what you can out of it? Maybe have a little fun together? Yes, we'll also have sex. But until you act more like a human being rather than a stolid robot, I will be perfectly fine waiting until our wedding night."

"And I am perfectly fine with that as well," he retorts so quickly that it almost feels like a slap in the face.

My eyes dart down to the floor ignominiously. Is Massimo really as apathetic as he's deemed to be? I knew he wasn't warm and endearing, but I didn't think he was this callous all the time. I could have sworn I felt a heart beating inside of his chest. But I guess I was mistaken. The blunt realization has my head spinning.

"Alright then," I say around the mass in my throat. I am now fully cognizant of what my future is like, and it's dark and grim. I won't be a queen reigning at his side. I'll be the lonely mafia wife like the rest of them. Like his mother. The thought of becoming anything like her puts a big rock in the pit of my stomach. My eyes bounce back up to the passive man. "I'm going to end up like her, aren't I?" I say quietly, but he hears me.

I can feel the backs of my eyes stinging, and it enrages me. No way in fucking hell will I end up like his mother. An empty shell who depends on pills even to wake up. Holed up in her room alone and broken. *Weak.*

I am *not* his mother. I am Alessia Bonetti. I am a future queen, and I will not let Massimo's attempts at making my life unhappy succeed. My life was never going to end with a happily ever after, but it will end with me at the top.

"Well, I'm glad we've cleared things up. I'll be having dinner at my family's tonight, so no need to wait on me." Spinning around, I leave his office in a whirlwind.

The small trek became a blur. It's like I blinked and was suddenly in my room, pacing and breathing fire. I'm feeling like I'm going to hyperventilate and keel over. My heart is pounding so loudly, and my vision is blurry, and I feel like it's getting harder and harder to breathe. A panic attack. Will my future be so desolate?

Okay, you'll be okay. You're strong enough for this. You can handle anything. You're a Bonetti and fucking mafia royalty. You weren't born into a life of rainbows and butterflies. It's guns, drugs, crime, and misogynists. You opted out of love for power. You've got this.

I pace my room, trying to get my breathing to slow down, when there's a knock at my door. "Who is it?" I snap.

"It's Massimo. May I come in?"

"Do you actually need permission?" Stomping to the door, I pull it open with a little too much force.

"Can we talk?" He shoves his hands in his pockets, and I silently gesture for him to come in.

When he walks to the middle of my room, he turns around, looking somewhat remorseful, but I need to stop being so hopeful. The man is remorseless.

I cross my arms over my chest, automatically feeling truculent and preparing for his subsequent censure. "I don't want to be like my father."

Well, damnit. Only he could manage to make my walls quake so quickly, maybe because it's the most candid thing he's said to me so far. Not wanting to ruin this moment, I keep my mouth shut for once.

"I don't want you to end up like my mother."

Everything about me suddenly crumbles. *Okay, I can work with this.* "Then let's not be like them."

"I'll start giving you more time. I'm not used to making anything but work a priority. I don't spend time with my family like you do, and I haven't had any long-lasting relationships. It's going to be a lifestyle change for me."

"Wow, okay. I was not expecting you to concede at all." I chuckle nervously, and he smirks.

"I'm not always so obstinate," he muses.

"I feel like I'm being tricked here."

"There's no trick." He smiles, shaking his head slowly.

"The man I spoke to down there is not the same man I'm speaking to right now. How did that so drastically change?"

"Like I said, I don't want to end up like them."

"Ahh, so now I know one of your weaknesses," I tease.

His smile grows. "Don't think it will work like that every time, *gattina*."

"Mhmm. We'll see."

He cracks a full-on smile, and I'm reminded of how damn handsome he is. It's impossible to stay mad at him when he's all cute and apologetic. "If you still plan on having dinner with your family, may I join you?"

"My family is yours."

CHAPTER FIFTEEN

Alessia

Massimo has taken our last dispute to heart, which may be backfiring on me.

We've been spending most evenings together, and he's found a way to loosen up some. Now, my growing feelings for him have doubled in size. It's beginning to feel too real.

Tonight, we're going out to one of his clubs where he has a meeting. It'll be interesting to see him in true boss form. To catch a glimpse of that 'scary man.'

I decided to forgo my modest style, even though we'd be meeting with the kind of men I should have my guard in place for, and wear something more...sexy. I'm dressed to kill in a mini drape dress that is half-red metallic and half-black silk. It stops midthigh with the center rising higher. I curled my hair, pinned some pieces up to stay out of my face, and painted my lips a deep red.

There's a knock on my door, and I grant them entrance—assuming it's Massimo. I disappear into my closet to get a light jacket and return to find Massimo in another bespoke suit that he deliciously fills out. His eyes light up and slowly drag up and down the length of my body, taking in my entire appearance.

I stifle a shiver and slip the jacket on, watching him as he watches me, then grab my small purse before reaching him. "You're trying to provoke me again, *gattina*." His voice dips dangerously low, and my pussy contracts.

"Yeah? In what way?" I say innocently.

He closes the gap between us and places a hand on my hip, and the amusement instantly drains from me. His warm hand slides around the silky fabric and lands on the small of my back. We're so close that I feel dizzy from his masculine scent and the fever extruding from his impregnable body.

"I might have to gouge a few eyes out tonight if I catch anyone looking at you for too long."

"I might like that." I grin. "But wouldn't that be bad for business?" I purr as I slide my hands up his chest and playfully tug on the lapels of his jacket.

His response is a grunt from the base of his throat, and his eyes keep darting down to my lips. I wish he would just kiss me already. I've been dying to kiss him forever, it seems, and I've never hesitated to make the first move, but for some reason, I want him to be the one to. It'd be like giving in, and I refuse to give in first.

"Shall we?" he breaks the spell and puts some space between us. I nod, and he takes me by the hand like he did the night of our engagement party.

How could I forget how incredibly manly and harsh they feel? It reminds me of how powerful they are and how rough around the edges he is, no matter how clean-cut he looks in those fancy suits.

It was Massimo who inspired my modest style. His comment at the gala was more impactful than I'll ever admit. In my sweet dresses, you'll never take me for a trained killer. And that's precisely how he wears his suits. He looks more like a nobleman than a gangster.

We get into the SUV between two others for departure. My father never travels with so many men unless leaving the state or the country. "Do you always travel this heavy?" I ask him after a few minutes of driving.

"I do now." He looks down at me as his large armrests over the back of the seat. I feel so tiny, practically tucked into his side.

"Oh, so this is because of me?"

"I told you. You're mine to protect now. For me to have a good time and relax with you, doubling my men will help me do so."

"Makes sense." I turn my head and watch out the window as we approach the city, trying to ignore his recent words.

You're mine to protect now. You're mine...

I feel my hair moving away from my neck and try to obviate a shiver, pretending to be unaffected. "You look incredible, *cara mia*," he rumbles close to my ear.

He doesn't bother to move when I turn back to him. Our faces are so close that my eyes have to bounce side to side to try to focus. One bump in the road would push us together. "I'm glad you think so."

Slowly, he moves in closer, and my eyes flutter shut. My lips part, hoping I'll soon feel his brush against them. Instead, I feel his breath move behind my ear and in my hair. His lips press against that sensitive spot between my ear and neck, causing me to go limp. My heart races and my breath hitches, and I find myself tilting my head to expose my neck. The way my skin pebbles when his tongue darts out and flicks against the skin there, I almost moan. I've wanted him for so long now; the craving and cupidity leave me famished.

The heat from his breath finds its way back to my ear. "*Dolcezza.*" *Sweetness.* If he doesn't fucking put me out of my misery and kiss me soon, I might explode.

The tender way he grips my chin and runs his thumb just below my bottom lip has me opening my eyes to be sure it's really him who's touching me. His gaze literally transfixes me, and I cannot look away. A bomb could be going off, or bullets could be flying, and I wouldn't be able to release myself from his seizure.

"We're here, boss."

Massimo gives me the hint of a smile and moves to get out, leaving me a mess inside and out. Taking a deep breath, I compose myself and allow him to help me out of the vehicle, taking immediate hold of my hand to head through the private entrance in the back.

I'm excited to finally come to this club that the De Luca's own. I've never been, and I've always been curious about it. They own quite a few legitimate businesses and do very well through them. Vineyards over in Italy, restaurants throughout the city, clubs, bars, strip joints, random investments. Without their illegal businesses, they'd still be rich as sin.

The entrance takes us through a long, darkened hallway that feels so tight with all these large men surrounding me; it makes me cling to Massimo a little more. He glances over his shoulder, and I give him a reassuring smile in response.

The hallway leads us to an elevator that opens to a balcony separate from all the others, overlooking the entire club. There's a glass partition along most of the railing, assuming it's bulletproof as an extra precaution. The colors around us are dark and luminous with black, sleek tiled floors. There are three large crescent-shaped booths all in a row and two small podiums between them with a pole going from floor to ceiling, presumably for dancers.

We're the first ones here, so I take the time to check out the place. I go to step around the partition, and Massimo stops me by my elbow. "I want you behind this until my guys finish scouting and hitting their posts," he lightly demands, and I nod my head.

He leaves to talk with some of his detail while I safely stay behind the glass to observe. It's a beautiful club, and I'm impressed. The club that we own is not as ritzy as this. But its sole purpose is to launder money from it, so we don't take much pride in it.

I sip on an extra dirty martini next to my sexy fiancé as he talks with a bunch of douchebags. Men from the Irish mob further up the East Coast whom I cannot stand. They're such barbarians, from their cliché bruteness to their obnoxious accents to their sexism. We've adapted to the modern gangsters, but they seem to be stuck in some time loop.

Typically, I enjoy being included in business meetings, but these pricks won't even acknowledge me when I open my mouth. I'd love nothing more than to pull out some of my knives from my thigh holster to use one of them as target practice.

I look around at the women they brought and wonder if I look anything like them. Okay, so my dress tonight is a little risqué, but I wanted to look sexy for my man. Looking at all their ring fingers, none of the women are wearing a ring, yet most of the men are indeed wearing one.

Fucking *stronzos*.

Massimo's head snaps at me, and he raises his eyebrows. *Shit, did I say that out loud? Oops.* The smell of whiskey wafts over me as he leans in close. "Are you bored, *bella*?"

"I'm okay." I smile and reach up to comb my fingers through some of his soft hair. I love its beautiful, natural waves and how the color is much darker than his facial hair. "Though my tolerance is waning."

I wasn't even thinking when I reached out to make contact, but the look in his eyes tells me he doesn't mind the caress. "I'll wrap this up soon. Then we can have some fun."

"Fun?" My tone is flirtatious as I lean into him, cozying up to his arm. "I can't wait to see how Massimo De Luca has fun." The music drowns out the sound of his chuckle, but I feel its vibration and have to look away before I become enamored with him.

Downing my third martini, I'm tired of waiting for these assholes to leave, so I get up and head over to the balcony and lean over it to enjoy people-watching. You'd think I'd envy their lives. They are so carefree, and their only actual obligation is paying their bills. They get to fall in love over and over and choose their own path. The only real expectations are from themselves.

But I don't want their lives. I happen to love mine.

Though I do miss my family like crazy, I wish Massimo could have been thrown into my life, not vice versa. It feels like I'm losing everything when he is only gaining. But Massimo is beginning to fill a part of me that I had no idea was lacking.

Alcohol and music both course through me, causing my hips to begin swaying to the beat. I can vividly feel his heavy presence behind me. I turn around to find that the *stronzos* have left, and my husband-to-be is now standing to his full height. One hand in his pocket and the other lifting his glass to his lips. Completely fixated on me, watching my hips continue to move.

I don't know if it's the martinis or the fact that he has been such a temptation since day one, but I want Massimo more than anything right now. The push, the pull, it has my insides quaking.

Getting only a small taste of Massimo and seeing what his massive hands are capable of has only left me desirous and needing more.

With a mischievous smile, I seductively make my way over to him. Pushing all thoughts of his other women to the back of my mind. No matter how much I compare myself to them, with the way he's looking at me now, he likes what he sees. He sometimes looks like he wants to swallow me whole after he's feasted on me for hours. For a man like Massimo to look at me in such a feverish way, it's electrifying. One single glance from him is so much more efficacious than any slight touch from any other man.

Setting his glass down as I reach him, I own all his focus. Placing my hands on his abs, they feel like steel as I lazily slide them up over his chest and to his broad shoulders. Wishing his clothes were gone as my eyes follow my movements.

When my swaying pelvis brushes against him, I feel the hardness in his slacks bulging. Arching my back, I slide my hands back down to his chest, then spin around to roll my hips, grinding my ass into that said bulge. I throw an arm around his neck and close my eyes.

Shivers run down my body when his breath tickles my ear. His large hands firmly gripping my hips, itching to flex. "You shouldn't tease me, *dolcezza*." His tone is dangerously low.

Darkness takes over his gaze as I tilt my head up towards him. "Why? You've been teasing me for months now." My voice comes out like I'm in pain because inside I am. I want him. His tongue darts out to lick his bottom lip slowly, leaving a shiny trail behind, torturing me. "*Baciami*." *Kiss me*.

"You want a kiss, *cara mia*?" Using the grip on my hips, he carefully spins me around to face him, then tugs me against his hard body. "I am yours to kiss any time you want."

One hand grips his massive shoulder, and the other finds its way to the back of his head. Fisting his hair, I yank him down to smash my lips into his. He made me give in first, and I can't repudiate the desire burning up inside of me any longer.

The way our bodies somehow mold together is surprisingly perfect, considering his size and my own. But we fit together seamlessly, and our mouths are in sync as our lips part and our tongues meet. He tastes like whiskey, and his lips and tongue are soft and smooth, a contrast to his rough hands. The way he's kissing me is both dominant and passionate. Everything inside of me liquifying and muddling my brain.

All I can think about is *him*. All I can feel is *him*.

If he doesn't take me to bed with him tonight, I might cry.

CHAPTER SIXTEEN

Alessia

"**T**i voglio, Massimo." *I want you*, I murmur against his lips.

"Then it's time for us to go home." His hand slides down to firmly grip my ass, and I lodge a whimper in my throat when he puts some distance between us.

The fire in my core is so intense it's throbbing, and I thank God I decided to wear panties. Otherwise, I'd be dripping down my thighs already. His firm grip on my hand as he pulls us back through the same way we came is more possessive than ever. For months, this storm of wanton and desire has been brewing and simmering merely confined. It's time to unleash it and destroy what we must.

Once we slip inside the vehicle and get moving, Massimo pulls me over his lap and teases me with his lips. Peppering tender kisses along my jaw line to my ear, my head cradled in his large hand. Breathing heavily, he kisses the shell softly, then starts dragging his lips down the side of my neck and to my throat. His bristly facial hair scratching my skin, adding to every sensation.

My fingers are tangled in the back of his hair as his hand slides down the column of my neck, and his lips drag back to mine. Our lips are slack as they rub together, and his hand continues going down until it cups my breast. He realizes I'm not wearing a bra underneath my dress, and the silky material is thin enough so that when he lightly circles my nipple, it's a vivid experience for us both.

"Touch me, Massimo," I beg in a hoarse voice, not recognizing it.

"*Cara mia*, my first time touching you will not be here," he whispers, and I gasp when he pinches my nipple. The sensation sends a zing straight to my pussy.

I wonder if he'll spank me again tonight or if that's just for punishment. If that's the case, I'll have to misbehave more often because I want nothing more than to relive that pleasureful pain.

His beard rubs against my cheeks as his mouth reaches my other ear, and he chuckles. It's deep and rumbly and sexy as fuck.

"It's like I can hear every thought going on inside of that intriguing head of yours."

"Yeah? What am I thinking?"

"You're thinking about that spanking, *gattina*. Are you hoping you might get another one tonight?"

"That depends." He hums in response. "What will you do as a punishment from now on?" I pant. "If spankings are for—" My breath hitches when he pinches my nipple again, but this time much harder making me hiss.

"The ways I could punish you are insurmountable, Alessia. Though I have a feeling we might go through the list relatively quick, and I'll have to get more creative," he muses. His finger makes its way into my mouth, and he hooks it to the back of my bottom teeth, cranking my mouth open wide. "I have a feeling you'll enjoy it too much."

I think so too.

Not only was the ride home a provocation, but it was also torture. All I wanted to do was straddle his lap and fuck him, not caring who could see and hear us. I think it was antagonizing for him as well because when we got home, he practically dragged me out of the car and in through the front door. When we hit the bottom of the steps, he hoists me up, wrapping my legs around his waist.

We're both grinning, our faces lightly touching as he ascends the stairs, holding me like it's nothing. His hands are large enough to cover my ass completely. The anticipation is driving me wild. All the things I'm conjuring up inside my brain of what's to come. Of what I'll allow him to do to me. The list is unending.

There's this tingling sensation I've never felt before in the pit of my stomach once we're closed inside his bedroom, and he sets me on my feet. It's like I'm nauseous and high from the nerves and excitement flowing through me. I've never been so overwrought with emotion involving sex. Sex has always been exciting for me, but never like this.

His hands make their way around my back as his mouth descends on mine once again. The kiss isn't hasty, but deliberately slow and penetrating as his tongue vulgarly explores me. The zipper on the back of my dress moves down at a measured pace, and I drop my hands from his neck to let it fall to the floor.

Removing his lips from mine, he creates some distance to take in my full appearance as I stand there in just a tiny pair of satin panties and my heels. His pupils dilate as they bounce all around my body for what feels like forever, causing me goosebumps, and palpitating in my chest.

"*Perfezione*," *Perfection*, he rumbles, setting off a shiver down my entire body, and a new flood of desire is sapped from me. His eyes snap up to mine, and his lips flicker with a subtle twitch. "The things I have been imagining doing to you, *bella*. All the things." He absorbs my body with his stare and licks his lips like a starved beast.

I'm immobile and frozen to my spot now, witnessing the effect he must have on all his victims. He's wholly entrapped me with his weighted power, making me picture the sick things he's been planning for me. I know it'll be like nothing I've ever experienced before.

Prowling back to me, he gently coaxes me, laying me down on his soft bed. The smell of him engulfs me, making me feel drunk and dizzy. His eyes are locked with mine as he picks one of my feet up and kisses my ankle then peels off my shoe. Placing it gently back down, he does the same with my other. We haven't even started yet, and I'm gasping for air as my chest pulses with accelerated breaths.

The thought of not having the upper hand in anything has reliably disrupted my calm and plunged me into panic. But with Massimo, I anticipate his total dominance over me. For one night, I won't be indomitable. I'll give into submission.

I finally break our connection when his shirt falls to the floor. My eyes widen at the taut muscles kept hidden from me. I anticipated he'd be built from solid steel, but I was looking at the most beautiful abstract art I have ever seen. The scars and tattoos that are scattered throughout his torso and mar his skin are storytelling and radiate more power. He looks intrepid and valiant, standing there showing off his years as not only a boss but a warrior.

Maybe it won't be so bad to let myself fall for him in time. I won't be diving in headfirst, but perhaps I can go ahead and dip my toes in one at a time.

When he strips down completely and his erection bobs in the air, my eyes remain wide. It's the most beautiful cock that exists. Long, *thick*, veiny, and just as hard as he is. He's fucking hung. The image of him stuffing it in my mouth, choking me, and cutting off my air supply has me salivating.

I open my knees for him as he crawls up on the bed. Settling his shoulders under my thighs, his hands slide under my ass cheeks to grip them and lift me up to his mouth. Over my panties, he takes one long swipe with his tongue, making my back arch and my mouth pop open on a silent gasp. Then he nuzzles his nose against me and hums. The vibration causes me to twitch and quiver. Even in the middle of an orgasm, I've never been so sensitive.

"*Dolcezza*," he rasps and nips at me making me jolt.

"Fucking hell, Massimo." I squirm, trying to get his mouth where I want it.

The grip he has on my ass tightens to the point of pain, making me hiss and clench up. "I have longed for this through years of patience, *cara mia*. Too long. You will let me take my sweet time with you." He places a gentle kiss on the inside of my thigh. "I'm going to savor the taste of your cunt first. Drink you the fuck in." He kisses the other thigh then makes a wet trail up to my core again.

Fisting the sheets in sexual frustration, he continues with a lick here, a kiss there, a nip there, all on top of the soaked satin still separating us, sticking to me and blocking him. I feel like such a beggar, desperate for the ultimate gratification.

I'm so close to screaming when he finally begins to peel my panties down. His eyes practically roll back when he shoves them under his nose and deeply inhales. It sends another delicious quiver through me, and he growls like a madman before tossing them to the side.

Licking his lips again, he stares down at my bare pussy. He whispers something inaudible under his breath as he kisses the inside of my knee and makes his way towards my center. Repeatedly teasing me by stopping just on the perimeter of my labia, his facial hair lightly brushing against my clitoris. Then he takes it away and does the same thing on the opposite side. But this time, he doesn't stop.

He kisses all the way to my center, and all the air rushes from my lungs when he tongues me there.

I can't tear my eyes away from him as he indulges. So articulate with his tongue and lips. Knowing exactly how to move them and where to move them. Reading every stifled noise and faint muscle spasm from me. His painful grip on my ass pulls me apart, pulling me taut and exposing me.

There's nothing he can't get to.

His tongue covers my whole pussy, moving strategically, edging me over and over. He isn't teasing me, though. He's stringing this out, and I can't hate him for it. I'm not ready for a crash yet. Not when the high will be unworldly.

He stabs his tongue deep inside of me as his dexterous lips continue to move around me, and the orgasm comes abruptly. Every single muscle in my body locks up painfully tight, and then I am convulsing, but I'm not at all coming down. He continues to devour, and my orgasm rolls right into another one where I soar for so fucking long, I'm not sure if I'll survive coming back.

As I finally do, thoughts of him inside of me fog my brain where I am literally his to do with as he pleases. As long as he is inside of me, and soon. No wonder how he has women willingly on their hands and knees for him. He's a fucking sex god.

My pussy remains sizzling as he kisses his way up my stomach, and my eyes blink open sleepily. Stars dance across my vision as I watch him gingerly kiss his way to my breasts. "So fucking perfect, Alessia. So worth the wait." He pulls one nipple into his mouth, and I suck air through my teeth when he clamps down on it with his teeth. I'm pretty sure if any other man would've done that, they'd have received a throat punch, but my body naturally arches up to him, offering him more of myself. His deft touch has me entrusting him with exotic bliss. But that's as far as my trust goes.

Diving my fingers into his hair, I fist it. He lets out the faintest of a groan as he plucks my other nipple, pinching and rolling and pulling. The sting immediately kicks in when he removes his hot mouth, and the cool air hits it. "Delicious." Grunting, he switches to my other breast to attack it. The one his mouth just abandoned, he replaces it with his fingers, and I feel it already bruising. Something about the fact that he has physically marked me has me ravenous.

"Massimo," I plead.

His teeth clamp down on my other nipple, and I whimper, but I don't beg him to stop. With my body, I'm begging him for more.

Dragging my fingers down the back of his head, my nails dig into him, instigating him.

His hand abandons my breast to snake down the flat of my stomach, delving into my wetness. I twitch under him, not at all in control of my muscles as he rubs my pussy and then hooks two fingers inside of me. My ass flies off the bed, and my head snaps back.

Fuck. Me. Holy fuck.

He's not prolonging my orgasm this time as he works his fingers harder and faster. My toes painfully curl, and my body binds up, and I cry out loud for the entire estate to hear. His teeth snap shut on my nipple in sync with my peak, and my vision goes black for a solid moment, leaving me completely blind and defenseless. Yet I give zero fucks.

Growling, my nipple pops out of his mouth, and he jumps up to kiss me hard on the mouth. His wet fingers dig into my hipbone as he grips it harshly. To accommodate the width of his hips, my knees fall wide, hitting the mattress. His steel rod probes me as our tongues are entangled, and our breathing intensifies. His facial hair rubs my face raw, and my nipples are chaffing against his chest.

Those large fingers of his wrap around my thighs, and he hikes my legs up high over his hips as he grinds his cock against me. I'm so overly sensitive from the ungodly orgasms he gave me that I spasm and mewl every time he nudges me. An indescribable sensation I can't stand but cannot reject.

The way he rolls his hips, he's entering me inch by tortuous inch. He's definitely the biggest I've ever had, and I know it will be an incredibly snug fit. Possibly tearing me.

Every inch he dips into me, I think there couldn't possibly be any more, but there is. Another inch, another, and another until his balls kiss my ass cheeks. He pulls back to look at me, stroking a tender hand down the side of my face and hair. There's this strange look in his eyes that's a combination of wildness, tenderness, and a dash of restraint.

"Don't you dare hold back with me now, De Luca. Now that you've got me."

"You're not quite ready for all of me yet, *gattina*."

"For what? Your whips and chains?" My purr is half taunting.

His hazel eyes roll all over my face in amusement. "I may have an unusual appetite, but I do not require them to take ownership of this beautiful..." My skin pebbles with tiny bumps as his rough hand gently slides down my body. "Sinful..." I hiss when he pauses to toy with my tender nipple. "*Seducente...*" *Seductive.* He makes his way to my hip bone to dig his fingers into it, making me squirm. He is totally dominating me in every way possible. "Goddess of a body."

I undulate my body underneath him as my hands run flat down his chest. Feeling out all the ridges and lumps that mark up his luscious body and rugged pulchritude. My nails find one of the biggest scars and curl into it.

His eyes become dangerously dark, but I barely have time to study them as he snarls and grips my jaw and neck in one hand to crash his mouth down for a punishing kiss. He pulls out to slam back in, jarring my body with the impact. I wrap my arms around his torso to hold on and keep close to him.

The entire length of his cock pulls all the way out and drills all the way back in over and over. Skin slapping and heavy breathing are all I can hear. My heart pounding and my pussy throbbing are all I can feel.

After the pounding continues to the point where I know for a fact I'll be very sore tomorrow, rapturous pleasure heats in my lower belly, swirling like a tornado and funneling through my core. The throbbing from him stretching me gets more intense as I whine into his mouth, and he pounds into me harder and faster until he pulls out abruptly and he explodes all over my aching pussy. Running down my slits, feeling blazing hot against the stinging flesh.

When he runs a finger down there, I flinch and take a sharp breath. He gets a little twinkle in his eyes as he doesn't let up. He is a sadist. And to my surprise, the anticipated wave of fear doesn't wash over me.

My jaw is slack as he roughly shoves multiple fingers inside of me, and he pumps them with measured beats. It burns, it stings, it has me quaking.

Fuuuuuck.

My neck snaps as my eyes roll back, and I try to scream, but nothing comes out. Fire wreaks havoc through my core as I convulse like an addict.

All I can comprehend is grumbling coming from him as his heat leaves mine, then it's a dreamy abyss I succumb to.

CHAPTER SEVENTEEN

Alessia

Before I open my eyes the following day, the soreness between my legs and the stiffness in the rest of my body remind me of where I am.

Peeking over my shoulder, I find a sleeping and very naked Massimo. His rich brown hair askew, the blankets tossed off him showing off his glorious cock, his muscular arms above his head, and his strong jaw locked even in his sleep. *Goddamn, he's beautiful.*

Although I could continue to watch him like a creep while he sleeps, I really need to get out of here. It's now morning, and it's time to go back to my room.

As discreetly as possible, I lift the covers to try and slip out undetected, but a heavy arm clamps down around me. He grumbles something inaudible as he molds his body to the back of mine, and I can't fight back the little smile.

"Uh," I croak and clear my throat to try again. "It's morning."

"And it's not time to get up yet," he mumbles. Then he pulls me closer to him and exhales into my hair. His breathing evens out only seconds later, and I don't know what to do, so I don't do anything. I close my eyes and fall back asleep with him.

The morning has never been so bright before. I moan, and my fingers find their way into his soft hair as he delicately sucks on my aching nipples. Before I can even blink, he's lodging his hips between my legs, his fat cock rubbing against my raw flesh.

There's no warning before he impales me, and my eyes pop open on a gasp as the fiery pain pierces through me. "You sore, *gattina*?" He doesn't pause to wait for my response as he makes languid strokes, his face buried in the crook of my neck.

"Yes," I rasp and grab at his broad shoulders.

"Mmm," he rumbles deep in his chest.

His hips dart forward with more aggression, and the burning pain subsides only slightly, enough to give way to the pleasure. My legs spread, begging him to deliver more pain for the little demon inside of me that craves it. Everything is so tender, and I'll walk around the rest of the day in salacious elation, constantly reminded of our tawdry time spent in his bed.

The unmistakable smell of sex in the air is palpable, and our skin keeps sticking together from the remnants of our desires. It's fucking nasty, and I love it. I want to bathe in our fluids and savor our mixed scents for days to come.

"Uh!" I moan and my body bows. The only way I can come from solely sex is when I'm on top, taking control of my pleasure. But his cock is bringing me to that perilous cliff and shoving me off. My body clams up, and a scream dries up in my throat as my pussy grips him.

"Yes, *gattina*," he rasps, his cock piercing me with bloodthirsty thrusts.

My muscles flutter when I seep back into reality, and my eyes go wide when I'm being flipped to my stomach and then forced to my knees. I'm unsure of how much more my pussy can take.

Pressure between my shoulder blades forces them down and my back to bend. "Oh, *gattina*. Seeing your blood on my cock..." I was just basking in the fleeting moment of the cool air soothing my inflamed pussy when I jump forward with a shriek in reaction when he gives it a good slap. The resounding has my pussy throbbing in pain and pleasure.

"Mass—" I go to scold him, and his harsh grip on my hips silences me.

His cock butts against me, and I shake with need and rock back, exposing myself like an offering. "Alessia," my name comes out on a growl. "Your body...it's perfection." He slaps one ass cheek and then fists it, causing me to clench up, but my hips still sway greedily.

"Just fuck me, Massimo," I warn. The frustration angering me. I don't care how badly my pussy burns and that it's bleeding.

He chuckles, and I swear my eyes roll back in my head from the beautiful sound of it. He presses his soft lips to one shoulder and drags his lips down my back. Then he flattens his tongue on my skin to lick his way back up. All the while, the head of his cock randomly bumps me. Even when it brushes against my thigh, I quiver from excitement.

His hot breath makes its way to my ear, and my mouth falls open as I begin panting. "You want it, *gattina*?" he teases. The stubbornness in me has me chomping down on my bottom lip, refusing to beg. "I bet you're tempted to take it, huh?" He slips his cock between my thigh gap and slides it against me. "Take it, baby," he whispers in my ear.

I'm afraid to move. I don't know why. In any situation like this, I wouldn't hesitate to take control. To do what I must to get precisely what I want. Maybe it's because what I want is him and his dominance. I want him to continue this total control over me and bring me that insurmountable pleasure only he has discovered inside of me.

So, I rock my hips back, silently demanding what I want from him. His fingers flex on my hips, and he stills against me. I'm close to screeching when he sits on his haunches and yanks me down, his cock abruptly spearing me. I don't know if it's from the angle or if I'm that swollen, but he stretches me, provoking my greedy hormones. I'm soaking his cock, causing that unique lewd sound as he thrusts in and out of me, using my hips to drive me.

I bend my lower back as far as I can, and it hits me differently, and I explode. I scream into the mattress, and he keeps at it, chasing his pleasure, tumbling right behind me. He growls when his hips pause, and he pulls out slightly to slam back in to pause and grunt. He repeats the motion a few more times before finally stopping.

Listlessly lying there, I can feel warm fluids dripping from me. I can't speak, I can't move, I can't even blink. All I can do is breathe and listen to my heart rapidly beating hard in my chest.

It's not until I feel his body heat leave me that I snap myself out of it. I roll to my side and sit up, unable to make eye contact with him right now. "I need to go shower," I murmur and scoot to the edge of the bed. When I swing my legs off, his big arm hooks around my waist again to stop me. "Come on, Massimo." The grin that spreads across my face is unavoidable.

"Then let's shower." I squeal when I'm easily yanked back and airborne, tossing me over his shoulder like a rag doll.

"Massimo!"

My ass jiggles when he gives it a good smack and takes several long strides to the bathroom. I'm still grinning as my head dangles behind him, and I have a great view of his rock-hard ass.

The water turns on, and he finally sets me on my feet in his lavish glass-enclosed shower. It's already steaming from the hot water, and he backs me against the tiled wall. "I don't have any of my shower stuff, and I need to wash my makeup off." I'm sure I look like a hot mess from falling asleep without washing my face.

He smiles down at me, and I can't help but beam up at him. His hair is messy, and there's extra scruff on his neck from needing to shave. "Tell me what you need, and I'll get it for you."

I snort and roll my eyes as I try pushing at his chest. He, of course, doesn't budge an inch. "I need to go shower up in my bathroom, Massimo."

"This is your bathroom," he says, causing me to roll my eyes again. "I want you moved into my room by the end of the day," he murmurs and nuzzles his face into my neck, making it hard to think.

"Not happening, De Luca. Not until we're married."

"Oh, it's happening. Today."

By the levity in his tone, I think he's actually serious. "Wait, Massimo. Stop." I try pushing at him again. "Massimo, I'm serious." He finally picks his head up and looks down at me in delight. "I'm not moving into the same room as you until *after* we're married. It's what we agreed upon."

"We also agreed not to sleep together until the wedding night. Things change."

"Well, consider this immutable." I try to be stern with him as possible, but it's hard to when he's standing so close to me in all his manly glory with a playful twinkle in his eye.

"What do you need from your shower?"

Knowing we'll just go round and round, I let him think he's won this tiny battle and tell him what I need right now. But he's not winning with the whole 'moving into his room' thing. It's complicated enough for an arranged marriage, so there's no need to complicate it any further by moving too quickly.

When he returns with the few products I requested, I'm standing directly under the water, soaking my tender and dirty body from head to toe. He goes to stand on the other side, only a few feet away from me, to do the same, his eyes full of intent.

I can't help but smile as I stare back, and my eyes take a gander at his impeccable physique. Every scar and tattoo over every defined line and muscle. He's glorious. Like a true gladiator. My eyes continue to roam, and his cock is growing larger and larger by the moment. I arch an eyebrow up at him.

"*Mi ecciti.*" *You're turning me on*, he says unabashedly with a crooked smirk.

Biting down a grin and shaking my head, I close my eyes and tilt my head back to wash my hair. My body is so fucking tender. My nipples raw, my pussy a little swollen, my lips puffy from kissing so much last night. But if he were to pin me against this wall right now, I wouldn't say no.

I'm almost disappointed when he doesn't.

CHAPTER EIGHTEEN

Massimo

Throughout the day, my thoughts are consumed by my woman.

The way her sweet cunt gripped me and swelled up after only the first time I fucked her. How her dark nipples puffed up and turned colors. Purple marks in the shape of my fingers decorating her sweet hips and ass. The mixture of her blood and cream on my cock. The sight was an exquisite, enigmatic masterpiece reserved exclusively for my admiration.

While she's been out handling wedding preparations, I've arranged for her belongings to be transferred into our now-shared bedroom. I know it will be a fight. Catastrophic. The thought of it elicits an involuntary twitch in my cock. Her vicious temper gets me harder than her seductive dancing. The woman is crazy, and I crave it and how it gets me riled up. Our first real fight will lead to phenomenal pleasure.

Thinking about how she tried sneaking an icepack up to her room this morning makes me chuckle, and Ezzo gives me a look. Clearing my throat, I try to play it off.

"You and Alessia seem to be getting along," he comments from his chair in front of my desk.

"We are."

"Is she as crazy as they say?" he muses.

I can't help the chuckle that erupts from me this time. "She is."

"Not afraid she might whack you in your sleep after one little tiff?"

"I think I'm safe. Unless I manage to *really* piss her off." We both chuckle, and I realize how long it's been since he and I have laughed together.

We're taught family is paramount, but is it logical to throw yourself into peril to protect those who are essentially strangers?

"I bought a vineyard in Tuscany. It'll be a good summer home for all of us," I blurt out.

"*Che cosa?*" *What*? He looks at me as if he couldn't have possibly heard me right.

"I wanted to buy a summer home as a wedding gift for Alessia. Thought it would be beneficial to purchase a vineyard for profit as well. It could be a nice family vacation home."

"*A family vacation home*," he repeats flatly.

"Yes."

"For *our* family?"

I feel the agitation climbing. "Why is this so hard to comprehend? I bought it as a gift to Alessia, but it's more than big enough for all of us to use." It's technically a castle sitting right between Siena and Florence, with twenty-five bedrooms and thirty-three bathrooms. It dates back to 1020 AD.

"Like at the same time?" I glower at him. "I'm just a little...surprised." He eyes me suspiciously. "We don't do family vacations."

"Look." I sigh. "I'm not asking for family dinners or celebrating every holiday together. I'm only suggesting a trip once a year to keep our family united. Family is important," I mutter in the last part, feeling like a fraud for saying so.

"Did Alessia put you up to this or something?"

"Never mind." I resist the urge to lash out, and force myself back to work.

"I'm not opposed to it, Massimo. I'm just wondering where all of this is coming from."

I ignore him, and he eventually gives up. I won't explain myself, and I shouldn't have to, for trying to bring our family together. Our parents are hopeless, but we can try to salvage what remains. We'll never be that kind of family where we sit around a Christmas tree exchanging gifts; we haven't since we were small kids, and that was only because of our mother.

Is it so wrong to want our relationship with one another to be more than a family obligation? It's how I already feel about Alessia. She's not only my family, she's someone I would die for, and if someone were ever to harm her, the consequences would be egregious and never-ending. And if she were to die...*Madonna*, I cannot even fathom that.

I want the real thing with her. I don't look forward to her being the person to reign at my side, but to the whole fucking package.

There's a knock at my door, and I know it's her before she opens it. She waltzes right in with the hint of a smile on her lips. "Oh, hello, Ezzo," she says politely with a bigger smile.

Ezzo stands up to greet her. "Alessia. How are you?"

"I'm good. How are you? I haven't seen you since the party."

"I've been around." He glances between us. "I was actually just getting out of here."

"Oh, I hope I didn't interrupt anything."

"No, not at all. I'll talk to you later, Massimo."

I don't say anything as he leaves us, and I keep my gaze on the gorgeous woman standing before me. Once the door is shut, she looks at me. "How's your day going?"

"It's hard to concentrate."

"Oh?" She casually clasps her hands behind her back, seemingly poised. She's wearing another innocent dress that she looks awfully dangerous in. "Is something distracting you?"

"I think I may need a break, is all." I stand to my feet and button my suit jacket.

"Are you hungry?"

"Famished."

"Did you not eat lunch?"

I round the desk towards her. "It's not food I want, *cara mia*."

"I'm not sure that I understand," she muses.

The floral scent drugs me as I stand a foot taller than her, even in her heels. "You have been making it hard for me to work all day, *bella*." Taking one finger, I twirl a lock of her hair around it, giving it a little tug.

"But I haven't been here all day, Massimo," her voice dips down to a sultry tone.

"Then how come I can't seem to stop thinking about you?" I murmur, and all humor drops from her face. We stand there unmoving, and I'm curious about her next move. My little kitten is awfully skittish at times.

Typically, I'm clairvoyant to the point where everyone is so predictable, but I do not see it coming when she goes for my belt with a straight face. Her fingers work hastily, and as soon as my cock is in her tiny hands, she drops to her knees. Her brown eyes stare up at me, desire dancing in them, and I suck in a breath of air when she darts her tongue out to swirl around the crown of my steeled cock.

"Alessia..." I rasp and slide my hand to the back of her head.

She takes me into her mouth painstakingly slow, sliding it as far as she can till it hits the back of her throat. She doesn't gag or squeeze her eyes shut. She remains calm as she glides it back to the tip and repeats it several times. Once she has my length slick with her saliva, she uses it to pump her hand on what she can't comfortably fit.

My other hand finds its way into her hair and grips it, but not harshly. I'm allowing her this moment, letting her acclimate to the size and girth in her precious little mouth.

She narrows her eyes at me, taunting me, daring me, telling me not to hold back like she had last night. Alessia doesn't want to be treated like some dainty princess. She wants to see that I am king.

The grip I have on her hair strengthens, and I know it stings her scalp, but she doesn't falter or shy away. I take over as I stop her and rock my hips forward to the point where her eyes water, but still, she refuses to gag or stop. My little psycho. She wants me to push her limits. She wants me to find them and send her over them because I don't think she even knows what they are. No man has been brave enough to explore them.

I fist my hand in her hair, using it to pull her back as I jolt my hips forward all the way to the hilt. Her eyes flinch, and I can feel her throat constrict, but she obstinately remains silent. I do it again and again, making sure to force the memories on her muscles, another part of her accustomed to me inside of her. Only one more part of her needs my cock's attention.

Has my *gattina* had anywhere back there before?

The thought of another man inside her gets to me. Especially with her heavenly mouth around my cock. My thrusts become more urgent, and tears start running down her face as she digs her nails into my hip bones, but she doesn't try to push me away, and she doesn't dare take her eyes off me. She takes it, and I can guarantee her cunt is pulsating.

Grunting, I can feel that tingly sensation in the base of my spine right before my balls tighten up. Just as I feel my seed making its way through my shaft, I hold her head down on my cock as I drown her in it. Letting it slide directly down her abused throat. I don't release her until I'm fully sated.

She gasps for air and sits back on her heels. Still, as she sits there on her knees, tear-streaked face, she looks sacrosanct and holy—like Hera herself, mightier than Zeus.

Tucking myself away, she catches her breath and goes to wipe away her tears, but I snatch her wrists into firm grips. On instinct, she becomes defensive from the restraint and begins to struggle against me. I soften my features and loosen my grasp as I pull her to her feet. I successfully allay her doubts. She yields, allowing me to frame her face with my hands.

"I hope that helps." Her voice comes out a little hoarse.

I almost smile as I admire her tear-streaked face. I use my thumbs to swipe through the wet trails in fascination. "I'm afraid you just gave me more to think about, *gattina*."

Her plush lips flutter. "Well, I will let you try and get back to work. I only wanted to drop in and say hi. Will we be having dinner together tonight?"

"Of course. And whatever you want to do for it."

"Hmm." She smirks. "Alright, Massimo. I'll see you later."

I kiss her gently on the lips and give her ass a little swat that makes her giggle. That fucking giggle will be the death of me.

I'd do anything to hear it.

CHAPTER NINETEEN

Massimo

I knew I wouldn't have to miss her for long as she came storming back into my office not even ten minutes later. The playful smirk replaced by a combative sneer.

"Miss me already, my love?" I muse because I just can't help myself. She's absolutely marvelous when her temper is spewing.

"I told you I am not moving into your bedroom," she vehemently scolds as she stops in front of my desk. Fists shaking at her sides, and her eyes wild with fury.

"*Our* bedroom, *cara mia*," I say calmly and lean back in my chair.

"You think you're funny or something? I'm just going to move all my shit back." The smirk on my face twitches, and she spins around to stomp out of the room.

Sighing, I wonder if I even have the energy for this when she just drained me of it only minutes ago. Aw well. I knew what I was doing, and now I must deal with the ramifications.

Peeling my jacket off and hanging it over the back of my chair, I head for the stairs. When I come to a stop in the hall between our two bedrooms, I hear her cursing and growling in rapid Italian as she leaves our bedroom with a pile of her clothing and stomps into her old bedroom.

When she storms back across the hallway and into our room again, I follow her. "You know, my love." I loosen my tie and unbutton the top button of my dress shirt. Getting comfortable. "I'll just have everything moved right back." She stops outside the closet with more clothes balled up in her arms. "I think you should know by now that I don't say anything that I don't mean. And eventually, I do get what I want."

She screams through her teeth and throws the pile of clothing to the floor. Plowing right through the pile, she aggressively advances on me. "We had a deal! You agreed to let me have my own room until we're married!"

"Lower your voice, *cara*," I warn.

"No! I will not lower my voice! You don't get to call all the shots! You don't own me! No one does!" she screams up at me.

Something inside me cracks, and I have her jaw firmly secured in my hand. Her eyes only narrow in wrath rather than widening in fear. Her instincts kick in, and she attempts to fight me off, but maybe it would work on a weaker man. But I easily conquer her, backing her up to the bed and shoving her back.

"Massimo!" she shrieks when she bounces off the mattress. "Do not manhandle me like that!" She pushes up to a sitting position, deranged as a feral cat, claws out and ready to spill blood.

"Do not scream in my face," I say coolly and crawl over the bed. She tries to scramble back, but I yank her down by her ankles. "I will not disrespect you like that, so I'd appreciate it if you do not disrespect me."

"Disrespect?! What the fuck do you call this?!"

Taking her wrists, I crank them up over her head and slam them down on the pillows as my legs straddle her body. She stops resisting and glares up at me as if she's calling my bluff. "Keep going, Alessia. You'll only make your punishment last longer."

"Punishment?! I didn't do anything wrong! You're the one who went against your word!"

"I did not go against my word," I quip. "I told you. Things change."

"Just because we had sex?! God, were you this clingy with all your women?"

I chuckle and reach over her to dig for the cuffs attached to the bed, buried behind the pillows. Without taking my eyes off hers, I restrain one wrist in the cuff, and her eyes finally reflect fear.

"Massimo," she grits out, causing a crooked grin to tug at the corner of my lips. "Uncuff. Me. Right. Now."

"I don't think so, *gattina*. You've tried my patience, and now you must pay." She begins thrashing and pulling on her restrained wrist. Tiny little thing is no match for me nor the steel. Easily enough, I pull her other wrist up to the second pair and click it around her wrist. "You fucking—"

"Tsk tsk." I cluck my tongue and wag my finger in her face as she screams through her teeth and flails about. "The more you curse and yell at me, the worse it'll be."

"I don't give a shit. You will uncuff me right now!"

Sighing, I lean back on my heels. "You'll be released once your punishment is over. And however long that will be is entirely up to you."

She begins swearing at me in Italian as I get up from the bed and go close the door. On my way back, I smile as I start peeling my clothes off. She's screeching and fighting, and I know her wrists will be a mess after this. I almost feel bad for that. I don't like to see her skin tainted unless it's from me and the pleasure we make together.

"Sshhh." I go and straddle her again, containing her flailing legs. "*Bambina. Calmati, amore mio.*" *Calm down, my love.* Her nostrils flare as she breathes heavily out of them.

"I'm going to kill you once I—"

"Alessia. Do I need to muzzle you?" I say sternly.

Her nostrils flare again as her eyes widen in outrage. "You will not fucking muzzle me."

"Then hush. Take your punishment like a good girl." Her lips thin as she sneers, and I think she'd rather silence herself than me silencing her with a gag. "You are so beautiful." I kiss her on the lips, and surprisingly, she doesn't try to bite me. She's learning. That's good. "I'm sorry, but I will have to rip this dress, *bella*." She's still silently glowering. The two thin straps of her dress easily snap. Reaching under her, I find the zipper. "Are you still sore, baby?" I rasp closely to her face. Her silence makes me chuckle. "Now, we aren't talking?" Nothing. "Very well." She remains quiescent and docile as I remove all her clothing. "Do you have any idea how ethereal you are right now? Red with rage, at my mercy, naked."

I nudge her legs apart to inspect her puffy little pussy. It's still swollen, but it's gone down severely since this morning. And what do you know? It's glistening. "Ah, *amore*." I remove my eyes from her cunt to look at her face. "You're fucking *gushing*." Her nostrils flare, and I know how much the invective inside her is raging.

Moving off the bed again to get a good look at my masterpiece, I decide to leave my pants on for now to abstain. First, she needs her punishment, then I can take my own pleasure.

Taunting her, I run my fingers down from her clavicle bone over her sensitive and raw nipples. I watch them pebble then continue down her smooth, slender legs.

"Knees up, *gattina*."

Face full of defiance, she not only hikes her knees up but spreads them nice and wide unabashedly. The daring look on her beautiful face has me laughing inside. *This woman...*

Crawling over her, I take a nipple harshly into my mouth, making her suck in a sharp breath through her teeth. I don't bite down, but I pull it to the back of my tongue and watch as she fights through the pain. Pinching her other nipple, I pull it, and her lips turn white as she strains them into a flat line.

I'm not necessarily trying to hurt her or even get a reaction from her. I'm just giving her a reminder of whose castle she's in. I'll treat her as my queen and, most of the time, as my equal, but she will learn not to disrespect me and fight me every time she may not agree with something.

I switch sides and do the same to each nipple. Her body tenses under me, and she fights back a whimper. Knowing I've made my point, I move down her body and cup her breasts, giving them a firm squeeze. She jerks her body to try and buck me off her.

I chuckle and sit back. My fingers wrap around her tight thighs to push her knees up at her sides. Such a beautiful sight. Her pink, puffy, wet cunt. "Keep your knees up." She obeys me as I let go. Taking one finger, I slip it through her folds to her entrance and slide it in. She's tense and tighter than normal. "Tell me. Are you sore?" I slowly pump it in and out of her, and she only stares at me. "Tell me, *gattina*. Or I won't be gentle at all."

"Yes." Her words come through her clenched teeth.

"Then I'll be gentle."

She scoffs. "Right. Do you even know how to be gentle?"

Chuckling, I continue pumping slowly with just one finger and place a kiss on her inner thigh. "I have yet to really let go, *gattina*."

"And have yet to be gentle," she retorts.

My heart thumps in my chest for some reason as I pause. "Is that what you want, Alessia? Gentle?" She's back to silence. "No, Alessia. You don't want gentle." I add another finger inside her, and her eyelids grow heavy as her chest heaves. "You need me to take your power and for you to feel mine."

Every minute of every day, she feels as if she needs to prove herself. Prove how strong, brave, and intelligent she is. Giving control over to me, she can, for once, be just a woman and not the ruthless daughter of a don.

"I hate it," she says in a breathy whisper.

"Now, *cara*. Let's not start lying to each other." I kiss her inner thigh, then dig my teeth into it, making her grunt.

"Are you saying you've yet to lie to me?"

My eyebrows arch. "I may keep things from you, but I will never lie to you." She tries scowling as I keep up a slow pace with my fingers. Her eyelids are growing heavier by the second, but she fights them. When I lean in for another kiss, the corner of my mouth brushes against her labia. The tiny moan that sounds in the back of her throat makes me smirk, but I don't comment on it.

"What happened with you and Arianna?"

My lips hover over her cunt as my body and fingers still. I could continue evading that subject since I should not remain in question. She shouldn't have asked me to begin with. I told her nothing happened, and that should've been the end of it. Then she went and accused me once again when I went away for a few days to go and look at the property in Italy for her wedding gift.

"I should not have to repeat myself, *gattina*. Nor should I have to ever explain myself. I've done nothing to earn your distrust."

"Trust is like love, Massimo. You can't demand it from me. It has to be earned, and it will not be easy. It'll take time."

"Trust can be broken. Are you saying your love can be broken as well?" She doesn't answer as she takes short breaths. "You can choose to trust. You can't choose to love because love is not a choice. Choose to trust me, Alessia. Until I prove you wrong."

"Will you?"

I start moving my fingers again and kiss her little bundle of nerves with a feather-light caress. "Will I what, *cara*?" I glance up at her and see the indecision on her face. She's not even sure what she's asking me. "If you're asking me if I'm choosing to trust you, the answer is yes. It's not something I've ever given to anyone willingly, but I'm giving it to you. If you're asking me if I'll break your trust, that is hard to answer. No, I will not lie to you. No, I will not ever be unfaithful or disloyal to you. But there are so many ways to lose trust in someone. It depends on how fickle your trust is. And back to the point of trust and love. I'm telling you right now, Alessia. My love is not a fickle thing. My trust, too, can be broken, but when I love, it's something that can never be undone." She stares down at me with this pained look on her face, and I continue to stroke her slowly. "Now, no more talking, *gattina*. Or I'll put a gag in you."

CHAPTER TWENTY

Alessia

I'm speechless. How can he really say that if he were to love me, he would never be able to stop?

He's wrong. Trust and love are the same. They take years to build and have to be earned, and they most definitely can be broken. Once broken, they take several lifetimes to fix.

"Now, no more talking, *gattina*. Or I'll have to put a gag on you."

And now I'm back to being bitter. Tying me up is one thing, but gagging me? The repercussions of that would be calamitous.

His fingers continue to thrust in and out of me as he teases me with light kisses to my pussy. He's already dissolving my refusal. I want him to devour my pussy and then fuck me. But he said this is a punishment. What if my punishment is this? To have me begging and pleading with him to get me off in one way or another? *Damnit, that would be a suitable punishment.* Turning me into a needy little bitch. He's right. There are so many ways he can punish me.

The prickly hair along his jaw stabs at my sensitive clit as he lightly brushes his lips up and down it. Mocking me, messing with me. My hips thrust up involuntarily, but he's quicker as he rears back some, not making contact. My heels had to come down to do that, and his eyes dart to mine.

"Put your knees back up, *gattina*," he commands, and I automatically obey. *Goddamnit.* He already has me tamed. "Don't put them down again," he warns.

Then he dives in mouth first, causing my breath to hitch and my muscles to spasm, devouring me like I've been wishing for. But as soon as he has me on the climb, he pulls back and even retracts his fingers.

Yup, this is my punishment. Orgasm denial. How very cruel.

The look on Massimo right now keeps my frustration at bay. To see him so out of order is unheard of. If I weren't seeing it for myself, I would never believe it to be possible. His lips parted, his eyes wild, his hair out of place, and his cheeks slightly flushed. He's a hot mess, and I want him like this every single day for the rest of my life. I may be restrained, and my control is taken from me, but I feel more powerful than ever.

The thought is terrifying, and it's like he can read my thoughts, or maybe my body is too revealing because he looks at me in question. His fingers leisurely trail up and down my slits, then they slip lower and lower until he hits that clenched-up hole.

"Have you had anyone here before, *gattina*?" His fingertip presses in just past the rim, and the muscles automatically tighten up.

"Yes," I admit to him honestly. There isn't much I haven't tried in bed. Other than being tied up, but I didn't exactly get a choice in the matter.

He grunts in disapproval and presses his finger in a little further, using the juices from my cunt. "Too bad." His finger pumps in up to his knuckle, and already I feel so stretched.

I've done anal a few times. Thinking about *his* massive cock going in there, it has me clenching up in fear. "Relax for me, *amore*." He places a kiss on my thigh. "Do not refuse entry from me. Ever." His finger bottoms out inside of me, and he stills. "Not in here." He pulls out a little, then pushes all the way back in, stilling again. "Or here." With his other hand, he drags his fingers through my wetness until he finds my center and pushes two long fingers inside, and my back bows off the bed. I'm fighting back a moan so hard I feel like I swallowed my tongue in effort. "Or that pretty mouth of yours."

He pumps in and out of both holes together, and I'm panting hard. Maybe if I act like this isn't the best feeling in the world right now, he won't pull back in time, and I'll come.

Always in my head, he pumps a few more times, and just as I'm so close to the top, he retracts from my insides, and I can't help it. I let out a frustrated growl, and the bastard chuckles.

When he grabs me by the hips and flips me over to my knees, I don't see it coming, and my arms twist unnaturally. But I don't let him know it hurt. I won't give him the satisfaction.

The cool air hits my seams as he positions me with my ass up and my head down in the mattress. My arms stretched out, and my knees widely spread. "*Perfezione*." *Whack! Whack!* He smacks each cheek with a firm hand, then rubs his thumb over my clenched hole. My eyes are squeezed shut and every muscle in my body cramps up from my muscles contracting. The back of his throat rumbles as he continues to rub over that hole. Then he caresses the globes of my ass and places a chaste kiss on each cheek. "Hold tight, *cara*."

The bed dips behind me as he climbs from it, and I hear some rustling around somewhere in the room, but I don't open my eyes to see. I'd rather not. He probably went to get some kind of toy to use on me—a whip or vibrator of some sort.

The rustling stops, and a moment later, the bed dips behind me again. "Suck." My eyes pop open to see a small object hovering before my lips.

"What is it?"

Whack! He smacks my cheek harder than before, making my bottom lip quiver. "Open your mouth and suck," he demands.

I glance down at the object and see that it's a butt plug. "I am not putting something in my mouth that has been in another woman's asshole, Massimo," I hiss. The audacity of him thinking I would do such a vile thing!

"It's clean. Now, suck." My lips seal shut in defiance. I know I'll pay for my disobedience, but this is across the line. It's degrading. "I'll shove it in dry if you don't," he warns, and I know he'll carry out his threat. Letting out a shaky breath through my nose, I tentatively open my mouth, and he slides the plug in. "Suck." Tightening my lips around it, I do as he says and suck. Making sure to slobber all over it because it's for the comfort of my asshole, after all. His eyelids grow listless, watching me, and I feel a little more power creeping back to me. Blinking his eyes a few times, he pops the thing out of my mouth and moves back behind me.

Cinching my eyes shut again, I wait for whatever is coming next. The tip of the plug begins to poke at my clenched hole, and I know from experience that if I tense up, it'll hurt more. So, I relax and arch my back more. He twirls the tip in the center of my hole and puts pressure on it as if he's screwing it in.

His other fingers find my wet folds, and he fondles them, making me loosen up even more on instinct. My hips begin rocking, gaining more friction, and the butt plug is set into place. My hips come to a jolting stop when he spanks me hard, once on each cheek. I growl again in frustration and anger.

It wasn't my fucking fault. My body was just moving on instinct!

"This isn't for you, *gattina*. This is for me."

A phone begins going off somewhere behind me, and I feel him getting off the bed again. "Yeah," he clips and pauses. "I'll be right down."

Yes! Any other time I would be outraged that a man answered his phone when I was naked on his bed, but not right now.

"Looks like we'll have to save the rest for later, *cara mia*," he murmurs, and I hear things moving around behind me. "Do you need to use the restroom?"

"What?" My head whips around as much as it can in this awkward position.

"Do you need to use the restroom? I won't be long, but if you need to use it, you should now."

"Massimo. You will not leave me like this." I grind my molars.

His fully dressed figure comes into view, and I roll my eyes to meet his twinkling ones. "Yes or no, Alessia?"

"Uncuff me right now!" I give the restraints a yank.

"I don't think you're in the position to make demands," he muses, and I pull more on the cuffs. The amusement drops from his face when he glances at my bound wrists. "I don't want you hurting yourself."

"Why? Because that's only for you to do?"

He looks back down at me and crouches next to the bed. "What I do to you is not bringing you any harm, Alessia," he says in a surprisingly soft voice. "I don't wish ever to see you hurt."

"And spanking me? Shoving things up my ass?"

Sighing, he stands up, buttons his suit jacket, and straightens his tie. "Are you in pain right now, *cara*?" I don't answer because the only thing hurting right now are my wrists which is my own doing. "I expect to come back to you in this exact position."

"Massimo."

"Don't move," he scolds with a finger pointed. "I won't be long."

I'm stunned into silence as he walks away, and I hear the door open and then shut. *He fucking left. He really fucking left me like this.* And there is absolutely nothing I can do about it.

The position I'm in is hurting my back and shoulders, so I fall to the side to rest them for a few minutes.

"I warned you not to move," Massimo's voice wakes me. Then he applies pressure to the toy still lodged in my ass.

"I didn't mean to. I fell asleep," I mutter sleepily. My mouth opens with a yawn. "Don't you think I've been punished enough, Massimo?" He doesn't answer me. "Massimo," I growl, getting really pissed off. "Get these fucking cuffs off me." I yank on them twice with more force.

Nothing happens for several moments, and I almost think he's left me again until I'm abruptly flipped to my back. I open my mouth in protest and he takes advantage by stuffing something inside of it. My fucking panties.

I snarl around the thin fabric and try to spit it out, but fucking hell, he shoved them in there good.

I'm breathing fire as he stands at the foot of the bed, looking like royalty in his sexy suit and the regal air clinging to him. I still when his fingers pop open the button on his suit jacket, and he peels it off. Using the restraints, I pull myself up to the pillows to prop my head up as I watch him slowly undress down to nothing. His muscled body illuminating power and strength.

On his knees, he makes his way over top of me and pokes my core with his erection. His hands are holding him up above me in a push-up position, and I pray to God he's going to fuck me now. I don't even need an orgasm; I just need his cock inside of me.

Slowly, he descends to give me his weight, brushing the shell of my ear with his lips. "You'll soon be my queen, but make no mistake. I will always be king of the castle, *amore.*"

Leaning back to his heels with a stony look on his face, he grips my hips and drives forward. My back bows, and the air rushes out of my lungs as he slams into me and does it over and over again. Long but harsh thrusts. My ass in his lap, using my hips to drill into me like a madman. Literally punishing my pussy. I won't be able to sit down for days without a reminder.

The climax comes rushing into me too quickly from the pent-up pleasure, and my muffled scream is impulsive. My muscles jerk and quake. He doesn't let up, though, not even for a second. Spots dance in front of me, and before I can see straight, I'm propped back up on my knees, and I don't even have time to catch my bearings as he slams into me from behind.

I already feel stuffed, so when he pushes on the butt plug, I arch my back more as an offering. Crazy thoughts invade my head about him replacing the plug with his cock and tearing me. Bleeding me again.

Both hands slam down on either ass cheek, gripping them painfully hard. They, too, are tender from last night and this morning. I grind my teeth as he fucks me savagely, and I should be in tears of pain, but my eyes water from another climax. He grunts behind me as his movements become uncontrolled, and he abruptly leaves me to spurt long ropes of cum to decorate my ass, crack, and creases. Dripping down to the mattress and coating me.

I'm spent and exhausted, melting into the bed. I have no idea what goes on for the next few minutes as I'm in and out of it, but when I come to, he's pulling my panties out of my mouth so I can gasp for air. When he frees my wrists, I remain motionless and confined by torpidity.

When he rolls me over to scoop me into his arms, my head rests against him and my body goes into a comatose state.

I'm wholly subject to his will.

CHAPTER TWENTY-ONE

Alessia

The shower was silent as I could hardly keep myself upright.

Who knew someone could fuck the life out of you?

He was so gentle and nurturing, and he even tied my hair up into a knot on top of my head before placing me under the hot water. He washed my body and gingerly pulled the butt plug out of me that I had forgotten about.

After washing me, he sat me down on the bench to clean himself quickly. Out of the shower, he wrapped me in a large fluffy towel and carried me back to bed like I was this fragile creature.

It's still light out when he joins me in bed, pulls me into his side, and covers us with the warm blankets. I tell myself I'm only going to shut my eyes for a moment, but I end up falling asleep against him.

From the steady beat of his heart, the feel of his breathing against my forehead, the warmth of his body, and the softness of the pillows and blankets. Yeah, it all lulls me right to sleep in no time.

I only know I slept for a while because my stomach rumbles in hunger when I begin to come to. "The night of our engagement party, when I excused myself to use the restroom, Arianna was waiting for me." Somehow, he knows I'm awake before my eyes open. "Yes, we have been together in the past, but it was never anything serious. She was a possibility for a union, but only that." He pauses. "She made advances at me, and I did what I could to decline her offers respectfully. That's all I will say about it."

Finally, I find the courage to open my eyes, and we lie there in silence for a while. I believe him, but we still have one more unresolved issue. "And your trip. I understand if it was something you can't yet entrust me with. But what am I supposed to think when you are so evasive about it?"

When he doesn't answer right away, I tilt my face up and find him staring up at the ceiling. "Because it wasn't for business." I swallow hard and almost look away until he ensnares me with his eyes. "It was for personal reasons, but I can't tell you what. You need to trust me, though. It was not to have an affair, and that's again all I will say about it."

Unless I want to drive myself mad with mistrust and paranoia, I need to start putting a little faith in his word, if anything. Otherwise, it'll only be me that I'm hurting. If he has anything to hide, it will eventually reveal itself.

"Okay." His face relaxes a little. "Did you know that your name means 'greatest'?" I practically blurt out, and a cute little crease forms between his brows. "Massimo means 'greatest'." I snort and glance down at his hard chest bashfully.

"I didn't know that." He pauses. "And what does your name mean, *bella*?"

I look back up at him to find him tucking one arm behind his head and focusing his attention on me. "Defender."

He gives me a little smile. "Was that intentional?"

I avert my gaze again. "My mother waited to name each of us until we were a few days old, claiming it was to get to know us, and give us each a fitting name. Tullio, one who leads. Armando, soldier. Santino, little saint." We both chuckle because Santino is no saint, but he's reticent, which can be deceived as one. "Paolo, small. Apparently, she knew he would be the last boy. And Gemma, precious stone." I roll my lips in and dance my fingers along one of his scars, fixated on it. "My father was actually the one to choose my name." I look up at him again. "*Babbo* said that when Gemma would cry, I'd remain silent. As if I were trying to be strong for her," I murmur the last part almost feeling silly with this little story. How could Massimo possibly understand the significance of it?

He seems unperturbed as he patiently listens to every word I say. My fingers lightly caressing a scar the whole time.

His hand flattens over top of mine as my eyes bounce around his torso, infatuated with all of them marring his skin. They land on the biggest one right under the left side of his ribs. "What's this one from?" I slip my hand out from under his and touch it lightly. It's raised and about an inch wide and three inches long.

"Machete." My eyes widen as I look at him. "I was young and overly confident. Would go into situations unprotected thinking I was invincible."

"I heard you've always liked to be a soldier more than a capo."

Exhaling through his nose, he shifts a little. "The business side of it has always been hard to keep my attention, but it's the duty of the eldest. It'll all be inherited by me."

"Do you want it?"

"Yes," he says with no hesitation.

"Just a different part in it," I say as more of a statement, not a question. "I know what you mean." I look away. "I'll never be taken seriously."

"With me, you will."

"Still not the king of the castle," I mutter, and we both chuckle.

"Is that truly what you want, Alessia? To be the king?"

I take a moment to answer him. "I long for recognition."

"I promise you will have it, *cara*."

CHAPTER TWENTY-TWO

Alessia

"**I** 'm telling you. He's definitely skimming some off the top, Massimo. These numbers do not add up," I repeat myself for the third time. It's the same result after we've gone round and round with the reports from one of his illegitimate businesses.

"He's been working for us for a decade. He's never skimmed from us."

"That you know of," I mutter, and he gives me a look. "I know it's hard to believe he would cross you, but like every man out there, he's capable of it."

Sighing, he pinches the bridge of his nose. "Get him to the warehouse, Vinny." Vinny is his second most trusted next to Monte who is currently on sabbatical. He shakes his head at me when I fight back a smirk. "Don't get excited, my little psycho. You will not be kneecapping him." He chuckles when I curl my bottom lip out in a pouty face. "Maybe just one if I do find him guilty."

"Oh, darling," I say sweetly as I make my way over to him. "You're too good to me." He turns in his chair as I place my hands on either side of his face and lean down to peck him on the lips. "Oh!" I squeal when he yanks me down to his lap and deepens the kiss.

Since the whole debacle with the bedroom situation, he has not been shy with his affection. If I'm anywhere near, he has to touch me profusely. It's getting more difficult to avoid my feelings from burgeoning. I feel like I'm going to fall headfirst one day, and that scares the shit out of me.

"I think we should take a trip," he murmurs as he makes a trail of kisses down my face and to my neck.

"A trip? Where to?"

His hand starts at my knee, sliding up my thigh, dipping under my dress. "Anywhere. Just get away for a few days."

"Could you really get away for a few days? The wedding is in less than twelve weeks." Massimo abruptly picked a different date last week, saying he wanted to be married by September.

"I'm sure everyone can handle things while we're gone." He nuzzles my neck with his facial hair while his fingers play with the hem of my panty line. "I want a few days with you uninterrupted."

"You could just cuff me to your bed and demand that I stay like that for days. I'm sure something you've done before," I muse and berate myself inside when he pauses.

I hate the fact that the things we do together, and the *toys* he uses on me, he's shared with other women. It's bratty of me to hold his past against him in any way. I know it is. But I cannot seem to help myself. I wish I could eliminate every female he has ever been even remotely intimate with.

"I've never wanted a woman like I want you, Alessia." He squeezes my ass cheek. "I never *not* want you." He kisses my collarbone.

"I'm going to go make some coffee. Do you want anything?" He lifts his head with a stare. I know he sees right through me. Whenever he says things like that, I flee. "I'll be back." I peck him on the lips and go to get up, but his grip around me tightens. "Mass—"

The door to his office opens aggressively without warning. *Angelo.* The distaste for me is immediate as he glowers at the two of us cozied up. Massimo isn't ignorant of the tension as he rubs a soothing hand up and down my thigh.

"Something urgent?" No warm greeting between the two.

"I need to speak with you."

Never being one to be ignored as if I'm not even there, I slap a cheerful smile on, not letting his unwelcoming gaze deter me, and get up from Massimo's lap. "Angelo. So good to see you. *Come sta?*" I reach up, and he actually leans down for me to place a kiss on each cheek, and he might as well be on his knees for me right now. He reeks of cigar smoke and cologne—nothing like his son's familiar scent.

"*Bene,*" he grumbles and looks past me to his son as if seeking assistance.

"Well, I was just leaving anyway." I keep my voice pleasant. "I'll leave you boys to it." I smile over at Massimo, and he flatly stares back. Obviously unhappy that I used this as an excuse to slip away. "I'll see you later, Massimo."

"*Ciao, bella.*"

Turning my back to them, I remain poised as I make my exit. When I close the door behind me, I hear, "She's certainly made herself comfortable," in Italian from Angelo, and I decide to stick around for a moment.

"She's my fiancée. She should be comfortable."

"So, she already has you under her spell. She's nothing but a malediction where nothing good will come from it. Her and the rest of the Bonetti's."

I stand there unmoving, waiting to hear what kind of response my fiancé will have. And it better be good or I'll go back in there to tell them both to fuck themselves. Disrespecting me is one thing, but disrespecting my family name is a death sentence.

"She's harmless and will soon be my wife." *Harmless?!* "Now, what did you need to speak to me about?"

I command my feet to move before I really do lose my temper and charge back in there. *Harmless?* Is he for real? I'm sure it was just an attempt to sway the conversation away from me and to placate his father, but *harmless?* I guess I could be presumed harmless when those who don't know me see me, but anyone who does know *anything* about me, harmless is not the word that comes to mind. Bold, audacious, psychotic, crazy...

How is the audacity of his father's slander taking a backseat for the stupid jealousy to seep back in? I've always been possessive but never jealous. It's making me feel petty, and I hate it. I know he has a lot of years on me, so of course, many women came before, but I loathe the thought of being anything like them.

Okay, not *like* them, but I guess our relationship being anything like he's had before. More specifically, our sex. I don't want cuffs he's used on someone else, or sex toys, or even the same damn bed.

His father accused me of having Massimo under some spell, but it's me who's struggling with the rooted hold he has on me.

The smell of rich coffee fills the kitchen as it brews from the fancy machine. The maids now know not to insist on doing every little thing for me. I am not at all helpless and enjoy doing things like making myself some coffee.

We grew up with maids and staff who did most things for us, but if I were thirsty, I'd go to the kitchen and get myself something to drink. Here? You're expected to pick up a phone and tell someone to deliver it. It feels like you're staying at some resort, as if this place doesn't already lack life.

It only took Massimo about ten minutes to seek me out. Knowing he isn't the type to let anything go, I had a feeling he would. The question is, did I want him to?

The firmness of his body presses up against the back of mine, pinning me to the counter. The nearness of him gets my heart rate going, and my body tingles all over. His fingers toy with my hair before moving it away from my neck, and he replaces his mouth there. "You should know, *cara*, any woman before you might as well have never existed."

I swallow hard. How does he always know exactly what is happening inside my head? It's invasive, and I'm not even sure what's going on up there half the time.

"You don't have to do that," I say quietly, heart pounding.

"Do what? Tell you how I feel? I know I don't need to." He kisses my neck, and my eyes flutter shut. "Feel free to let me know what's inside this beautiful head of yours at any time." I swallow hard again. Afraid to move or speak. Unsure of what will come out of my mouth if I do. I'm not ready to make myself so exposed to him, especially since I am still trying to process it. "Stop running from me when I do tell you what's on my mind, *gattina*. I'm not going to stop, so you better get used to it."

"I don't mean to hold the past against you," I whisper.

"If it makes you feel any better, I want to murder any man who has ever touched you. If I come across any of them, I might."

I grin. "Does that mean I can kill anyone who has touched you?"

"If it'll make you feel better."

"Even Arianna?"

He chuckles and spins me around. "Not that I would care." He tucks some of my hair behind my ear. "But you know that would mean war."

I pout. "Fine. But if she ever touches you again, I will have to pop her."

He snorts and props me up onto the counter by my waist. "I'll even hand you my gun."

"You know I carry my own." I wrap my arms and legs around him. "All this talk about whacking ex-lovers turns me on." I kiss him on the lips.

His lips respond immediately, kissing me harder and hiking up my dress around my waist. He said he doesn't ever not want me, and I can say for sure that I feel the same. Even when I'm sore as hell and exhausted, I want him inside of me, pounding me into the mattress. Or behind me, pounding into me so hard his balls slap my pussy. And when he leaves marks on my body, I want to look at them and admire them for hours. Little reminders of what it feels like to be seized by Massimo.

"Are you going to fuck me or what?" I tease.

"After I indulge myself first," he says cheekily and drops to his knees. Having Massimo on his knees in front of me is otherworldly.

My panties come down my legs gradually until they make their way into his pocket, and I know I won't be getting those back. *Dirty little man*. He probably takes them out to smell them when he's alone in his office.

Prying my knees apart and wide, he hooks his hands underneath my thighs and jerks me to the edge of the counter. My palms slam down behind me to steady myself, and he's already savoring me.

Moaning, I rake my nails through his hair, and he grunts. I love how his facial hair rubs my skin raw when he does this, adding sensation.

Sucking my entire pussy into his mouth, I gasp and begin riding his face. Fucking him right back. It eggs him on as his breathing becomes erratic, and he pushes my thighs back to spread me wider.

Spots dance around in my vision as I explode in his mouth, and I'm eager to feel him moving inside of me. When he stands up and starts undoing his pants, I go for the buttons of his shirt. I love the feel of his muscles and scars under my fingers.

Tugging his arms free from his shirt, my hands immediately start roaming his body as he lines himself up with my entrance. My head falls back as he bottoms out inside of me, and he takes that opportunity to start kissing my neck as his hips begin to move. My nails dig into his strong shoulders, and my back arches to get as close to him as possible.

"Boss—" I gasp and hide my face into his neck as he stills. Then a gun pops off only a second later, making me jump a little and cling to Massimo.

Glancing over, I expect to see a dead body lying there in the entryway to the kitchen. "I missed," he rumbles against my neck and moves his hips again. Picking right back up where he had left off.

Giggling, I find his lips with mine, and I can't wipe the grin off my face as I kiss him. "You're crazy."

"You're one to talk, *bambina*."

Giggling some more, I start attacking him with kisses, totally enamored with him.

CHAPTER TWENTY-THREE

Alessia

I admire my wedding gown one last time before I stuff it into the back of the closet.

My mother about keeled over when I mentioned wearing a black gown on my wedding day. I don't embody virtue, and red would be a bit risqué, so I thought black would still be elegant enough. But after her reaction, I decided to appease her and go with a champagne and cream color dress. And it's the most gorgeous thing I have ever seen in my life. It's a nude mesh with an overlay of cream lace, and there's a detachable skirt that attaches to my hips to create this floor-length bustle. It's fucking magnificent.

I shove it into its hiding place when my phone goes off, and I see that it's Tullio calling. *"Salve!" Hello!*

"Where are you?" he rushes out tightly, and a wave of alertness washes over me.

"At the De Luca's. What's wrong?"

"Santino is on his way to pick you up. We need to get to the hospital."

"Okay, I'll be waiting." I hang up the phone without asking questions. Whatever it is, I'll find out as soon as my brother comes to get me, and peppering Tullio with questions on the phone will distract him.

Slipping on my small heels, I grab my phone and shove it into my small purse. Promptly, I make my way downstairs, calling Massimo on the way.

"*Gattina.*"

"Hey, I'm not sure what's going on yet, but Santino will be here soon to pick me up and take me to the hospital."

"I'll meet you there."

I hang up without another word, and Joey, my new guard, is hot on my heels as he sees me heading out. "My brother is coming to get me. Massimo knows."

"I'll wait with you."

Santino pulls up in front of the estate less than ten minutes later, and Paolo jumps out of the passenger seat, leaving the door open for me, and I slip inside. He closes the door and jumps into the backseat just in time for Santino to practically peel wheels out of there.

"Where's Massimo?" Santino murmurs from behind the wheel.

"Out. He's going to meet me at the hospital."

"Call him and tell him not to come."

"Santino—"

"Now, Alessia," he clips, and I know to always listen when he speaks.

"Yeah," he answers after the first ring.

"Don't come to the hospital."

"I heard what happened." The tone in his voice is not at all reassuring.

"Well, I haven't yet." I swallow hard.

"It wasn't me, Alessia. You have to know that. And I will find out who did it. I swear to you I will." The dark timbre has a beseeching underlining, and I have yet to learn why.

My heart is now pounding in my ears. "I'll call you later."

"Start talking," I say as soon as I hang up.

It's Paolo who speaks up. "Mamma and *Babbo* were in an accident."

"What kind of accident?" My stomach immediately binds up, and I twist my neck to look between them.

"Car accident," Paolo says, which doesn't make sense. Why would Massimo say it wasn't him, and he'll find out who it was? That must mean... "It was a hit," Paola confirms my fear, and I nod my head as I try to hold it together. Already everything inside of me wants to either burn up or crumble.

Santino grabs my hand and glances over at me, looking a little pale. "*Babbo* didn't make it, Alessia." Everything around me tilts, and I place my hand on the door to steady myself as my heart dissolves to the pit of my stomach. I might either puke or pass out from the instant pain it brings me. *Babbo* didn't make it, meaning he's *dead*. "And Mamma is in an induced coma."

Silently, I nod my head again and face forward. Watching the world go by in a blur and putting myself into a safe place. One where no one can reach me. Right now, I have to be strong. I cannot fall apart just yet. "Gemma?"

"She's on her way to the jet right now," Paolo murmurs.

When I try swallowing, my throat aches. "You think it was the De Luca's," I say quietly, praying I'm wrong.

"We have suspicions," Santino says.

I deflate into my seat with lamentation. *Babbo*...The thought of Massimo having anything to do with the hit on my parents is something that will kill me, so I don't argue with them or ask any more questions. Hospital first, accusations later. Pushing all thoughts of Massimo to the back of my mind, I cling to Santino's hand as we race the rest of the way to the hospital in silence.

One of our foot soldiers is waiting out front of the hospital to move the car for us as we jump out and run inside the building. The woman at the front desk knew we were coming as her eyes widen, and she rattles off the floor and room number.

Instead of taking the elevator to the next floor, Santino barges through the heavy door to the stairwell, and we take the steps two at a time. Santino, being a foot taller than me, ends up ahead of us as Paolo keeps pace with me out of chivalry.

It's not hard to find where we're supposed to be as we easily spot the group of large and menacing looking men standing at the end of the hallway. Tullio pacing, and Armando wiping at his reddened face. They both snap to attention as they see us running to them.

Armando takes me in his arms first, and his body shakes as he cries against me. I squeeze my eyes shut and don't let myself go. Not yet. If I break down now, I won't be able to keep it together for Gemma.

. *"Alessia. You remember what your name means?"*

"Yes. Defender. And Gemma's means precious stone."

I'm my sister's defender. Have been since day one, and I will be until my last dying breath. I'll make *Babbo* proud. Live up to the name that he picked out himself.

When we break apart, I reach up and dry Armando's tears, and he closes his eyes. "*Babbo* told us it was our job to keep you girls safe." When he opens his eyes again, they're hardened in anger. "I'll never let anything happen to you and Gemma."

I give him a sad smile. "I know, Mando."

Tullio comes over to me and brings me in against his chest for a crushing embrace. His hug is stiff and not as warm as usual, but it's strong, giving me much-needed strength. "I'm so sorry, Alessia. I'm so sorry."

I pull back to look up at him finding his eyes dry. "Any word about Mamma? Have you been able to see her?"

"Not since they had to put her under." His jaw ticks as he looks out over my head. "She'll make it, though. Just has a lot of healing to do."

Looking around, our men are all grim-faced as they silently mourn the death of our father. He was loved and revered by his men. Respect usually grows out of fear, but absolute devotion comes from both fear and adoration.

Paolo wipes at his tears with angry motions as Santino leans against the wall, flat and passive. Armando is still a crying mess as Tullio looks like he's about to explode in rage. Barely hanging on by a thread.

It grows eerily silent as we all stand there without knowing how to move forward from here. The life of a mafioso is always risky; our lives are constantly in danger, but we've been fortunate so far.

But good fortune always runs out.

CHAPTER TWENTY-FOUR

Alessia

G emma has finally exhausted herself with tears hours after getting home from the hospital.

After our brothers passed her around, she fell into my arms and
hadn't left since. We were finally able to see Mamma after what felt
like forever waiting. We all filed into the room, filling it with our
presence, and sat with her for hours, praying.

I'm still stuck in some kind of numb state where the tears won't
come as I tuck Gemma into her bed. As I head downstairs to talk
to my brothers, my stomach rolls, knowing what I will be walking
into. Something I have put half of my energy into ignoring.

They're all stuffed inside Father's office, and my eyes immediately
go to the loveseat in there. Memories try to flog my brain, but I shove
them back.

They all stop talking when my presence is known. All looking at me with caution. For fear of me finally breaking down or my reaction to whatever they've been withholding from me.

"So, tell me," I say when no one speaks.

"We have one of the butchers in custody," Tullio states.

"Then why the hell are we here?" My vitriolic tone doesn't faze them.

"We're here because this is where we all need to be right now." He uses a stern voice with me as his nostrils flare.

"So, no one's even questioned him yet?"

"Not yet, but we don't need to, to know he's one of De Luca's guys," Paolo sneers.

"How do you know that?"

"One of our guys recognized him," Armando says as he sniffles.

"And that's what we're basing this off of?"

Tullio slams his fist down on the desk. "Yes. For now, we are. Until I go and question him myself."

"Massimo says it wasn't him." I cross my arms.

"It was the De Luca's," Tullio says as a matter-of-fact.

"Massimo wouldn't lie to me."

Tullio chuckles and shakes his head. "You don't even know him, Alessia. Smarten up. He's Massimo De Luca. He's capable of anything."

I hate the way he's talking about Massimo. He might have a lot of blood on his hands and capable of a lot of things, but not lying. He didn't lie to me, and he wouldn't be involved in the murder of my parents. He wouldn't do that to me. I know it.

"You're wrong, Tullio. I'll admit, Angelo may have been involved. I won't deny you that since he has never been shy about his hatred towards our family, but not Massimo. He wouldn't do this. I'm telling you."

He couldn't.

"Just stop it, Alessia," Tullio hisses, looking like he might combust at any given moment. "The De Lucas have been our enemy for decades, and we should never have tried to ally with them. The marriage is off, and you are to never speak to Massimo again!" His voice bellows out at the end, feeling like he just slapped me.

My temper sizzles just under the surface, but there's no speaking to him when he's restive like this. Usually, I would lock horns with him and push back, ready to refute, but it wouldn't help my cause to fight him now. It'll only anger him more and also myself. "You're upset, I get it. We all are. I think what we need is a strong drink and a good night's rest. We can pick up this conversation in the morning."

I turn on my heels and ignore my brothers, who obviously don't have my back since they haven't said a word in my defense.

"Do not leave the estate unless I give you permission," Tullio calls out, and I stop in my tracks. My fists shake at my sides as I refrain from retaliation. *I cannot lose my temper on my brother right now.*

Swallowing my pride, I continue making my exit and flee to my room. I'm jittery and anxious and so fucking high-strung by the time I lock myself inside. I'm pacing the room like a caged tiger, ready to rip apart anyone who dares enter it. Tullio may be the man of the house now, but he will not speak to me like a child and think he can ground me like one.

I stomp over to the mini bar and pour myself something substantial. The only thing to help allay the grief and rage trying to rip me in half. I keep going to my phone, anxious to call Massimo, but I have a feeling it might only make matters worse at this moment.

The vulnerability I'm currently plagued with will have me believing only what I want to. I need to speak to Massimo with a less grief-stricken state of mind.

After three glasses of whiskey, I'm finally able to put myself to bed and pass out next to Gemma.

One fire at a time.

The house is dead quiet when I get up and head into the kitchen to make everyone breakfast. Mamma would be the one to do that, but she's not here right now. Gemma and I are the women of this house until she returns home.

I have breakfast already cooking when Gemma comes down and joins me. Preserving a stoic silence, she jumps right in, and we work side by side. Her eyes are pink and puffy, and she looks drained. I wish I knew what to say or do to help her through this. Help ease some of the pain for her. She's too fragile for any of this.

"Hey, have you seen my phone?" I ask her after a while.

"No, sorry," she mutters.

"Huh." I could have sworn I put it on charge on the nightstand before falling asleep, but it wasn't there when I woke up. I had told Massimo I would call him in the morning. I guess I'll look for it after breakfast.

One by one, our brothers begin trickling in. Salvatore comes and hugs me around my hips with his little arms. "I'm sorry about *Nonno* and *Nonna*," *Grandfather* and *Grandmother*, he sniffles.

I smile down at him and ruffle his hair like I always do. "Thanks, Sal."

"I'm going to miss *Nonno* so much." He sniffles more, trying to hide his tears.

Crouching down, I cup his sweet face in my hands. "Me too, tough guy. But we'll never forget him."

"Are you sure?"

"Yes, I'm sure. I won't let us."

Everyone sits down at the table, and the energy is lifeless and somnolent as we pass around the plates of food. The guys all dig in as I pick at my food with Alba in my lap. I bury my face into her soft curls and inhale. Her scent is soothing, and I feel at peace for just a moment, feeding off her innocence and oblivion.

I'm still sitting there with my food hardly touched as everyone around me finishes up and they're clearing the table. Time vanished imperceptibly as if I were at a standstill. That's the thing about loss. The ceaseless motion of the earth continues, indifferent to your paralysis. Life goes on with or without you.

People out there are happy, living without a care in the world when a huge part of me just died. Not able to see the light at the end of the tunnel, where my heart will ever be whole again. I envy them, those who have yet to feel the great pain of such tragedy. To be spared the abrupt departure of someone so vital to your existence. To be denied the solace of a goodbye.

I'll never get one more hug. One more smile. One more chance to tell him how much I love him...

"I need to speak to you in *Babbo's* office," Tullio says in a low voice, breaking my trance, and walks away before I can respond.

Sighing, I hand Alba to Gemma and head to the office. It's just him in there waiting for me, so I close the door to give us privacy. There are dark circles under his eyes, and he hasn't shaved yet, and I'm pretty sure he's still in the same clothes as yesterday.

"You didn't get any sleep," I comment.

"Sit down, Alessia." He motions to one of the chairs in front of the desk. Trying to make this as civil as possible, I sit without a fuss. "The guy is one of De Luca's crew. Questioned him myself last night."

My stomach turns. "And what did he say? He said they ordered the hit?"

"Yes."

"But who? Did he say it was Angelo or the De Luca's?"

"Does it matter?"

"Yes, it matters," I growl. "It could have been just Angelo, and Massimo was out of the loop. You don't even know what their work dynamic is like. They hardly word together! He knew Massimo wouldn't go along with it."

"You don't know that!"

"Yes, I do! Massimo cares about me! He wouldn't do that! And why would he? Why would any of them? Why would Angelo want us to marry if he just wanted to take us out?"

"It wasn't Angelo's idea! It was Massimo's!"

"What?" I rear back.

"Massimo came up with the arrangement, not Angelo. In fact, Angelo was against it and wasn't exactly secretive about it either."

Okay, I can process all that later. *One fire at a time.* "Okay, but why would Massimo agree to the marriage if they were just going to kill *Babbo*?"

"To sweeten the deal."

"To sweeten the deal," I parrot back dryly. "No. I don't buy it. I'll call him right now and find out." I get up and go to leave. The sooner I talk to him, the sooner we can get this straightened out. We should all be focused on mourning the death of our father and praying for Mamma. Not pointing fingers and fighting.

"Good luck. It'll be hard to call him without a phone."

I come to a halt and then slowly turn around. "What's that supposed to mean?"

"It means you're without a phone and confined to the estate grounds until further notice."

He is really testing my forbearance here. "You're grounding me? *Cazzata*, Tullio. Give me my fucking phone back," I demand.

"Not happening."

"What the fuck, Tullio?!" I yell.

"I have a lot of shit to deal with right now. I'm not dealing with your tantrum. You can go."

"This is insane! You can't do this!"

"I can, and I just did."

Staring at my brother as if he's a stranger to me, I realize I can't win this one. Not this time. "I'll just use Gemma's phone then." I turn to leave again.

"Took hers away too." I stop. "Don't make me lock you in your room."

I spin around now, *fuming*. All restraint flying out the window. "You wouldn't dare," I caustically hiss.

"If I have to, I will."

"Santino wouldn't let you do that," I try using as a lame attempt.

"He'll do whatever I ask of him. Especially if it has to do with your safety."

"How is taking away my phone and locking me up keeping me safe?" He doesn't answer. "Tell me!"

"You'll just call Massimo and let him manipulate you."

"So, now I'm some naïve neophyte that lacks intelligence and a mind of my own?"

"Didn't say that, Alessia."

"You pretty much implied it! You think I would be easy to manipulate! Same fucking thing!"

"Look, I know you care about Massimo. Possibly even love him." I scoff and cross my arms. "So, whatever lies he tells you, you're most likely to believe them."

"He isn't a liar, Tullio."

"This is exactly what I'm talking about."

"You don't know him! I've been living with him for the past few months! He isn't a liar!"

"In time, the truth will reveal itself."

"You can't keep me here like this, Tullio. I want my phone back."

"No."

"I cannot believe you right now. I am not the enemy here, and you're treating me like one." He's silent as I stand there, combusting with rage. The backs of my eyes sting, and I swallow around the achy lump in my throat. No, they'll be tears of sadness, not anger when I finally break down and cry. "I won't forgive you for this." Giving my brother one last hard look, I leave.

A maelstrom of every volatile emotion churning within.

CHAPTER TWENTY-FIVE

Massimo

I've been trying to get a hold of Alessia all day, and when her phone goes straight to voicemail several times in a row, I know something is wrong.

I had nothing to do with the hit on the Bonetti's, and my father has been out of town, so it couldn't have been him either. And what would be the point in starting an unnecessary war with them?

"De Luca," Tullio Bonetti answers after two rings.

"I'd like to speak with my fiancée. Is she alright?" I rush out, unable to contain my eagerness.

"She's fine, and she's where she belongs. Home." I stand up to my feet with hostility. "The marriage is off, and so is the truce."

"The fuck are you talking about? It wasn't us, Bonetti," I snarl like a rabid beast.

"We have one of your crew, and he says otherwise."

"Who," I snap.

"His name is pointless."

"*Sti cazza.*" *Fuck that.* "Let me speak to Alessia."

"Not happening." His serenity only infuriates me more.

My blood begins to boil as a dark haze veils my vision. "I want my fiancée back," I clip every word out on another snarl.

"You two are done. And you will pay for what you did."

"The fuck—" I'm met with silence as he hangs up on me.

Roaring at the top of my lungs, I fist my phone and miraculously refrain from smashing it. The thought of Alessia being unable to reach me has me thinking with somewhat of a lucid head. Tullio didn't say anything about her not wanting to speak with me, only refusing to let me speak with her.

"Boss?" Vinny questions, somehow breaking through my pernicious smog.

"Pack heavy. We're going to get my fiancée back."

Three SUVs are packed and loaded, and we head for the Bonetti estate. I will gun down their soldiers if I must to get to Alessia. She's mine, and she will not be kept from me. Not locked inside a tower or kept inside a cage. She belongs to me, and if she ever needed to be held prisoner, it would be me as her warden.

We're met at the gates with their armed men as if waiting for us. "Boss, don't," Vinny says when I open my car door. He's been trying to talk me down the entire ride here.

Ignoring him, I get out, and he and the four other men in the car join me. "Tell the others to stay in their vehicles," I tell Vinny and walk up to the gate to stand before Jino, their cousin. "I'd like to see my fiancée."

"Not happening, De Luca," he says evenly.

The urge to storm their estate is so prominent I can hardly think straight, but if I want to live to see my fiancée again, I need to find some tranquility and be less rash. Again, thinking of Alessia has me able to clear my head from the bloody haze.

"Tell Tullio that if he does not return her to me, it's war."

"It's already a war that you've started." I can see his composure broken and his emotions leaking into his tone. Everyone around him stirring uncomfortably.

"I didn't start shit," I growl, spit flying at him through the gate. "So, if he does not give her back to me, I will fucking burn down the city until he does."

He cocks his gun and lifts it to aim at me right between the eyes. Guns cock back all around us on either side of the gate. "If you don't leave, I have the authority to shoot," he warns.

My nostrils flare as my molars crack. The plan was to shoot our way inside, but what good would that do with me dead? Knowing I have to devise a better plan, I turn and get right back in the vehicle. My attack needs to be strategic and well thought out. Not impulsive. No matter how much my insides are roaring to go through whatever I have to, I know I'm not invincible, and I could lose everything I'm dying for.

"It's now war. Find me a Bonetti. I want them alive," I murmur lowly to Vinny.

It's been four days since I approached their gate. Still no word from Alessia, and I've been making good on my promise. We invaded two businesses they launder money through, and I'll hit up another one today. Then I'll take another one and another one until I have my bride back. I'll fucking bleed them out.

Even if Alessia told me herself that she didn't wish to speak to me, I still wouldn't back down. She. Is. Mine. She was promised to me, and I will have her back.

"Your father's plane just landed," Vinny says after he pockets his phone.

My father has been avoiding me for the past few days, not answering my phone calls or calling me back. It only leads to suspicion, and I'm eager to get in the same room as him and question him myself. I know a liar when I see one, no matter how skilled they are. But if he did have anything to do with the assassin, he's pompous enough to admit to it openly.

"Did you seriously order another hit on a Bonetti business?" Ezzo demands as he storms into my office.

"Yes."

"You have to stop, Massimo. You've started a war, and for what?"

"According to them, we have already started a war. And they're holding Alessia against her will."

"You sure about that?" He pauses. "The Bonetti's are convinced it was us who took out Marino. Alessia thinks you helped kill her father."

"She knows I wouldn't do that," I growl through clenched teeth. I know she doesn't believe it and that Tullio and her brothers are keeping her as a prisoner. I refuse to think otherwise.

"How do you figure?"

"If Alessia thought I had something to do with it, she wouldn't ice me out. She would confront me herself, swooping in like a bat out of hell. Trust me. I know her."

I know my batshit crazy woman well enough to know that if she thought for even a second I was guilty, the cold shoulder would be the last thing she would give me.

"Fine. Let's say her brothers are keeping her against her will. It's not like they would hurt her." He tries to reason.

"Alessia belongs to me, and until they give her back, people will die."

He exhales dramatically as he drops down into a chair. "At least wait until you talk to our father for another raid."

I study my little brother closely for a moment. "Do you know anything?"

"I don't. I swear it. My loyalty is to you, Massimo. Always has been and always will be."

"Don't ever let him catch you saying that." I glance over at Vinny, then back to Ezzo. "Or anyone else." If our father even caught a whiff of disloyalty, he wouldn't hesitate to take us out. Son or not. "Fine. I'll wait till I talk to him."

"And what if you find out it was him?"

"I'll do what I have to do." Whatever I need to do to make things right and get my bride back, I'll fucking do it. If handing over my father as a bargaining chip will make peace, *I'll fucking do it.*

My phone starts going off, and I pick it up without looking. "Yeah."

"Boss, we got a Bonetti," one of my men rushes out.

"Who?"

"The youngest. Paolo."

"Is he unharmed?"

"He's alive but not exactly unharmed."

"Do not fucking harm him," I order.

"Got it. Do you want us to bring him to the warehouse?"

"No. Bring him here."

"Yes, sir."

I hang up and run my hands through my hair. "They got Paolo. He's on his way here now."

"*Porca troia*, Massimo," *Fucking hell,* Ezzo curses.

"I'm not going to kill him. Just using him as leverage."

"*Cazzo*, Massimo. You need to rein it in some."

"I'll rein it in once I have her back." He doesn't even understand how much I'm already reining in. I want to charge the estate guns blazing, but I'm trying to be prudent and not emotional.

"She's really worth it to you?"

"Yes." The word is out before he's even finished his sentence.

His eyes widen in shock, not only because of my honesty but how I didn't even hesitate. "Well, then, I guess I can be somewhat understanding. Okay. I won't give you any more shit, but please don't let your actions be so ardent."

Ezzo finally leaves me to my morbid thoughts and self-loathing. I need to focus on my father, though. Search for any clues before confronting him. He was never bashful with his enmity toward the Bonettis, but never said anything more than snide comments.

That doesn't mean I wouldn't put it past him.

CHAPTER TWENTY-SIX

Alessia

The sound of the doorknob twisting doesn't disturb me as I lay in bed staring at the wall.

Tullio had confined me to my bedroom after I tried to get a hold of a phone and put a gun to someone's head. Twice.

No matter how much Gemma cried and begged them not to do it, they did it. All of my brothers locked me away in my old bedroom with several men guarding my door around the clock, knowing one man wouldn't be enough to hold me.

Santino comes into my line of sight with a tray of food. "Come on, *piccolina*. Come eat." He sets the tray down over on the coffee table.

"*Vaffanculo*," I mutter halfheartedly.

Standing in front of me, he sighs and shoves his hands into his pockets. "You know we're only trying to protect you. Your insubordination is only punishing yourself."

"Your nearsightedness is only turning me against you," I retort.

"Look, if we find out Massimo had nothing to do with it, we'll let you speak to him. But as of right now, we're unsure."

I pick my head up to look at him. "Unsure? I'm locked up because of uncertainty?"

"It was the De Luca's, we're certain about that. But it is possible that Angelo was working alone."

I sit up and scoot off the bed to my feet. "Then let me call him and talk to him, Santino. He really wouldn't lie to me. I know I can get the truth out of him."

"I'm sorry, Alessia. I can't do that."

"Can't or won't?"

"Can't."

I pause, knowing that Santino really is not the enemy here. Tullio is now a capo, and just because we're family doesn't mean we can disrespect the boss whenever we're in discord. "How long are you guys going to keep me here?"

"I don't know. Maybe until you come around to reasoning or when the problem is dealt with."

"Dealt with." I take a deep breath through my nose. "Can you at least promise me one thing?" He waits. "Whatever you find out, can I please talk to Massimo before you do anything to him?" The thought of his betrayal is like acid in my throat.

"I'll do my best and advocate for you, I promise. But you know I don't call the shots around here. Now, come eat."

Unable to argue with Santino any longer, I sit with him, and we chat while I eat. He lets me know that Mamma is stable, and if she continues to improve while her body is trying to heal, they'll try to pull her out of the coma soon.

Another thing I will never forgive Tullio for is keeping me from visiting our mother.

There's a knock on the door, and I call out to whoever it is to come in. It's one of our men who pokes his head in. "Tullio needs to see you, Santino."

"I'll be down in a minute."

"He says it's urgent."

I frown. "What's going on?"

Santino stands up. "I'll be back."

"Oh, come on," I whine and stand up to follow him to the door. "I'm not going to try and run, I swear. Please let me go with you." I don't even try to disguise the desperation in my voice.

"I'll see if you can come out. Just hang tight for a minute."

I growl and slap the door when he closes it in my face. "Damnit!" I fucking *hate* not having a clue as to what is going on outside of these walls. Gemma is the only one who would tell me anything, but she's no use. She never knows anything.

I'm pacing my room when Santino comes back, not much later. "Alright. Come with me." He looks tense, so whatever is going on, it isn't good. Santino is hardly moved by anything.

I follow him out and down to our father's office, which I guess Tullio has now taken over. We walk into Armando and Tullio having some heated conversation. It comes to a halt when their eyes snap in my direction.

"I'm going to fucking kill him," Armando growls as he runs his hand through his jet-black hair.

"What's going on?" I ask.

"Massimo is at our gates," Tullio says calmly.

My heart rate automatically picks up from the mention of his name and knowing that he's near. It's been over a week since seeing or speaking to him, and I miss him so fucking much. "Right now? Let me go talk to him."

"Alessia." Tullio stiffly approaches me. "Massimo has been on a rampage. He's cleaned out three of our businesses so far."

"What? Why?"

"Because he thinks he's still entitled to you," Armando says, his anger and disgust directed at me, and I choose to ignore it.

"He's here for me?" *He wants me back.*

"You sound excited," Armando says through his teeth and stomps towards me. Santino turns to stand in his way. "Like this is somehow all one big romantic gesture for you."

This gesture is the epitome of romance.

"This wouldn't have happened if you guys didn't take away my fucking phone! I could've talked to him and prevented it!" I yell.

"You're right," Tullio says when Armando opens his mouth to argue.

"What do you mean I'm right?" I look at him with apprehension.

"Massimo is here...with Angelo."

I narrow my eyes and stare at him in confusion. "Okay...?" As in joined forces? Because if that's the case, then—

"As a contribution," Santino fills in.

"He has Paolo!" Armando roars.

"He has Paolo?" I ask, still trying to get my brain to play catchup.

"He's okay. He took him as collateral," Tullio says with a sigh, no malice in his tone. Tullio can be stubborn, but he isn't bullheaded, and he can see when someone is shedding light on something. He's fair, just like *Babbo* was.

"And we're just going to let that go?!" Armando yells, Santino still holding him at a safe distance. I know my brother would never hurt me, but he may cross a line in a moment of passion. He and I definitely compete for the shortest fuse.

Tullio ignores him as he talks directly to me. "Angelo and Paolo for you in exchange."

"Fine. Then let's go make the exchange," I say, trying to mask the excitement.

"You're not leaving with that psycho!" Armando yells.

"I'm not being held here prisoner anymore!" I yell back.

"You don't have to marry him, Alessia. With *Babbo* gone and Angelo calling the hit on him, the truce is automatically broken," Tullio speaks gently.

If the truce is broken but Massimo still demands me back, does that mean he still wants to marry me, alliance aside? Well, I won't know until I get to talk to him.

"Let's make the exchange, Tullio." He studies me as we both tune out Armando and his hysterics. He's silently asking me if this is what I want, and I'm telling him it is. I want to be with Massimo. He unleashed a wrath on the city for me because he wants me back. Truce or no truce. And I want to be back with him. Truce or no truce.

Santino makes Armando hand over his piece before we go out there, and Tullio finally gives me my phone back. Walking down the long driveway with armed men surrounding us, Massimo comes into view, and every fiber of my being screams to close the distance between us.

I'm so fixated on him that I almost didn't notice the gagged and beaten Angelo De Luca on one side and a bruised and gagged Paolo on his other. He has a firm grip on his father, but I don't see him holding back Paolo.

His hazel eyes bore into mine as we get closer. The pull between us becoming too overwhelming to function. He inspects my body from head to toe as if making sure I'm unharmed. My eyes clash with Paolo's as he starts screaming around the gag and struggling against his restraints, making Massimo place a firm hand on him.

I look up at Tullio, and he looks back at me. "He would never hurt me, Tullio."

"I'm only doing this because I feel as if I don't have any other choice. I can't keep you locked up forever." He pauses and glances at the other side of the gate, then focuses on me again. "I've already talked with Massimo, and the fact that he's handing his father over to us not only to exonerate himself but to get you back, shows he cares for you. This isn't about proprietorship." He glances over there again. "He's doing it out of despair. He may have been enraged and on a warpath, but I know a man in agony over a woman when I see one." He gives me a sad look. "I'm sorry for—"

I shake my head. "No. Don't. You were doing what you thought you needed to do. We just lost *Babbo,* and we're worried about Mamma, and emotions were high. I'm sorry for being so rebellious."

He snorts and gives my chin a playful pinch. We have an audience, so he won't go over the top with his apology and affection. "No, you're not." I crack a smile, knowing he's right. I'm only apologizing to get this thing moving along. "I love you, *piccolina.*"

"Stop sounding like this is goodbye," I murmur.

"Life is uncertain."

We *all* know that now more than ever.

The gates open, and I give each brother a subtle smile, reassuring them that I'm okay. Massimo tells his guys to lower their weapons, and without reservation, he shoves his father into the arms of my brothers.

His gaze is locked on me as he stomps forward, and I quicken my pace towards him. The space between us diminishes, and I throw my arms around his neck as he crushes me against his body. "I swear I had nothing to do with it, *amore,*" he rasps into my hair as he strokes it and holds me close. Not giving a shit that we have eyes on us. For him to be so bold with his longing in front of his men and in front of another family is a proclamation that says much.

"I know. I knew the whole time. I knew you wouldn't ever do that," I say in a hurry, clinging to him and unwilling to let go. Basking in his scent and the heat from his embrace. It's precisely what I've needed during the most agonizing week of my life.

"Can I take you home now?"

"Please." I pull back, and we stare at one another. He looks at me as if he hasn't seen me in years, and I know exactly how he feels. It was painful to be separated like that, and I wish to never be torn from him again. My family home will always feel like home, but he is where I belong.

I look back and see that Paolo is safely back with my brothers, and he and Armando have joined forces in their dismay. I look between

Tullio and Santino. Neither of them wants to let me go, but they know they have to.

I turn back to Massimo. "Let's go home," he says, taking my hand.

CHAPTER TWENTY-SEVEN

Massimo

Having Alessia back, I feel like I can eat, breathe, and sleep again.

I was miserable without her.

On the way home, we don't speak as I hold her in my lap and bury my face in her hair. "*Mi sei mancato molto, amore mio.*" *I missed you so much, my love.*

"*I knew you had nothing to* do with it."

"I know." I lift my head and caress her cheek. "If you thought I did, you'd come for my head."

She smiles and rests her head on my shoulder. "I'm glad you know me so well." Her lips gently press against the side of my neck.

"I do."

"They're going to kill him," she whispers.

"I know." My jaw ticks, and I look up to discover that we're already rolling up to the estate.

She lifts her head and stares me in the eye, her beautiful golden-brown eyes bouncing all around. The vehicle comes to a stop, and we put the conversation on hold to head up to our room, where we can speak freely.

"What will his men do when they find out?" she asks as we both stand there with some distance between us.

"I'll have to get rid of some. Between Ezzo, Sarita, Vinny, Monte, and myself, we'll be able to weed out the ones who were most loyal to my father."

"Why did you do it? Why would you give up your father to get me back? Tullio called off the truce. You don't have to marry me," she says gently.

I stalk her. "I never *had* to marry you, Alessia."

"Tullio also said it was you who procured our arrangement. Not your father."

I dip my chin once and stop right in front of her. "I've wanted you for years."

"The gala."

"Yes."

"So, was that a test or something?"

Amusement lifts one side of my mouth. "Sort of." I let a gap of silence hang between us. "Ask me again why I traded my father for you. Why I was going out of my mind without you."

She licks her plump lips, and they fall slack with short breaths. "Why, Massimo?" Her voice comes out as soft as a whisper.

Threading my fingers into her hair, I hold her close. "Because I love you, Alessia." Her eyes widen slightly. "I'm so sorry I couldn't prevent it," I say with absolution and remorse, referring to the accident. "So damn sorry." Knowing the pain she now lives with, it's a burden I will, too, carry.

A tear escapes her beautiful eyes and trickles down her cheek. Calming her trembling bottom lip with my thumb, I brush the lonely tear away, and another follows. "Thank you for what you did, Massimo. It won't bring back my father, but your actions speak volumes."

I move in closer when she sniffles. "I hope it proves to you my loyalty and devotion." Lifting her left hand, I press a kiss to her finger, still adorned with the ring I gave to her.

"It does." She attempts a watery smile.

"I understand if you want to postpone the wedding, *cara mia*. If you need time, take all that you need. Know that I'm not going anywhere."

Her face falls as she gawks up at me. "You...really still want to marry me?"

"I do." I tuck some of her hair behind her ear and caress her cheek. Admiring her beauty I missed so much. "Were you not listening to a word I said?" I muse.

"You said you loved me and chose me, but we don't have to get married. At least, not yet. We can just be together."

There's this weird twisting feeling in my chest. "You don't want to marry me..." I despise the fragility betrayed by my own words.

"It's just that...we don't have to."

I thought we were on the same page. That she possibly loved me back. Seems I've read the situation wrong. "Sure." I swallow hard and take a step back. Fighting the urge to demand what I want.

"Massimo." She jumps to me and cups my face. Panic in her eyes as she searches mine. "I love you too, I do," she rushes out. "But if we're going to do this thing for real, for love and not for an alliance, shouldn't we try and do this right? We still hardly know each other and—"

I take her around the waist to pull her body into mine. "We know each other enough. I told you my love is not a fickle thing. When I love, it's perpetual and set in stone. I don't see the point in waiting, Alessia. I want to marry you." I tighten my arms around her. "*Sposami*." *Marry me*, I rasp. "Be my wife, my *regina*."

Her eyes dance around, then her pouty lips curl into a seraphic smile. "Okay," she whispers.

"*Ti amo*." Another tear slips down her other cheek, and I'm reminded once again of her loss. Tullio warned me that she has yet properly mourn and to be gentle with her. She's been doing her damnedest to be strong for everyone else, completely neglecting herself and her grief.

"*Ti amo tanto*." Her arms go around my neck, and her head falls back. "*Baciami*."

CHAPTER TWENTY-EIGHT

Alessia

"Hey, Mamma. Let's get you looking more like yourself," I say as I brush the dry shampoo through her hair. I set the hairbrush down to pull out the makeup bag. "A little too thin and pale, but still beautiful," I mutter as I begin to sweep some powder on her life-lacking skin.

The door to her room creaks open as I apply some blush to her cheekbones. We have guards outside her room twenty-four seven, so I'm not concerned and continue catering to Mamma. Sleeping beauty, we like to call her.

"She looks good," a dry but feminine voice comes behind me.

Turning around, I come face to face with Vita. The youngest De Luca, also known as the family's recluse, is always disappearing or finding herself in some trouble. Someone I always thought I would get along with, but she does her damnedest to be unreachable. However, her desperation for attention is quite apparent.

"Hey, Vita. How are you?"

"Better than you." She comes further into the room and makes herself at home on the sleeper couch. She'd be stunning if it weren't for the permanent sour look on her face. Her hair is lighter than Massimo's, but her eyes are dark. She's not as tall as her sister, but she's still taller than average height for a woman.

"Most people are." I sigh and focus on pampering Mamma. "So, to what do I owe this great pleasure of an impromptu visit from the infamous Vita De Luca?"

"Just bored."

I glance over at her and find her inspecting her nails, feigning boredom. "So, you thought you'd take a trip over to the hospital to visit a woman you could give two shits about that is still in an induced coma?" I arch an eyebrow at her, and her eyes roll up to meet mine.

"Yup," she pops. A giggle bubbles out as I shake my head and turn back to Mamma. "So. Do you...know what's going on with my father?"

Keeping a phlegmatic front going, I don't flinch or falter. "He's getting exactly what he deserves." Meaning a lifelong sentence of torture and pain.

"And what is that exactly?"

"Punishment for killing my father and almost killing my mother."

"It wasn't right, you know." She pauses. "Massimo turning in our father was treachery." Now, I falter and still, unable to keep my serenity. "Whatever the reasons for him doing what he did, it was his call to make. Massimo wouldn't have turned over our father if it weren't for you."

"Your father was unhinged, and like a rabid dog, he needed to be put down."

"They're all psychotic assholes. My father was no different."

My head whips around as I itch to grab for one of my knives tucked in a holster under my dress. "My father was *not*. Yes, he was a capo and did things to get to where he was, like his father before that, but he was not psychotic. He was fair and treated everyone who worked for him fairly. Ask anyone who knew him. Your father? He couldn't even be good to his children. He would have turned any of you in if it suited his ambitions. He went after my parents for some ancient vendetta he probably doesn't fully understand himself. It was a needless murder, and he's paying for it and will continue to pay for it until he dies of old age."

We sit there locking horns, and the air thickens. "My father may have been a shitty one and an even shittier man, but he deserved respect." She stands to her feet, and my basic instincts also have me on my feet.

"As did mine," I sneer.

"That was between the two capos."

"You know nothing, Vita. Attacking my parents was starting a war between both families. If you knew anything, you would know that. Yes, Massimo may have turned in your father because of me, but because of me, you and the rest of your family are pardoned. You're blaming me for what happened to him when you should be thanking me. You're alive and will remain alive because of my love for Massimo. Any other family would have been obliterated as a whole for sharing blood with the enemy."

She begins prowling forward. She's half a foot taller than me, but I could take her down in two seconds flat. "I'll never accept you as a De Luca. You're going to get my brother killed, I'm sure of it."

"Like I said, I am what is keeping him alive. Now, get out of my mother's hospital room and never come back. You are officially blacklisted."

"You'll pay for it someday."

I step forward out of reaction. "Do not fucking threaten me, Vita. I am not afraid to cut a bitch."

"Neither am I," she says confidently, sneering down at me.

"Leave now, or I will make you. Do not make me do that, Vita." I'm not sure if I could stop myself from actually killing her if I end up having to put my hands on her. To threaten me, to say that it was Angelo's *right* to take us out...She's practically begging for a beatdown.

"I just got my nails done, so..." She cocks her head to one side with a fake smile. "I'll take my leave. It was great chatting with you, Alessia. We should do this more often."

My fists are literally shaking at my sides as she turns and nearly skips out of the room. Giving it a few moments to collect myself, I charge to the door and rip it open.

"Vita De Luca is not allowed here ever again. Do you hear me?" I say with venom to one of the guys on duty.

He nods his head. "Yes, Miss Bonetti."

"Call Jino right now and let him know. I swear, if Vita even gets past the hospital entrance, heads will fucking roll." I slam the door shut and take a deep and soothing breath.

How fucking dare she come in here and make threats! How dare she try to justify Angelo's actions! How fucking dare she try and make me her enemy!

I jump a little when my phone starts going off from across the room. Walking swiftly, I pick it up. "Hey."

"Hey, I heard Vita was just there," Massimo says, and I smile.

"Yes, it was definitely a surprise to see her here." I sit in the chair beside Mamma and place my hand over hers.

"Is everything okay? Do I need to—"

"Everything is fine, Massimo. You know I can handle Vita."

"Of course, you can, but she's my responsibility, so if I need to set her straight, I will."

"I banned her from visiting again. Told the crew not even to let her step a foot inside the building. It's handled."

"What happened?"

"It's nothing. Just petty drama, that's all." I don't need Massimo to fight my battles for me. Vita isn't a threat. She's all bark and no bite.

"Alessia," He growls.

"Massimo," I mock him.

He sighs heavily through the phone. "I know you can handle her, but I'm beginning to think she's more than just audacious these days. I've ignored the problem for too long."

"She's just a little girl inside a woman's body who never got the attention she craved. I almost feel bad for her," I mutter.

"Don't feel sorry for the overprivileged rich girl," he muses, making me smile.

I chuckle. "You're right about that. So, you have daddy issues. Boohoo."

"Well, now you're just being mean." His voice dips down low. "That's still my sister you're talking about. You might have to pay for that last comment."

"I look forward to it." I grin.

"Little psycho," he mutters. "You coming home soon?"

"I am. Leaving in probably ten minutes or so."

"Might as well head right upstairs when you do."

"Yes, sir."

"I love you. Be safe."

"Always. I love you too."

I hang up the phone smiling from ear to ear like a dumbass. "Alright, Mamma." I pack up my stuff and lean down to kiss her cheeks. "I love you, and I can't wait till you come back to us. We need you. Now, more than ever."

CHAPTER TWENTY-NINE

Massimo

"How is she?" Santino asks from beside me as we sip on our dark liquor.

"Still trying to be strong."

"She *is* strong."

"You know what I mean," I grumble. "She doesn't even want to postpone the wedding and spends her time either finalizing it or here tendering to your mother."

"Fia's concerned."

"Aren't we all?" I watch Alessia talk with her sister and Fia. All of us still dressed from the funeral at the Bonetti estate. Alessia still hasn't had any breakdown. If she has, it's been in private, and she hid it well, but I'm reasonably sure she hasn't, and she's still painfully holding it together. "I think she'll be okay though. It's been less than a month since it happened. There's still plenty of time for her to concede to her grief."

I feel his eyes on me as I keep mine on my woman. "So, you love her," he states flatly.

"I do." I sip my drink.

"And you're going to marry her."

"I am." I turn my head towards him. "I hope you don't expect me to ask any of you for your permission. I already got it from your father."

"You know damn well Alessia will do whatever the fuck she damn well pleases. Permission or no permission. Blessing or no blessing."

"One of the many things I love about her."

He snorts. "I suppose you're one of the rare few capable of handling her."

I turn my attention back to her. "I'll take that as a compliment."

Truth is, Alessia eats most men alive. I know I'm the only man to be able to go head-to-head with her and manage to keep mine. Sure, a man would have to be blind not to find her drop-dead gorgeous, but she's too much woman for average men.

My father once told me that women can only weaken you, but she drives my ambition. Makes me see clearer even when she makes it hard to even breathe around her.

She's majestic as she holds her head high and makes her way around the room, being sure to talk to everyone who came. She excels with diplomacy when her temper is in control. Poised and cogent. Hiding behind her resplendent veneer of an innocuous woman as if she couldn't even hurt a fly.

I clear my throat. "How's your mother?" I mutter lowly. Small talk isn't exactly part of my nature, and I know it isn't for Santino either.

He sighs and rubs at his knee. "Confused, devastated, lost..."

The words are accurate to the way I would feel losing Alessia. I couldn't imagine it, especially after decades and several children later.

With her amicable smile firmly in place, Alessia politely says her goodbyes to those leaving. Family from Italy flew in and are staying here for a few days, which has occupied her more lately, and she continues to use that too as a distraction.

Once she tends to her mother and shows some relatives back to their rooms, ensuring they are well-fed and have everything they need, she starts whirling around the place to clean.

"*Cara*, let the maids do this. Let's get you into a hot bath." I spin her to face me.

"I—" I observe her face run through several emotions. She's so used to fighting when someone tries to tell her what to do. "Okay." She finally deflates in defeat.

We head up to her old bedroom, where we'll stay for the night. I'm not sure if her brothers were so quick to grant me pardon for Alessia's sake, or if they're too burdened at the moment to hold a grudge, but they let bygones be bygones. They accepted me at Alessia's side for the funeral and welcomed me into their home.

"Can I pour you a drink, *mia amata*?" *My love.* I offer as soon as we're closed inside the room.

Turning into me, she wraps herself around my torso. Her nose buries into my chest to breathe me in. "Thank you for being so wonderful, Massimo."

I smile as I hug her back. "Wonderful. Never thought someone would ever refer to me as wonderful."

"Well, you are." Her gold eyes sparkle as she props her chin up on my chest. "To me, that is."

"I'll make you a drink and draw you a bath." I press my lips to her forehead.

"You mean *us* a bath?" she says smiling.

"If that's what you want." I kiss her again, then peel myself away from her.

Ten minutes later, we're together in the lavish bathtub with the jets going and her resting between my legs. She had tied her hair up on top of her head, and there are little dark ringlets at her neck from the heat from the water. Her perky breasts are peeking out of the water's surface, and I'm hungry for her, but I restrain myself out of respect.

"I think I'm in shock," she says after a while. "Or I'm heartless."

"You are not heartless." I kiss the side of her head.

"You sure about that?" She pauses. "At first, I was just trying to be brave. For Gemma. But then I wanted to cry...but I couldn't. I *can't*." She tilts her face up to me, not shielding her vulnerability from me. "I want to cry, Massimo. I want to get it all out. I feel like it's all trapped inside of me, festering and burning, spreading. But it won't come out." Her eyes glaze over.

"With me, you can let go, Alessia. Crying will not make you weak."

"How?"

"Running from your feelings is a weakness. Confronting what weakens you will only strengthen you."

"Crying feels weak." Her voice is so tiny. I wish I could absorb the grief for her.

"I know." I drag my fingertips down the side of her gorgeous face tenderly. "But you have to get it out. Otherwise, it will take over and consume you. Drain you. Reduce you down to a weaker self."

"I can't," she chokes out and closes her eyes. Her beautiful body quivers against me, so I tighten my arms around her. "I want to, but I can't."

"Take your time, baby. Take all the time you need." I press my lips to her cheek. "I'll be here the entire way, and no matter what, I know your strength. It's okay to show me your weakness."

Her eyelashes flutter as she opens her eyes. "Is it?"

The tension in my head tightens as I draw my eyebrows inward. "Yes, Alessia. You can put all your trust in me. I won't ever betray you. Never use your weakness against you." She stares up at me, skeptical and weary. I have to keep in mind that she isn't herself. "Let yourself go with me. You're safe, baby." I kiss her lips. "You're always safe with me. Your heart." I place a hand over her heart. "Your body." I run that same hand down her body slowly, and her eyes flutter shut as her head rests back. "And your head." I grip the back of her neck firmly, making her pliant in my grasp as I crash my lips down on hers.

Her back arches as my tongue dives into her sweet mouth. She twists her body in my arms and climbs on top of me. Straddling me and wrapping her entire self around me as if she can't get close enough. "Massimo. Make me feel," she rasps as her hips roll and rock.

"What would you like me to make you feel, *amore*?" I kiss her back and dig my fingertips into her shapely hips.

"Anything. Everything," she breathes.

"I think I know what you need, *gattina*." She needs the control taken from her. She needs pain added to her grief. "Up on your feet," I command. With glossy eyes, she rises. I use her hips to pivot her around and she loses her balance, catching herself with her hands on the edge of the tub. Exactly the position I needed her in.

"Just like that, *gattina*," I rasp, and admire her exposed backside. She moans loudly when my mouth makes contact with her cunt and I eat her.

On reaction, she pushes against me, greedy for more friction. My mouth inches up to that taut ring of muscles. And slide two fingers inside her needy cunt. She moans and continues rocking. I curl my fingers and begin fucking her and my tongue jabs at her other hole. She stills in desire and I look for that sweet spot inside of her.

When her legs start to tremble, she mewls and her back hollows. I don't let up, knowing she's right there. A feminine cry comes out of her when a clear liquid ejects from her cunt, running down my hand and splashing my chin and chest.

Standing up behind her, I rub that liquid up and down the crease of her perfect ass, then stroke some on my cock. My mouth hangs open in awe at the sight and sensation.

Gripping both meaty globes, I spread them and rub the head of my cock against her. Warning her of where I plan on fucking her.

Her muscles relax on instinct, and opens up for me like a flower blooming. Using one hand, I grasp my shaft and push forward with my hips. She hisses through her teeth as I sink in. I continue pressing forward until I finally bottom out. Her muscles contract around me, and I give her body a moment to accommodate.

"Please, Massimo," she whispers hoarsely.

"I got you, baby."

Pulling out to the tip, I slam back in, letting her ass swallow me whole. I know she needs more, so I rut into her with savagery. Not withholding my brawn or craving. I catch her around the waist when he arms gives out without falter.

Every time my pelvis hits her, it jerks a moan from her. My balls feel heavy as they sway and slap her pussy. Her hands claw at my arm circling her waist and she whines.

Hissing through gritted teeth, I feel my balls clench up right before I explode. My hips become immobile when my pelvis kisses her ass and my cock twitches inside of her to empty.

Sound and sight eventually come back to me and I realize Alessia is shaking and I hear a sniffle. Gently removing myself from inside of her, I turn her to face me and everything drops.

I don't say a word as I gather her in my arms and sit down with her to purge herself of the dormant grief. To lament her suffering.

To face her pain, and allow me to share it with her.

Chapter Thirty

Massimo

A piece of Alessia was taken from her when her father died. I can do my best to give her pieces of me, but I can never replace them.

Ever since her mother came home from the hospital, it has undoubtedly brightened her days. I thought tonight would be a good time to go out and have some fun, for Alessia's sake. Unfortunately, I only have more things to stress over.

From a liable source of mine, I heard that the Bortsovs are finally coming out of the shadows and making moves. They're a Russian family that came to Jersey about a decade ago and kept to themselves. But we knew it was only strategic thinking on their part. Being a new family moving in so close to already claimed territory, they became public enemy number one. One wrong move, and they would've had every family on the East Coast on them. So, they kept their heads down and slowly encroached on territory lines.

With Marino Bonetti and Angelo De Luca out of the way, they assume they could capitalize on our collective low point. What they don't know is that the Bonetti's and De Luca's are not at war over it, and we're at the height of our accord. The fortification of our union has made us into a revered powerhouse.

They do have one advantage, though. Their connections with the Abramovs, the most prominent Russian family on the entire East Coast with the latest and greatest weapons and tech. We may have always had a good relationship with them, but Russians tend to stick together. So, if it comes down to it, they'll likely side with each other.

I'm just getting into the shower when I get the alert on my phone for the gates. Alessia is finally home from spending the day with her mother, which is perfect timing. She can join me in the shower.

Not even five minutes later, I see her silhouette move across the fogged glass, and my cock hardens, watching her remove her clothing. I smirk when she opens the door and steps inside.

"*Amore*," I rumble, and she comes to wrap her arms around my waist.

She sighs in content. "I missed you."

My hands move all over her backside, and I press my lips to the top of her head. "I almost called in the cavalry."

She giggles and turns her face in to kiss my chest. "I think you mean firing squad."

"Yeah, that does sound more like it." She props her chin up on my chest. "How's your mother?"

"She's doing really good." Her face dims some. "Doctors are even impressed with her tenacity."

"Definitely runs in the family." She tries to smile but fails. "And how is she dealing with your father's absence?"

She sighs and rests the side of her face on my chest, still holding onto me. "I don't think it's really hit her yet. She only came out of the coma less than two weeks ago. Woke up to her world so drastically changed." She goes quiet for a long moment. "I couldn't imagine losing you," she whispers.

I selfishly find satisfaction in her statement and tone. To know Alessia would be so affected by the loss of me. But I'm at a loss for words. I can't promise her tomorrow or the next day.

"Are you still up for going out tonight?"

"Absolutely." Her hands slide down to my ass to squeeze it, and she grins up at me. "After you fuck me."

Picking her up by the backs of her thighs, she squeals as I pin her up against the tiled walls. "You read my mind, *mia amata.*"

I fist her ass, using it as leverage to hover her cunt's heat over my erection. Inhaling her kiss with my mouth, I impale her. Her cheeks hit my groin and I jerk my hips to make sure there isn't a sliver of me not inside of her. She moans and takes a deep breath through her nose as her tongue thrashes against mine.

Keeping her fused with the wall, I begin grinding into her by rolling my hips. I don't stop until we're both satiated.

My *regina* is killing me in her dress. Departing from the modest attire reminiscent of vintage housewives fashion, a pink satin dress clings to her silhouette. It comes up high on her thighs showing off the tan she's gotten from the summer and the muscles from all her training. The top looks like a corset with jewels decorating it, showing off her ample breasts.

"You're trying to have quite a night tonight, aren't you?" I murmur into her ear as my hands explore her body.

"Why is that?" Her fingers toy with the back of my hair.

"This dress, *amore.* It'll get some people killed." She giggles, and I kiss her neck.

Miraculously, I'm able to resist her temptations on the way to the club. We get ourselves comfortable in the private VIP section, and drinks are being poured as her family and mine begin showing up.

I'm sitting down next to Ezzo and Sarita when Alessia comes over and sits in my lap. "You know, I never thought you could actually be cute," Sarita says, talking to me.

I chuckle, and Alessia kisses my cheek. "He can be pretty cute, can't he?" she teases.

Grunting, I narrow my eyes at her and give her butt a little swat. "Cute, huh?"

"And sweet," she adds.

Ezzo barks out laughter from beside me. "You two really are fucking crazy together."

"What? Don't say that!" Sarita chastises and reaches around us to smack his knee.

"Are you kidding me?" Ezzo continues. "Their idea of the perfect date is kneecapping."

With a shocked look, Alessia twists her head to address my brother. "That is so not true! I mean, yeah, it's definitely a nice time, but I wouldn't say a *perfect* date." She turns to me, grinning, and pecks me on the lips. "Thanks again for letting me do my first kneecapping."

Leaning in, I brush my lips across hers. "You're welcome, baby."

"Oh, God." We both turn to Sarita, and she's staring at us, horrified. "You guys really are a pair of nutjobs."

"I prefer mentally deranged," Alessia says, grabbing my face to kiss me deeply, and I chuckle against her sweet lips.

Sitting back, I watch and enjoy seeing Alessia, her unrestricted self, as she smiles and laughs with Fia and Sarita. Witnessing the merging of our families before the actual nuptials is a promising sign of our shared future.

"Mmm," Alessia hums against my mouth as we kiss. She's back on my lap as the crowd we started with starts to trickle off. "You're so tasty."

"So are you, my love."

"Mmm," she moans as we kiss some more.

"Keep moaning like that, and I can't be held accountable for what happens." I'll fuck her right here and now in front of everyone.

"Don't tease." She pouts.

"Alright, we're heading out," Armando says to us, and one by one, everyone else leaves, and I have Alessia all to myself now.

Giving Vinny a look, he makes himself and the other men scarce. I don't waste any time as I capture her lips and thrust my tongue inside of her mouth. "You really love my crazy ass?" she asks with a breathy voice.

"Yes. I'm crazy about this crazy ass." I give said ass a good squeeze.

Her arms snake around my neck as she thrusts her breasts forward. "I'm fucking delirious for you."

"Yeah?"

She nods her head, biting down on that bottom lip of hers. "I especially love it when you fuck me like you hate me."

God, I love this woman.

"Can we go home now?" she murmurs as she kisses my neck.

"Not just yet. I have plans for you that cannot wait."

She leans back to look at me with a mischievous grin. "Yeah? What kind of plans?"

CHAPTER THIRTY-ONE

Alessia

I have spent my entire life trying to subdue my crazy side, thinking no one on this planet could harness it, but that man really did exist. And his name is Massimo De Luca. Don of the De Lucas and king of my soul.

He doesn't ever try to domesticate me or kill my temper. He urges me to harness it, and at times, he likes to feed off it to unleash the beast inside of him.

Like right now, he has both of my wrists bound behind my back in one of his powerful hands, and his face is buried between my thighs from behind. The noise from the club in the background drowns out my cries as I'm bent over the suede couch.

My knees wobble as he indulges. The crude way he slurps and savors me...he surely knows how to eat a pussy.

His arm hooks around my waist when I almost collapse from the orgasm that smacks into me without much warning. I go limp against the couch with my ass in the air. He releases my wrists, and I hear him chuckle when I don't move.

My eyes flutter when he coaxes me into his lap to sink down on his cock. The very breath in my lungs still when I'm fully seated and filled with him. He gazes up at me with tension in his jaw and I can smell myself on him.

Rising up on my knees, I begin to ride him. I ride him until I wilt against him from our simultaneous orgasms. My head rests on his broad shoulder as I try to catch my breath.

"*Now*, we can go home, *cara mia*," he murmurs into my ear.

I'm spent when we slip into the back of the SUV, and Massimo keeps me in his lap. His light caresses keep me sedated as he pets me like a kitten. "*Potrei guardarti tutto il giorno.*" *I could look at you all day*.

"Mmm." I rest my head on him. I feel wetness sticking between my thighs and leaking out of me. "I might be leaving a wet spot on you in a moment here."

Pressing his lips to my forehead, his hand begins sliding up my thigh from knee until it stops at the peak. His calloused thumb rubs through the wetness in circles. Then he dips behind the delicate fabric, and I take in a sharp breath when he rubs me.

"How do you do this to me?" I whisper as I look up at him through hooded eyes.

Everything grows fuzzy as he continues to circle my clit, and he kisses me lightly on the lips. "Do what, *gattina*?"

"Make me like this. Defenseless." I pant. "Unguarded."

"It's nice, isn't it?" he rasps as his lips tease mine. "Giving up control momentarily."

"I don't like giving up control."

"But you do with me."

"I trust you with it."

Handing over control to Massimo is freeing and liberating, like taking a break and letting him pull my strings. I never realized how exhausting it was to be me until I didn't have to be, suddenly finding it easier to breathe.

Massimo enhances my life in countless ways. He might enjoy dominating me, but he never makes me feel inferior to him.

He's the king of the castle, but he knows that a powerful queen only amplifies his sovereignty.

CHAPTER THIRTY-TWO

Alessia

"**I** cannot believe you'll be a De Luca in three weeks," Gemma says as soon as the seamstress for her final dress fitting leaves.

"Ah..." I sigh as I throw myself back on my bed with a blissful look on my face. "I know." I'll always be a Bonetti at heart, but holy fuck. I'm really marrying Massimo De Luca.

"And it's not because of some alliance," she mutters, and I feel the bed dip beside me.

I turn to my side and prop my head up on my hand. "It's not. I love him. Like a lot."

She grimaces. "Massimo De Luca. That's who you fell in love with."

"Yes. And he happens to love me back." I grin with zero fucks given.

"Well, of course, he loves you back. You're awesome and gorgeous. He's...*scary*."

"And a lot of people would say the same thing about me." I shrug. "We're like twin conflagrations."

She actually laughs at that one. Then she grows quiet, screwing her lips to the side in deep thought. "And you swear he treats you right? Like...in the bedroom?"

I waggle my eyebrows at her. "He definitely treats my right in the bedroom." You can see the curiosity written all over her face. "And yes, there are handcuffs and spankings."

"You mean to tell me that you let him handcuff you and spank you?" she asks in astonishment, and I nod my head. "For real. My sister, Alessia Bonetti, allows a man to handcuff her, leaving her exposed and helpless, and she likes it?"

"God, you make it sound less sexy. But yes. He handcuffs me to our bed and has his way with me."

"And he spanks you. Like you let him strike you?"

"Once again, not making it sound as sexy as it is. And it *is* sexy. Ask my soaked puss—"

"Gross, Less!" she shouts, making me crack up. She's such a prude! How the hell is she my twin sister? She manages to crack a smile and shake her head at me playfully. "You really are insane, aren't you?"

"Sure am. And you all still love me."

"Only because we'd be afraid to turn our backs on you," she utters under her breath, biting back a smile.

I let out a giggle. "Bullshit. My insanity is the best part of my charm."

She snorts. "If that's charm, then I guess I know exactly what it is that you see in him then."

"I'm his dark half to his darker half."

"Romantic," she mutters dryly.

I'd like to think so. It's definitely not your princess and white knight fairy tale, and more like your maleficent and dark knight romance, but it's ours.

Gemma jumps as my head snaps to the closed bedroom door when we hear *pop! pop! pop!* in the distance. There's only a short pause before gunfire begins going off back-to-back and nonstop. It's rapid-fire, not single shots. The sound was too precise to be outside the gates surrounding the estate.

We're both up off the bed and on our feet. I run for my bag, which has my two Glocks in it. "Gemma, we need to get to the panic room." She runs into her closet. "Where are you going?!" I shout as I make sure my guns are loaded and the safeties are off.

"Getting my gun out of the safe!"

"Why the fuck is your gun in the safe?! Just get your ass out here, Gemma! Forget about your gun!" It's not like she really knows how to use it anyway, and the gunshots are getting louder, which means they're getting closer. *How? This place is a fortress!*

She comes running out of her closet in a frenzy, and the gunshots sound like they're now inside the house. "Oh, my God!" Gemma shrieks.

I run over and grab her hand to drag her with me to the door. "We need to run for the panic room *now* before it's too late." She starts resisting and shaking her head frantically. "Gemma," I growl. "I know you're scared, but we have to run. *Now.*"

Practically yanking her arm out of the socket, I wait a second to listen before pulling open the door with my 9mm raised. "Come on," I hiss, and pull her out the door with me.

When I hear boots stomping up the stairs and unfamiliar voices, I shove Gemma back into the bedroom. *Fuck, we don't have any time left.* I turn to my sister. "Gemma, I'm going to hold them off. As soon as I start shooting, I need you to run your little heart out and do not stop. You understand me?"

"What?" she squeaks. "I'm not going without you!"

"There's no time to fucking argue, Gemma. I mean it. As soon as I start shooting. Fucking. Run."

A tear slides down her cheek as she shakes her head like crazy, and I can hear them getting further up the steps, even with bullets being fired back and forth. "No. I'm not leaving you."

"Yes, you fucking are. Ready?"

"No! Alessia, please!" She tugs on my arm, and I spin on her, knowing that only tough love will work on her right now.

"Gemma. I need you to put your big girl panties on right fucking now, or the both of us are dead. Do you understand me?" Her chin trembles, and tears begin to rain down her pink cheeks. "If we both run, we're dead."

"But if you stay, you're dead," she rasps.

"You know I can take care of myself." My nostrils flare as I remain firm. "Ready?"

She sniffles and slowly nods her head. "I love you."

"You can tell me that when we get out of this." I know our brothers won't let us die like this. Neither will Massimo. They won't. They can't. *I* won't let us die like this.

I can hear the men right at the top of the stairs now. Someone is barking orders to check the rooms, and I don't even hesitate. It's literally now or never. My Glock raised, I come out of the room and just start shooting. "Go, Gemma! Now!" I roar and take down the two men who made it to the top of the steps. It should make however many men behind them pause just long enough to give Gemma time to dart down the hall.

I duck and dive back into the bedroom when the doorframe behind me explodes from someone blindly shooting back. The sound of heavy boots hit the steps collides with men shouting in Russian.

Great. What the fuck are the Russians doing here?

Before I barricade myself inside the bedroom, I take out two more men who make it to the top of the stairs. Then I slam the door shut and run to take cover. Knocking over the loveseat, I jump behind it.

"Fuck," I hiss when I realize I shot more rounds than I thought, and I'm out of ammo. Now, I'm left with my .22 and my knives.

More of them make it up the stairs, and the sound of bullets popping off is nonstop from inside the house. Gemma had to of made it inside the panic room by now, and if she's waiting for me, I'll fucking kill her if they don't.

I'm aware the door won't hold them back for long, and if my brothers haven't come to the rescue yet, something is desperately wrong.

Thank *fuck* Mamma was out. And I won't let her come home to another loss.

The door is peppered with bullet holes, but I keep my eye on it. Preparing myself for the ambush. As soon as the door is kicked in, I start picking them off one by one. It's not easy with a .22 and when they're wearing tactical gear, but I'm a crack shooter and hit my mark every time, at least putting them down. Still, it takes more than one bullet, and I'm now out of ammo on my second gun.

They don't delay as four men rush into the room armed with some heavy shooters. All I have are two of my knives on me, so I'll have to use them wisely. I can fight, and with my size and prissy dress, they'll underestimate me without my guns.

Raising my arms in surrender with a forced look of fear, they advance towards me. They eye me up and begin to circle me like sharks in the water. I might be the tempting bait, but I am no fucking chum.

Come and get me, boys.

I bide my time patiently, preparing to strike when they get closer and their defenses are down. Totally taking them off guard as I throat-punch the guy closest to me and go to attack the next one. I get him in the groin and then in his throat, too, when he's distracted. But that's only half of them.

The other two are smart enough not to allow me time to turn on them, and one tries to grab me from behind, but I'm quicker as I duck out of his way and I side kick him as hard as I can right between his ribs and hipbone where I know there's a gap in his vest there. As soon as I make contact and he howls in agony, the last guy charges me. I can be the best fighter out there, but when a man uses their weight against me, I'm fucked.

We go down to the ground hard, and I'm easily overpowered with his pure strength. The other guys are all slowly getting up around me, and I really start to panic inside. I should've gone for a knife sooner, probably after putting down the second guy. I wanted to impair them first before pulling out my only weapons, giving them less of a chance to be able to swiftly disarm me.

Fuck, I should've been smarter. Should've been faster.

The sorry fuck that has me pinned down leans in and murmurs something in Russian, licking his lips. The rest move in around me and chuckle as they murmur their agreement to whatever he says.

"Zhopu porvu margala vikoliu, suka," *I'll rip your ass and poke out your eyes, bitch*, I sneer one of the only sayings I know in Russian and top it off with a massive wad of spit to the center of his ugly face.

The other men all cackle like hyenas, but the one wiping my spit from his face is unamused. He cranks his arm back to sock my right in the jaw, knocking my head to the side, and the instant taste of copper bursts on my taste buds.

I snap my head back in place to look him in the eye as if unfazed. I was pissed before, but now I'm ireful. "You all will fucking pay for this. We don't simply kill *porcas* like you." *Pigs.* "We make you our bitch," I spit.

They chuckle around me. "Looks like we bagged ourselves the crazy one," the man still on top of me says. "We were hoping to enjoy you and your sister together. Where did the little *zaychik* run off to, huh?" *Bunny.*

"Eat a dick," I seethe. And he will...his own, that is.

He grins, and I can feel the others licking their chops, eager for a taste. *Okay, Alessia. Time to think with your tits here.*

Out of breath, I finally stop struggling against him as if I can't anymore. They laugh at me, and one guy bends down to tear my dress down abruptly. The straps easily snapping, and both of my breasts pop out. They all hoot and nod in approval. The same man who ripped my dress reaches down and gropes both breasts with his dirty hands. Bile instantly rises, but I numb my mind to it all. All I concentrate on is blood.

"I'm going to save you for last when I get out of this, you fucking bitch," I hiss, and the man on top of me punches me square in the face, taking me completely by surprise and making me see stars.

That's going to leave a mark.

He sneers something in Russian, and I gather up a big wad of blood and spit in my mouth and fling it up at him. When he wipes away my spit from his face for the second time with his shoulder, I'm a tad bit rattled despite my grin. I probably shouldn't have done that. I planned on playing it cool and getting them to relax, but I can only take so much without reacting. Plus, I need to get rid of some of the blood in my mouth anyway.

The man still holding me down makes the grave mistake of removing one hand from my arm that he had pinned at my side to wind up and punch me in the cheek, snapping my head to the side. I don't even have time to shake it off or even feel its effects as I go for one of my knives, and once again, they don't see it coming as I shove it home, right between his legs thrusting upwards. My teeth clench, and my nostrils flare as my arm shakes from using so much force, and his mouth falls open in a silent scream. The other men are all frozen in shock to react in time.

My father always told me never to hesitate. It'll cost me my life, and he was right because the men here who have hesitated let me arm myself with the now dickless man's gun and start shooting before he's even slumped over. I effortlessly take two out, and when the last one turns and starts to run like a coward, I take my other throwing knife out of its holster, and I throw it with precision, and it lands like a dart in the back of his neck.

Wow. I have killed a lot of men today.

Shoving dickless the rest of the way off me as he whimpers and moans in pain, I get to my feet and swipe at the blood coming from my nose with the back of my hand. Picking my knife up off the floor, I kick him over to his back as he's trying to cup his hands around his crotch, where a river of blood is coming from.

I stand over him, grinning. "Do you know what happened to the last man that tried to defile me?" He tries growling something I don't understand because I don't speak fucking Russian. "You heard I'm crazy right?" I get down on my knees and I raise my knife above my head, then arc it downwards as I drive it right through one of his cupped hands. He howls out and removes it as he stares at it in horror, shaking like a leaf. "That's because I am fucking crazy. Do you know how I got such reputable status?" He attempts to drag himself away, now blubbering, begging for mercy. My grin turns sinister as I stab him in the thick muscular part of his thigh above his kneecap to end his retreat. He cries out in agony, foaming at the mouth. "You're about to find out."

With my hand still gripping the hilt of my knife that's embedded in his leg, I crawl on my knees to him and then sit back. With too much enthusiasm, I tear open the crotch of his pants, and without even a second to pause, I slice through what's left of his tiny pecker, dismembering him with one cut. His jaw becomes unhinged as he screams out and gurgles on his own blood.

He miraculously tries again to escape me, and I get up with a maniacal grin. Slowly stalking him, he tries desperately to drag himself across the carpet, staining it a crimson red. His will for survival is impressive.

He finally comes to a stop, too weak and quickly bleeding out. I crouch down near his head and tilt mine to one side. "Consider this a mercy, *fica*. If I let you live, you'd spend a lifetime down in the catacombs where you would endure pain for many years to come." My lips thin as my teeth clench, and I shove his own cock inside of his mouth, stuffing it as far down as it can go. It doesn't take long for him to choke to death on it, and I rip his shirt open.

"ALESSIA!!" Massimo's voice bellows out from somewhere inside of the house.

I ignore the shouting as I gingerly carve my pretty initials into his chest. I go to sit back to admire my handy work when something out of the corner of my eye catches my attention. The guy that went down with my knife in the back of his neck is still alive. Not for long, though.

"Alessia! Gemma!" my brothers all start shouting.

I thought that maybe I had gone deaf when I heard the gunfire finally die down, or perhaps I was tuning it all out in a state of fear. You know, the whole about to be gang raped then killed thing.

I stomp over to the pitiful sack of shit and take my knife out of him before kicking him over to his back. Blood dripping from his mouth, he spits some Russian up at me, and the veil of calmness I've been wearing gives.

I completely black out.

CHAPTER THIRTY-THREE

Alessia

"A lessia!" Massimo's roar finally breaks through to me. "Alessia!" It grows closer, and I look down to see my knife still stabbing into flesh and blood. The face unrecognizable.

I'm covered from head to toe in blood, including my exposed breasts. Shit, he can't see me like this. None of them can. I jump up to franticly find something to cover myself with. Racing over to the bed, I snatch the small throw blanket to wrap around myself just in time.

Jino, our cousin, is the first familiar face to appear behind the stacked-up bodies inside the doorway. "Up here!" He climbs over the dead men and rushes to me. "Alessia. Are you alright?" I nod my head. "Let me see." He tries to reach for my face, and I rear back some on reaction.

"Gemma," I croak.

His eyes widen in fear as he scours the room with his gaze. "Where is she? Is she okay?"

"She went for the panic room up here. Go."

Just as he turns, Massimo literally comes barreling into the room, looking deranged and utterly mad. "Alessia!" he yells again, even though he can clearly see me standing here. I hug the blanket closer, feeling so ashamed. It's unfair the way a man can so instantaneously make a woman feel violated.

His hands cradle my face as soon as he reaches me, making me wince in pain as he inspects me. His chest is rising and falling, and his eyes are wildly jerking all over the place.

"I'm okay." My voice is hoarse coming out. "I swear I'm okay." My face hurts like hell, but it could have been much worse.

He takes notice of the blanket I'm tightly grasping, and he tries tugging on it with flaring nostrils. "Drop the fucking blanket, Alessia," he warns, his voice sounding like nothing I've heard from him before.

Not having much of a choice because I'm temporarily out of fight, I drop the blanket, and my hands jump up to hold my ripped dress over my breasts. "I'm okay, Massimo. Really."

His breath is coming in ragged as he snarls at my torn clothing. Then he tries to yank my dress up my legs, and I smack at his hands. "Massimo! Stop!" I glance at all the men in the room as they inspect all the dead bodies. Without taking his eyes off me, he orders everyone to leave. He's looking more wrathful by the second, like the growing cloud mushrooming from an atomic blast.

"Pull your dress up now, or I will rip the rest of it off you." Spit comes flying out, and I feel like combusting into tears of embarrassment. Men never have to worry about anything like this.

Taking a breath, I bunch my dress up for him in humility, feeling like I'm being violated all over again. He drops down to his knees to examine me up close. My panties are still in one piece, and there aren't any signs of struggle down there.

Jumping to his feet, he crushes my body against his. My face is killing me as it's smushed into his chest, but I don't dare tell him. I'm pretty sure he's more fucked up about this than me right now. The adrenaline keeps the trauma at bay, and I'm sure the scene is more gruesome to any onlooker.

"Massimo. Please tell me everyone is okay. Please," I whisper.

"We haven't found Gemma yet, but your brothers and your mother are fine."

"Gemma went to the panic room. I don't think anyone got past to get to her."

The tension in his body intensifies, and he gradually leans back. "And why didn't *you* go to the panic room?" His voice is like ice causing me to physically shiver.

"There wasn't enough time. They were already coming up the stairs so I had to hold them back so Gemma could make a run for it," I rush the words out.

"You didn't have to do *shit*. You could've hidden and waited it out!"

"You weren't there! You didn't know the situation!"

He's deathly silent and still for a moment, then his grip on my upper arms is now bone-crushing, and he trembles as his face turns a shade darker. "You're also a smart woman, so act like it. It was you against an army."

"Yeah, and I handled them," I chop out each word.

"No. You got lucky."

"Fuck you, Massimo. I did exactly what I had to do. If I hadn't held them back, Gemma wouldn't have been able to get to the panic room, and you and I both know she'd be completely helpless against those men. I'd be trying to protect both of us from getting gang raped and then murdered," I vehemently seethe, then throw my arm out, gesturing to the small army of men dead around us. "I knew what I was doing. It was either risk my life, or risk *both* of our lives."

"No, you had to try and prove something. To show everyone you can play with the big boys. There's a difference between being smart and being smug."

"Oh, yeah? And what would you have done, Massimo?!" He doesn't answer, and I nod my head. "Exactly. You would've done exactly what I did, but that's okay, right? Because you're a man and expected to fight, whereas I'm a woman, and I'm expected to cower under the fucking bed."

"Is it so wrong that I want you safe?"

I let out a bitter chuckle. "Look around you! You act as if I went out there looking for a fight! The fight was brought to me simply because of my last name. I'm in the mob. I'll never *be safe*."

The lines on his forehead deepen. Suddenly, the background noise comes rushing in, and I know that my brothers need to see that I'm alright.

I go to step around Massimo as I mutter something about needing to go, and he blocks me. "Massimo. I'm not up for games right now."

"We're not done talking."

"Well, I am. Now, move your big ass out of my way."

"Not until we're done talking."

I try shoving by him and he makes the mistake of trying to detain me. I'm still in fighting mode. I scream through my teeth and start swinging at him while he tries to catch my fists and dodge them at the same time.

"The fuck is going on here?!" Tullio says, rushing in. Massimo and I both pause as we seethe at one another. Then Massimo's eyes dart to my uncovered chest the same time I remember it, and he turns his back to block me as I try to cover myself back up.

"Nothing," I snap, glaring up at the back of Massimo's head. "This male chauvinist is being a *stronzo* right now."

Tullio steps around Massimo and turns me to him to begin inspecting me, panting in rage. The more he sees, the more he fumes. He swears under his breath in Italian as his hands shake against me.

"I'm okay, Tullio." His wild eyes snap up to mine, and then he's crushing me against his body for an embrace.

The rest of my brothers begin trickling in, and they all do the same. Hugging me, examining me, cursing the dead Russians. But not one of them gives me shit about what I did today.

I can hear the voices of Mamma and Gemma, and I the shame burns my cheeks. "I didn't want them to see this," I murmur quietly to Santino, but it's too late.

They come running into the room both in tears and engulf me. Ignoring the cuts and bruises on my face, my mother squeezes it as she peppers my face with kisses, and Gemma sobs. "I'm okay, I'm okay, Mamma. I swear."

She hugs me again and then suddenly freezes in my arms and gasps. "*Mio Dio.*" *My God*. She slowly pulls back, staring away in horror, and I can't look her in the eye, nor Gemma. What they must be seeing. How they must see me now.

Crazy Alessia. Little Psycho. They're no longer just names my brothers tease me with.

Gentle hands cup my face and make me look at Mamma in the face. "Gemma told me how brave you were, *piccolina*," she says, looking at me like she always has. "*Babbo* would be so proud."

"My defender," Gemma adds in a shaky voice as she laces her fingers with mine, giving me a watery smile. I smile back, thinking about how she was like a precious stone locked away safely inside a vault, and I was the one guarding it.

After tossing my ripped and blood-soaked dress and grabbing some of Gemma's clean clothes, I rinse off quickly in the shower and then let the doctor patch me up. Luckily, my nose isn't broken, and with some painkillers and some ice, I'll be good as new in a couple of weeks.

Massimo and I keep our distance from one another, and every time we make eye contact, he scowls and quickly averts his gaze. I don't have the energy to deal with his little tirade, so I don't. It infuriates me how badly I let it hurt me.

I had already planned to stay the night here, but it's necessary for more reasons than one. Gemma and Mamma need me, and Massimo can go home to sulk alone.

I survived today and protected my sister. I know *Babbo* would be proud. At least, I hope he would be.

Hours later, I have Mamma and Gemma tucked into bed in my old bedroom. Both of them were so emotionally exhausted that they passed out soon after their heads hit the pillow.

So, I finally make my way down to the office. It's still too hard to refer to it as Tullio's office now, hence why it's now *the* office.

I enter the room, and everyone glances at me. "Hey, there's Jane the cock ripper," Armando makes a jab, and it makes me bite back a bashful smile as everyone else laughs and takes their stabs at me. Everyone but Massimo, Tullio, and Santino. None of them are at all amused.

Because I'm a glutton for punishment, I say, "I should totally get it tatted." I plop down onto the loveseat, trying to act as casually as possible.

The room quickly grows dead silent, and I soak it all in. The looks on their faces become grim and stricken as if suddenly remembering how I've earned yet another nickname, and it makes me snicker some. Something I tend to do when I'm slightly uncomfortable...or I should say when I'm making *others* uncomfortable.

Tullio clears his throat, and I've felt Massimo's eyes practically singing my skin since I walked in.

"I need to speak with Alessia," Tullio says, breaking the tension. "In private." No one questions him as everyone files out quietly except for Massimo, who stands there still looking at me. "I'm sorry, Massimo. I won't be long."

"I'll be waiting right outside," he murmurs, reluctantly leaving us.

As soon as we're alone, Tullio joins me on the loveseat. The soft fabric runs under my palms as I slide them around the surface. "If you ever decide to redecorate, promise me you won't get rid of this couch. Or at least give it to me."

Tullio has always taken his role as the eldest seriously. The only time I remember him anything less than serious was when Agnella was in his life. So, it's warming when he smiles like he does right now. "I promise."

"Massimo is pissed at me," I mutter. "Thinks I should've run to the panic room with Gemma."

He sighs and runs a hand through his hair, then over the scruff on his face. Poor guy has aged so much in the past few months. "As your older brother, I wish you did too." I huff and fall back against the couch. "We can't help the fact that we'd rather you do whatever it takes for you to be safe and not risk your life."

"What don't you guys get?" It hurts knowing that the only man who would be proud of me isn't here to tell me so. "If I had run rather than held them back, Gemma wouldn't have made it to the panic room. Neither of us would. And what do you think would've happened then? I'm not stupid *or* over-confident, and I know I could've been raped and killed, but it was either me or both of us. Be pissed at me all you want for doing that, but I would do it again in a heartbeat if given the choice. Even if I died."

"I'm not upset with you, Alessia. I'm proud of you."

"You are?" My voice raises.

"Of course I am. And *Babbo* would be too. I'm sure of it. He's always been so proud of you. Even when he found out about you cutting off the Gallo's boy's cock and fed it to him."

I bite back a smile. "Tell me."

Tullio puts an arm around me, and we both lean back. He begins to tell me about that day. How he was horrified for a whole two seconds before bursting out in laughter. I needed this. To reminisce on the good memories.

"He always knew you could take care of yourself, Alessia. We all do. But we also wish you, Gemma, and Mamma could have a better life. Even Alba."

I rear back, frowning. "A better life? I love my life, Tullio."

He stares at me for a long moment. "Only because this is what you know."

I sit up straight and twist my body inwards. "It's because I'm a Bonetti, and it's in my blood. This is all I know because it's all I want to know. *Babbo* understood that. That's why he let me train, why he didn't have me go to college, why he arranged a marriage for me."

"*Babbo* would see things differently if he had lived through everything that has happened recently."

"You can't say that!"

He sighs heavily and leans forward, dragging his palms down his tired face. "You're right. It isn't fair to speak for him, but I can speak for the rest of us now. The ones who are still here and love you immensely. I have lost too many loved ones already." His voice tightens towards the end, and his eyes glaze over with that anguish still just under the surface. "I don't know what I would do if anything happened to you girls."

"It's part of this life, Tullio. I won't ever put myself in danger if there's another choice. I didn't have one today. Please see that," I plead with him gently. I can see him breaking inside, and I don't want to give him any more grief. He's had enough.

He nods his head solemnly, and we grow quiet for a moment. "Did you really have to make that guy choke on his own dick again?" he mutters.

I snort. "He had some naughty plans with it. Mine were better."

CHAPTER THIRTY-FOUR

Alessia

Massimo has been oddly reticent lately, more than usual.

It's been a week since the attack, and we've hardly spoken. Even more bothersome, we haven't had sex. He'll come to bed late without a word, and I'll pretend to be already sleeping.

I don't know if he's stressed out or still shaken or if he thinks I'm too fragile at the moment. I have no idea what to think when he's like this, but it's eating me up inside.

More so than the initial incident. I've never felt so helpless in all my life. It wasn't the fear of dying, it was the terror of being defiled and ravished by those pigs. I would've chosen death over that.

But I got out of it nearly unscathed, though I don't think Massimo has.

I miss him. I miss the Massimo I had before all this. The one who could crack me like an eggshell. Who couldn't keep his hands off me or even go an hour without tracking me down. Initially, he was aloof and a little cold towards me, but this is different. He's not only distant, but he's also dour. Even when I'm tucked into his side with his arms around me, he feels miles away.

In a crime family, conflicts and unexpected events always occur, but maybe being with me is an unnecessary complication. Between losing my father and him having to lose his, and my mother being in the hospital for so long, and then the attack on our estate. What if it's all too much for him? What if I'm not worth the added strain?

The only thing I can do is get him to talk to me. I demand that he delineate in words exactly where his head is at.

I put a little effort into my appearance before confronting him, mainly to hide some of the bruising on my face, or possibly distract him from it. I slip into one of my urbane dresses and stare at myself in the mirror for a long moment to gather more courage.

Knocking on his office door, he calls out for me to come in. He doesn't even look up from his desk as I enter and close the door behind me. Not until I come to a stop right in front of his desk. For a second, he seems like I have him ensnared by my presence, then the shield goes back up, and he feigns indifference. I don't let him see how badly it hurts as I, too, feign indifference.

"How are you?" I ask coolly.

"I'm good. How are you today?"

So fucking formal. What is wrong with us? "I'm good. Just miss you." He gives me a tight smile and returns to whatever he was doing. Doesn't he know how difficult it is for me to force those words out, showing even a sliver of vulnerability? Again, I remain withdrawn and round the desk to prop myself on the surface next to him. "Talk to me, Massimo. Whatever is going on with you, with us, I have a right to know."

He stills but keeps his head down. "We'll talk tonight." Then he goes back to whatever the fuck he was doing.

I snatch the pen out of his hand and white knuckle it. Trying to contain the outburst trying to explode from me. "No. We'll talk now." He slowly looks up at me. "You hardly look at me, we haven't had sex, you won't talk to me, you do your best to avoid me until it's time to go to bed. Tell me why," I rush the words out and leave a pause for him to respond, but he gives none. "Do you think they raped me? Is that it? I said they didn't, and I meant it. So, if you think I'm ruined or broken—"

"I don't think that," he snaps.

"Then what is it? Tell me what's going on." He doesn't answer me again. "When you said we should postpone the wedding, did you really mean postpone? Or did you mean cancel it?" I've been trying to avoid that thought ever since he said it days ago. I thought it was because of my face and the aftermath of it all, but in the back of my mind, I've been terrified that he doesn't want to marry me anymore. When he still doesn't respond, my heart drops and my worst fear is made real. "Do you still love me, Massimo?" I curse myself when my chin trembles and my throat aches from trying not to cry. I want to scream at him for making me feel so weak. For making me sound so fucking pathetic.

Still, he gives me nothing and I feel like I'm going to be sick. I wish the ground would open up and swallow me whole. "So much for your love not being a fickle thing," I spit, my anger quickly baited to the surface, leaving my heartache on the backburner for now. I hop down from the desk, more than ready to flee.

"Alessia." He goes to grab for my hand, and I dodge it. His eyes instantly darken, and his face hardens.

"No. You had your chance to speak and chose to stay silent which says a lot." So many things I want to sling at him right now. Let him know how much of a coward and a liar and a fraud he is. But if I do, I might end up breaking down, and he no longer holds such a privilege.

"Alessia," he says more firmly as he grips my upper arm tightly, stopping me as I try and leave.

"Get the fuck off me, Massimo. I am so serious right now."

"Don't you dare deny my touch," he growls.

"Fuck. You." I'm shaking with gritted teeth.

His wild gaze mirrors my feral one as we have a standoff. Then his mouth comes crashing down on mine and he kisses me hard. I kiss him back at first and then I chomp down on his bottom lip and he rears back in shock. I don't dare blink as I lick my crimson lips and he wipes at his and gapes down at the blood on his fingers. When he looks back at me, I quiver. He's savage and I'm here for it.

Gripping the back of my hair harshly, I let out a hiss just before he smashes his mouth against mine again. "Do that again, *gattina*, and I will tie you to the bed and torment you for days."

I don't even give him a response as I kiss him back and we tear at each other's clothes. He has me naked in record timing and his shirt is gone and his dick is out. Propping me up on the desk, he shoves his cock inside of me with brutal force and begins his violence. Our kissing remains rough and sloppy, both of us desperate to send a message.

I'm silently begging him to tell me he still loves me. To tell me that we're okay. That he only needs more time to coop with the trauma the attack may have caused.

He pounds into me for a while then abruptly pulls out and repositions me. Yanking me down from the desk and spinning me around to pin me against it and drive back into me from behind, causing my hipbones to crunch on impact.

My body is bent in half when he shoves me down on my face by my hair and his other hand grips my ass cheek so hard it'll leave marks. I have to reach up and grip the edge of the desk to hold on while he removes his hand from my hair and snakes it around to roughly toy with my clit.

Arching my back and angling my hips towards him, he hits a new spot, and I'm so close to coming. The way his hips speed up, and he grunts, he is too. His plan was clearly not to make this last.

Fisting my hair again, he jerks me upwards making me cry out. His mouth is crushed against my ear forcing me to listen to his ragged breathing. He doesn't whisper any sweet or dirty words to me like he always does. He just pants and fucks me until we both erupt.

I come hard and fast and I'm barely spiraling down from it when he pulls out of me to come all over my ass. Something he typically does when we're fighting, so I don't let myself read too far into it.

When he gets himself dressed and leaves the room while I'm still bent over his desk naked and fatigued, I do.

What is happening?

CHAPTER THIRTY-FIVE

Massimo

THE DAY AFTER THE ATTACK…

Alessia spent the night at the Bonetti estate last night and I let her. I was torn between never letting her out of my sight ever again, and not being able to look at her without hostility.

I love her for her audacious side, but she is so fucking arrogant and reckless at times. She could have helped Gemma get to safety and then taken safety herself. We were only minutes away. Instead, she had to go all fucking macho trying to prove something. It was stupid and I could've fucking lost her.

I requested some time with Tullio while I was there to pick Alessia up and bring her back home. He agreed, claiming he wanted a private word with me as well. So, here I am with Tullio and Santino closed inside their office.

"With the Bortsovs making some ballsy fucking moves and having a rat inside, it isn't safe for her here right now," Tullio cuts right to it. "With you or with me."

"I know," I say lifelessly. She was made to be my queen, but I love her too much to lose her. I would selfishly rather have her stripped of the life she is so faithful to and have her hate me, than to than to have her taken from me, leaving me breathing when she no longer can.

"So, you're on board with this. Sending her away," he asks.

Before I answer him, Santino speaks up. "If you do this, she'll never forgive you. Either of you. She'll hate you both for as long as she lives. You can never take it back or undo it once it's done."

"I understand that," I confirm. I've tormented myself with the idea all night.

Twice now, there was a hit on the Bonetti's. The first was my father's doing, but it couldn't have been him this time. And the Bortsovs have to be working with someone on the inside, and until we know who, none of us are safe.

Santino studies me as I sit here sulking inside. "I can't tell if you're doing this because you love her, or because you don't."

My fists clench, nails biting into the flesh. "Does it matter? Either way, I'm going to let her go so that she's safe," I raise my voice more than I ever do in present company.

"It does fucking matter," he snaps back and I'm a little taken aback by his sudden change in tone. Santino is always calm, no matter the situation. "I'm going to have to stand by and watch you break her heart, and I need to know if you deserve a good pounding afterwards or not. I have never seen my sister in such a condition as when we forced your separation, and that was only for a week. So, I'll ask you one more time. Are you letting her go because you love her, or is it because you *don't*?"

"It'll break my heart too."

I'll never love anyone like I love her, and I will never agree to spend the rest of my life with any other woman. I'll find someone eventually to give me an heir or two, but never a wife. Alessia Bonetti was it for me. The core of my being. Walking this earth without her by my side for the rest of my life will be my atonement for breaking every vow I gave to her.

"She's not going to go easily," Tullio says. "Especially if she thinks you don't want her to."

"I know what I have to do," I flatly state, already feeling desolate inside.

Santino scoffs and shakes his head. "So, you two are really okay with losing her, of her hating you. And don't forget she won't just leave and accept it. She'll seek revenge, or even worse. She'll self-destruct."

"It's not forever," Tullio mutters, visibly unconvinced by his own lies. "And this isn't just for Alessia. This is for Mamma, Gemma, Lesina, Alba..." He eyes me briefly as if I am to add any names. But the danger of the females in my family are not as dire as theirs. "And I'd rather have her hate me than to see her dead," Tullio adds taking the words right out of my mouth.

"Yeah, well, she might as well be dead to the two of you after this," Santino says.

"As long as her heart still beats, I can live with that," I end with.

CHAPTER THIRTY-SIX

Alessia

I ended up sleeping in my old room across the hall last night. And Massimo never came for me, not even to talk or drag me back to our bedroom.

But this morning, he had no problems hunting me down to tell me Tullio requested our presence today. He delivered the message, then left.

I'm an emotional mess inside, but I gather up my wits and head out to the waiting SUV. I'm almost surprised when he slips inside the same one as me, and I hold my tongue about it. How much his sudden change in character hurts will remain mine to bear, as is the severe impact these silent moments take on my heart.

The entire ride is painful as he stares down at his phone and I look out the window watching the world whiz by. I feel like we're further away from each other than when we first met. When he was cold towards me then, it was obvious he just didn't know how to relax around anyone. He needed time. Now, he's trying his best to ice me out and he doesn't even have the decency to tell me why.

Whatever my brother wants to talk with us about, I want to speak to him about coming back home. It's clear that Massimo no longer wants me. Last night, he redacted every promise he had ever made to me, and it killed me.

I hate myself for obsessing over where it might've gone wrong. What *I* could have done wrong. Is he really so turned off by my decision to fight to save my sister?

I've never tried to hide who I was. I'm the same tenacious woman I've been from the beginning. The very one he's been encouraging to soar.

How could he shape me for a throne, only to deny me its seat?

As soon as we pull up to my family's estate, I practically throw my door open and jump out. I don't bother waiting for Massimo as I saunter up to the door and let myself in and head right back towards the office. Ready for battle and hyped up for war.

Santino, Armando, Paolo, and Jino are all hovering right outside the door with penitent faces and can barely make eye contact with me. Whatever is going on, they're all bracing themselves for my reaction, which means I'm at the center of this.

The fucking coward I was obligated to marry didn't have the fucking *cogliones* to tell me himself. He needed backup from my brothers. Good fucking ridden then. But *fuck* does it hurt.

Entering the room, Tullio is sitting behind the desk per usual and the door closes behind me. Glancing back, I see Jino standing on one side of it and Vinny stationed on the other. Why do I feel like I'm about to be accused of a crime and then proscribed and banished? My perception may not compare to these men, but I know premature remorse when I see it. Especially when Tullio isn't even trying to hide it. If he thinks his puppy dog eyes will help mitigate the blow he's about to deliver, he's sorely mistaken. My anger is already simmering, and I'm still in the dark about what's coming.

I sit down without having to be told and Massimo takes the chair next to me. "How are you, *piccolina*?" Tullio asks.

"Cut to the fucking chase, Tullio. What the fuck is this about?"

He hesitates for a moment. "I need to ask you to hand over your piece."

"Fuck off. I'm not handing over shit until you tell me what's going on."

He takes my hostility in stride, knowing it's merely a prelude to the storm his forthcoming words will unleash. "I figured you'd say that," he mutters, and Massimo remains silent next to me. "You know I love you so fucking much. I—"

"Just stop, Tullio," I choke out, not able to hear any of this shit. "Please. Just get it over with."

"You're leaving" He finally rips it off like a bandage. "You, Gemma, Mamma, Lesina, and Alba. It isn't safe for you all right now. Not until we have dealt with the Russians and whoever they are connected with."

"The only place I'm leaving is the De Luca estate to come home," I state.

"Not an option, Alessia." The gravity in his tone is solid.

"Fuck it's not! You cannot tell me what to do!"

He slams his hand down on the desk making me jump a little in my seat. "I can tell you what to do as head of this family."

"Why?" I say just above a whisper. "Why are you sending me away? I get wanting to send Gemma, Mamma, Lesina, and Alba away, but why me? You know I can take care of myself."

"Because we love you, that's why."

"No." I swallow hard. "You're dismissing me." He doesn't say anything. "What about Paolo and Armando and Santino and even, *fuck,* Salvatore! What about your son?! Oh, wait. Because he's a male!"

"It's not about you being a female," he says evenly.

"*Cazzata*! Yes, it is!" I lean forward waving my hands everywhere. "I'm just as much a part of this family as any of you! I have the same blood running through my veins! This isn't fucking fair!"

"You had to kill almost a dozen men, Alessia! That's what you want for yourself? To have to take on a small army and kill people? You made it out alive this time, but what about the next time?"

"It's the life I signed on for! I haven't been hiding under a fucking rock!" I turn on Massimo. "And *you*," I seethe, and he turns his head to me. His eyes dead as they glare back. "Every promise, every vow, every *word* you've ever fed me. It was all bullshit, wasn't it?"

"Not all of it, but things have changed."

My heart sinks. "Like your feelings for me." The bastard doesn't answer. "Or are you pretending not to care to make me go away?"

"I do care for you, but I need to put my empire first."

"Enlighten me."

"You're a liability. I have enough enemies as it is, with the Russians coming after your family, it puts a hit on mine for our association."

"Our *association*," I repeat, and the word dries up on my tongue leaving a sour taste in my mouth. "That's how you sum up everything we were." I shake my head in utter disappointment. The rancor inside of me growing and building up more momentum.

I jump to my feet and both my betrayers slowly rise to theirs. "You are such a fucking liar and a fucking coward." *His love isn't fickle? Once he loves, it's for life?* I pry the engagement ring that feels heavier than ever from my finger and chuck it at him as hard as I can. He dodges it by calmly stepping to the side. Then I reach up to the rose gold chain around my neck, a necklace he had gotten me, and give it one good yank. It easy snaps, and I fling that at him too. He turns his head to dodge it, but part of the chain grazes his cheek. He ignores the blood trickling down his face as his eyes firmly meet mine again. It feels good to see him shed blood because I know he won't be shedding any tears for me.

I pull out my .22 and aim it at his head. Two other guns cock back and then a third. Vinny pointing one at my head, Jino and Tullio pointing one at Vinny. Massimo just stands there like a statue not evincing a single emotion. Everything from the inside out made of stone. "You." Then I point my gun to my brother. "And you. Both of you. *Dead* to me."

I abhor them. I hate them so fucking much. I'm on the verge of insanity and there's no talking me down from there. If I don't leave now...

I turn to escape, and I just cannot contain the roaring rage inside. Pointing my gun, I pull the trigger. Shooting Vinny right in the foot on my way out. I don't miss a beat and continue past the rest of those who have betrayed me and walk right out of the front doors.

Tullio tried to feed me the bullshit of this being temporary, but this is the last time walking out of the place that used to be my home. I will never step foot inside of this place again. I have no home, I have no family. All of them a bunch of traitors.

The short drive back only has me stewing, working myself up more. I'm sure my things are already being packed for me. Once I get up to *his* bedroom, I lose it completely. Fisting one of my knives, I scream and slash. Destroying the bed first. The one he bought brand-new so it could be just ours and not tainted by other women. Stabbing the mattress and slicing through it over and over again. Then the pillows all get ribboned and the blankets until it looks like it's snowing in here. Everything he bought brand-new for me. They can all rot in hell along with his fucking black heart.

Next, I storm over to my closet and thank God there isn't a maid in there. She would probably find her way at the wrong end of my blade. I dig out my wedding dress that I was obviously never meant to wear, and I tear it to shreds too. "You fucking lying sack of shit! You never loved me! You never meant anything! You fucking played me! You *stupid motherfucker!*" I scream as I stab and slice my gown until I double over as a sob abruptly rips through me. "You *fucking motherfucker!*" I wail and continue slashing through the extravagant material. The hardwood floor becoming collateral damage in the massacre.

Surrounded by the fabric of my torn gown, I cry my fucking lungs out as the world is caving in around me. As if I haven't experienced great loss recently, the two most important men in my life collectively broke my heart, tearing the rest of my life apart. Taking everything that means most from me.

Why did you leave me, Babbo? Why?

He wasn't supposed to leave me like this. Not when I need him more than ever. He wouldn't banish me. He wouldn't force me away.

I'd give anything to run into his arms like a little girl, and have him squeeze me tight. Keep me in his embrace where I feel most protected. Most loved.

Regaining a bit of stability, I use the soiled dress to wipe the snot and tears from my face and stand up. Holding my head high, I exit the closet, and my phone starts going off. I pull it from my pocket to see that it's Mamma calling, and there's no way I can talk to her right now.

When I decline the call, it goes to the home screen, where I have a rare picture of Massimo and me set as my background. With a high-pitched scream, my ire bleeds from my pores, and I throw my phone as hard as I can against the wall, knowing it shattered the screen.

Rage takes back the wheel and I trample through the estate in a destructive frenzy. I obliterate anything in my path while barking orders for my shit to be packed immediately. I'm ready to be rid of this place.

It was beginning to feel like home to me. It was quiet and cold compared to the warm house I grew up in, but because of Massimo, it was becoming home. Because *he* was becoming my home, as well as my heart.

Now, they're both broken.

Do they not remember who I am? Sending me away is severing any connection. *Infinitely.* It can never be repealed, yet they went ahead and did it anyway.

CHAPTER THIRTY-SEVEN

Alessia

ALMOST THREE YEARS LATER...

I've been so eager to try this bad boy out. One of the many perks with my new career choice are the fun toys I get to play with.

My relocation across the country to the desolate southwest had me doubting I would ever recapture that thrill—the one that comes from staring death in the face, by living with the constant shadow of death.

After moping around for weeks in a spell of despondency and self-pity, I emerged with newfound resolve, ready to take back ownership of my life. It's my path to forge.

Still, I oscillated between melancholy and anger and contemplated building my own empire or devising a plan of retaliation. My insider knowledge could certainly take those down who hurt me.

Yet, despite my longing for vengeance, I could never truly repay their betrayal in kind.

And the headache of running an empire wasn't enough for me. The only way I could cope was to feed the bloodthirsty beast raging inside. I knew just the person that could assist me in that. Well-known assassin, Komodo.

To my recollection, at the time, I knew him to be a loner, loyal to whoever pays the most. But when I found a way to contact him, I learned he now works for The Organization. I told him I wanted in on impulse. He checked my alias to make sure there would be no way of tying me to the mob, and once he cleared me, he set me up with a meeting.

It wasn't hard to prove my worth to them. My life of training led me up to that moment.

A couple of years later, here I am. On top of a tall building with my new Dragunov aimed at my next assignment. Because what would a markswoman be without the best marksman sniper rifle out there?

Edwin Edwards has been a very dirty little man with a thick file of corruption. Another CEO of some pharmaceutical company that is progressively in moral decline. He thrives off the sick to get rich. He has the only effective product on the market for a rare pediatric disease, and it's pricy. Most families cannot afford it. The bastard could cut the cost down by 50% and still maintain his multi-millionaire status.

Supposedly, the people he borrowed money from to start his company were out of patience. He thought that with all the money he'd made, he was somehow untouchable.

I'm no vigilante, but I enjoy executing people whom the world would be better off without. I wish this one didn't have to be a quick job. I'd love nothing more than to play with my food first, but I was given orders.

It's become my catharsis for the pent-up anger inside me that never seems to dull or fade. It's what gets me up every day.

Popping in a piece of cinnamon gum, I get down and peer through the scope. Yup, still there, utterly oblivious, as he sips his top-shelf liquor with a bunch of big kahunas. One of which is the man who hired someone to kill him.

Even if this weren't a sorry sack of shit, if I'm told my mark, I execute it, not at all diffident or hesitant, and once you're in, you're in until they decide to release you. And the sentence for refusing a job, is death.

It's not like we're paid to shoot up schools or hospitals. They're people that got themselves involved in dirty money one way or another.

And we all die eventually, right?

I know. I'm a heartless bitch. Blah blah blah.

No one knows what I do these days. When the Bonetti women were sent away, I went my separate way off to live alone in the desert. I check in with them every couple of weeks, but I haven't spoken to any of my brothers since we left.

Despite missing the men, Gemma, Mamma, and even Lesina settled into their new, suburban lives reasonably well. Armando is the only one to visit, unable to be entirely out of his daughter's life. But when he comes to town, I make a point of being elsewhere.

Scoping out Mr. Edwards' security detail one more time, I see nothing has changed. All just as oblivious as the loser himself. Some security he has. I could probably wave a red flag and they wouldn't even spot me.

Chomping down on my gum, I sight my target. Going for his chest since he seems to move around a lot as he's talking. I rather not miss and risk one of his security guys catching me before I take a second one.

Releasing the air from my lungs through my mouth, I pull the trigger. *Boom!* Hits home. Square in his chest, sending him down like a sack of potatoes. "Oooooooooohhhhhhh!!!!" I gleefully squeal in excitement as I duck down out of sight completely and kick my feet in the air like a kid. *That was fucking amazing!* I wish I were assigned to more sniper jobs like this one so I can play with the big guns.

"Mwuah!" I give my rifle's stock a big smooch and pack it up as chaos unfolds from down low. Screaming and shouting. I hit the tiny inconspicuous earpiece in my ear to tap into the local cop's frequency to see how far they're out. The closest one seems to be a few miles away, so I have time. No time to waste, though.

Slinging the case over my back, I stay crouched down as I run for the back of the rooftop and I glance over. No one is back here scouring the area yet. Wow, his security team really fucking sucks. Good for me.

There are two more buildings at the same height as the one I'm on, with a large gap between them. It might not be Olympic distance, but it damn sure seems like it when you're carrying a large bag on your back. My crazy ass has already done a test run for it, and I can clear it with no problem. Tall people might be able to jump, but this short bitch can fly.

Standing back several feet from the edge, I run my ass off and soar through the air and onto the next rooftop. I land on my feet but drop to my knees from the momentum. Springing back up, I don't skip a beat as I take off into a sprint towards the next one. I pump my legs even harder, knowing I used a lot of energy on the first one. Biting back a scream, I clear the second gap, but not so gracefully this time. I still manage to get up and walk away, though it'll most likely hurt like a bitch tomorrow.

A coiled black rope is tethered to a pole at the edge of the building. The fire escape stairs are too close to the threshold of the alley to stay obscured, so I have to repel myself down. With all the chaos going down on the next block, no one will ever suspect the little redhead with glasses and what looks like a cello case slung to her back coming out of the shadows.

Everything goes according to plan.

Just another average yet exciting day in the life of Freida Marina Lopez. Time for a drink and maybe some sex.

CHAPTER THIRTY-EIGHT

Massimo

The thin rose gold chain with the tiny swan hanging from it stares up at me as I open the top drawer of my desk and slam it back shut.

Mia cigna. My Swan. Proud and effulgent-looking but dangerous when provoked. They happen to be very protective, as well as monogamists, mating for life.

It's been three years, and it still feels like a knife twisting in my gut. It only took three hours to change my mind and call Tullio to ask if we really did the right thing.

"It doesn't matter. It's too late now. She wouldn't come back no matter how much we begged her to."

I was notified that Alessia had departed the grounds before I arrived. I walked into the maids and several of my men scrambling to erase the remnants of the wreckage she left in her wake throughout the house. However, my quarters were off-limits so that mess remained untouched.

The bed was the first thing I noticed. Nothing was left from the nights we spent together but my own memories.She tore the mattress and everything on it to bits—pillows, blankets, everything. After glimpsing her slight insecurities about my past, I had our bed replaced as well as anything that might have come near another woman.

Then I walked into our closet and saw a pile of torn-up gold and cream intricate fabric in the middle of the floor. Her wedding dress. I didn't even know she already had it. I dropped to my knees and fisted the fabric, wishing I could see her in it once. To have a vivid picture of her in a wedding gown inside my head. I'd envisioned her plenty of times, but to see her with my own eyes only once would've lasted me a lifetime.

Willing myself off the floor, I ventured back out into the room and found her phone with a broken screen. The screen lit up as soon as it was in my hand, and my heart skipped a beat. It was a picture of the two of us. I remember exactly when she took it. We were sitting out on the patio and she'd told me about the plans she had for a garden back there. She was so zealous and passionate when she talked about it, and I was willing to give her the most outlandish garden there ever was. Then she came over to sit on my lap as we enjoyed a bottle of wine together, and she held out her phone to take a picture of us because the point where the sun was in the sky created this magnificent glow. She stared at me in awe as I reflected the same expression.

After punching in the passcode, I sat down to scroll through her phone to see what else she had on there. There were not a whole lot of pictures of us because neither of us is the type to take selfies and pose for the camera, but there were quite a few. More than I have taken in several years combined.

I explored everything she had on her phone, and when I found letters she had written to her loved ones in case anything ever happened to her, I slumped to the ground, strength deserting me.

To the love of my life,

The Don of the De Luca's and the king of my heart. Who knew love was ever really in the cards for me? I never thought that in my wildest and dirtiest of dreams, I would ever end up with a man like you. One who could somehow harness my temper but not tame it. One who could take control but make me feel all-powerful. One who could make my knees shake with one single touch. You've grounded me in so many ways yet made me feel like I was empress of everlasting paradise on Mt. Olympus.

Massimo, *amore mio*, my *re, cuore mio. My love, my king, my heart.*

Know that you have made me the best version of myself. The most fierce. The most driven. The most loving I have ever been in my life.

If you're reading this, it's because something happened to me (or you're snooping) and I need you to remember how much you truly meant to me in case I've been too stubborn to tell you or if we've recently gotten into one of our epic battles with one another and it didn't end up with me tied to your bed and me screaming in ecstasy.

I love you, Massimo De Luca. My greatest one.

Love,

Alessia

After I read it over and over, I wanted to call it all off with or without Tullio's approval. But he was right though. If my woman is anything, she is tenacious. Also, I am a bit of a grudge-holder. And I loved her for every bit of stubbornness in her body as long as she yielded to me eventually. But there's no coming back from this or rescinding.

My phone starts ringing, breaking me from the haunting memories and displaying a blocked number on the screen, which is impossible to do. A blocked number wouldn't be able to get through the cyber security on this phone, nor could my phone be traced. Warning bells are going off inside my head as I answer with trepidation.

Placing my phone to my ear, I wait for whoever it is on the end to speak first. "Massimo De Luca. It's been quite a long time."

"You have two seconds to tell me who this is," I say evenly.

"It's Komodo," he says with a Polynesian accent, and I glance around the room for anything that might be out of place that I haven't noticed before.

"How the fuck did you get through to this number?"

"I come with information, Massimo."

He's a busy man and he made the effort to track down my number and break through all the firewalls, so it must be some tangible information he has. "I'm listening."

"It'd be best if I came to speak with you in person."

"Not happening, Komodo." Mercenaries don't reach out to you unless they're contracted to kill you. You reach out to them when you need their services. "Tell me what I might need to know."

"It's about the Bonetti girl."

I shoot forward in my chair, my heart in my throat. "*Cazzo*," I hiss and growl. "Talk."

"In person, Massimo."

"Sir, someone just pulled up to the gate," Vinny says as he and Monte enter my office unannounced.

"I assume that's you," I say in a lowered voice.

"I swear I come in peace, my friend."

"I'm not your friend." He chuckles, and I'm too desperate for answers to react to his levity. "Get out of the car, no weapons. Once my guys check you out, you'll be walked through."

"I'll see you soon."

As soon as I hang up the phone, I tell Vinny and Monte to grab some men and keep their weapons raised as he gets out of the car and to check him thoroughly. Then to cuff him and walk him through the estate, bringing him straight to me.

Komodo is a legendary contracted killer in the underworld. He's who you call to get a job done and done right, a man with no conscience. You pay him enough and he'll take out anyone for you.

About fifteen minutes pass before Komodo is escorted into my office, surrounded by my men and cuffed. Vinny forces him down into a chair, and I give Vinny the okay to clear the rest of the men from the room.

"Start talking."

"First thing's first. I'll tell you what you'd like to know, and you get me out of the country."

"You need help getting out of the country?" His justifications seem dubious, considering he can usually hop from country to country undetected like a flea.

"Yes. Once I give you this information, the price for my head will double. So, I need your word first." So, he's done something to make the organization turn on him.

"And it's about Alessia Bonetti."

"Yes."

"Why didn't you go to the Bonetti's with this information? Why me?" I casually lean back in my chair and study him.

"That I would like to keep to myself if you don't mind."

I wait for a minute to reply. "Tell me what you know, and I'll let you know if I do mind or not."

"You'll help me out of the country."

"Yes." There's no reason not to help him even if the information he gives me isn't as valuable because he's a well-respected and venerable marksman. Though, if it involves Alessia, it's priceless.

"Do you know what your ex-fiancée has been up to these past few years?" I don't answer because I don't. If I kept an eye on her, I'd break down and go to her, or I'd hunt down every man she involved herself with. "I figured, and her family obviously doesn't either because I don't see how they would let her, considering you all made the effort of removing her from danger."

"Stop prattling. Just spit it out."

He ignores my curt tone. "Just a few months after you guys banished her." I don't correct him because it isn't essential. "She contacted me." I swallow hard, afraid of where this might be going. "She wanted a job." My fists clench. "After I checked into her new alias to ensure your tech guys did their job correctly, I didn't have a reason to tell her no. Plus, you don't tell Alessia Bonetti no," he muses, but I'm not in the mood. "Anyways, I got her an interview, and she was in."

"And that's what you came to tell me? That she's a contract killer?"

"Not exactly. She's a big girl, so who am I to blab? No, I came to tell you that the people I worked for found out who she really is. I'm not sure how, but they know, and there's now a hit on her."

I jump up to my feet and roar, "*Che cazzo!*" *What the fuck*! "You wasted this whole time rambling when there's a fucking hit on her head?!"

He's awfully calm for a man who is about to fucking die. "There's time. I was the one contracted for the kill, which obviously I'm not carrying out, but once they realize that, they'll go to the next contact and put me on the chopping block for refusing the job. So, you see my dilemma here?"

I do. Refusing to kill her, he's putting a hit on his own head. He'll lose most of the connections he would typically use to get in and out of countries, so he needs some outside help, hence why he came to me.

"How much time do we have?"

"Enough to get there before someone else does. Even if someone does beat you to it, it'll take a lot of time getting past all her own security she has put up around her property." He smirks, obviously amused by something about that.

"Why haven't you told her?"

"It wouldn't be safe to do so."

"You're saying if I call her to warn her, I'm endangering her."

"Yes. I'm not positive, but it's not worth the risk."

"She needs some kind of heads up."

"I'd say it would be safe to call her once you're close."

"*Cazzo*," I spit. "Ready the plane. Get a team together," I bark orders out to Vinny, and he swiftly leaves my office. "What I don't understand, though, is why you didn't carry out the hit."

"If I killed Alessia Bonetti, I would have at least three prominent families who wouldn't stop looking for me. Especially you now allied with the Abramovs." He's right about that. And how the fuck does he know about the Abramovs? That'll have to wait till later. Right now, the exigent dilemma is getting to Alessia in time.

"I'll get you out of the country. *After* I get Alessia home safely."

And after I spank her ass black and blue for her senseless temerity.

CHAPTER THIRTY-NINE

Alessia

I'm rolling my body with my hands in my hair as the music flows through me.

The adrenaline from earlier only rolled into more energy, and I needed a night out to release the steam. Otherwise, I would've spent the entire night feeling trapped and jittery. Also, very alone.

I've been fending off male after male since I decided to take myself for a spin on the dancefloor. It isn't time to pick out my victim to lure back to my place tonight yet. I only just got here.

"Hey, baby!" Someone comes up behind me and breathes their hot breath down my neck. His groin touches my ass, and it may not have been the crudest grope I've endured tonight, but it was uninvited, and I've had just about enough of it.

Just walk away, Alessia. Walk away.

I plan on doing just that, but as soon as I take a step forward, his hands grab at my hips to pull me back. "Where you going, sweetness?"

I grit my teeth so fucking hard my jaw groans under the pressure. I fist my hands trying to quell the trembling in them.

"Just one dance, baby." His puny erection rubs against my ass, and it's more than I can take.

My actions are out of my control as I spin around with a toothy grin, facing the guy with a death wish. He returns my smile, utterly ignorant of the danger. "You want to dance?"

He nods his head with enthusiasm, licking his lips as he violates me with his eyes. When his perverted gaze reaches my face again, he must sense something disturbing in it because his expression drops simultaneously with his hands. But it's too late.

I have no recollection of taking my shoe off, but it's in my hand one second, and then the next, the heel of my stiletto is piercing through his left eye socket. Blood instantly bursts from him, and he goes down, howling like a baby. His entourage I was oblivious to jump back, but keep close with concern. Though they avoid me with caution.

I grimace with a girlish gasp, adding a hand over my mouth for theatrics. "Whoopsies." I step over the writhing punk, planting my feet on either side of his torso. "Aw, what's wrong, baby? I thought you wanted to dance," I say with a pouty tone, but I can't wipe the gleeful look off my face.

"You bitch!" he cries out, holding his damaged eye with bold hands. "You got my fucking eye!" he screams with blood dripping into his mouth and staining his teeth.

My head cants to one side in amusement as music and lights continue to blare around us. The rest of the patrons are too far gone in alcohol and desire to pay us any attention.

"You fucking bitch!" Spittle comes flying out as he rolls around on the floor.

I take a seat on top of him, plopping down with unnecessary force and pinning him down on his back. He grunts and groans. "No one touches me without a formal invitation," I coo, dragging my nails up and down his chest seductively.

"Goddamnit! My fucking eye! My eye is gone!" he cries over and over like a little bitch, and I don't appreciate being ignored.

Pulling out a knife, I lean down and hold the blade to his neck. Luckily, he still has one good eye and freezes under me when he catches the glare of the shiny metal. I grin and take a look at the rest of him. "Too bad. If you could've been a good boy and remained patient, we could've been going back to my place tonight."

He pants beneath me, giving me that look I know and love. The one that tells me I wield all the power.

"I guess we still could." I drag the dull side of my blade back and forth against his skin, toying with him. "You're actually really sexy like this," I purr. "All bloody and vulnerable."

"You're fucking crazy," he rushes out in a choked voice.

I stop. "I am." Leaning in all the way, I flatten my tongue against the side of his jaw, not completely tainted in his blood, and swipe it all the way up to his hairline. "Mmm," I moan. "You're tasty." I giggle and lean back some.

He's even more petrified as he gapes at me, his good eye unblinking. "Okay, you've had your fun," my new friend Kamea says, appearing out of nowhere with two grizzly men flanking her as always.

I give her a pouty lip. "But I was just getting started," I whine, causing her to smile and shake her head at me.

"Is anyone going to get this crazy bitch off me?!" One-eyed Willy shouts for anyone to listen. He tries to sit up, and I shove him back down without taking my eyes off Kamea.

"Come on," she says patiently, holding her hand out for me.

My shoulders slump as I look back down at Willy. "I'm sorry, baby." I play with the collar of his shirt. "Looks like this is where we say goodbye." I lean down, and he recoils from my proximity. "You should know," I rasp against his ear. "Chicks dig scars. And eye patches."

Planting a wet kiss on his cheek, I place my hand in Kamea's and let her pull me to my feet. There's a commotion behind me as one of her men handles the situation, and I let her drag me through the unaware patrons and back to her VIP section in the club.

"You really do not know how to lay low, do you?" she sasses as we take a seat on the suede couch.

I shrug a shoulder and pick up the drink sitting on the table in front of me. Not bothering to check who it belongs to. I know I have nothing to worry about here in this private section surrounded by security to protect little Princess Kamea. She's mafia royalty over here on the West Coast.

"You do need to cut that shit out though, Less." I eye her over my drink, and she rolls her eyes at me. "*Frida*," she corrects. "My dad can't have you drawing attention like that in here."

"He touched me," I grumble.

"So knee him in the face next time. A bloody nose can go unnoticed. But not when you take someone's eye out."

I look at her as she calmly waits for a response. "Okay." I sigh. "I'm sorry, Kam. I'm just a little tightly wound tonight."

"Any particular reason why?"

I stare at the crowd beneath us as they all dance to the music and with each other. *So carefree*...I'm reminded of times with Massimo, and it instantly sours my mood.

I finally shake my head. She doesn't know what I do now for a living. No one does. She'd be horrified if she did. She might come from a crime family like I do, but she did not grow up knowing that, nor has she embraced it like I have. She dresses edgy and has dark, exotic features, but she's a real sweetheart. She and I couldn't be more opposite.

I turn my attention back to her and find her staring off into space, her usual smile missing. "What about you?" She looks at me. "There's obviously something going on with you." I get up to sit back closer to her, so I don't have to shout over the loud music. "Spill."

"He's back," she says solemnly.

I frown. "Who?"

She stares back at me silently for a moment. "Anson."

"Oh." I pause. "What do you mean by back? Like back into town, or...?"

Her eyes dart around. "I can't really talk about it here. I'll fill you in later, though."

I nod my head in understanding. "So, have you seen him yet?"

She nods. "Yup."

"And?" I question. "What happened?"

"He fucking hates me." She leans forward to grab the bottle of liquor and pours two shots.

"Why?"

She hands me a shot, and we both take them. She slams her empty glass down on the table. "Because I ruined his life."

I join Kamea in drowning in alcohol to numb our pain, and dancing late into the middle of the night before calling the quits.

It's still dark outside when I wake up to the annoying chirping going off. I yawn and stretch before padding my way through the quietness of my home.

Hmm, perimeter breach. Probably just a coyote or deer or whatever else lives in these deserts. Grabbing my rifle propped up beside my back door, I pull up the surveillance on my tablet and check all the cameras out there. "Definitely not an animal," I mutter as I turn all the lights out and grab my night vision goggles. I'm in the middle of nowhere, and there'd be no other reason to stumble across my property unless it were intentional.

Whoever is moving in the dark out there comes to a stop. Probably realizes I know they're there and now waiting on me to make the first move. *Good luck, buddy*. I can wait all night long. I flinch a little when my phone starts going off, and I see it's a blocked number.

"If you're here to kill me, then at least stop pussyfooting around," I say plainly to who I assume whoever is trespassing.

"Alessia. Where are you?"

The feelings of longing and heartache are both short-lived but violent enough to throw me off kilter when I hear the sound of a much too familiar voice. It's quickly replaced by enmity. Ignoring the urgency in his voice, I tell him to go fuck himself and hang up. I can't waist time staring at my phone or entertaining these twisted thoughts. I need to focus on my current situation.

Peering through the night vision lenses, I see the trespasser still hasn't moved. My phone goes off again with the blocked number. "Look, I don't have time for your games right now—"

"Alessia, listen to me," he growls. "Where. Are. You?"

"None. Of. Your. Fucking—"

"Goddamnit. Are you at home?" he snaps.

Needing to end this call soon so I can focus, I answer him truthfully. "I'm at home. Why?"

"I need you to stay put. Get away from all the doors and windows. Do you have a panic room or bunker there?"

"Now, why would I need a panic room or bunker?" I sass. "I moved here to be safe, remember?"

"Stop fucking around, Alessia. I know what you do."

I roll my eyes. "Don't know what you're—"

"Hey, what's going on?" I turn around with the rifle raised. "Whoa." He raises his hands in surrender and backs up some.

"Who the fuck is that?" Massimo barks over the phone.

Shit, I forgot about the guy I brought home last night. *Oops*. "It's no one," I murmur, embarrassed for some reason.

"Kick his ass out. You have trouble coming your way."

"Who?" I ask, then address whatever his name is. "You need to leave."

"Why? What's going on? Maybe I can help."

"You can help by leaving, and not telling anyone you were ever here." It was stupid and impulsive of me to bring back one of Kamea's guard dogs. No one is supposed to know where I live. Especially not someone close to another crime family.

"But, I—"

"Go!" I shout, raising the gun higher.

"Yeah, no problem." He throws the rest of his clothes on and goes out the front door without another word.

"Alessia!" Massimo shouts over the phone, and I jerk my ear away from the phone.

"Okay, okay! Stop shouting. Just tell me what you know."

"Your employer put a hit out on you. They found out who you are."

"Fuck," I hiss.

"Yes, fuck."

When I hear an engine revving, I go to check out the front window, standing at an angle so that I can't be seen. Thankfully, my intruder allows my one-night stand to leave in one piece.

"How do you know all this?" I go back to my post at the back of the house.

"Komodo came to me."

"Komodo? Why?"

"He was hired to take you out."

"Then why the fuck did he come to *you*? Better yet, why didn't he carry out the hit on me?" An alarm sounds. "*Cazzo*," I hiss.

"What was that?"

Another side of the perimeter has been breached. Pulling up surveillance, I see that I've got some more company. "Huh. Sending more than one mercenary to take out little old me. I'm flattered."

"This isn't fucking funny."

"I'm not laughing." I sigh and put him on speaker so I can set the phone down.

"I'm about three miles out."

"What?" My eyes snap to my phone. "Why?" My voice pitches higher. "I don't need your help, Massimo. This is my land, and it's littered with shit that'll blow them to pieces before getting within a hundred yards of my house. And so far, it's just two pussies who've yet to make a move."

"It's more than two pussies, Alessia."

"How do you know?" I say defensively.

"I have drones circling over. You have a small army coming your way."

"I've taken down a small army before and was less prepared for it."

"Well, you're getting my help whether you like it or not."

"Whatever." I disconnect the call and toss it aside bitterly. Why the hell am I sitting here waiting on them? I know why they're here, and I won't let them even think they can take me out.

"That's right motherfuckers. I'm Alessia Bonetti, and you *pompinaras* are trespassing, and you can literally *mangia merde e morte.*" *Eat shit and die.*

Lining up my shot at the corner of the closed window, I pull the bolt back and then slide it back forward, locking it down. *God, I love that sound.* I pull the trigger, and the glass shatters around a perfect hole. I watch through the night vision scope as the man goes down. I snort as I reload. "Sorry, Charlie," I mutter and pull up the surveillance again as I move through the house.

This other guy is on the move, and I watch him in excitement as he nears a landmine. I grin when he steps directly on it, and he's blown to pieces. The little enjoyment doesn't last long, though.

Damnit, here comes the firing squad.

One by one, my property is surrounded by men on foot. All prudent to keep their distance since they're now aware of the landmines. Little do they know I apparently have backup coming, but it doesn't matter anyway. I have the advantage of knowing each and every one of their locations, but they can't see me. I can do this all night with all the toys I've been collecting.

I don't need Massimo's help. I didn't back then, and I damn sure do not now.

Alright, eeny meeny miny moe. I'll start with the one closest to the front of my house. Going into the living room now on my hands and knees, I skip the reload and switch my Remington out for my Dragunov, and begin to unload. Right away, they all start firing back blindly. Bullets come from every angle, hoping they'll randomly get me.

I begin picking them off one at a time, varying my positions to prevent them from pinpointing me. As long as my location remains unknown, they won't coordinate their fire in one direction.

"Whoa!" I drop to the floor and take cover when I realize one of these *stronzos* brought smokin' aces to the party as drywall and plaster explode from the wall behind me. "You *stronzos* are ruining my home!" I yell as I army-crawl to safety. I have a .50 cal too, but it's on the other side of the house in my arsenal. This would be an excellent time to use it too. When the hell else would I be able to use that thing?

I'm taking cover behind the metal coffee table I flipped over as holes are being blown through my walls behind me, and shots are being fired from every window in my house. *Okay, so I might need backup.* They clearly aren't going to try and approach the house. They're just going to pepper it until there's nothing left.

Bright headlights shine through the front of my house, and the gunshots double in sound. I whip off my goggles and take a deep breath in part relief and part anxiety. My nightmare in shining armor has arrived.

Fuck, I hope they brought the big guns too. Just as that thought enters my head, I hear a heavy machine gun begin to go off.

"Oooohhhhh." My mouth falls open in awe. "Fucking sweet."

The shots being fired into my home begin to die off as they're now directed at the cavalry, and I get back in the game. We pick them off quickly together, and I see that they sent more than a small army to take me out. *What the fuck?* I'm aware of my reputation for being crazy, but if it weren't for Massimo coming, I would have been taken out with the small army that first started coming for me. Let's be honest. Maybe they also got tipped off and knew Massimo De Luca was coming.

Finally, the shots come to a stop, and I stand up with ringing ears and adrenaline coursing through my veins like fire. *Wow. What a rush.* I look around my house at all the damage done, and there isn't an untouched surface. Everything is in ruins. "Damnit," I groan and drop my head back. I really liked the little home I made here.

"Alessia!" Massimo bellows out, and it's like I've been thrown back in time. "Alessia!"

"I'm alright!" I shout back. "You can go now," I mutter to myself.

The door splinters open, and there stands Massimo in the doorway, bathed in the headlights' glow.

The devil himself has come to my rescue.

Chapter Thirty-Nine

Alessia

His wild gaze scans me from head to toe.

When he reaches out to touch me, I recoil. "I'm fine. Not even one shot got me," I say monotonously and avoid looking at his handsome face. God, why does he have to be so handsome? And his hair is longer, all the way to his chin, with the brown waves tucked behind his ears. And did he get his hands tatted?

His fists clench at his sides, turning them white and red. "How could you be so *stupid*?" he spits in outrage, triggering my own.

"I am none of your concern, Massimo," I snap and turn away from him to do who knows what? Clean? Pack up anything that survived and leave?

"You'll always be a concern of mine. Get whatever you want if there's anything left. You're coming with me."

"No, I'm not," I say, picking up the broken picture frame of myself with the other banished Bonettis. The only family I have left. I'd be a liar if I said I didn't miss my brothers and the rest of my family. My heart hurts thinking about how much time I've missed with my nephew.

"You are," he says firmly, tearing me from my thoughts. "You know damn well I'll make you if I have to."

I spin around and point my rifle at the man I once loved with all my heart. "I'm not going anywhere with you," I hiss venomously. "Thank you for the heads up and coming to my aid, but I can take it from here. Now, kindly get off my property."

"You wouldn't shoot me," he foolishly taunts.

I cock my head to one side. "You don't think so?" I cock back the bolt and slide it back forward, locking it. I might not kill him, but I *will* shoot him.

He steps forward some. "Do it then."

I can totally shoot him. Why not? I know where to hit without killing him. He believes he still wields power and control over me. I'll have to demonstrate how far I have outgrown his significance. The only reason why I don't kill him is because his men will rush in here and shoot me dead on sight. But not if I just injure him...

Taking a breath, I place my finger on the trigger. Just as I'm about to pull it to graze his arm, a shot goes off from somewhere behind me and hits me on the back of my shoulder. My eyes widen as I gape at Massimo in shock. "You shot me?" Then the world tilts just before everything goes black.

"Ugh," I groan as I begin to come to. "What the...?" My limbs feel leaden as I gradually pry my eyes open, squinting against the harsh light. I try to rub at them and realize I'm unable to. I yank on the cuffs that are restraining me to a chair. Or a seat more like it. I'm on a plane, cuffed to one of the seats in an upright position. That's why my fucking neck is killing me.

"Couldn't have at least given me a neck pillow?" I say dryly as Massimo stands in my peripheral.

"I wasn't trying to make you comfortable."

"Yeah, no shit." I look up at him, seemingly unfazed. "What's up with the cuffs? We're in the air. Do you think I'm going to crash the plane with me on it?"

"Wouldn't put it past you."

I look away and lean my head back. "Can I have some water? Maybe let me take a piss?"

He leans over to uncuff me without reservation, and I hold my breath, fearful his scent might compromise my resolve. "Come on."

Surprisingly, he let me go to the bathroom alone, giving me privacy. I wash up a little, and he's waiting outside the door when I come out. Silently, I follow him back to the seat, and he goes to cuff me again. "Seriously, Massimo." I hold my arms to my chest. "I'm not going to try anything. Where would I go?"

His eyes narrow on me for a moment. Then he snaps the cuff around one wrist and rises back to his full height. "I'll get you some food and water."

"Oh, what a great host you are." I give him a cloying smile to add to my sarcasm. He doesn't react as he turns and leaves.

When he comes back several moments later with a sandwich and a bottle of water, he hands them to me and sits beside me. *Because this won't be awkward at all.*

"I assume Tullio and the rest of the Bonetti brigade will be waiting for me with the welcome wagon?" I ask as I uncap the bottle of water to chug it.

"He doesn't know anything yet."

My head whips around to face him. "What do you mean?"

"I haven't told him," he says coolly, giving me his profile and a moment to admire his robust features.

"Why?"

"Didn't have time to."

"But you're taking me to him, right?"

He doesn't answer right away. "I'm taking you home."

"Whose home?"

"Ours."

I scoff and shake my head as I look away. My appetite completely gone. "And I'm the crazy one," I say in disbelief. What the hell is he actually thinking? "I'm not going home with you. If you really think I am, then you certainly are dense."

"I'm dense?" he blanches and finally looks at me. "You thought you could go all *Kill Bill* and become a fucking assassin."

I bite back a giggle, and it only enrages him even more. "I'm sorry. It's just kind of funny hearing you make any movie reference."

"You still think this is all a joke. That you almost died back, there is a fucking joke. We sent you away to keep you safe, and you put yourself in even more danger by becoming a professional killer. How could you be so arrogant and reckless?"

"I prefer audacious," I say smugly, and his face somehow darkens even more.

"Alessia, I swear—"

"Judge me all you want, Massimo, but it wasn't my choice to be sent away. It's *my* fucking life, and I'll do with it as I please. If you ever knew me, you would've known I wasn't going to just settle down in the suburbs and meet a nice guy, get married, and have a normal life. I never wanted that, and I never will. Go ahead. Try and ship me off somewhere else. I'll just find myself another thrill there as well." We both sit there seething, our nostrils flaring in detest. "I'm not going home with you. If you try, I'll do my damnedest to escape and make it so you *never* find me again." Each word is more spiteful than the last, leaving my lips.

"Thanks for the warning, *gattina*."

"Do not call me that," I growl, and he finds amusement in it as his lips twitch. Giving me a small taste of my own medicine.

He invades my space, and I don't dare move an inch. Standing my ground proudly. "I'll call you whatever I want, *gattina*. Especially *mine*," he rasps in my face, and it takes every ounce of strength not to be affected.

"I'll never be yours again. Just so you can toss me to the curb for the second time? No fucking thank you. Fool me once, and you're dead to me."

He chuckles and leans back in his seat, allowing me to fill my lungs with air. "*Siamo fatti l'uno all'altra, amore mio.*" *We're made for each other, my love.* He lightly trails a finger down my forearm, then back up again. I keep still as my skin breaks out in little bumps. "I made the mistake of sending you away, and I won't make the same mistake twice. So, get used to it, Alessia, because I am *never* letting you go."

It's me who invades his space this time. "In your twisted ass dreams, *cornuto*," *cuckhold*, I whisper against his lips, then flick my tongue out to swipe from his lips to his forehead before falling back into my seat and facing forward.

His eyes remain on me. "Eat your sandwich." He stands up. "We'll be home soon."

I take three bites of the sandwich and then toss it in the seat next to me. I'm not hungry, and I'm not going to be his obedient prisoner. I'd rather be Tullio's. I'll have to find a way of contacting him. Once he learns of the attack on me and Massimo's intervention, he'll undoubtedly come to confront the De Lucas, insisting on seeing me. I'll beg him to take me home with him, and unless Massimo is willing to jeopardize his alliance with his new best buddy, he'll have no choice but to let me go.

CHAPTER FORTY

Massimo

C ornuto.

I didn't let her get a reaction from me, but I was burning inside to wring her little neck and fuck her silly.

Tullio will likely be displeased to find out about my independent actions and the delayed notification. But dealing with Alessia takes precedence. She faces severe punishment.

Right now, though, I can't even look at her. I had to jump inside a separate vehicle from the airstrip to go home. I cannot stand her dry tone and bitter remarks as if none of this holds any weight. Her stupidity and immaturity and lack of self-preservation...

"Oh, shit!" my guy behind the wheel shouts and slams on the brakes as we all brace ourselves.

My head whips around to the vehicle Alessia is in behind us, watching it roll. My heart plummets, and I'm already out the door before we're even safely on the side of the road. I run towards their vehicle as it does one more roll and comes to a stop on its side.

"Alessia!" I slide down the slight decline in the grass. Vinny kicks out the windshield and starts crawling out with blood coming from his head. I ignore him to climb up on the car.

"She fucking attacked Bruno," Vinny groans.

"Fucking—" I growl and punch out the broken glass of the side window so I can peer inside. If she isn't dead, I'll fucking kill her. The little psychopath. My hands around her slender neck are getting more and more enticing. Choking her until she passes out, only to let her wake up to do it again. "Alessia!"

"Shit." I hear her whine and see movement under the limp body of one of the guys riding with her. "I didn't exactly think that through," she utters under labored breath.

"Can you move?"

"I think so. Hold on." I see her push the guy off her and then put her fingers to his neck, checking for a pulse. "Got a live one!" She has the audacity to try and lighten the mood with humor.

Shaking with rigorous rage, I lean my upper body over the edge of the broken window and reach down for her. She hisses when she gets up to her knees and goes to reach her arms up but quickly snaps them back down with a look of pain on her face.

"What's wrong?"

"My ribs are definitely broken, and possibly my arm too." She moans in pain and falls to her butt.

"Well, suck it up and give me your fucking hand," I snarl, patience long gone.

"Oh, let me just hop to it," she sasses. "Give me a fucking second." She gets up on her knees again. "Can you at least throw the key down so I can uncuff myself? It'll make this a hell of a lot easier."

"Should've fucking thought about that before you decided to try and kill yourself."

She glowers up at me in response and is quick to realize I'm not fucking around. So, she ungracefully gets up to her feet and lifts her elbows so I can scoop her up from under her arms. When I begin to lift her, she chomps down on her bottom lip and whimpers some.

"Is everyone else okay?" she murmurs as I cradle her and begin making our way to the vehicle still in one piece and right-side up.

"Like you fucking care?"

"Just asking," she mutters, refusing to look at me.

She doesn't deserve a fucking answer, so I don't give her one. Let her sit and wonder. Even though I'm infuriated and want to fucking kill her, I'm gentle with her as I place her into the car.

Vinny didn't look good when I passed him, but he'll have to stay back to clean up his fucking mess because it's he who let it happen. He knew to keep a close eye on her.

As soon as I'm settled in next to her, we're on the move, and I call the doctor to demand he meet us there as I tune out Alessia's ragged breathing. As soon as I hang up, I uncuff her wrists. She's not going anywhere for a while.

Pulling up to a stop in front of the estate, I gently cradle her in my arms again, and she has the nerve to fucking chuckle. "This totally backfired on me."

An avalanche of words tumbles from my mouth, their content lost to me in the heat of the moment. I have never been so angry in all my life and never thought I could be so angry at *her*. I thought I could lock her inside my bedroom, removing anything and everything that could be used as a weapon, but her complacency has pushed me beyond my endurance. She wants to act like an insolent ingrate, then I'll deal with her the same way I would a prisoner, until she's begging for me to restrain her to my bed instead.

"Wait, where are we going?" I don't answer. "You're not really going to keep me down here," she says as I descend the basement stairs. Her voice is hoarse, and she's obviously in a lot of pain since she's not struggling against my hold.

"Until you come to your senses."

"And by senses?"

"I mean, until you're ready to behave." Meaning begging and pleading because that's what it'll take for me to let her out.

"Then I guess this is home sweet home for me."

One of the things I love most about her is her ferocity, but does she have to be so fucking bullheaded? I can't tell if her lack of fear of death comes from courage or a belief she's untouchable.

After the doctor's assessment, I help her change into some clean clothes. Broken ribs, a broken arm, and a shit ton of knots, bruises, and cuts up and down her body. But she'll live. Doc gave her some pain pills, and as soon as I got her settled into her tiny cot, she passed out without any more of her caustic sass. The woman's tongue is the most wicked thing I've ever had to tolerate. But I do because she's still mine. My love for her remains in every bone and blood cell in my body, no matter how tempted I am to kill her.

"How is she?" Komodo's voice rings out when I close the door to Alessia's cell and slide the lock into place.

Heading over to his cell, I crank the latch and open it. Gesturing with my arm, he walks out. "She's home, and other than the consequences of her actions, she's safe. I'll help you get out of the country."

Some in my position may want to tie up loose ends, but Komodo, although not entirely ethical, is straightforward and reputable. Completing every job with discretion and immediate precision. He's still useful.

He claimed that if he had taken the hit on Alessia's head, it would've caused him more grief than to disobey The Organization. I call bullshit. I know I am not an enemy you want, nor are the Bonetti's, but everyone knows there is no going against The Organization. Whatever his ulterior motive may be, I couldn't give two fucks, because Alessia is alive and now home.

So, I sit and have a drink with the man. "You do understand that they will not just forget about her."

I nod as I stare at the condensation forming on the glass in my hand. Even though they failed to eliminate Alessia, and she has returned to De Luca territory, they won't cease their efforts to send more for her.

"I would offer to stick around to assist in any way, but I'm afraid they'll sis their enforcer on me." That catches my attention. "They'll send whatever other mercenaries they can muster up to come at you guys, which I know you can handle, but you won't be able to shake their ultimate weapon."

"And you can?" I arch an eyebrow.

"I've been studying her for years now. It's best to know your competition well."

"Her?" He nods once, and I cast him an appreciative glance. So, Russia's most infamous assassin is a female. I snort when Alessia immediately comes to mind.

After we finished our drinks, I sent him on his way with what I could give him. Then out of respect, I plan to meet with Tullio in person to update him on the latest with his lovely sister.

We've been on great terms for the last few years, and I'd like to keep it that way. We'll once and for all become family in the very near future.

"Massimo. How are you?" Tullio says as I take a seat in his office the next day.

"I've been better." More so now. "I'm here to let you know that I have Alessia."

"Excuse me?" He leans forward with a deep frown on his face.

"Do you know what your sister has been up to over the years?"

He sighs and rubs at his eyes, looking aged and overworked. "I have a feeling I won't like it," he mutters.

I recap on the last two and a half days, from Komodo's impromptu visit to Alessia's new profession to the attack on her and to the part where she almost killed herself in the car accident.

"How the fuck didn't we know what she was doing?" he spits as he paces on his feet. Then he comes to a stop facing me. "And why the fuck am I just finding out? You needed to fucking tell me as soon as you knew!"

I keep my cool. "There wasn't time, Tullio."

"*Cazzata*! A phone call would have sufficed!"

"My mind was a little preoccupied." I couldn't focus on anything else but getting to her in time.

"Where is she now?"

"Home."

"*This* is her home. I want her here."

"No," I don't skip even a fraction of a beat. "She's perfectly safe with me."

"She's my fucking sister, De Luca. She isn't yours anymore. You gave her up, remember?"

Exhaling, I stand to my feet and button my suit jacket. "And you did too." If I don't extricate myself from this office soon, I will lose all self-restraint and elicit every bit of resentment I've had towards him since he talked me out of going after her as soon as we let her go. "We were wrong sending her away the way we did. Because of that, she almost got herself killed." She did try to warn us all, as did Santino.

"I want to see her," he says more calmly, giving in and consigning his sister over to me.

"Sure. Come by tomorrow."

"No, I want to see her now."

"She's resting. Tomorrow will be better."

"De Luca," he growls. "I need to see for myself that my sister is safe."

"I think you should be worried about the safety of your mother and the others first. They could be planning to get to her through them."

His eyes widen slightly as if the thought hadn't even occurred to him yet. "*Cazzo*."

"Let me know if there's anything I can do. Otherwise, I'll see you tomorrow." I excuse myself and head back home.

I have a scorned woman I need to tend to.

CHAPTER FORTY-ONE

Alessia

"**G**et the fuck off me," I sneer at the two goons escorting me back into my cozy cell. I was allowed to bathe in an actual shower today after who knows how many days. Supervised by a surly Massimo.

He didn't say a single word the entire time. He showed up with his goons, they escorted me up to the first level to a random bedroom with a bathroom, and Massimo closed us inside. He silently gestured for me to shower as he stood outside of it.

I spin around in a fury, expecting the door to be slammed shut in my face when I almost crush my nose against Massimo's chest. I jump back as if he's on fire, unable to bear the proximity. Not a single muscle on him flinches.

His face is still in that permanent glower, and I roll my eyes. "What?" I bite out bitterly and go to lie down on my cot. My ribs and arm are throbbing from moving them around so much to shower and change.

I stare up at the ceiling in agitation as he remains stoic near the door. "Say whatever it is you want to say, De Luca. I'm tired." The silence is suffocating. Huffing, I turn my head to look at him. His fists are red as they pulsate at his sides. I glare back at him and can see the rage burgeoning. I know he wants to choke the life out of me, and the thought has me squeezing my thighs together and gulping.

I realize what he's here for and what I am in for. He gave me a few days, probably for his sake, not mine. In fear he might actually kill me.

My chest begins rising and falling with shallow breaths, and his expands with his own labored breathing. The tension boiling. The air too thick to breathe comfortably.

He puts one foot in front of the other with determined steps, and I'm paralyzed. I refuse to show fear when he abruptly pauses only a few feet away from me. Our eyes remain welded, and I swear my heartbeat can be heard as it pounds.

"Get up," he coldly demands.

My nostrils flare. "Fuck off."

His joints creak as his fists coil, and they begin to tremor, seconds away from snapping. I'm now shaking, no matter how hard I fight it.

"Up. On. Your. Feet."

"No."

My eyes pop when he roughly grips the upper arm of my unbroken one, and I scramble to get my feet under me as he hoists me upwards. My ribs scream as our noses touch, and his grip constricts. He might actually break my other arm.

"This is how it's going to go, Alessia. You are going to do exactly as I say from here on out, you feel me?" His voice is unlike anything I've ever heard. It sounds more animal-like than human.

"What the fuck makes you think I'll do that?"

"Because you will remain down here until you do."

"Then so be it." I remain defiant as I stare back at him.

An eternity passes before he finally cracks. I screech when I'm spun around and slammed against the cement wall. My face slams into it making me see stars and I scream through my teeth out of pain from my broken ribs being crushed under the weight of his body pinning me there.

"Why do you have to be so fucking infuriating?" His lips move against my ear as we both pant in rage.

"I didn't ask you to bring me here!"

"Well, too fucking bad. You're here now, and still alive thanks to me. And let me tell you right now, Alessia. You are never leaving. If you ever make it outside of this cell, you'll be lucky if I ever let you out of my sight for even a fucking second. You are mine, and you will accept it."

I chuckle. "You are out of your goddamn mind if you think I will *ever* accept you again."

His body goes completely still and I'm pretty sure my heart just stopped beating. His silence is always most threatening. As if the calm before the storm.

I'm flipped back around and grit my teeth when my back is shoved against the wall. "I have broken ribs, you asshole," I spit through my teeth.

He's right back in my face with his. "And I am so tempted to break more." He's absolutely unhinged, I believe him.

I narrow my eyes at him. "Do it."

He takes a ragged breath in and then slowly lets it back out. It does nothing to quell his temper. He slams his fist on the wall over my head and I can't help my body's natural reflexes when I flinch. His eyes light up in demonic delight, and he does it again. This time closer to my head. This is what he wanted from me. To see me in fear.

Fuck that.

I roll my shoulders back and grapple with my rebellion. My eyes bore into his darkened ones, daring him to hurt me like I know he wants to.

His mouth collides with mine, so belligerently our teeth clash and I have no choice but to oblige. I want to bite him, refuse him, but I'm physically unable to as he eats me alive with his lips, teeth, and tongue. He kisses me viciously and uses his weight to adhere me to the wall, immobilizing me.

He gnarls and rips the oversized t-shirt of his I'm wearing down the middle and hoists me up, forcing my legs over his hips. Ignoring my whimpers from the pain it causes me, he fumbles with one hand between us all the while still brutalizing my mouth with his.

There's no attempt to tear my panties off. He shoves them to the side and pillages me with maddening force. I dig my nails into his shoulders over the fabric of his shirt and whimper, but he doesn't let up at all. Not with his kiss or his violent thrusts.

There's agonizing pain in my ribs, but the pleasure in my pussy balances it out to a beautiful harmony. I'm beginning to forget why I would deny this. Why should I deny myself this overdue pleasure?

I gasp in his mouth when the pain becomes unbearable, and I pound on his shoulders. He rips his mouth from mine, gasping for air, but his hips do not stop. "My ribs," I say through short breaths. "Massimo." He doesn't respond or stop and I bite down on my trembling bottom lip. I try pushing at him with my good arm and he starts rutting me harder. Growling, I use my head to clobber him.

With our faces so close, I wasn't able to aim correctly, and I ended up headbutting him right in his nose. He finally pauses and I'm frozen in fear. I watch as blood drips from his nose and I'm too terrified to look him in the eye.

His chest rumbles with an animalistic sound and I'm airborne for only second before I'm slammed onto the cot. "You just don't get it, do you?" he seethes.

"You were hurting me, you fucking asshole!" I start struggling against him, twisting my body and pushing at his chest.

Nothing fazes him, even when I hit him in the face and claw at his neck. He hovers over me, wedged between my thighs. "Get off of me!" I shriek. "Get the fuck off me!"

His long fingers wrap around my neck, his arm locks to hold me down, and his other hand grips his cock to guide it back into me. I tear at his hand and arm and gnash my teeth at him. "Massimo! I'm going to fucking kill you!"

His hips ram forward and I lose a little bit of my fight. Partly from sexual gratification and partly from lack of oxygen as his hand tightens around my throat. My head spins and spots begin dancing in my eyes. "Ma—" I try to speak but it's near impossible. I use my casted arm to swing at him and I catch him on the chin.

He stills over me and violently jerks me up to a sitting position by my neck, crashing our noses together. "Stop. Hitting. Me." Spittle hits my face.

I bare my teeth back at him. "Fuck. You." My eyes widen and I take a sharp breath of air when his fingertips stab at my broken ribs. They hurt so fucking bad I want to cry, but I refuse to. Hardening my face I chomp down on whatever I can. It happens to be his cheek.

He ferociously growls, slamming me back down by my neck and begins fucking me again. Instead of fighting him off, I wrap my legs tightly around his waist and smirk up at him in provocation.

I didn't think he could fuck me any harder than he has before, but he does. With his hand around my neck, anchoring me down, his hips piston forward with cruelty. He succeeds at hurting me, but he's unsuccessful at punishing me because it still feels so fucking good.

No matter how willful I can be, the orgasm wreaks havoc through me. My mouth falls open on a raspy scream. He grunts and growls through bared teeth until his hips come to a halt. My inner muscles contract and throb, sapping him.

The afterglow is already clearing, and the pain diminishes any pleasure that I just experienced. I know Massimo can see it all over my face, but he remains unconcerned. His dead gaze is unwavering as he climbs off me and tucks his cock away unabashedly. His mask almost slips as I grit against the pain, holding my ribs involuntarily.

Without spitting any more threats or hateful words, he exits my cell, slamming the door and locking it behind him.

CHAPTER FORTY-TWO

Massimo

Three weeks, Alessia has been in the confines of her cell.

Her arm is still in a cast, and her ribs are still healing, but I still hold no remorse for how rough I was with her the last time I paid a visit. Especially how she's made every effort to escape any chance she gets as soon as she began feeling better, she's craftier than I could have ever imagined. Must've learned quite a few tricks when she was being hired for *murder*.

"Oh, hello, my love," she chirps as I approach her door. "I was beginning to think I'd never see you again." She's lounging on her cot in only a bra and panties as she tosses a roll of socks up in the air and catches it over and over again like a ball. "Come to revel?"

"Came to see if you're ready to rejoin society."

She leans up on her elbows, her supple breasts perky and an evil smirk on her lips. "Not a chance, De Luca. But nothing is stopping you from coming in here to play again." She rubs her thighs together seductively. It's tempting.

I tear my eyes away from her legs and look at her face. "If I come in there, it won't be playing."

She holds my gaze with her own. "Then come on in, and let's...not play." Her hand snakes down her flat stomach and rubs over her tempting cunt.

"Don't tease me, *gattina*. I'm already restraining myself so that I don't wring your pretty neck. If I come in there to remind you who you belong to, we'll be locked in here for days."

The amusement drains from her face as she sits up all the way. Her seductive façade gone. "I'm not yours, De Luca. That was a hate-fuck, make no mistake."

My mouth twitches. "Whatever you say, *mia amata*." We have a standoff for an intense moment. "Would you like out of your little cage?"

"That depends." She stands up and stretches her arms above her head. My eyes make a leisurely path up and down the length of her body in reaction. "Are you just exchanging this cage for another one?"

"Yes."

"Then I think I'm okay where I'm at." She casually walks over to the sitting chair in there and sits down, crossing one leg over the other.

"So, the hard way it is," I mutter, and she glowers at me.

"You better not dart me again like some kind of wild animal." She clenches her teeth.

"Then you need to behave, *gattina*."

"I hate you," she hisses and stands back up. I can physically see her struggling with her own forbearance as she tries to decipher whether or not her pride should outweigh her comfort and dignity. "I'll *behave*."

"Good girl." I fight a smirk when her nostrils flare out of response. "Come on out."

CHAPTER FORTY-THREE

Alessia

"**Y**ou *bastardo*! Get these fucking cuffs off me right now!" I scream and thrash. "*Ti ammazo*, De Luca!" *I'll kill you.* I yank and pull on the cuff locked around my wrist as I screech and sling all kinds of profanity at the sorry bastard that put me here.

"You brought this upon yourself with your petulance. I was going to let you have free range of the bedroom, but you decided to be a brat instead." He hovers over me with his hands inside his pockets, all calm and relaxed on the surface.

"You can't keep me like this forever. Once I'm free, you're a dead man."

He sighs and shakes his head, then clucks his tongue. "Naughty *gattina*." He crouches down, his face level with mine now. "Do you know what happens to someone who threatens me? Huh?" He

247

pauses. "You have now threatened me several times, and I will not keep letting it go," I growl and yank on the cuffs. "I'll give you a moment to rest because you'll need it for what I have planned for you."

"Massimo," I sneer. "Let. Me. Go."

"Never." He stands up and straightens his jacket. "I'll be back in about an hour." He reaches towards me to touch my cheek and I turn my head to dodge it. "You'll pay for that too, *amore*," he says on a heavy sigh.

I hate him. I hate him so much. I hate all the feelings that instantly came back the second I heard his voice over the phone and the way my body absolutely aches for him. I miss him so fucking much and I know I can't deny him forever. It's only a matter of time before my body gives in ultimately and my heart won't be far behind it. It isn't fair.

I've killed people. A lot of people. And I didn't care what they did to deserve it. I was able to point a gun at a complete stranger and pull the trigger, taking their life. So, why can't I stop loving this cruel man who purposely broke my heart?

I lay there staring up at the ceiling for who knows how long. All I know is that it was light out when we came up here and now it's dark. I don't even know what day it is or if it's even the same month. I tried to keep track in my cell, but then it felt like it was only making it worse.

I was blessed with the privilege of being outside of my confines only to shower every couple of days, and every time I tried to run. Obviously, my attempts ended in spectacular failure. I know there's no getting out of here, but I won't stop trying, purely out of spite.

I anticipated Massimo bringing me to his room to keep a close eye on me. Then his bed came into view, and I panicked. Depressing thoughts of Massimo fucking other women in my absence had me backpedaling. I'm sure he figured it was my final attempt to fight him, but it was my heart weeping for what we once were and begging him not to mar those precious memories of mine.

I honestly thought that what we had was real and that everything he'd ever said to me was absolute. He fucking played me. He's nothing but a pompous canard with an alluring veneer that I will never trust again. If I let him anywhere near my heart, he'll squeeze the life out of it.

The door creaks open then clicks shut. I don't bother to look; I just know that it's him. When he comes to the side of the bed and looks down at me, I keep my eyes averted. "Would you like to join me for dinner, *bella*? Or would you like me to feed you?" I don't answer. He sighs and sits on the edge of the bed. "If you don't choose, I'll choose for you, and I think we both know which option I'll go with." If he thinks his nonsensical threats get to me anymore, he's fucking clueless.

"If I give in. If I behave. What then?" I state, my voice remaining uninterested. "What do you want with me, Massimo?" I turn to look at him.

Two creases appear between his dark brows. "I want *you*. I thought that was obvious."

"You want to toy with me."

"No, *amore mio*." He tucks some hair behind my ear.

"Then what?"

"I love you, Alessia. I never stopped."

My entire body feels like it might fall through the mattress and through the floor, and I have to swallow through the constriction in my throat. Blinking back the threatening tears, I divert my gaze to the ceiling. "Please, don't. I'll give in, I'll behave. Just don't say those things to me. I fell for them once, and it almost destroyed me when you took them back."

He once had me convinced that our love was interminable and unequivocal. Then he tarnished it when I learned the poignant truth. Love is not at all unconditional. There are always limits.

"I won't ever part from you again." His voice is soft and kind, yet concrete.

Shaking my head, I close my eyes and say, "Please don't. I can't take it. I'll go insane. Do whatever you want with me, just stop saying things like that."

"It's the truth."

The ceiling comes into view when I slowly blink my eyes open. "I don't believe you anymore, De Luca. Remember that fickle thing called trust?" I turn to him. "I have lost all trust and faith in you. Your words have lost all credibility. There isn't enough time in a lifetime to earn it back."

He stares at me, his jaw ticking underneath his dark facial hair. His hazel eyes unblinking. "Well, good thing I have all the time in the world to remedy that." He pulls his fist out of his pocket. Reaching up, I realize too late what he's doing as he uncurls my hand then slips the ring into place. "These last few years should have never happened, Alessia. We should've been married and having our first child by now." *Oh, you cold bastard.* My throat becomes painful trying to knot up my emotions. "We'll get back to where we were."

"You can't erase the last few years just because you wish they didn't happen. They did. I'm not even the same woman anymore. You might not even recognize me."

"Well, like I said." He uncuffs me from the bed and takes my wrist in his hands to tenderly rub it. "We have all the time in the world." Bringing my hand up to his mouth, he kisses the back of it then moves to kiss the bruising around my wrist.

"Can I have some privacy please?" I ask when he takes me to the bathroom to use the toilet. He turns his back to me but doesn't leave. "You're fucking kidding me, right?"

"You may seem docile now, but I'm not stupid, *amore*. Now, do what you need to do, so we can get some dinner."

"As in leave the estate?"

He chuckles. "What do you think?"

"So, you're really going to stand there and listen to me pee?" He doesn't answer. Grunting my disapproval, I drop my panties and pee. It was humiliating enough to have a toilet out in the open in my cell where anyone could come by to catch me sitting on the pot. Relieving myself in private will feel like such a privilege after this.

When I walk past him after I'm done, he's hot on my heels, expecting me to run or fight. I stop at the sink and pick up his toothbrush to use since there isn't another one for me. I shrug my shoulders at him in the mirror as I brush my teeth. He doesn't say anything as he stands there and waits.

Once I'm done, I leave the bathroom and take a seat in the sitting area. "Can I have some clothes to wear?"

He pauses just short of where I'm sitting, regarding me with condescension. Like I'm some inept peasant from whom he expects undue reverence. His eyes finally meander south, causing a heat wave. I strain to maintain a stoic façade. He's already eroding my resolve and wearing my resistance.

"I like you like this, *cara mia*."

Defiance seeps back in, but I keep the outburst at bay. Instead, I stand up and head to the closet. I almost trip over my own feet when something abruptly stops me. My clothes are already in here and neatly put away as if I never fucking left. *What kind of sick joke is this?* If this is his way of fucking with me, he's beyond cruel and cunning. I was planning on coming in here to throw on one of his t-shirts, but here they all are, deriding me, taunting me.

"*Bastardo*," I mutter as I grab a comfy shirt and soft shorts to throw on. As I spin around to exit the closet, I stop again and this time, so does my heart.

"Is this some kind of sick joke?" I'm shaking when I burst out of the closet with smoke coming out of my ears, holding the custom-made wedding gown of mine in one piece. He's standing in the same spot I left him, still so relaxed. I slam down the dress and stomp on it like a petulant child, and scream through my teeth. "I hate this dress! I hate this ring!" I pry it off and fling it at him. "And I hate you! You might be king of your castle, but you will never be anything above me! I let you play me before, and I will be damned if I let you do it again! You built me up only to tear me down! But you didn't fucking break me! You'll never break me! Ever!" I go flying at him, talons extended. Pounding my fists into him wherever I can get to. "You fucking piece of shit! You can't have me! I'd rather die than be yours again!" The fervid rage that has been building and coiling inside of me is now erupting. No longer able to harness or subdue it. "You fucking lying sack of shit! You're a fucking monster! I wish I never met you! I wish you would just—"

Between my hair covering my face in my fit of rage and the speed at which he moves, I'm suddenly pinned down to the mattress with my arms above my head and my legs pinned down with his weight. The position and the force he's using stabs at my still healing ribs and arm making me whimper in pain.

"You done?" he clips sharply, not raising his voice, though he's lucidly peeved.

"With you, yes. I've been done with you," I spit with my hair still in my face.

"You think that's supposed to discourage me? Even if I really thought you were done with me, it wouldn't matter. I'm not done with *you*. Not now, not *ever*. It's up to you when you decide to accept it."

"Never," I growl through my teeth.

"Now look who's full of shit, *gattina*."

My arm and ribs are killing me now. "You're hurting me, Massimo," I say in a softer voice. Setting my pride aside for the excruciating pain.

The severity of his look diminishes, and he eases up on me to provide slight relief. His hazel eyes hold mine with unvoiced sentiments, yet uncertainty holds his tongue.

To my surprise, he allows me to feed myself and shower alone. We don't speak at all unless he gives me orders, and I yield without argument. The fight in me is suppressed for the night.

Even when he locks the cuffs around the wrist to my unbroken arm, I turn on my side with my back to him, and I beg for sleep.

There's always tomorrow.

CHAPTER FORTY-FOUR

Alessia

This morning, I woke up alone and no longer restrained.

I stretched out my stiff limbs and noticed a glass of water on the side table, along with a folded piece of paper addressed to me.

Alessia,

You are one wrong move from making the cell your permanent residence. Do not think for a moment you are pardoned for everything you have pulled so far. I'm only allowing you more time to heal.

I'll be down in my office most of the day if you wish to speak to me.

Your brother is coming over for dinner tonight.

Remember. This is your last chance.

Behave.

Balling the note up, I toss it across the room. "Behave," I mutter and scoff. "*Stronzo.*"

No matter my evil plans for the day, I need to wash up first. When I head into the bathroom and grab for the toothbrush, I freeze. The damn ring I yet again threw at him is on my finger. Again! How the fuck did he slip it back on without waking me? I stare down at the colossal rock, then glance over at the toilet and then the trash can.

One wrong move from making the cell my permanent residence.

Not worth the risk. And though it's in my nature to be stubborn and irascible, I might need to play nice for a bit if I want out of here anytime soon.

Besides, it's just a ring. It doesn't mean anything if I don't let it. Just a big, gorgeous ring that I felt naked without for years. It means absolutely *nothing*.

Even though I took a shower last night, I need a minute before making any moves. I tie my hair up and sit on the bench with hot water running to bask in the steam. I need to switch up tactics. I can't physically fight my way out of this. I'd have to really build up some trust with them first. Find someone I can easily manipulate and use to get me out of here.

The only problem with conceding, even if only for a moment to gain his trust, is that I risk falling into his trap, forgetting what's real and what's not. I risk falling madly in love with him again and I cannot allow myself to do that. If he were to break my heart again, and he will, I know I could pick myself back up and move on, but who would I become?

After hurting me once, I turned to killing people for money to cope. Hurting me a second time when I have yet to heal from the first, how would I cope with it then? Become a terrorist or something?

He had taken my heart, then crushed it. Now, he threatens the entirety of my being, and I will not allow him to lay waste to it.

Feeling as if I have detoxed enough of the bitterness to function, I get out of the shower to get ready for the day. I head into the closet to stare at all the clothing, completely at a loss for what to wear.

Part of me wants to dress sexy to toy with Massimo some. Part of me wants to dress like my old self in a modest dress to mess with him more. But then there's a part of me that wants to show him that I am no longer the Alessia he knew. No longer the one who wears pretty dresses and an angelic smile, trying to disguise my demons.

Massimo wants to pretend like nothing ever happened, then let the games begin. Debutant it is.

When I open the bedroom door, I come to a halt. I knew there would be guards standing outside, but I didn't expect to see his cousin. "Monte."

He smiles and there's no sign of what Massimo had done to him. "Alessia." He closes the small gap and we kiss each other's cheeks. "How are you?"

"I've been better." I shrug. "So, he put you on babysitting duty again?"

He chuckles and rubs the back of his neck. "Yeah, seems like it."

"Well, I promise not to taunt him with you again. I'll pick on someone else." I waggle my eyebrows and he laughs.

"Please don't get anyone's face bashed in."

I glance at the other guy standing guard and don't recognize him, but he must've had a good talking to because he won't even look at me. "I'll try not to. But you know I can't promise you anything," I joke.

We turn and walk side by side. "It's been close to four years."

"It has. So, tell me what you've been up to."

"Well, other than the usual, I met someone."

"Oh? Tell me about her."

"Her name is Gia and we've been dating for about a year now."

"Gia what?" I ask casually.

"Nuh uh. I'm not giving you her last name so you can case her out."

Giggling, I stop at the top of the stairs. "Why not? I'm bored and I have a feeling I'll be under house arrest for the unforeseeable future." Until I can escape.

"You really think Massimo will give you access to the internet?"

I deflate. "True." We descend the steps. "Well, tell me about her then. Entertain me."

He tells me all about his girl next door Gia and how they met the old-fashioned way at the supermarket, and he thinks she's the one. She's clueless to what he does for a living and I'm sure it will be a major issue when she finds out. To the sound of it, a girl like her will never accept his lifestyle. A girl like her wants an ordinary man with a desk job or one who does something noble like construction. She'll eventually want a church wedding and a house in the suburbs with a white picket fence and several kids and a dog.

Even as a young girl, I never dreamt of a life like that. I always saw myself marrying someone in power and staying in the mafia, though, in that dream, I had power, too. Right now, I feel powerless. Nothing is like it was before with Massimo. He put me on a pedestal, only to pull the rug from underneath it.

Monte walks with me to Massimo's office, and I enter without knocking. "Hello, *caro*." I saunter in and notice Ezzo sitting in front of his desk.

Massimo doesn't respond right away as Ezzo stands up with a cheeky smirk to greet me. "So, good to see you, Alessia." He kisses both of my cheeks. "How are you feeling?" He glances down at my cast.

"Feeling good. How've you been?"

"Good." His smirk turns into a smile and goes to take his seat again.

Before addressing Massimo, I believe I owe someone an apology—a plethora of apologies, really. Turning around, I face Vinny, who is posted near the door. "Vinny, how are you?"

He remains stolid like a good little wooden soldier. "I'm alright."

"And your foot?" I chew on my bottom lip biting back a smile.

The corner of his mouth twitches. "It healed."

"I'm happy to hear."

He nods his head once, silently accepting my half-assed apology because that's as good as he'll get out of me.

Still holding back my smile, I nod my head then spin back around to find Massimo watching me. "Have you eaten yet?"

"Don't act like you're not keeping tabs on me." I can't help my sharp tongue. The thought of being under twenty-four-hour watch is utterly affronting.

Narrowing his eyes at me, he visibly takes a breath. "Sarita requested to see you."

"Is she here?"

"Somewhere."

"Then I shall go find her." I give him a cloying smile with my head tilted. "Unless you need me for anything, my love." I bat my eyelashes dramatically.

Not finding any amusement in my theatrics, he says, "Go ahead and find her. I'll find you later."

"Alrighty then. And don't you worry, my love. I'll *behave*. You boys have a wonderful day." I blow Massimo a kiss and leave as briskly as I arrived.

As soon as I'm out of his office with Monte again at my side, the smile drops from my face and I exhale. Frankly bored with the ongoing performances. Monte tries to hide a chuckle making me give him a look.

We find Sarita in one of the sitting rooms, sipping from a fancy teacup and reading a book. She literally looks like something out of an old English movie. Her light hair is perfectly styled into silky curls, and her dress is even more modest than mine, showing off the bottom half of her long and slender legs. Her head pops up, and she gives me a radiant smile, standing to her feet.

"Alessia." We kiss cheeks and she genuinely looks happy to see me which is quite endearing. We may not have been close when I lived here, but we were almost friends. "It's so good to see you. I cannot tell you how relieved I am to see you back here. Massimo was not at all himself while you were away."

While I was away? She makes it sound like I was on some sort of sabbatical or retreat. They tried to put a temporary spin on it, but I knew none of them ever planned on us coming back. I'm only here because I got myself into some trouble and Massimo decided to keep me as his little pet once again. No need to burden her with my drama though, so I don't correct her in any way.

"Come sit with me. Would you like some tea?"

I go and sit. "I could actually use a cup of coffee."

Monte says he'll be back with coffee for me and leaves us. Of course, I automatically think about using this opportunity to make a run for it, but I know I won't make it far. It's better I wait until I'm at one hundred percent.

"I, uh, asked my mother to join us. I hope that's alright with you." She drops her head slightly to one side as she studies me.

"Oh," I say a little surprised. "Sure, of course, that's alright. How is she?"

"Same as always." Her shoulder hitches briefly. "How is your mother? And your sister?"

"Last I heard they're good. They're home now too."

"That's a relief to hear. So...a hitman?" She shields her amusement with her teacup.

I return it with my own. "I prefer hit*woman*." I sigh. "It was fun while it lasted."

She giggles. "You really are a wild one. I wish I had more of your spirit."

"You do just fine without it." Monte comes in with a coffee for me and I thank him. "So, how's Vita?"

The engaging smile on her face slips, giving way to a confused expression. "Massimo didn't tell you?"

"Tell me what?"

"Vita's gone."

"What do you mean gone?"

"She packed up her stuff and left. About two years ago. Managed to completely disappear."

"What? Are you sure she wasn't taken?"

"Doesn't look like it," she says sadly.

"And you guys don't know where she is?"

Her eyebrows draw in as she shakes her head. "We're still looking, but wherever she is, she's definitely trying not to be found."

"Oh, shit. I'm so sorry."

Just as she opens her mouth to say something else, Celia enters the room. "Alessia," she says smiling and I stand up to properly greet her. "Let me look at you." She holds me by my shoulders to do a once over then frowns when she looks at my cast. "Oh, no, *piccolina*. What happened?" It's not surprising she's clueless about what's happening. She's usually oblivious to everything.

"Uh, got in a little accident." She gasps. "It was quite a few weeks ago. I'm okay now."

She joins us at the small table and pours herself a cup of tea. Her frail arms peek out of her what I like to call a moo-moo dress, and even though she applied makeup, you can see the wear on her from the depression she's struggled with for so many years. You would think being free of Angelo, she would've gotten a little better, but I guess it was too late.

The afternoon I spend with Sarita and Celia is quite pleasant. I can't hold anything against either of them because it isn't their fault Massimo is a douche bag. And it's a nice reprieve to put down the boxing gloves momentarily.

It was a pleasant way to distract myself from thinking about dinner with Tullio tonight. He came by to visit me once while I was behind bars in the basement. I thought he was there to rescue me, but after he saw that I was all in one piece, he decided to ream me out. He did so for so long I ended up passing out before he was done due to the pain killers I was on.

Now, I'm out of my cage that was located inside a bigger cage.

Time to mentally prepare for this.

CHAPTER FORTY-FIVE

Massimo

I observe with mild amusement as Alessia and Tullio go back and forth with their ongoing dispute.

Their hands flailing around, and my *gattina* red in the face from anger. He began laying into her as soon as they parted from their embrace.

Finally, they both take a breath. "Why don't we sit down to eat, huh?" I suggest, standing up.

They grunt their last words under their breath and take my lead into the other room to sit around the dining table. Alessia avoids looking at either of us, and Tullio's scathing look alternates between us. Leaving me guessing who will be the recipient of his next tirade.

He still harbors resentment towards me for the communication delay. So far, only Tullio has seen Alessia. Her other brothers were responsible for retrieving the remaining Bonetti women. I antic-ipated they would return to demand a meeting with Alessia, but according to Tullio, they are too enraged to face her.

So, she has yet to reunite with the rest of her family, and I know it hurts her. She can act tough all she wants, but I know her family still means everything despite all her begrudgery.

"I haven't told Mamma yet," Tullio mutters once the first course has been served.

"What *are* you going to tell her?" Alessia replies meekly for once, showing some guilt.

"I don't know yet. I should probably tell her the truth so you can get a scolding from her as well, but I don't want to hurt her." She scoffs. "What?" he snaps.

"Nothing." She thins her lips.

"No, no. Say what you have to say."

"I have nothing more to say to you."

"Why am I the bad guy here? You're the one who went out and fucked with the wrong people and almost got yourself killed."

"No." Her eyes are brimming with fire. "You did this! Assum-ing any of you could dictate my life, you sent me away, breaking my fucking heart!"

I've already endured her guilt trips several times. Not to men-tion I've been haunted by my own regrets ever since she left. Eating away at me and driving me mad. She wasn't the only one thirsting for blood out of resentment. So many have received the wrath of my longing, but I can't do anything about what has already been done. All I can do is focus on this day forward.

Tullio's demeanor softens as I remain silent. "We weren't try-ing to break your heart, Alessia. I swear, we were only trying to protect you while we took care of the Russians." She scoffs again and rolls her eyes as her arms fold in under her breasts. "It wasn't right the way we went about it." Alessia's attitude mellows, surprised by his candid admission of regret. "I'm so sorry for sending you away, *piccolina*. I'm not always going to make the right decisions, but from now on, I won't make them for you."

"You really mean that?" Her voice is gentle, and I envy the way she's quickly giving into her brother. Possibly even forgiving him.

"I do."

"Then can I come home now?"

"No," I answer for him, and she snaps her head in my direction. "You *are* home, *cara mia*." I sip my glass of whiskey.

She looks back at her brother. "Tullio?"

Scratching the back of his head, he sighs. "I think you should stay here for the time being." I grunt my disagreement, and he throws me a look.

"What! So, all that not making decisions for me was bull-shit?" she shouts.

"You still have a hit on your head, and until Massimo and I have tracked down the rest of The Organization and—"

"Wait." She looks between the two of us. "You two are going after The Organization?"

"Yes." Tullio looks at her tentatively then looks at me. "You didn't know?"

"No." She looks at me in disbelief. "I cannot believe you guys! And you guys say I'm the stupid and reckless one?!" She throws her arms in the air, for once taking something seriously.

"We know what we're doing," her brother argues.

"No, I don't think you do. Do you even know who the head of it is?" Neither of us respond. "Exactly. No one does. And they have the Black Widow under their control!" We both frown. "Black Mamba. The Lynx. The Wolverine. The King Cobra. The Russian assassin!"

I'm cognizant of what she's talking about and think back to my conversation with Komodo. "We aren't ignorant, Alessia," I speak up. "We are aware of who we're dealing with."

She shakes her head in dismay. "You two are going to get yourself and a lot of people killed. Me included." My fists clench. "He hasn't sent his assassin here yet, but if you provoke him, he will. And there will be no way to protect me or any of us." She downs the rest of her wine, draining her glass.

I look over at Tullio and he looks at me. *Is she at all right in any way?*

The rest of dinner is quiet, and we only make some small talk. I let Tullio and Alessia have a moment as she walks him to the door, and I go ahead up to our room without her. I know she has too many questions to try and take the opportunity to run. I feel like I've aged several years since she's been back in my life. I'll be lucky if I make it past the age of sixty married to her.

I'm sitting on the edge of our bed when she comes in. I loosen my tie after peeling my jacket off and kick my shoes off, preparing for a confrontation over everything, but her actual topic of concern surprises me.

"Why didn't you tell me about Vita?"

"What's to tell?" I respond flatly.

"Um, that your sister is missing. The fact that you haven't been able to find her should be disturbing. Aren't you afraid that she's dead?"

"I know where she is."

"What? But Sarita said—"

"Sarita doesn't know. She thinks we can't find her."

She stops a few feet in front of me and crosses her arms. I'm longing to reach out and touch her. "Why are you lying to her?"

"If I tell Sarita where Vita is, she'll go and try to bring her home."

"So? Maybe that's what she wants."

"Of course, that's what she wants."

"I don't mean Sarita. I mean Vita." I frown and she rolls her eyes. "Do you know her at all?" She sighs and drops her arms when I don't answer. Then she comes to hop up on the bed next to me leaving too much distance between us and letting her shoes drop to the floor. "Vita is constantly crying out for attention. Are you trying to tell me you never saw that?" I still don't respond out of fear of what I might say. I honestly do not want to talk about this, but she's finally talking to me and not yelling. "The girl was constantly getting herself into trouble desperately trying to get your attention."

"Mine?"

"Yes, yours. Or Sarita or Ezzo or even your mother. Hell, even your father."

"She could care less about our father."

"Not from what she told me," she utters under her breath.

"What do you mean?"

"Nothing." She exhales loudly. "It was stupid and in the past. Point is, Vita is most likely doing this to see if any of you will come after her. Try to bring her home. *Want* to bring her home."

"Is that what you were trying to do?"

She narrows those brown eyes at me. "I didn't run away. And if I were trying to get your attention, I would've gotten married to the president of a biker gang or someone of a rival family."

"You've thought about it," I muse.

"I've thought about a lot of things, Massimo. I had a lot of time on my hands." There's no amusement in her tone.

"You could've done anything with your life."

"*My* life. Yes. It was *my* life, and it was taken from me. So, I chose another one because it was mine to choose."

We're quiet as we stare at each other for a heated moment. I'm pleasantly surprised when she doesn't react as I reach up and tuck some of her dark hair behind one of her ears. She claims she isn't who she used to be, but it's a complete lie. It's still her. Only a few years older and wiser with a chink in her armor.

"You really didn't know what I was doing?" she asks quietly.

My body goes rigid. The sight of her standing in the center of her home in ruins, untouched and unscathed, sent emotions swarming inside of me. Part of me saw her as a goddess standing in the middle of a tornado, unmoved. Another part of me felt like I had failed her.

"Tullio assured me he would have some kind of eye on you to make sure you were okay. If I kept an eye on you, I wouldn't have stayed away."

Her eyes dart to the floor and I can see her walls shoot back up. "I wasn't doing it for attention. I needed an outlet, that's all." She looks at me again, face hardened. "I don't think I can ever forgive you, Massimo. In order to survive in this world, I cannot give second chances. Just because I cared for you and even loved you doesn't make you an exception."

"You've forgiven Tullio."

She looks away again. "I've forgiven him because he didn't play me. You did." She stands up and heads into the closet.

The conversation is over for tonight. If I try and defend myself and tell her that she couldn't be more wrong, it'll turn into an argument ruining the tiny bit of progress we've just made.

Going to bed without yelling is a success and I'll take what I can.

CHAPTER FORTY-SIX

Massimo

Alessia's words pertaining to Vita hit me and left me reflecting on the last however many years.

How could I not see Vita's cry for help?

So, I sent someone out to California to check in on her, and what they found was unsettling. If I do not intervene now, she will soon be dead.

It's time to bring her home.

There's a polite knock on the door to my office and I call out for entry. Sarita pops her head in and smiles. "You wanted to see me?"

"Yes." I lean back in my chair, and she closes the door behind her. "Have a seat."

"Sure." She sits down.

"I hope you don't have any plans today."

"Nothing important."

"Good. We're taking a trip."

"We are? Where to?"

"California. All of us."

"Okay…? Mind filling me in?"

"It's where Vita is."

Her eyes light up. "You found her?"

"Yes."

She sits forward with wide eyes. "What? How—how is she?"

"She's not doing well."

"What do you mean she's not doing well? Is she sick? Is she in trouble?" she rushes out genuinely concerned for our sister.

"She's gotten herself into some heavy stuff."

"What, like drugs?" I nod my head. "She's always dabbled in some stuff here and there."

"Not like this. She's going to kill herself if we don't get out there."

"Okay, right. Yes, let's go."

"I need you to talk to Mamma. It has to be all of us."

She gives me this wistful look that I can't face. "Okay. I'll make sure we're all there." She stands up. "Massimo." I look up at her. "Thank you."

"Don't thank me," I murmur.

"Why not? You're showing you care, and I know it isn't easy for you. For any of us. We're not like…the Bonetti's."

I never told anyone else other than Ezzo about the property I bought in Italy and the family vacation that obviously never happened. Once the dust settles, I'd like to rectify that.

"Thank Alessia. She's the one who talked me into going to get her."

She smiles and nods her head. "I'll be sure to thank her."

"I want to be leaving in the next hour."

"Got it. I'll see you later after I round up the troops."

She takes her leave, and I go back to looking at the facility I plan to put Vita in as soon as we get back. I'll have to put some guards on her there to be safe, but it looks like it's the best one on the East Coast.

Since we'll all be out the entire day, I decided it was time for a family reunion for the Bonetti's. Not only will they occupy Alessia while I'm away, but it'll increase the chances of her not escaping. I have Tullio's word that they will not give in and let her leave with them.

Alessia was not at all pleased, as I thought she would be when I told her. She was visibly anxious and uncomfortable. I think she's somewhat apprehensive about finally facing everyone, especially her mother. Again, she showed a sliver of remorse.

Only wish I received the same treatment.

CHAPTER FORTY-SEVEN

Alessia

The family reunion is emotional as *fuck*.

Gemma and Mamma erupted into tears as soon as they embraced me. Between hugs and kisses and sobs, they peppered me with questions and accusations.

"Why did you have to get yourself into trouble?"

"We were supposed to be laying low."

"Did you get involved with another family?"

"Were you trying to get yourself killed?"

"I knew something would happen with you living out in the middle of the desert by yourself."

"I could have lost you," Mamma cries and cradles my face in her hands.

"Mamma, I'm okay."

"You're not okay. You have a cast on your arm and broken ribs," Gemma points out.

I glance at my brothers who're all waiting in line to give me their two cents. "That was from the transportation here," I mutter a bit sheepishly.

"Oh, *Madonna!*" Mamma exclaims, making me smirk.

"What happened?" Gemma asks and everyone is waiting for me to explain.

Glancing over at Tullio who knows what happened, he's not at all willing to throw me a bone here. "It was just a small accident. No need to fuss over it."

"No, no. It's a really good story. Tell them what happened, Alessia," Tullio baits and crosses his arms with a smug look.

"Oh, yes. It's a very good story," Paolo says, glowering at me. Then I look at the rest of them, and they all have the same knowing look.

Okay, so my brothers are definitely pissed about the accident. I'll allow this tiny moment to be angry with me.

"Let's have a seat, Mamma." I bring her over to the couch in the room we're all congregated in, and Gemma sits on my other side. *Perfect. I'm surrounded.* When my brothers all come to stand in a straight line in front of me, I swallow hard. This is going to be a long day. No wonder why Massimo made himself scarce.

With each revelation about why I came home and how I sustained my injuries, my mom and my sister became increasingly shocked. I shouldn't be surprised Tullio wouldn't show me any mercy, not at all softening the blow for me ahead of time. It's his way of punishing me.

I give my first apology, for *anything*, to my mother. It'll be the only I give because her and my sister are the only ones I regret worrying.

Paolo and Armando drop the tough guy act and give me some leniency knowing that I have been punished enough by making Mamma cry. They each give me a bear hug making me suck back the tears threatening to spill as they express how much they genuinely missed me.

Last is Santino. He's been mute the whole time, but I know he has a lot to say. He gestures with his head for me to follow him outside of the room. The rest of the family fills the room with chatter and we're able to sneak away.

"Let me have it, Saint."

We stop somewhere down the hall and face each other. "You don't owe me an apology."

"No?"

"I warned Tullio and Massimo that sending you away would be severely consequential. I knew your resentment would evolve into something toxic."

"So...you're not angry with me?"

He takes a deep breath in then lets it out slowly through his nose. "I'm not proud of your actions, but I can't be angry at who you are, *piccolina*." He playfully pinches my chin. "*Babbo*'s little warrior."

My nostrils flare in restraint. "I thought that nickname he gave me was reserved for private."

He snorts. "When we would call you little psycho, he would correct us in saying you're his little warrior."

I swallow around the rock lodged in my throat. "I miss him, Saint." My heart aches with the fact that I didn't get nearly enough time with him and never got the proper chance to mourn him. Just as I was beginning to accept from grief, I experienced my first heartbreak.

"I know. I do too." He pulls me into his arms and I wrap mine tightly around his torso. Santino is the tallest out of my brothers, even taller than Massimo, but he's not the gentle giant he's perceived to be. But to me, he always is.

We turn to go back to the room. "That reminds me. Do you think I could pay Angelo a visit soon?"

He chuckles and wraps an arm around my shoulders. "Only if you promise not to chop his cock off and make him choke on it."

I roll my eyes grinning. "I won't make any promises I can't keep."

By the time my family decides to leave, I'm exhausted. I tried to weasel my way into leaving with them by using Mamma, but she turned out to be a complete traitor. She said that I needed to stay with Massimo and that he'd keep me safe.

"You really don't care that I'm being held prisoner here?"

She frowns and looks down at my hands. "I don't see any shackles."

I give her a dry look and drop my head. "I'm not shackled, but I am not allowed to leave. I want to be home, not here."

"Alessia." She cups my cheek with her hand. "I know Massimo hurt you, but he thought he was doing the right thing." I open my mouth, but she doesn't let me speak. "Although he may not have gone about it the right way in making you feel unloved by him, he knew it was the only way you would leave."

"They didn't give me a choice." I swiped at the tears that managed to slip out. "I don't think I can forgive him, Mamma."

"I know your stubborn streak is hard to get past, but you will. You'll find a way, bambina.*" She kisses my forehead. "I love you."*

It's late by the time I make my way up to Massimo's room. He's still not home, and Monte wouldn't tell me where he's been all day. In a torpid state, I become disgustingly sentimental when I glance down at the ring I'm forced to wear. Normally, I only wear it around Massimo, but I forgot to take it off when he left today.

Sitting on the edge of the bed and staring at the ring, I feel a wave of disheartenment instead of anger.

Massimo and I were so good together, then he demolished everything. No matter if what he said in Tullio's office to make me leave was bullshit or not, it does not erase the pain it caused me. If it was a ruse to let me go, then he purposely hurt me, and I can't see past that.

Even if I wanted to forgive him, I don't think I know how. I'm stubborn by nature and he doesn't even seem contrite. He's more eager to disavow his mistakes than to take real accountability for them. Admitting you're wrong and expressing your remorse are two different things.

I'm already asleep when the sound of the bedroom door clicking shut wakes me up announcing Massimo's homecoming. Sitting up in bed, I adjust my eyes to the dark. "Hey," I say quietly, and he comes to my side of the bed. His tie is loose, and his suit jacket is draped over his one arm, seemingly exhausted. "Where were you?"

"California."

I sit up more and turn some. "What were you doing in California?"

"Getting Vita."

My eyebrows jump up to my forehead. "You were getting Vita? Like as in bringing her home?" He nods his head. "Oh, wow." My thoughts are a bit staggered right now, realizing he actually heeded my advice. "So, she's here?"

"For now." He sighs and sits down on the bed. My family seriously messed with my head today because all I want to do right now is hug him and rub his shoulders to relieve some of the tension he's burdened with. "We're taking her to a facility tomorrow."

"What kind of facility?"

"A rehab. She's in poor shape. Gave her some sedatives to keep her out most of the night."

"But she's alright?"

"She will be." He turns his head and gives me a tight smile. "How did it go with your family today?"

"Better than expected. Though my brothers forced me to tell Mamma about the accident I caused," I mutter.

"Well, that's what you get," he teases making me crack a smile. "Monte said you didn't try to use them to escape."

"Oh, I tried," I admit truthfully, and he arches both eyebrows. "I even told Mamma how I'm being held here against my will." His lips twitch in response. "But she told me I had to stay put."

"Did she? And why's that?"

"She's obviously losing it." I sigh and lay back down.

"Mhmm," he mumbles unconvinced. "Well, she obviously has changed her tune since we talked."

"You talked to Mamma?" He nods. "When?"

"A few days ago." He reaches up and unknots his tie to slip off all the way. The movement I find myself transfixed by.

"And what did she say?"

"You first."

I screw my lips to the side as my eyes narrow on him. "Whatever."

He chuckles and stands to his feet. "I'm going to shower." He looks at me over his shoulder. "Care to join me?"

"No, thank you." I settle into the covers with a slight smirk.

"I could make you." His voice lowers an octave, and I glare at him even though my stomach flips. *Please, make me. It won't take much effort.* "You're lucky I'm too tired right now."

He closes himself in the bathroom and the water to the shower turns on a moment later. Turning on my side to face the bathroom door, I'm so tempted to walk in there and join him. To run my hands all over his scarred-up muscles. Water dripping down his olive skin and washboard abs.

My family has seriously put my brain in a blender tonight.

CHAPTER FORTY-EIGHT

Alessia

assimo didn't come home last night, and I'm worried.

Monte is being strangely on edge and refuses to provide me with any answers when I question him on Massimo's whereabouts. I don't even think he would prevent me from leaving if I tried. I ended up caving this morning and tried to call him, but his phone was off and still is several hours later.

Something is obviously wrong, and I plan to get to the bottom of it.

I'm just about to go and hunt Monte down again when he rushes into the room around noon looking frantic. "What's going on?" I rush out, my heart automatically sinking in fear.

"Phone's for you," he says quickening his pace.

"Is it Massimo?"

"No, but it's important."

"It better not be another woman telling me he's two-timing us," I mutter and take the phone from him. "Hello?"

"Alessia. Nice to hear your voice."

"Komodo?" I recognize the accent instantly.

"Sorry, I don't have your new number."

"Well, I just got my phone privileges back for being a good girl," I muse.

"Good to hear."

"By the way, thank you for not killing me." Monte clears his throat grabbing my attention and I find him baring his teeth at me, prompting me to roll my eyes. "But this obviously isn't a friendly phone call to catch up. What's going on? You know something about Massimo? Is he two-timing me?" I ask without any real intent.

"I warned him about going after them."

"So, did I."

"Well, he's gotten himself into a little trouble."

"Tell me everything you know," I demand.

After I get as much detail as possible out of Komodo, I get off the phone and face Monte. "Get the crew together and pack heavy. I need to go see my brothers. Meet us at our airstrip when you're ready."

"Wait." He halts me, giving me the impression he's going to prevent me from leaving. "Where is he?"

"Fucking Russia. The Organization is hot on his tail and will have him in their custody within hours. We have to move." He knows not to question because that'll waste precious time.

Clad in combat gear—form-fitting black clothing, combat boots, my Kevlar, and my hair pulled tightly back in a ponytail—I don't bother asking for any weapons, knowing I can get them at my family's estate.

I call Tullio on my way to give him the shortest version and he says he'll call in the Abramov's. Which is a total shock to me, but questions will have to wait.

Only my brothers and their most trusted men are gathered in the office when I get there. "Since when are we so cool with the Abramov's?" I ask right away.

"It's a long story, but we are," Tullio says. "Take that old Kevlar off, Yulia has something better for you."

"Better than my Kevlar? And who the fuck is Yulia?"

"Yulia Abramov. Now, take it off."

I start undoing the vest, and Paolo comes to assist me. "I need to visit the armory."

"We'll see what Yulia brings," he mutters.

"Tullio?" He looks at me. "You're not thinking about making me sit this one out, are you?" The room grows quiet, and I try to suppress my instant temper. "I *am* coming."

"Alessia—" Tullio starts.

"No. I have the location, and I will fight my way out of here and go at it alone if I have to." I purposely left out the exact location where they plan on holding Massimo for the same reason.

Tullio's shoulders wilt as my brothers and our crew all look to him. "Alright. Fine," he concedes resentfully. "My orders though."

"Got it, boss." I salute him, making him smirk, and my brothers smile. It feels good to finally be part of the gang.

"Alright, boys. I brought some brand-new toys." A beautiful woman sweeps into the room with a bunch of men carrying large artillery boxes. The way she holds herself, it's obvious she's the one in charge. Her dirty blonde hair is pulled back into a long braid and her dark eyes are somehow bright when they land on me. "And I finally get to meet *the* Alessia Bonetti." She approaches me grinning, and I remain impassive. I politely accept the proper greeting, though I'm weary of this new relationship with the Russians. "I'm Yulia. Between your brothers and Massimo, I feel as if I already know you."

Right away my hackles are up. All I can think about is Massimo and this beautiful woman alone together...If they fucked...God, I cannot think about that right now.

"I heard you have quite a collection of your own," she says not at all deterred by my silence and gestures to the weapons being unpacked around us.

I glower over at Tullio. "I used to, yes." The cheeky bastard has the audacity to grin.

"When you get back, we'll have to make some time to get to know each other," she adds.

"Yeah, sure."

"Alright, let me get you suited up." She peels off her leather jacket revealing her tattoo covered arms and shoulders. *Damn, this girl is hot as fuck. Omg, am I seriously getting jealous right now when Massimo is facing dire peril?!* I'm actually stunned by my own pettiness.

Several minutes later and I'm sucking it in. "Holy shit. I cannot breathe in this thing." I try to twist around in the vest she put me in.

"It's tight, I know, but feel how light it is. It's stronger, too," she explains.

"But what's the point of it being lighter if I can barely breathe in it?"

"Oh, don't be such a sissy," Armando jabs making me stick my tongue out at him.

Taking another deep breath, I twist and turn some more, and I feel like my body is already getting used to it. I guess it wouldn't be so bad if my ribs weren't still a little tender.

"Believe me. It's better trying to breathe through this than trying to breathe when you get shot with the Kevlar on," Yulia says confidently.

"It's really that much stronger?" She nods her head. If she's saying it has better protection, then she's right. A slight shortness of breath now is better than breaking more ribs with a single shot. Or worse, something getting through.

"It can withstand getting shot with a .50 cal," she adds.

My eyes literally turn into two saucers as I gawk at her. *"Santo cazzo Madre di Cristo!" Holy fucking Mother of Christ!*

She giggles and it sounds so feminine coming from a badass woman who just suited us all up with these insane weapons and new protective gear. "It'll knock you on your ass for sure and leave a mark, but you'll live."

Huh, maybe I could stand to make a new friend.

I stuff my combat boots and my tactical thigh and back holsters with throwing knives and a couple of handguns, and I get to strap two heavy arms to my body—ones provided by Yulia that I am unfamiliar with, which are light in weight yet high caliber. Then we load up several vehicles and head to our private airstrip.

Monte, Ezzo, and a sizeable crew are already assembled there. We quickly file into the plane, filling it to capacity. If we were to crash, the cargo we're hauling could potentially blow up an entire country.

"It's him again," Monte says, handing his phone over.

"What's going on?" I ask as soon as the phone touches my ear.

"They have him in custody and on their way to the location," Komodo says.

"Just him?"

"That I know of, yes."

"And same location?"

"Yes, there hasn't been a change from what I've intercepted."

"Okay. Call if you hear anything else."

"Be safe, little one."

"I will."

When I hang up, I face the two-dozen pair of eyes on me. "They have him." Everyone mumbles their curses under their breath and my nostrils flare as I contain my rage. "Look. I'm not going to lie. They captured Massimo to try to draw us out. They knew we'd come for him, and they'll sick the Russian assassin on us and lot of people will die."

"Are you talking about the *prizak*?" One of the Russians speaks up and I look at him in question. "*Ghost*. Some call it the ghost though it goes by many names."

"It?" Paolo asks.

"No one knows their identity," another Russian says. "Only that they've seen long raven hair from under their hood."

"It won't matter though. Word has it, the assassin has gone rogue, and Sergei Petrov is ripping through the country to find them."

"Sergei Petrov?" I ask in shock.

"Yes, your old boss," the first Russian says, his tone dripping with accusation.

"Sergei Petrov is the head of The Organization?" A bunch of us ask in unison.

"*Da*." *Yes*. He nods.

Sergei Petrov. His name and his family are no secret. It's fascinating to think of how well he hid not only his connection to The Organization, but his ownership of it.

And if it's true that his trusty assassin is going rogue on him, we might not actually die trying to save Massimo after all.

CHAPTER FORTY-NINE

Alessia

Apparently the Morozov's are letting us land on their airstrip and will be waiting for us there.

The Morozovs are another Russian family allied with the Abramovs. They agreed to lend us some of their men to help us, but it isn't their fight, so it won't be much. The Abramovs lent us a group of their soldiers as well, which is much more generous than most.

Vladimir Morozov was the one to meet us when we landed, giving us safe passage, and vehicles, asking for only one thing in return. We leave Sergei Petrov alive. We weren't in the position to say no seeing as we're on their turf and they're helping us. Getting Massimo back is our sole priority anyways.

"Tullio?" I ask once we're settled into the provided vehicles and on the move. He turns his head to me. "Can I *please please please* shoot the minigun?" I even flatten my palms together under my chin. "Please?"

He sighs and rolls his eyes. "Maybe."

"Yes." I bounce a little in my seat. I've always wanted to unload with a machine gun, and the minigun mounted to the top of the vehicle is calling my name.

"I said maybe."

"Good enough for me." I grin.

"Little psycho." He shakes his head smiling.

"This is nice."

"What? Charging into Russia with an army to save your boyfriend?"

"My fiancé, and I meant the part of being a part of the team." Okay, so Massimo's life being in grave danger has fast-tracked the forgiving process. I didn't think I even had it in me.

"You've always been a part of the team."

"Not like this."

"We haven't done anything like this in a long time, Alessia. Last time we did anything close to this you were still a teenager. Of course, you weren't included."

"If I were a few years older, would you have included me?" I arch one eyebrow.

"Probably not," he admits. "I know I'm starting to sound like a broken record, but I only want to keep you safe. All of us. *Babbo* did too. Your capabilities never escaped his notice, *piccolina*, but to him, you would always be his little girl."

His way of putting it recasts everything in a new light. The different treatment I resented wasn't rooted in gender bias, but out of love. I wasn't limited for being a female, I've been cherished.

"Tullio?"

"Yes, *piccolina*?"

An apology hangs on the tip of my tongue, but I'm still me. Stubborn bitch and all. "I love you," I say instead.

"Don't get all soft on me now." He bumps his shoulder into me. "Now, is not the time."

I smile and nod my head. "Right. I'll save that for when we get De Luca back."

The next hour or so is one big blur. Adrenaline at its peak, especially since I got to use the fucking minigun. Literally razing their soldiers surrounding the abandoned building.

Next thing I know, Armando and I have some Russian mother-fucker held with my knife against his throat demanding the exact location of my betrothed. As soon as he pisses his pants and spits the words out, I slice his throat and move forward.

"*Cazzo*. Alessia, you are savage," Armando says, shaking his head with a faint smile.

"Let's go."

With my ears ringing, we rush up to the corner, and Armando quickly peeks around. "Go." He motions for the soldiers to go first. They rush around the corner and start popping off right away. Armando and I go in behind them, guns raised, and shoot our way through the hall and to the stairwell the guy told us to look for. Our men cover us, and we send two ahead of us downstairs to clear the way.

Descending the stairs, we aren't met with anyone right away. Not until we reach the bottom and turn to the left like instructed. We unload, and one of our guys goes down, but we have to keep moving. We manage to shoot our way through again, and I begin peeking in through each little window on the closed doors. It's not until the third one that I see Massimo.

"In here," I bark out.

"Go. I'll cover you."

There's a big metal latch on the outside that I crank, and the heavy door makes a loud screeching sound as I open it. Massimo is tied to a chair in the middle of the empty room, his head limply dangling down. "Give me a minute," I say to Armando, and I close the door on his face as he starts shouting at me.

"Damnit, Alessia! You have one fucking minute!"

Yeah, yeah...

Walking swiftly over to Massimo, I can't help the smirk that stretches my lips wide. To see Massimo being the one restrained for once. I'm tempted to pull my phone out and snap a picture of him.

"So, this is what Massimo De Luca looks like tied up," I muse.

He gradually lifts his head, and my stomach churns when we lock eyes and gape in sheer horror. I rush to close the gap and brush his hair out of his face to get a better look at him. The bruising and swelling aren't what tears my gut up in anguish and agony. It's the fact that his lips have been sewn shut. Seeing me, his chest heaves with growing tension.

"Oh, baby," I whisper and move his hair back again. I used two hair ties to hold my ponytail in case one broke, so I remove one to tie half of his hair back to stay out of his face for me, and I get a better look at his face. I hold back a grimace as I gently sit in his lap and cup his face with just as much caution. "And I was so looking forward to stringing this out." I give him a sad smile and reach for one of my knives tucked inside my boot. "Okay." I take a deep breath in and out to help steady my hand. "Stay completely still for me, baby."

As delicately as possible, not to nick his lips, I cut through the thread and he gasps for air. My forehead falls to his and my breathing begins to match his. Letting my nerves surface. *My poor baby.*

"*Baciami*," he hoarsely rasps.

My eyes fly open as I pull back slightly. Instantly, I'm hesitant. Not because of my pride, but because I don't want to hurt him. But anything can happen once we leave the safe confines of this room. I could soon lose him, or he could lose me.

Pressing my lips gently to his, he growls and jerks his head forward to deepen it. He tastes like blood, his tongue is coarse most likely from dehydration, but I don't care. It still tastes like him, and it's been years since I've felt this complete. It's so familiar and yet as exhilarating as experiencing something for the first time.

"Are you two almost done in there?!" Armando calls out from the other side of the door as gunfire continues in the background.

"Almost!" I call back and slide off Massimo's lap. "So, I got to use the minigun," I brag with a big grin as I cut his limbs loose.

He chuckles roughly and shakes his head. "I'm sorry I missed that." He stands up and rolls his head around on his shoulders.

"I'll let you pick." I hold up my Glock and the heavy gun. He reaches for the Glock and I have a hard time parting with it. It's my favorite. He eyes me and I pout right before letting it go. "You be good to her." I turn and pound the door twice with my fist. "Done!"

Armando opens the door. "About time," he grumbles then acknowledges Massimo with a head nod.

Stepping one foot out of the door, Massimo pulls me back. "Don't even think about it, Massimo," I warn him with a murderous look.

His nostrils flare and he takes a soothing breath. There's no doubt in my mind we was planning on locking me in here until it was safe. "I love you," he says instead.

I grin then raise my gun. "Let's get the fuck out of here."

CHAPTER FIFTY

Massimo

I'm overly keen on finishing what Alessia and I started back in that room.

Especially as we pick off the rest of the Russian bastards that captured and tortured me. To watch Alessia in action with her slicked-back ponytail and combat gear, looking like a mod-ern-day Viking, I'm not a mess inside with worry over her safety like I thought I'd be. I somehow fall for her all over again. She's fucking fearless.

We end up gathered in one area once all the gunfire has died down. "Happy they didn't kill you, *fratello.*" *Brother.* Ezzo pats me on the back.

"Nice ponytail," Armando teases, making others chuckle.

I smirk down at Alessia, and she reaches up to toy with some of my hair left down. "I think it's sexy." She grins.

A rumbling noise sounds in the back of my throat as I take her around the waist. "Sexy, huh?"

"Very," she purrs and slides her hands up and around my neck, giving my hair a little tug.

"So, I assume you two have finally kissed and made up?" Tullio asks.

"More like calling a truce," she responds without taking her eyes away from me.

I pick her up off her feet, and she wraps herself around me. Her brothers all begin to protest, but we tune them out as I pin her against the wall. The rest of the world seems to melt away, and we're caught up in our own little reality. I stroke her face in disbelief that she's really here. I thought I was going to die today. I thought I had reached my limit, and everything had finally caught up to me, with this being my only contrition.

"You didn't leave me to die," I murmur with no seriousness.

"I didn't." Her eyes dart all over my face and I can only imagine what she sees. "Sorry for getting you into this mess." Her mutter is hardly audible.

If I could move my eyebrows right now, they'd jump up in shock. Though it was a half-assed apology, Alessia does not apologize. So, when she does, she means it wholeheartedly.

"But if you ever do that to me again, I will feed you your own dick." Our lips come together as I chuckle, but all humor quickly fades when I have to pull away due to the pain it causes me. "Let's go get these stitches out of you," she says softly as she strokes my cheek amorously. I've longed for this softer side of her.

"*Sposami, amore mio.*" Her face drops completely as she studies me for a long moment. "Tomorrow."

Her eyes narrow. "You still have a long way to go, De Luca." Then her face softens with a smile. "Plus, I want a wedding, which could not be put together in one day.

"I want you as my wife."

"I want the dress," she retorts quickly.

"You have the dress."

"I want the flowers and music and chapel and everything. I want it all."

I'm quiet as I admire her beauty and defiance. "A week."

Her green eyes widen and her luscious lips part. "A year," she finally counters with.

"Two weeks."

"Two years," she says with an eyebrow arched and I full-on laugh.

I missed her so fucking much. "This is the one and only time I'll do this. You have six months." She grins in victory. "But we sign the marriage license in one week."

"Massimo Antonio De Luca. You—"

I cut her off with a kiss that is too painful to deepen. "I love ruffling those pretty feathers of yours," I murmur against her lips.

"And I'll admit I love it when you ruffle them." She kisses my cheek. "Can we go home now? I fucking hate Russia."

"You and me both, baby."

Alessia isn't parted from my side the entire journey back to the airstrip where both planes are waiting. As soon as I take a step outside the vehicle, Vinny comes rushing towards me despite all his obvious injuries. The guy has been through it over the last several weeks. "Oh, thank fuck." Then his eyes widen when he gets a good look at me. "Holy shit."

"Yeah, holy shit," I mutter.

Alessia saw me trying to pull some of the stitches around my mouth out myself and chastised me before grabbing her brother. So, Santino joins us on my plane for the ride home.

Fucking sewed my mouth shut. I'm almost impressed by their level of sinisterness.

Once we're up in the air, Santino sets up the medical supplies. "You're going to have some gnarly scars," he murmurs as he cleans the area first.

"Chicks dig scars," Alessia says with a sliver of enthusiasm.

"*You* dig scars, Less. Little psycho," Santino teases though he's serious. I eye her and she shrugs her shoulders totally unoffended.

"Alright. Now, stay still for me," Santino says, and I close my eyes purely from exhaustion. The adrenaline has been slowly leaking from me draining me of energy and causing my other injuries to throb.

The stitches definitely do not feel good coming out, but a hell of a lot better than going in. It's not like they numbed me or carefully did them. They made sure it fucking hurt.

"And...done," he says several minutes later, and I feel something soft pressed to my mouth. Opening my eyes, I find an angel smiling as she holds some gauze against me. "Now, what else needs urgent attention other than your eye that has doubled in size?"

My hand is obviously broken, which will have to wait for x-raying after we land, but he was able to stitch up the gash on the back of my head and another one on my chest. Not much else he could do, though, for the bruising and broken ribs that will also need to be x-rayed other than give me ice to help manage the swelling.

Santino says he'll be back with some ice packs and I lift my hand up in gratitude as Alessia verbally thanks him. He nods his head and disappears to sit somewhere else, giving us privacy.

"Well, it doesn't seem like your lips are bleeding too badly." She lifts the gauze then cringes before putting it back. "Maybe not." I drop my head back, and my eyelids feel heavy with a crushing weight of fatigue. "Let's lean you back, baby." She leans across me and hits the button to recline my seat. "I'm going to go help Santino get you some ice and make sure to get you some water and painkillers." I nod my head in response. "I'll be right back. Hold onto this." She lifts my hand to replace hers and then kisses my cheek before getting up.

My mind practically goes numb from overwhelming exhaustion. The only energy I have is to think about the fact that I'm alive.

"Alright, pain killers, water, and a shit ton of ice," she says when she comes back. "Here." She uncaps the bottle of water and hands it to me along with the pills. "Shit. You definitely need new gauze." She takes the soiled stuff from me while I drink and she replaces some clean ones in my hand and I rest my head back down.

We're both quiet as she begins sticking ice packs around me. One to my side with noticeably broken ribs, a couple of others in my torso where I'm black and blue, and one to my knee even though I haven't said a word about it—she must've noticed me slightly limping.

"I'm going to hold this icepack on your eye for a little while." I'm hardly able to nod my head as my eyelids finally succumb to fatigue and droop shut.

The ice pack is placed gently over my eye, and I'm out.

CHAPTER FIFTY-ONE

Alessia

"What are you doing?" I mumble as I'm jostled awake inside of Massimo's arms.

"I didn't want to wake you," he murmurs, carrying me off the plane.

"I can walk, Massimo."

"Why walk when you can be carried?" He smirks.

"You're the one that's been through the wringer. Put me down."

"No."

"Stubborn ass," I mutter and wrap my arms around his neck to help hold some of my weight.

We slip into the waiting SUV and I look around. "They'll be landing in less than an hour." As always, he's able to read my thoughts. He takes my hand in his and sighs. Then he rolls his head around his shoulders.

"Did you get some sleep on the plane?" I yawn and the vehicle starts moving.

"A couple hours."

"That's it?"

"Yes."

"The bleeding stop?" He nods his head.

The rest of the ride home is completely silent, and although his hand firmly grasped with mine is reassuring, it still gives me flashbacks of when he suddenly went quiet on me before. He could be too tired to talk or maybe it hurts to, but it gives me anxiety, nonetheless.

A feast is prepared for when we get home. Most of us haven't eaten in well over twenty-four hours, but I notice Massimo has barely touched his food.

"Does it hurt to eat?" I ask from beside him.

"I'm alright, baby." He gives me a tight smile.

"We can go up anytime you want. I'm pretty full now." I place my fork down.

"I have some things to take care of first."

I mask the sting caused by his minor rejection. I thought he would be equally eager as me to be alone. "You should really relax and get some good sleep." Despite everyone's strong urging, he stubbornly declined any medical attention tonight. "Massimo—"

"Later, Alessia." He kisses my forehead then stands up. Paralyzed by disbelief, I find myself unable to argue or protest.

I watch as he says something to Vinny and Ezzo and they leave the room together. *He is not already trying to leave me out.* I went to Russia guns blazing in a bullet proof vest that killed my ribs, I'm pretty sure rebreaking them, to save his ass when I was supposed to hate him. *Not happening.*

Getting up, I leave the room and head right to his office. The door is left cracked open and I don't even try to eavesdrop or knock. I make my presence known and barge right in.

They all stop talking and Massimo sighs when he sees me. "I'm too tired, baby."

I plant my hands on my hips, my temper quickly baited. "Tired for what?" He rubs at his temples then winces when he rubs too close to the swollen side of his face. "Massimo. If this has anything to do with the fucking Russians we just took on, I think I deserve to be in on it. I am the one who brought in the cavalry, and without me and my intel, no one would have come for you because they wouldn't know where the fuck you were. I'm pretty sure after the last forty-eight hours I have more than earned my place."

No one speaks as his shoulders visibly sag. "Okay, *gattina*. Have a seat."

Wow. Two for two now. Wait. Three for three. First, Tullio including me, then Massimo not stopping me, now this. I'm finally getting somewhere. At almost twenty-five years old, I'm finally getting some respect. Respect I should not have to still fight for.

I yawn for the fifth time in ten minutes when Massimo says we're calling it a night and the room empties. I know we're both too tired to argue tonight, but I'm still fucking bitter.

"Alessia," Massimo says firmly, demanding my attention.

Anger sizzles on the surface as he stares at me, and I avoid eye contact. "Let's just go to bed, Massimo." I stand up and finally look at him.

"Not until you speak your mind," he says casually, remaining cooly seated behind his desk.

"It can wait until tomorrow. We're both tired and you need to put ice on your eye again. Come on." I turn and begin to head towards the door.

"Alessia, we are not going to bed until you get what it is off your chest," he says so vehemently I come to an abrupt halt.

Slowly, I spin back around to face him, now wide awake and the anger that was sizzling is now boiling. "Fine. You want to have it out with me right now?" I stomp forward and start pointing my finger at him. "You were *again* going to leave me out!"

"And you were right, so I conceded," he tries to cut me off with.

"After I invited myself into your little secret meeting! I shouldn't have to at this point, Massimo. Either see me as your partner, or I swear to God I am gone," I threaten.

He stands up quicker than I thought possible despite all his fresh wounds and injuries. His eyes now just as ablaze. Exhaustion completely obliterated as rage feeds us the strength we need for this blowout.

"Gone, *gattina*? And where would you go?" he taunts.

"Anywhere I fucking want!"

"And you think you'll find someone out there that'll see you as I do? As the woman you are?" he says lowly as he begins to circle his desk.

My eyes widen in outrage. "I don't need anyone, especially a fucking *man*, to tell me who I am, and what I am worth," I seethe. *How fucking dare he?!* I used to think I needed to marry into power to gain power, but after being on my own, I'm acutely aware I can embody regal status solo.

His expression crumbles as he positions himself before me. Suppressing my emotions from spilling over in the form of tears consumes what little energy I have left. "Alessia," he says with less anger. "I—"

I recoil, fighting the rise of sadness that's rapidly replacing my anger. Each shake of my head brings me closer to breaking down. "That might be one of the most hurtful things you have ever said to me," I strain through a sore throat. "To imply that I need you, or *anyone*, to be someone."

He deflates all together and takes a soothing breath. "I did not mean that, *cara*."

"Then what did you mean?!" A rogue tear escapes, running down my cheek.

He glares at me for a solid moment. "I didn't mean anything by it. It was my anger speaking. The thought of you trying to leave me..." he visibly swallows hard. "I shouldn't have said that."

I don't move or make a noise. If I do, I might shatter.

"Alessia," he says my name so softly as he cautiously takes a step forward. "I did not mean that. You don't need me, or anyone, or money, or an eminent surname, or fucking cock to prove yourself." He brings himself toe to toe with me. "You are ungodly revered, Alessia."

"Don't patronize me, Massimo."

"I would never." He shakes his head slowly with a straight face. His arms tenderly slip around my waist, and I again have to fight the tears. "I'm so sorry, *amore*." His eyes plead with mine and his face drops closely. "Please understand I am just under a lot of stress, and combined with the lack of sleep and—" he stops to take a deep breath and I can feel his utter exhaustion. "Forgive me, *amore*. Please."

I nod my head silently, mentally lashing my temper to stay down.

"I love you so much, Alessia." He presses his soft lips to my forehead, causing my eyes to close in reaction. "I guess you discovered another one of my weaknesses."

That has me smiling and rearing back to see him. "Yeah? What's that?"

He scowls at me, but there's no real threat behind it.

I bite my lip to resist a giggle. "I won't taunt you with it, I promise."

I won't say the words out loud, but I know the weakness he's referring to. The thought of me leaving...

"Do you want me to grab some food to bring up for you?" I ask him as we leave his office together.

"I'm alright, *mia amata.*" The torpidity oozes from his tone.

"Are you sure? You hardly ate anything."

"Food can wait till tomorrow," he murmurs. "I want to shower with you." He nuzzles his face against the top of my head. "And go to bed with you."

"Sounds like perfection."

The shower is spent in silence as we robotically wash ourselves and climb out as soon as we're done. I check his wounds for him after we brush our teeth and head off to bed dragging our feet the entire way.

Peeling the covers back, we slip into bed and both sigh. "Come here, my love," he says slipping his arm under me and I slide over into his side and use his chest as my pillow. I begin tracing one of his scars absentmindedly. I haven't done this since before I left, but it's a habit I never kicked. "You'll certainly have more scars to caress."

His depressing tone has me looking up at him with my eyebrows pinched. He stares blankly up at the ceiling with one arm tucked behind his head. "Does that bother you?" He doesn't answer, and I cannot believe my eyes. Is Massimo...self-conscious? "Massimo." I climb up to my knees and straddle his waist to get his attention. "You could have scars all over your face, and I would still find you the most sexy and handsome man known to this world," I say so earnestly that he actually cracks a smile. Grabbing his face, I force him to look at me. "I fucking love you, Massimo. Scars, no scars. Even if you didn't have a face at all. I love *you.*"

The tension in his face vanishes, and he reaches up to cup the back of my head, pulling me down to him. "Say it again. Tell me you love me for me."

"I love you for you, Massimo. *Siamo fatti l'uno all'altra.*" *We were made for each other.*

His twilight meets my midnight, yet somehow, we create light.

CHAPTER FIFTY-TWO

Alessia

"**I** don't like surprises," I whine.

"You'll like this one, *cara mia*." He bends his head down to capture my lips. My body automatically arches to fit against his and his tongue sweeps in to brush up against mine making me moan.

"How about we postpone this surprise just a little bit?" I murmur.

"I promise we'll have plenty of time to do this with the surprise."

I cling to him with my arms around his neck and pout. "But I want you."

"Oh, *gattina*. You make it near impossible to say no to you."

"Then don't. Let's fuck." I kiss him.

Massimo chuckles when I climb him like a tree and wrap my limbs around him. I swallow it up and begin kissing him deeply. He does not disappoint or deny me.

Quickies are never unsatisfying or underwhelming between us. The orgasms are always just as earth-shattering, and we're still gasping for air by the end.

"Pack your bags, *bambina*," he says when we peels his hot body from mine. "We're going to Italy." He smacks my butt and uses my state of shock to slip away from me.

"Italy?"

It turns out the whole De Luca clan is headed off to Italy. Our wedding was two months ago, and because of so much going on, we only had time for a short honeymoon to a private island in the Caribbean. And when I say short honeymoon, I mean way too short. I could've spent weeks with Massimo on that island.

At first, when he informed me his siblings were coming, I was a little disappointed not to have him all to myself, but then he assured me that where we're staying, we'll have plenty of privacy. As long as I can have him as much as I want, I'm satisfied because he will be satisfying me multiple times a day.

The flight to Italy is about nine hours, so we leave around midnight. I cuddle up to my husband and fall asleep in the private room. My husband, whom I now trust wholeheartedly.

I was again faced with the same decision I had years ago. I could choose to trust him, or I could spend the rest of my life driving myself mad with doubt and paranoia. I may still hold a tiny grudge, and I'm not too proud to admit that I can be morbidly petty. But he'll have to accept that because there are certainly many things I have to learn to accept about him, like the constant power struggle.

So, we both agreed to raze our walls and put our faith and confidence in each other. Equally. And there's no one on this planet I trust more than him now, including my own family. He'll always know me best inside and certainly out.

Mamma of course has been pestering me about when she'll be getting some grandchildren out of me, but I keep tossing the attention back over to Armando and Lesina who still only have little Alba and they've been married for years now.

And I happen to know about Tullio and Sarita's secret affair, and it's so tempting to out them just for a bit of drama. But something makes me want to let them be for a while so I can continue enjoying the entertainment it brings me. It'll be interesting to see how it ends.

I wake up to kisses being gently placed all over my face. "Mmm." I flutter my eyes open and find Massimo's handsome face hovering over me. "*Ciao, bello.*"

He smiles. "*Ciao, bella.*" He kisses my lips. "We'll be landing in an hour. Come eat something."

"Mmm." I stretch my arms up above my head. "Okay." I stand up. "Let me go wash up first."

After washing up and changing my clothes, I head out and everyone is sitting around chatting and having breakfast at the table. The only open seat is between Massimo and Vita.

Vita spent sixty days in rehab and has been clean ever since. Her homecoming has gradually brought their mother out of isolation, reviving life into Celia's faded gaze.

Vita and I still don't speak to one another unless it's in passing or in greeting. The hospital room altercation lingers unpleasantly, and her lack of acknowledgement only souring the memory further. I suspect the animosity towards me stems from somewhere deeper, more personal, than the issue of her father. Perhaps she's envious of the immediate connection I've established with her family. Envy is an insidious emotion that festers and preys on its host from within.

I don't pay her any mind as I take my seat, and Massimo automatically kisses me on the lips. There's a plate of food in front of me, so I dig in and join in on the conversation. "Ezzo, I hear you might meet your future wife while we're here?" I ask.

"Possibly," he replies.

"Not possibly," Massimo says in a low voice. "You *are* meeting your future wife."

Ezzo sulks and I bite back a giggle. "Arranged marriages aren't always so bad," I muse and pop a grape into my mouth.

Massimo relaxes in his seat, draping an arm around me. He twirls a lock of hair around his finger and gives it a playful tug. He smirks when I shoot him a look.

"And sometimes they are," Celia says lightly, raising her glass in salute making us chuckle.

"Have you seen pictures of her?" Vita asks.

"No," Ezzo replies.

"I have." Sarita grins.

"And I've asked her not to say a thing," Ezzo rushes out looking at her sternly.

"Why not?" I ask, enjoying the way Massimo nonchalantly plays with my hair.

"He says he doesn't trust my judgement," Sarita answers dryly.

"If she's ugly, I'll soon find out for myself. But if Sarita says she's pretty and gets my hopes up and she turns out not to be..." he trails off.

"You *chooch*," *Ass*. I chide him, and everyone laughs. Ezzo throws me a wink and I shake my head smiling. He and I effortlessly slipped into a brother-sister dynamic. He's nicknamed me Harley and I couldn't be more flattered. Maybe I'll ask Massimo for a giant mallet for my birthday to use at the warehouse.

Trips with him to the warehouse is kind of foreplay for us. Something about watching him bleed information from someone gets me going. Sex is always nasty as fuck afterward.

I haven't been to Italy in almost five years and I cannot wait to feel close to my Italian heritage. Mamma was born in Italy and didn't come over to the states until she was almost a teenager, but my father was second generation in the states. We used to visit Italy quite often, but it had already been close to a year before Massimo and I got engaged, then so much has happened since then.

Massimo and I get into our own vehicle when we land. "Are you ready for your surprise, *amore*?"

My legs are draped over his lap, and he has me tucked into his side, making a light trail up and down my exposed leg. I look up at him. "I thought this was my surprise."

"It's not."

I turn into him. "What is it?"

"You'll have to wait and see."

"Massimo," I whine, and he shuts me up with his lips. The scars around his mouth are hardly noticeable, mainly because of his facial hair. But even without the hair covering them, I meant what I said. I love this man. The scars honestly only add to the appeal because I am batshit crazy in love with him.

By the time the car stops moving, I'm a mess. I want Massimo so badly. "If you don't take me as soon as we get out of this vehicle, I will kill you and have my way with you anyway."

He laughs against my lips. "You sick bitch."

"Yes," I croon. "So, you better give me what I want."

"Yes, Mrs. De Luca."

"That's *signora* to you." I finally peel my eyes away from my handsome husband and they widen when I take a look at where we stopped. It looks like a castle in the middle of the countryside. "This is where we're staying?" No wonder why he said we'd have no problem having our privacy.

"No, my love," he rasps in my ear. "This is for you."

I almost bump heads with him when I whip mine around. "For *me*? What do you mean?" I practically shriek.

"Come." He opens his door and slides out then offers me his hand. It takes me a moment to shake myself from the stupor and climb out. "Remember when we first got engaged and I disappeared on you for a few days?"

"You mean when I accused you of having an affair?" I ask, my eyes bouncing everywhere, trying to take everything in.

"Yes," he growls. "I was here, buying this as a wedding gift."

I stop in my tracks abruptly and face him. "You bought this for a wedding gift? To me?"

"Yes, Alessia. A queen deserves a castle."

"I—" I stare up at him, wholly speechless and astounded. "I don't even know what to say."

He uses his knuckles to drag down my cheek. "You don't need to say anything, my beautiful wife." Threading his hands into my hair, he wraps them around the back of my neck to pull me in for a passionate kiss. "Before giving you the full tour, let me show you to our room first."

I thought he'd never ask.

CHAPTER FIFTY-THREE

Massimo

Picking my wife up into my arms, I relish the way she kisses my neck like she can't seem to help herself.

I had thought she once let her guard down for me before her banishment, but compared to how she unabashedly clings to me now, I see that there is a difference between Alessia *letting* her guard down, and Alessia *having* her guard down. Her now prioritizing me over her family was the pinnacle in our relationship for me personally.

She stops to look around the room as we enter it and I kick the double doors shut behind me. "Oh, my God. Wow," she gasps.

I admire her every reaction as we venture further inside. I left the majority of the property as it was, only renovating a master suite for us. I'll leave it up to her to make any changes.

This in fact is a castle and the previous owners for many generations tried to preserve as much as possible. I don't want to destroy history, but considering we will be a part of its history, I think it'd be safe to put our stamp on it as well.

"I love it. I can't believe you bought this for me." She beams at me, but I see the smugness behind it. She was already entitled to begin with, but now she's spoiled rotten. "It's seriously like a fucking castle."

"It *is* a castle, and also on a vineyard."

"Seriously?" she squeals, and I nod my head chuckling. "Well then, as gratitude, I am yours to do with as you please."

Chuckling again, I pin her down on our bed. "You're already mine to do with as I please," I murmur and dip my head to kiss her neck.

The woman still feigns abhorrence for my utter dominance and being spanked until her ass is too painful to sit on for days, but she is constantly provoking me.

We both hastily undress, and I begin to worship my wife.

Our ceremony resembled a coronation. She ascended the altar as if it were a throne. She stood resplendent, an embodiment of regality, enveloped in a sacrosanct aura. The crowd visibly swayed, barely resisting the magnetic pull urging them to their knees in veneration.

Taking both of her wrists in one hand, I hold them down above her head and take a nipple into my mouth. Sucking it until she hisses. It pops out of my mouth and I move to the other one and do the same. She's arching her back and panting as I move my mouth slowly down her body. Every inch of her delicious.

When I get to her sweet cunt, I flip her over to her knees and bury my face into her. "Fuck, Massimo," she rasps and rocks her hips, so I clamp my hands down to keep them in place. The little mink knows I'm the one in control.

Using the heel of my palms and my thumbs, I spread her cheeks open so I can get to everything. Because that's where I'll up with my cock.

She whines and moans into the mattress as I gorge on her cunt and the tight back hole I cannot wait to feel band around my cock. Once I have her quivering for me, I'm up on my knees lining myself up to dip into her cunt first. She's so fucking sexy from this angle. Her hips look wider and her ass bigger and the way her waist is stretched out and her beautiful back exposed to me, it's hard not to want to take her like this every time.

Her cunt is so wet, it's creamy for me and sticks around the base of my cock when I pull out and line up with her ass. She resists the urge to clench up as she arches her back.

The slicked-up head of my cock rubs around the tight hole, and I press forward slowly. "Mmm." She fists the sheets harder and pulls. Then she sucks in a sharp breath through her teeth as it goes in past my head.

Taking my hand, I flatten it on her back and rub up and down to help keep her relaxed. She's such a tiny thing. And me? I'm more significant than average. It's a stretch for any woman of any size.

My cock is in halfway, and I pump it. It already feels extra-mundane and heavenly. Everything about her does. Her personal dopamine alone heightens all my senses. Making everything feel...*more*. Fate has delivered me my perfect counterpart. Something I thought unattainable. My formidable queen of the underworld, who loves me with the same fierce passion.

The shaft of my cock disappears into her more, and I'm getting closer to bottoming out. "Go ahead, baby. Let go."

My nostrils flare as I still for a moment. Telling me to let go is like taking the leash off a rabid tiger. "Alessia," I choke out.

"Do it, baby." She rocks back, taking it upon herself to swallow the rest of my cock.

"*Cazzo*," I spit, and my hips punch forward. Drilling into her hard but leisurely, slamming in, then slowly pulling back.

Hooking my arm around her waist, I pull her down to the side with me and begin rolling my hips. My one hand grabs at her breast as the other snakes down to slip against her creamy cunt, and she pushes her ass back and moans.

She moans louder and rolls her entire body. My hand leaves her breast to squeeze around her throat, stealing the air from her, and her moves halt. Accepting my dominant position.

Moving my hips faster I really let go. Skin slapping and both of us panting. "*Ti amo*, Alessia."

She moans and turns her head. "I love you so much."

Kissing her hard, she begins convulsing, and my balls jump up to succumb to my release.

After we catch our breath, I give her sweet ass a swat as she heads off to the bathroom and I go to run the water in the tub that's in the main room overlooking the outdoors. I had fantasized about Alessia, wet and nude in the clawfoot tub, with our motherland as the backdrop.

I'm just sinking down into the warm water when she comes sauntering out, wearing only a smirk and her hair up on top of her head so that everything is on display for me. Nothing in the way of her beauty and the smoothest skin I've ever touched.

She has me chuckling as she climbs over me and wraps her arms around my shoulders when she joins me. With a contented sigh, she closes her eyes and rests her head on my chest.

"So, how long are we really staying here?" she asks after a moment of serenity.

"Eight days."

"Mmm. Perfect. So, I get eight days of this?"

"More or less." I rub her backside with both hands. "Although I do love having you naked around the clock, I would like to leave the bedroom at some point to show you the rest of the property."

"As long as we can come right back to do this."

I smile. Sometimes I honestly think she is just as insatiable as me. Her fingertips start lightly seeking out my scars, and I watch her in a daze. "Do you know when you do that?"

"Do what, my love?" Her eyes are still shut.

"That."

Her fingers still, and she looks up at me. "What?" I dip my eyes to where her fingers are, and she follows. "Oh." She snorts. "Not anymore. I love outlining their forms and letting my imagination roam with intricate backstories." She turns in to place a kiss on one scar. "But it's become a habitual fixation of mine. It's soothing for me."

She places another kiss on my chest. Then another and another. Her lips begin moving their way up my chest, and she ends up straddling me as her mouth is all over my neck. My cock comes back to life and bobs up behind her.

"Massimo," she rasps and lifts her face up to mine. "You empower me in every single way possible." She reaches behind herself to wrap her fingers around my cock and pulls.

"Your existence has forged me into an unparalleled version of myself."

She grins and strokes my cock some more. "That's the most flattering thing you have ever said to me." Her lips collide into mine for a ravishing kiss. Lifting her hips up, she sinks down on me.

CHAPTER FIFTY-FOUR

Alessia

Waking up in Italy with a nipple being sucked on and my pussy being fondled is what dreams are made of.

"Mmm, Massimo." My fingers find their way into his hair. He's kept it long, knowing how sexy I find it. My eyes stay shut as he thrusts one finger up inside me and my back bows with a moan.

I'm so close to an orgasm when my eyes pop open to the loss of his fingers inside me. He replaces it with his cock and I replace my disdained look with a smile as he starts fucking me. The weight on his body pinning me down against the mattress. His hips moving forward in sharp thrusts.

"Wake me up like this every single morning," I whisper.

"I'll hold you to that, *amore mio.*" He clamps his teeth down on my earlobe.

He fucks me until I'm crying out his name and then he abruptly pulls out to come all over me, but I want it elsewhere. "In my mouth," I pant.

He doesn't waste any time as he straddles my upper body and strokes his cock. Picking my head up I take his cock in my mouth and suck hard. His hand slaps against the wall and lets out an animalistic groan.

His cum is warm and thick and also smooth as it shoots into my mouth, filling it up. His hand comes under my jaw to squeeze and I know not to swallow. He pulls out slowly and I leave my mouth open for him to admire his dirty work.

Pinching my chin, he smiles a little. "Swallow, *gattina*."

I do as he says and gulp it down. Then my tongue darts out to lick my lips making sure I get every single smooth drop. His body collapses down onto mine and I wrap my entire self around him.

"What did you put in my water, Massimo?" I rub myself against him feeling like I want him all over again. "How do I still want more?" We had sex so many times yesterday, and last night, we had to set some records. It's been like that ever since we came back from Russia, but this is more. I feel like I'm in heat.

His body vibrates against mine as he chuckles. "Breakfast, then tour." He kisses my cheek and goes to get up, but I'm feeling clingier than ever right now. His chuckle when I refuse to let go of him does nothing to extinguish my desire.

Scooping me up with him, he brings us to the bathroom where we shower and wash up for the day. We keep our hands mostly to ourselves as we get dressed and finally leave the room.

Now that I'm not attacking my husband, I can actually take in the place. It's all traditional Italian style, with the archways and out-of-date décor and structure, but it's beautiful and all-around perfect. "I love it so far," I tell him with a beamish grin.

"I'm glad." He smiles back at me.

I hear voices up ahead, and we find his family all clustered there. "Hey!" Sarita is the first to greet us and they all fall in line to do the same.

Between Sarita and Ezzo, I link arms with them and we begin walking through the estate. I turn my head over my shoulder to find Massimo smiling back at me and I blow him a kiss before turning back forward.

The estate is even bigger than theirs back home. It is, after all, a castle on a vineyard. Everything is more beautiful than the next and I just cannot believe that Massimo had bought this for me as a wedding gift almost four years ago. I accused him of sneaking off to have an affair when he was really in Italy buying me a fucking castle. He could've just told me he was doing something special for a wedding gift instead of being evasive. He talks about how I provoke him, but he definitely does the same in return.

After we're done with the tour, we walk through the courtyard, where the entire structure is built to make a circle around it, and we head to the back of the property, where the pool and gardens overlook the vineyards.

"Why the hell didn't we get married here?" I turn back to Massimo.

"Because the wedding was yours to plan, and I wanted to leave this for a surprise," he says with his head tilted down and his hands in his pockets. For once, he isn't wearing his power suit; he's wearing dark-washed jeans that fit him well and a plain black T-shirt. He looks just as sexy and just as threatening.

I notice Vita is missing, but I don't comment on it as I turn back to what lies ahead of me. The fantastic view and my in-laws. "Well, someone should use it for a wedding venue." I look at Sarita, and her eyes drop from my gaze. I turn to Ezzo then. "What do you think? Would this be good enough for your Italian princess?"

He laughs and shakes his head. "I would hope so."

Celia comes to stand next to me. "You have brought such joy to us, *piccolina*," she says quietly.

Me? Bringing joy to people? She must be crazier than me. I don't bring joy. I bring chaos and disruption.

"I know you don't see it, but you have somehow brought us all closer together whether you intended to or not." She turns and hugs me, and I don't know what to say. To be given credit where credit is not due, what can I say?

But it does give me a warm and fuzzy feeling inside.

CHAPTER FIFTY-FIVE

Massimo

On our third day here, we're all gathered in the pool area and patio. Some are in the pool, including my gorgeous wife, and some are lounging around, enjoying the beautiful weather and scenery.

I've never seen my siblings or my mother so happy and blithe. It has been ingrained from birth to believe in the supremacy of blood ties, but why? Witnessing Alessia's family dynamic revealed a deeper truth. Authentic kinship is built on connections that run deeper than genetics. It's an intangible connection, a profound bond.

As soon as Vita joined us, late as usual, she's been edgy and almost acting paranoid. Nonstop looking at her phone and all around, sometimes gazing up at the sky as if she's waiting for something to happen.

"Massimo," Vita calls my attention. "I was hoping I could have a word with you and the family."

"Now?"

"Yes." She tries giving me a smile, but it's forced. "You, Sarita, Ezzo, and Mamma. It's important."

I'm immediately suspicious. "Why now?"

She frowns, but she's more thrown off than offended. "Um, because it's just urgent. I have something I need to tell you guys right now. Can we please go inside to discuss it?" she rushes out and looks around again. "It'll only be a minute."

I scrutinize her intently, sensing an ulterior motive. Deciphering her hidden agenda becomes my pressing priority. "Massimo! Chopper coming in!" one of my guys shouts.

My gaze snaps sharply back to Vita as she gawks at me with tide eyes. There's no time for questioning as I hear the chopper in the distance.

Jumping to my feet I shout for everyone to go inside and take cover as I run towards Alessia. She's already swimming towards the edge of the pool and I bend down to yank her up and out as soon as I can reach her. I yell at her to get inside and help Sarita and my mother out as well, pushing them towards the house.

The chopper is in sight as I run behind them towards the house. Bullets rain down, hitting the pool water and the patio stone. I bolt inside through the doors, and we're all diving to take cover.

Spotting Alessia, I run towards her on instinct as the bullets come flying in through the estate shattering everything left and right. Alessia dives around a corner behind a brick wall and I follow her to wrap myself around her. She clutches my shirt as we brace ourselves and wait for the firing to stop.

Eventually, they do, and the sound of the chopper fades away. I cup Alessia's face in my hands, and her head snaps up. I start quickly inspecting her to make sure she isn't hurt, and I find her doing the same to me.

Once I see that she's unharmed, my head begins turning in the direction of everyone else, and so far, no one is hurt.

My search lands on Vita, huddled against the wall in a quivering ball with an ashen expression. She looks haunted as if she's just seen a ghost.

Yesterday...

I watch as Alessia loops arms with Sarita on one side and Ezzo on the other to walk around the estate. A smile stretches across my mouth seeing her happy like this. She pivots her head to smile back at me and send me a kiss.

"You're kind of pathetic with her, you know," Vita murmurs with a petulant tone.

"And you need to grow up sometime, Vita." She and I stop to face each other. "We all had shitty parents. The same shitty parents. No one else is crying out desperately for attention. We're doing what we can to make up for the past. Either get on board with it or hang back." I go to walk away then stop again. "And your blatant disdain for my wife needs to end today. We would have let you rot in California if it weren't for her." I turn and walk away from her, so tired of her shit.

It was our father who tried to kill Alessia and her family, yet she's forgiving of that. Vita is hanging onto a grudge for our father, and she needs to let that shit go, or she's out. If it's between my sister and Alessia, it'll be Alessia. No question about that.

I kiss Alessia on the forehead and go to step away, but she stops me. Pity clouds her eyes, confirming her grasp of the situation. My wife's perceptiveness so often goes overlooked. She reluctantly relinquishes her grip, freeing me to manage the crisis.

Standing over Vita, it pains me for the little girls she once was and still is deep down. As someone fifteen years her senior, I should have taken on a more paternal role. None of us got the parents we needed, but Vita needed that support, and no one provided her with it. I take full responsibility of that failure, and now I must bear the repercussions of it.

Her eyes come up to meet mine with tears already streaking her face. "I just—I—I'm sorry, Massimo." It's her confession. I was hoping that in some other way, it wasn't her. That her paranoia was really mine.

"The attack with the Russians at the Bonetti's." It's always been a mystery who really helped place a rat inside.

"I wanted *Pápa* back." She cries harder. "They were just supposed to free him. No one was supposed to get hurt." Tears and snot are now both running down her face.

"Oh, *bambina*," Mother coos, and she goes to comfort her, but I block her with an arm.

"Alessia was there." She sniffles and shakes. "And here." She looks down. "Why?" I snap, now seething. Twice she has tried to have Alessia killed. My wife. My love. My heart. My life. That is unforgivable.

"She makes you weak." The venomous bite and change of tune makes it easier to see her transgressions without obstruction or hindrance. "If it weren't for her, we'd still have our father."

"Why the fuck do you care so much about him? He never cared about us."

"He was still our father!" she shouts.

"And that is my wife you tried to have killed today! The woman who almost died twice! And the rat has been right under my nose the entire time!" I roar, now murderous with ire. Every muscle in my body screaming to choke the life out of her. In this moment, I don't see her as anyone else other than my wife's assassin.

"And I'll do it again!" she screams suddenly looking mad, the youthful innocence exterminated. "I will fucking kill that bitch! Father was right! The Bonettis are nothing but a curse!"

I gape at her, not having a clue what to do now. What do I do with her? It's evident she is unrepentant and completely devoid of remorse. She will try it again if I don't—

Her body slumps to the side at the same time the sound of a gun goes off. A hole appearing on one side of her head, framing the inlet of the bullet, as the ruins of her skull explode out of the other side. My mother shrieks and screams in horror as I whip my head around to look at Alessia. She only stares back at me in genuine shock, her hands clean. My mother collapses to the floor, wailing as I look around for the one holding a gun, and I find the last person I would have expected.

Sarita lowers the handgun slowly to her side. Her face blank, and her hand steady. No one says a word and the only sound is our mother's sobs. Moments tick by as we all stand there in utter shock.

"We tried fixing her," Sarita finally speaks. Her voice eerily even. "She was never going to be right, and she was going to keep trying to go after Alessia. Or any of us. There was nothing we could do."

It's as if she is in some trance and quickly shaking herself out of it, dropping the gun in dismay. She's now frantic as she looks around at all of us, abruptly taking off through the estate. Ezzo looks to me, then goes after her.

I watch as my mother weeps for Vita, a pool of blood multiplying. "Massimo," Alessia's gentle voice is close by. "I'm—I'm so sorry. What can I do?"

"Don't," I quip, not ready to deal with any of this just yet. I was still trying to wrack my brain on how to deal with Vita and her sins, and now I have to deal with her death and Sarita deeming herself as judge, jury, and executioner.

"Let me—"

"I said don't!" I shout as I spin on her. "Just—" I say through clenched teeth, trying to keep it together. "Wait for me in our bedroom."

She doesn't take my harsh tone to heart as she nods her head and walks away without argument.

"Mamma." I crouch down next to her and place a hand on her back. "Mamma, come on." She turns and falls into my arms and sobs against me as I embrace her and pull her to her feet. I throw Vinny a look to get this all cleaned up as I steer Mamma away from Vita's lifeless body.

Another family member down.

CHAPTER FIFTY-SIX

Chapter 56

I f Alessia doesn't want to leave me, I might really come to question her sanity.

My family is beyond fucked up.

Now, my conversation with Sarita yesterday is really plaguing me. Along with the guilt I have for not seeing Vita for who she really was much sooner. I'm failing this family miserably.

It's late when I get back to our bedroom. Sarita wouldn't see anyone as she locked herself in her bedroom, and I handed Mamma off to Ezzo to deal with. I'm sure she'll be turning right back to her pills, and I cannot deal with that on top of everything else right now. Right now, I need to grovel. Beg my wife not to leave me. Ensure her that she is still safe with me.

Entering the room, I find Alessia pacing, and her eyes snap in my direction. We both stand there unmoving momentarily, then she sprints to me. "Are you okay?" She cups my face and stares up at me with worry tensing her face.

Bending down, I capture her lips in a tender kiss, savoring every moment. My tongue gently sweeps into her mouth, tasting the sweetness of honey, soothing the ache within me. I yearn for her to make me feel whole again, to help me forget my failures. I want to feel like the warrior she trusts completely, the one she puts all her faith in.

Backing her up to the bed, we begin undressing each other. No words are spoken as we get naked, and I climb over top of her. Our mouths find each other again, and I slowly enter her. No cuffs, no manhandling, no dirty words, no foreplay.

No, this is different. This is me showing her my pain and this is her letting me do it without words. She's trying to shoulder some of it for me and only this once, I'll let her. Because for this one instance, I can't do it alone. It's too much for me to bear. I've never felt like this before. So overwhelmed and a little lost. Everything in my life leading up to this day is finally coming to a head.

My strokes are long and thorough, our mouths never letting up their assaults on each other. Even when my name leaves her lips on a cry and I'm grunting through my climax. I only stop when I need to come up for air, my head falling against her shoulder.

"What can I do for you, baby?" she whispers, and I finally open my eyes. Her brown eyes bore into mine, face still full of concern.

"Don't leave me," I rasp.

The worry lines between her brows increase. "Leave you? Why the fuck would I leave you? If anything, you will try and send me away again for my protection."

I shake my head and stroke her hair. "No. Never again."

"Well, I'm not going anywhere." Her arms wrap around my torso.

"I should've seen it coming. I should've known that Vita was up to something."

"How could you, Massimo? She's your sister, and it's been no secret that she hates me, but I never would've thought she was capable of anything like that. I never took her threats seriously, so it should be me that should've seen it coming and didn't."

My hackles shoot up as my face tenses. "Her threats? She's threatened you?"

Sighing, she moves some of my hair away from my face. "That day when she showed up at the hospital."

"When you told me you could handle her."

"Yes, and I did. But I still should've told you. That's on me."

"Tell me now."

"She was pissed off about your father and said that I was to blame for that. I explained to her that if it weren't for my love for you, then we would have declared war on all of you for your father's actions. It didn't matter though. She still blamed me and even blamed you."

"If you would've told me—"

"What would you have done, Massimo?" I don't answer because I'm not entirely sure. "You wouldn't kill your sister for a stupid threat that you wouldn't have taken seriously either."

"I would have kept my eye on her. Maybe even saw the Russians coming and..."

"And you wouldn't have sent me away," she says softly. She takes a deep breath and closes her eyes for a second. "There's no point in going back to think about what any of us could've done differently. We're here now, and I am so sorry you lost your sister, but what's done is done." She stops and studies my face as I just stare back at her. "You're taking the blame, and you shouldn't."

"How can I not? I almost lost you again today."

"But you didn't. I'm still here. You protected me." She smiles. "The way you yanked me out of that pool and then wrapped your body around me." She wiggles her hot little body under me.

I manage to crack a smile, but it quickly fades. I stroke her hair more. "I have something to tell you." Her expression drops. "I think Sarita is playing your brother."

A giggle bubbles inside her as she tries to choke it down. "Of course she is." She giggles more look at her in confusion. "Look, if you did to me what Tullio did to her, I probably would've killed you. He's getting far less of what he deserves for humiliating her like that and breaking his word."

"I thought you'd be upset."

"I'm proud of her." She shrugs. "Don't get me wrong here. I love my brother to death, and if she were to try and physically harm him in any way, I would, of course, go after her whether or not he deserves it. But she will just play him the way she felt he played her. Only better."

I stare at my wife in actual awe. "How the fuck are you so cutthroat one second and so angelic the next?"

"Angels fall all the time, baby," she muses, moving her arms around my neck. "So, what makes you think she's playing him?"

Yesterday...

We're finishing a nice dinner and wine tasting out in the garden, where there's a lovely venue in the center. The sun is setting, there's music playing, and everyone is enjoying themselves. Everyone except Vita.

"I don't know what to do about her," I mutter.

"Who?" Sarita, the only one near me, asks.

"Our sister."

She sighs. "I don't think there's anything any of us can do."

"We've all gone through the same shit."

"We can't all be like you, Massimo. Strong."

"You're strong too. I don't see you walking around with a chip on your shoulder."

"Though my demons may be hidden, they are no less potent. I'm simply better at masking them. Believe me." She sips her wine, and we grow quiet for a while as we watch everyone.

"We know." She looks at me. "About you and Tullio."

She snorts. "Of course you do. You know everything."

Not everything. "Why? He made a mockery of you."

"Oh, I know." She smiles and gets to her feet. "And I won't ever forget."

"I like that girl," Alessia says, grinning.

"Little psycho." I look at her with disappointment. "My father went after your family, my sister went after you, and now my other sister is going after your brother. You sure you don't want to leave me?"

"You sure I'm worth the constant headache you must have trying to protect me? Not to mention you're down two family members because of me."

"If I can't blame myself for my sister's actions, then you can't blame yourself for theirs."

"You really don't resent me for it? Even a little?"

"Not even in the slightest." Her eyes dart away from me. "Hey." I turn her head back. "I do not resent you, nor will I ever. If I have to choose between you and any member of my family, it'll always be you. You're my wife and the best part of my life."

The smile comes back to light up her face. "I don't think I'll ever get used to hearing you say sweet things like that."

"Good."

"I love you, Massimo De Luca."

"I love you, Alessia De Luca."

Want to know how it turns out between Sarita and Tullio?
Signup for my newsletters for extra chapters and free novellas.
StasiaMars